The Stars Alig...

"This **absorbin**...
Highland Groom...

"**Expert storyte**...
starred review...

"An **absorbing** ...
—*Kirkus Review*...

"Julia London writes vibrant, emotional stories and sexy, richly drawn characters." —*New York Times* bestselling author Madeline Hunter

"Julia London strikes gold again. Warm, witty and decidedly wicked—great entertainment." —#1 *New York Times* bestselling author Stephanie Laurens

"[London writes] singular, outstanding Regency romance… Her masterful ability to bring characters to life makes this romance entirely absorbing." —*Publishers Weekly*

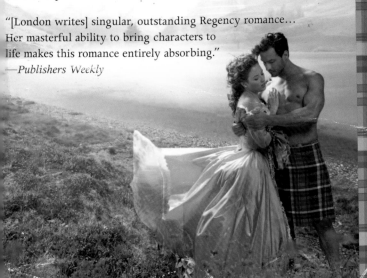

Praise for *New York Times* bestselling author Julia London

"Veteran author London entices readers.... Expert storytelling and believable characters make the romance between Arran and Margot come alive in this compelling novel packed with characters whom readers will be sad to leave behind."
—*Publishers Weekly* on *Wild Wicked Scot* (starred review)

"London's writing bubbles with high emotion... Her blend of playful humor and sincerity imbues her heroines with incredible appeal, and readers will delight as their unconventional tactics create rambling paths to happiness."
—*Publishers Weekly* on *The Devil Takes a Bride* (starred review)

"This tale of scandal and passion is perfect for readers who like to see bad girls win, but still love the feeling of a society romance, and London nicely sets up future books starring Honor's sisters."
—*Publishers Weekly* on *The Trouble with Honor*

"The complexity of the relationship between Daisy and Cailean sets this novel apart from many in its genre."
—*Publishers Weekly* on *Sinful Scottish Laird*

"Julia London writes vibrant, emotional stories and sexy, richly drawn characters."
—*New York Times* bestselling author Madeline Hunter

JULIA LONDON

HARD-HEARTED HIGHLANDER

HQN™

ISBN-13: 978-0-373-78999-3

Recycling programs for this product may not exist in your area.

Hard-Hearted Highlander

Copyright © 2017 by Dinah Dinwiddie

This edition published by arrangement with Harlequin Books S.A.

For questions and comments about the quality of this book, please contact us at CustomerService@Harlequin.com.

® and TM are trademarks of Harlequin Enterprises Limited or its corporate affiliates. Trademarks indicated with ® are registered in the United States Patent and Trademark Office, the Canadian Intellectual Property Office and in other countries.

www.HQNBooks.com

Printed in U.S.A.

To the Scottish Highlands,
fueling the fantasies of readers for hundreds of years.

Mackenzies of Balhaire

John Armstrong, *Lord Norwood*

Anne Armstrong

- Knox Armstrong *(bastard son)*
- Bryce Armstrong
- Margot Armstrong, b. 1688
  m. 1706
- Arran Mackenzie, b. 1680

Conall Mackenzie

Jane Mackenzie

— Cailean Mackenzie, b. 1711
  m. 1742
  Daisy Bristol, b. 1713
  Lady Chatwick

———————————— Ellis, *Lord Chatwick*
  (Previous marriage)

— Vivienne Mackenzie, b. 1713
  m. 1733 ———————————— Maira Mackenzie, b. 1735
  Marcas Mackenzie, b. 1710 ——— Bruce Mackenzie, b. 1736
  (distant relation) ————————— Gavin Mackenzie, b. 1738
  ———————————————————— Nira Mackenzie, b. 1741

— Aulay Mackenzie, b. 1714
  (Captain Mackenzie)

— Rabbie Mackenzie, b. 1715

— Catriona Mackenzie, b. 1722

Ivor Mackenzie

Lilleas Mackenzie

- Griselda Mackenzie, b. 1685
- Jock Mackenzie, b. 1679
  m. 1713
  Nell Grady, b. 1690

CHAPTER ONE

The Scottish Highlands, 1750

HE STOOD ON the very edge of the cliff, the tips of his boots just over the crusty rim, nothing below them but air. It was quite a long way down—one strong gust of wind would do it.

He wondered how it would feel to fall. Would his body soar like the seabirds that leaped from the edge of the cliffs to glide above the surface of the water? Or would he fall like a rock come loose from the edge? Would he be alive when he crashed into the water? Or would his heart desert him well before that final moment?

No matter how he fell, Rabbie Mackenzie knew he'd be dead the moment he hit the water and was impaled on the rocks that lurked just beneath the froth. Likely, he'd feel nothing. The water would recede and carry his body out to sea like so much detritus.

He watched the waves crashing against the wall of the cliff as the tide rose, spellbound by the violence of them. It was true that he wished himself dead, but it was also true that he'd not found the courage to die. It was the height of irony—what he wished, what he longed for, was the Highlands of his youth, when Highland men were not afraid to die.

And yet, here he stood, afraid to die.

Rabbie wished for the prosperity of those years before the battle between the Scots and the English on the moors near Culloden, for plaids and the armaments of a mighty clan, now all of it outlawed. He wished for the *feills*, where he once measured his strength against men in rousing contests, and for the bonny lasses who carried ale to quench the men's thirst. Those Highlands were gone. It was a wasteland now, entire settlements burned by the English, the people either hanged or dispersed to lands across the sea. Farmland stood empty. Cattle and sheep had been rounded up and sold. The land was devoid of color and life.

Even Balhaire, the seat of the Mackenzie clan for centuries, had not gone unscathed. They had kept apart from the Jacobites, the rebels who wanted to restore Charlie Stuart to the throne. The Mackenzies had let it be known to all Highlanders they wanted no part in the rebellion. Even so, after so many Highland clans had seen their men slaughtered on the moors of Culloden by English forces, half the Mackenzie clan had been chased away by fear and false accusations. Rabbie himself had been forced to flee, hiding away in Norway for a little more than two years like a bloody coward.

Aye, he'd been sympathetic to the rebel cause, but he'd not taken up arms. He held no love for the English, no matter that his mother was a foreigner, a *Sassenach*, and his brother's wife an English viscountess. Rabbie had agreed with Seona's family—that Scotland would be drowned under the weight of taxes and excises as long as George ruled them.

He'd agreed with it, but he'd not spoken publicly against the crown. They'd come looking for him all the same, had burned more than half the village about Balhaire before the flames could be doused, had seized their cattle and laid waste to their farms.

Aye, Rabbie longed for the days of his youth.

He also longed to know what had happened to Seona. Was she dead? Was it somehow possible she was still alive? He would never know.

A movement at the entrance of the cove caught his eye. The prow of a ship was emerging, bobbing up and down in the waves as the captain negotiated the granite wall and the rocky entrance to their hidden shelter.

That would be his brother, Aulay, just returned from England.

Rabbie looked down at the water once more, wishing for a gust of wind to make the decision for him. He watched a bit of seaweed ride out from the rocks and into the center of the cove, and then, with the next wave, disappear altogether.

He stepped back from the edge. He'd not jump today. Today, he would meet his intended bride.

RABBIE TRUDGED WEARILY up the high road of what had once been a bustling village surrounding the fortress of Balhaire. Many of the shop fronts were shuttered, and with the exception of a smithy and an inn that also served somewhat as a dry goods shop, there was hardly any commerce to be had.

He walked through the massive gates and into the bailey of the old castle fortress, Balhaire. No one but a few men were about. Even many of the dogs that had once roamed this bailey had left for places unknown. He carried on, into the old castle, past walls stripped of their historic armaments, save those they'd managed to hide away.

His boots echoed on the stone floor as he made his way to the study where he'd find the laird, his father, the head of what was left of Clan Mackenzie. He was inside, as Rabbie knew he'd be, his brow furrowed as he studied a ledger at his desk. He was still quite robust in spite of a bad leg. His hair had been turned to silver by the events of the last few years.

His father didn't notice him at the open door. *"Feasgar math, Athair. Ciamar a tha thu?"* Rabbie said in greeting.

"Rabbie, lad, come in, then," his father said, waving him in. "I am well, very well." He removed his spectacles and rubbed his eyes. "We missed you at breakfast this morning." He repositioned his spectacles and glanced at his youngest son. "Where might you have gone, then?"

Rabbie shrugged. "I walked."

His father looked as if he wanted to say more, but did not. Rabbie was aware that his family worried about his state of mind. He worried about it, too. He'd tried to hide his restlessness from them, but it was no use—a man could not create a pleasant mien out of thin air, could he?

He walked to the sideboard and poured a dram of

whisky, which he tossed back before holding up the container to his father with a questioning look. His father shook his head. His gaze fell to the container, apparently waiting for Rabbie to put it aside.

Rabbie didn't put it aside—he poured more. "The ship has come," he said. It wasn't necessary to say which ship—they'd lost one of their fleet of two to England and now relied on the oldest ship. They'd been expecting Aulay for a day or two now.

"Good," his father said. "I donna like my second son in England any more than I like my first there."

He was referring to Cailean, who had married Lady Chatwick. They resided at the northern estate of Chatwick Hall, away from politics and trouble...except that a Scot was never far from trouble in England.

His father didn't mention the bridal party. Rabbie drank a second dram of whisky, felt the warmth of it cut through the clawing in his throat. His drinking had been a source of contention between him and his mother of late, and for good reason. In addition to battling his dark thoughts, Rabbie was also drinking too much. He just couldn't seem to help himself on either front.

He walked to the window and away from the temptation to drown his despair in whisky, and stared down at the empty bailey. "It's decided then, is it?"

"What is?" his father asked.

His father knew very well what he meant, and a moment later he sighed, as if he was weary of discussing it. "I've said it before, lad, I'll say it again. You must be the one to decide—I canna make the decision for you, aye?"

But hadn't he made the decision for him? Hadn't the decision been made the first time his father and mother approached him?

"Have you changed your mind, then?" his father asked.

Rabbie laughed with no small amount of derision. "Changed my mind? What, and leave Balhaire unprotected? Allow them to come in and dismantle it completely?" He shook his head. "No, *Athair*, I've no' changed my mind. I'll do as I must, I will."

"It's no' ideal, no," his father said.

A blatant understatement.

"Cailean has said she is bonny," his father suggested. "That eases you a wee bit, aye?"

No, that pained Rabbie most of all. No one was as bonny to him as Seona MacBee had been, she with the dark red hair and deep brown eyes. *A Diah*, why hadn't he married Seona before the war? If he had, she'd have fled to Norway with him. She'd be alive.

A sharp pain sliced behind his eyes and Rabbie squeezed them shut. "As if that matters to me now," he muttered.

"Rabbie," his father said. Rabbie could hear him coming to his feet, the labored drag of his bad leg and cane across the floor until he reached his son. He put his hand on Rabbie's shoulder. "The lass is young. She'll bend to your will, she will. She'll become what you want of her."

What Rabbie wanted of her was to become Seona, and that was impossible.

"See here," his father said quietly. "Marry the lass. Put her in your marital bed and then take a mistress."

Surprised, Rabbie turned to look at his father.

"Spend your time at Balhaire, or send her to England for long summers. You need no' lock yourself away with her at Arrandale." At Rabbie's baffled look, Arran Mackenzie merely shrugged. "Desperate times demand desperate measures, do they no'? This is no' what your mother and I want for you. Unfortunately, we've no other options. If there was an Englishman in want of a Highland wife—"

Rabbie instantly shook his head. It is one thing for him to marry into an English family, but he would never wish that on his free-spirited younger sister, Catriona. "No," he said firmly. "It must be me, aye?"

"No' if you donna want it."

"I donna want it," Rabbie said. "But I'll no' leave Balhaire without hope."

His father smiled sadly, patted Rabbie's shoulder and then, leaning heavily on his cane, started for the door. "Then we'll seal the betrothal tonight." He paused in his trek across the study and glanced back. "Unless you say the word, lad. You need only say it."

There was no word Rabbie could say—he was trapped like a mouse behind a door with a cat waiting on the other side, no way out but death. If he didn't marry this woman, her father, who had bought Killeaven from the crown after the Somerleds had deserted it, would buy up lands around Balhaire, including those that had been abandoned by Mackenzies that had fled. Lands his family could not afford to purchase from the crown, not with their sea trade cut in half, their smuggling brought to a halt by war and the fact that there was no one left to buy their goods.

If the land around Balhaire was bought, and sheep installed, there would not be enough land to sustain the Mackenzies that were left. No land for food, no land for livestock. They were struggling to rebuild after the rebellion and the destruction it had wrought across the Highlands. If Rabbie took this *Sassenach* girl to wife, and Killeaven with her, the Mackenzies could at least control the erosion of their livelihood.

He truly had no choice.

THE BRIDAL PARTY had arrived with quite a lot of commotion. Sixteen in all, Frang, the butler, said—servants, the girl's parents, an uncle, he thought. And a governess.

"A governess," Rabbie repeated disdainfully. "Is the lass no' seventeen years of age? Is she still in need of a *governess*?"

"Not a governess, precisely," his mother said, patting his arm. "I'd venture she is a governess turned lady's maid for lack of a better occupation."

"What, then, am I to feed her, too?"

His mother frowned and managed to look elegant while doing it, a feat that he'd never seen matched in another woman.

Rabbie and his parents were in the great hall. They'd taken their places on the old dais above the tables, where Mackenzie lairds and their families had sat for two centuries. They could hear the arrival of the *Sassenach*, could hear the voices chattering merrily at the entrance. They watched silently as Aulay led the English contingent into the hall.

At the head of the *Sassenach* party was a tall, slender man with a face powdered as white as snow and who, judging by his dress, was the Baron Kent. He paused to glance around, his expression one of amazement, as if he'd never seen the inside of a castle. When Cailean and his wife, Daisy, had come a few months ago with the news of their discussions with Baron Kent, Daisy reported that Bothing, the Kent home, was quite grand. "Three stories tall, with long wings," she'd said. "Grander than Chatwick Hall."

Rabbie had never seen Chatwick Hall, but he'd noted the way Daisy's eyes had widened and had supposed the Bothing place must be very grand indeed. Perhaps Balhaire was more rustic than what he'd anticipated. He wondered what the baron might expect of Killeaven, the estate he'd purchased sight unseen.

Aulay walked briskly to the dais ahead of the group. His blond hair had grown too long, and the sun had browned his face after so many days at sea. He looked leaner than the last time Rabbie had seen him. He swept his hat off his head and bowed to his parents, then spoke in Gaelic, greeting them both, and then Rabbie.

"So then," his father responded in Gaelic. "How do you find them?"

"No trouble," Aulay said with a shrug, and looked at Rabbie. "The lass is meek."

Rabbie said nothing. He didn't want a meek lass. If he had to do this, he wanted a woman. He looked to the group for a glimpse of the lass in question, but the only woman he noticed in that gaggle of *Sassenach* was one standing slightly apart from the group, leaning insouciantly against the wall. She was tall, dark-haired and plainly dressed. She'd crossed her arms across her middle and her gaze was fixed on the hound sniffing around her hem. She looked a wee bit as if she was inconvenienced, which he thought was rather odd. If anyone here was inconvenienced, it was certainly not she.

Rabbie's father stood. "My lord, *Ceud mile failte*—welcome to Balhaire."

"Bit of an unusual place you have here," the man who looked like a ghost said as he strolled forward. Behind him, another man waddled after him like a fatted pig. Both of their wigs were ridiculous. "How good of you to receive us. I understand Killeaven is a bit of a drive yet from here?"

"Four miles through the hills," Arran Mackenzie said. He picked up his cane and began to make his way down from the dais. In spite of that cane, Rabbie's father was still a commanding figure, and he dwarfed Lord Kent. "You and yours are most welcome in our home tonight, aye? Rest here before carrying on to Killeaven." He turned partially as Rabbie's mother stepped off the dais to join them. "My wife, the Lady Mackenzie."

His mother curtsied and greeted them. Kent turned quite jovial at the sight of his mother, no doubt pleased with her English accent and her beauty. He introduced the man with him as his brother, Lord Ramsey.

"May I introduce you to our son?" his mother asked pleasantly, and gestured toward Rabbie.

Kent's head snapped round, and he eyed Rabbie through a squint as Rabbie came to his feet and began to make his way down from the dais. "Well then, you're a fine specimen, are you not? As physically fit as your father and brother, I dare say. Look here, Avaline, here is your future husband," he said, and turned back to his group.

Someone nudged the pitiful lass forward. She stumbled slightly, found her footing and curtsied. She had hair the color of barley, green eyes and cheeks flushed to the color of plums. She was a wee thing, and the only thought Rabbie could summon was that he would crush her on their wedding night. He'd have to put the virgin on top of him.

He approached the group. The lass would not look at him. "My lord," he said to her father, and bowed. He glanced again at the girl, who had yet to meet his gaze.

"A strong young man," Kent said, taking Rabbie in, nodding approvingly, as if Rabbie were a prized cow. "You'll give me heirs, I dare say you will. May I present my daughter, Miss Avaline Kent of Bothing," he said, and took his daughter's arm, drawing her forward. "She's pretty, isn't she?"

Rabbie looked at her fair complexion. She was chewing her bottom lip. Her hands were quite small, suitable for nothing useful as far as he could see. "Bonny enough, I suppose, aye," he said.

With the exception of the startled cough from the woman leaning against the wall, no one said a word for a moment.

And then Baron Kent laughed roundly. "Good enough!" he jovially agreed.

Rabbie's mother managed a kick to his ankle. He moved forward lest she kick him again and presented his palm to receive Miss Kent's wee little hand. "How do you, Miss Kent."

"My lord—sir," she said, and curtsied again, as if she hadn't noticed his hand at all. And when she did sink into that curtsy, Rabbie happened to glance at the woman by the wall. She had dark hair, quite dark, like Rabbie's sister, Vivienne. And hazel eyes. She was frowning at him, and not in an elegant way like his mother. And then she looked away, as if annoyed by him.

Rabbie was slightly shocked. Who was *she* to judge him? And what did she bloody well expect?

"Miss Kent, please, do come and sit. You must be exhausted," Rabbie's mother said, and took Miss Kent's hand, pulling her away before wrapping an arm around her shoulders.

"My wife. Where is my wife?" Lord Kent asked, as if he'd misplaced her somewhere. Another woman appeared from the huddled group. She was small and meek, too, her gaze downcast as she shyly greeted Rabbie's mother.

For the love of Scotland, that's who his bride would become.

Rabbie sighed heavenward as the English party was seated, and glanced over his shoulder, to where the mysterious woman had stood frowning at him as if he was a naughty child.

But the woman was nowhere to be seen. She'd just… disappeared.

"Rabbie, darling, perhaps you might sit with Miss Kent and put her at ease," his mother said, her cheerful voice belying the murderous look in her eye.

"Aye," he said, and reluctantly moved to the table where the wisp had been seated. He couldn't help himself—he glanced back over his shoulder once more.

The woman with the dark hair and piercing hazel eyes was gone.

CHAPTER TWO

BERNADETTE HOLLY LOOKED around the dank room to which she'd been assigned. Or rather, the room to which Avaline had been assigned. Bernadette had been given the small antechamber attached to this room, where she was to sleep on a straw mattress so that she might serve her mistress in the event the girl couldn't find the chamber pot in the middle of the night.

If Bernadette ever uttered such a thing aloud, one would think she was ungrateful for her position and disdainful of Avaline. Nothing could be further from the truth—she was grateful and she was not the least disdainful of Avaline. But she was a bit uncertain if the girl possessed a full head of brains.

The room was quaint if not medieval in its appearance, and quite drafty—Bernadette could feel the gusts of wind coming through the windows. She shivered and walked to the window, pushed aside the heavy brocade draperies, then sneezed at the dust collected in their folds. The window rattled with another gust of cold air, which seeped in around the edges of the old panes.

Bernadette leaned forward over the deep sill and looked out. The sun was just sliding down behind the hills, its golden light turning the hills red, which in turn cast dark green shadows onto bright yellow rapeseed.

She found the landscape stark and barren, but strangely beautiful. England was scenic country, too, but Bernadette had never seen anything quite so severe in its allure as this landscape.

Avaline, however, had found the land intimidating. Worrying a knot of ribbon at her waist, she'd stood beside Bernadette at the bow of the ship as it had glided toward the harbor earlier today. "There doesn't seem to be anyone about. It looks...*bleak*."

Behind Bernadette, the door of the room suddenly swung open, startling her. She dropped the drapes and turned around to see Avaline backing into the room, profusely thanking whomever had delivered her here. When she had gone well past the point of polite thanks, and the person had tried to dart away into the dark corridor, Avaline leaned forward, craning her neck around the doorframe. "Good night!" she called out, then shut the door very quietly, as if she feared she might disturb someone, and turned to Bernadette.

"Well?" Bernadette asked brightly. "How did you find him?"

Avaline looked as if she might collapse at any moment. But then again, Avaline often looked near collapse. "He's so *big*," she said in a near whisper.

He was certainly that. A tall, ruggedly built man, with very dark, cold eyes.

"Oh, Bernadette," Avaline moaned, and staggered to the bed, sinking onto it. "I don't know how I shall ever manage."

"Now, now, you mustn't despair," Bernadette said, and moved to sit beside her charge. "It's the first meeting, after all. Everyone is on tenterhooks. Mr. Mackenzie was undoubtedly as nervous as you," she said kindly, although she sensed, having observed him, that the man hadn't a single nerve in him. He'd appeared insouciant, overly confident and quite secure in his idea that he was much grander than the girl he was meant to wed. A rooster, if one wished to put a name to it.

"Do you really think so?" Avaline asked.

"Yes, of course." That was not true—she didn't believe it at all.

Neither did Avaline, and she fell over onto her side, distraught. "They are negotiating the terms of our betrothal now. My father and—and *him*, naturally, and his father, and his brother. He is so *distant* and he seems unfeeling, and yet his brother has been very kind, has he not?" she asked anxiously, pushing herself up again. "Don't you think the captain is kind? I said as much to my mother, but she said I was not to think of him at all. I wasn't *thinking* of him. I was merely pointing out that he seems kinder than his brother."

"Where is your mother?" Bernadette asked curiously. She often lost track of Lady Kent, who was as quiet and unobtrusive as a mouse. Avaline was boisterous in comparison.

"She is with Lady Mackenzie somewhere in this huge and wretched place," Avaline said morosely, and gestured lamely to the walls around them. "Lady Mackenzie bid me join them, but I begged her pardon and said I was so very tired after the journey, but *re-*

ally, Bernadette," she said. "*Really*, I thought I might burst into tears if I remained another moment."

"Then it's good you came here," Bernadette said, and put an arm around Avaline's shoulders.

Avaline suddenly burst into tears and buried her face in Bernadette's shoulder. "I can't believe I must *marry* him!" she wailed.

Neither could Bernadette, frankly, but it was the way of things for a girl born to Avaline's station in life. They married men who strengthened their families' connections and made them all richer. "Men always appear much fiercer when they are unknown," she said, patting Avaline's back. "It's natural for them to appear so."

"It is?"

No, of course it wasn't natural. Had the girl learned *anything* from Bernadette in the last six years? "Yes, always. They must preen and show their fierceness to attract a mate. Much like a rooster."

"Like a rooster," Avaline repeated, sounding hopeful now. She sat up again and folded her hands primly in her lap.

"Avaline…" Bernadette stood from the bed and kneeled down before her, so that she was looking her in the eye. "You must reserve judgment of him. In situations like this, the first meeting is truly the hardest. But when you are alone with him—"

"Alone!"

"Not *alone*. You know I'll be nearby," Bernadette said soothingly. "Say you are invited to walk with him. You might use that opportunity to converse with him, ask him questions about himself and assure yourself he is not as…" *Boorish. Primitive. Savage?* "As distant as he has appeared to you," she said, and smiled. "Men are quite eager to speak of themselves and need only the *slightest* encouragement. I've no doubt you'll find him a wonderful companion if you allow him to focus his attention on himself."

Avaline seemed highly skeptical. Bernadette would have to improve her powers of persuasion, but her belly chose that moment to growl with hunger. And rather loudly, too. She hadn't had a bite of food since early in the morning.

Avaline looked at Bernadette's belly. "Oh, dear! You haven't eaten!"

No, she'd not eaten, because that craggy old bastard of a butler had *instructed* her to come and prepare her lady's bedchamber. Firstly, Avaline was not a *lady.* Secondly, Bernadette was not a bloody chambermaid. Granted, she was scarcely a rung above it, but she had her pride. She was, after all, the daughter of a recognized knight, Sir Whitman Holly, and his wife, her mother, Lady Esme Holly.

"How very careless of us," Avaline said.

"You mustn't give it another thought," Bernadette said. She would be thinking about it all night, enough for the both of them.

"No, I am going to summon them now, and tell them—"

"I've an idea," Bernadette said. "I'll help you ready for bed, then I'll go and seek out the kitchen. I shan't disturb anyone—they'll be quite well occupied with putting the house to bed."

"Well…" Avaline said uncertainly, and bit her bottom lip again. Bernadette pointed to her own lip, and Avaline stopped chewing at once. It was a dreadful habit the girl had, and on more than one occasion, she'd ended the day looking as if someone had slapped her across the mouth.

"Come," Bernadette said. "I'll brush your hair."

When she'd brushed and braided Avaline's hair and put her in bed with a book she wouldn't read, Bernadette said good-night and went in search of the kitchens. She was not accustomed to missing her supper and she didn't much like it. She hoped she was not too late.

The castle was a confusing maze of winding corridors, some of them poorly lit, but Bernadette possessed a keen sense of direction and found her way to the great hall. It was empty now, save for four dogs that had staked their places before the massive hearth and the warm embers there. They scarcely lifted their heads when she paused to look inside.

She walked on, turning down one of the more brightly lit corridors. She heard voices, and realized the sound was coming from an open door. She moved closer. The voices were male, and she paused just outside the door, listening. She couldn't make it out, really, and honestly didn't care what they were saying—she only wanted to sneak by. She darted past the open door, but realized, too late, that in the shadows just past the open door was another door that closed off the hallway. *"Of all the bother!"* she whispered, and tried the handle, but it was locked.

Bernadette turned around, prepared to dart past the open door once more, but she realized with significant consternation that she was plainly visible from the room where the men had gathered, and they were visible to her. And there, facing the door, sat Avaline's intended. Or was he now officially her fiancé? Whoever he was, he was staring at Bernadette, his expression unreadable...unless one looked at his eyes.

She didn't know the man's eye color, but from here, it looked as black and as hard as obsidian. His gaze moved over her, slowly and deliberately, as if he found her wanting. His casual perusal felt as if it had singed her, leaving a tingling trail down her chest to her abdomen. He was a beast! An uncivilized *beast*.

Bernadette glared right back at him. Men didn't scare her as they did Avaline. Quite the contrary.

She lifted her chin and walked on, aware that his gaze followed her for the space of that open door.

"Madam?"

Bernadette had been so intent on showing that wretched man she was not the least bit intimidated by him that she hadn't seen Captain Mackenzie moving down the corridor toward her, and almost jumped out of her skin.

He smiled at her obvious surprise. He was carrying a bottle in one hand.

"I beg your pardon, Captain," she said as he neared her. "I'm a bit lost. Would you kindly point me to the kitchen?"

"The kitchen?"

"I, ah… I was tending to Miss Kent's things during the supper hour," she said, wincing slightly with apology.

"Ah. Come then," he said, his warm smile returned. "You'll be quite lost if you attempt to find it on your own, you will. Our ancestors didna think much of efficiency when they built this fortress." He gestured for her to come with him.

He had such a lovely smile and even lovelier light blue eyes. He'd been unfailingly kind to them all since the moment they'd boarded his ship, and Bernadette couldn't help but smile now, happy to have been rescued by him.

"Miss Kent, she's well, is she?" he asked pleasantly as they took another turn into another corridor.

"Quite. A bit tired, what with the journey, but very well, thank you."

"Aye. Here we are then," he said, opening a door and allowing Bernadette to pass through before him. A wooden table stretched long through the middle of the kitchen. On one wall were the many pots used for cooking. On another wall, jars of spices. The smell of lamb roasting made her stomach growl, and she smiled sheepishly at her escort.

Captain Mackenzie walked to the bell pull and tugged on it. A moment later, a woman appeared. Her gray hair was knotted on the top of her head and her apron was wet from the chest down, as if she'd been washing.

Captain Mackenzie spoke to her in Gaelic. She re-

sponded in kind and disappeared through the door from
where she'd come. The captain turned to Bernadette
and bowed. "Barabel will prepare something for you,
aye?"

"Thank you," she said gratefully.

"Will you find your way to your room, then? I'll
have Frang come and—"

"No, please. I am confident I know the way." She
wasn't the least bit confident, but she'd as sooner wander all night than see Frang again.

"Aye, verra well. *Oidhche mhath*, Miss Holly," he
said, and walked out of the kitchen with his bottle.

Bernadette watched him go, marveling at the way
nature worked. How on earth could two brothers be
so entirely opposite of one another in both looks and
mien?

Barabel returned with a platter of brown bread,
cheese and meat. She very unceremoniously slapped
it down on the table in the center of the kitchen with a
pointed glare for Bernadette.

"My apologies for the inconvenience," Bernadette
said, and smiled.

Barabel did not return her smile.

"Do you speak English?"

Barabel responded to that by turning about and
walking through the door. A moment later, Bernadette heard the clink of china and the slosh of water.

She moved cautiously to the table and looked around
for a stool. There was none. Neither were there any dining utensils. Well, that wouldn't deter her, not when she
was this hungry. She hoisted herself up onto the table

and put the platter on her lap and ate with her fingers, listening to the moans and groans of the wind moving through this heap of stones, sighing with relief at the taste of food.

She had managed to have some bread, some chicken and a bit of cheese when she heard footsteps coming down the hallway toward the kitchen. She assumed it was the captain, and looked up, smiling self-consciously.

It was not Captain Mackenzie at all, but his darker, gruffer, angrier brother. He paused just inside the kitchen door and fixed his gaze on her. His expression was hard, unyielding. He reminded her of the granite face of some of the hills around here—she didn't think he could possibly smile if he tried.

Bernadette needed a moment to collect herself. Judging by the way he looked at her, she didn't know if he intended to give her a tongue-lashing or hang her. Or…well, she didn't want to think about what else he might intend. She licked the grease from one finger for lack of a napkin, then another, and carefully moved the platter off her lap and onto the table before hopping down. She realized, now that she stood before him, that he was even bigger than he'd first appeared across the great hall. Quite broad of shoulder and powerful. And with waves of enmity rolling off of him and lapping over her.

No wonder Avaline was so shaky.

He didn't say a word, but continued to stare at her, and she could feel that look piercing clean through her as a muscle worked in his jaw, as if he was biting his tongue. Bernadette stared back at him. Did he want to speak? Then speak. Did he want something of her? *Ask.* Was he perhaps only surprised to find her here? Or did he always stomp about looking so displeased and disgruntled?

Barabel returned to the kitchen, dipped a curtsy to him and spoke in the Scots language. He responded with few words in a tone so low and silky that Bernadette suppressed a small but surprising little shiver. Barabel disappeared once more, and he sidled up to the table, staring down at her plate. He picked up a piece of chicken and ate it.

Well, then. She could add ungentlemanly to her growing list of dislikes about him.

"Have you had your fill, then?"

The beast spoke after all. No, she hadn't had her fill, and yes, she was still hungry. But she resisted the urge to look longingly at her food. "Yes. Thank you."

He ate another bite, then folded his arms across his chest and turned away from her a moment. Then back again, those dark eyes piercing hers again. "Is it the custom in England for a servant to invade the kitchen of another man's house?"

Invade? He made it sound as if she'd entered with an army demanding bread. "Not at all. Unfortunately, I missed—"

"Aye, my brother has told me."

Then why, pray tell, did he ask? "I beg your pardon," she said, and moved to pass him. But he shifted slightly, blocking her path. Bernadette lifted her gaze to his— she could see nothing but hardness in his eyes, could feel nothing but coldness radiating off of him. There was something very dark about him that Bernadette was certain there was not a bit of kindness in him. She thought of Avaline, how gentle and young and naive she was. To be married to this man? She couldn't help herself—another shiver ran down her.

He noticed it. "Do you find the Scottish night too *fuar* for your thin English blood?"

"I hardly know what that means. But I will own that my thin English blood finds churlishness to be jarring."

Her remark surprised him, clearly—she saw something spark in him, and one brow rose slowly above the other. "You are bloody well bold for a maid," he said, his gaze moving over her body, taking her in so boldly and unapologetically that she could feel her skin begin to heat under his perusal.

"And you are bloody well discourteous for a gentleman," she returned. She tried to slip past him, but he refused to move, and her arm brushed against his chest as she maneuvered around him. Once clear of him, she refused to sprint, as she very much wanted to do. She walked calmly away from him in spite of her racing her heart, her back ramrod-straight, her chin lifted. She could feel his gaze on her back, could feel it slicing between her shoulder blades and piercing her through.

It is no small miracle that Bernadette found her way back to her small antechamber. She dressed for bed and collapsed onto the straw mattress, her heart still beating faster than it ought to have. She tried desperately to sleep, but she kept seeing his dark eyes, the color of a stormy sea, boring into her.

CHAPTER THREE

THE TERMS OF the *tochradh*, or dowry, were agreed upon the next morning while Bernadette was at breakfast, a meal she was determined not to miss.

She noticed that the other people in the hall sat as far from the Kent party as possible, looking askance at them if acknowledging them at all. She had never in her life met with such inhospitable surroundings and was quite relieved when it came time to gather her and Avaline's things and depart that gloomy castle.

The Kent family, including Bernadette, would travel to Killeaven by means of an old coach. She couldn't guess where his lordship might have come by it, but it looked ancient, the paint having faded and the wheels on the verge of rot. The rest of the party, including Avaline's uncle and the servants, would come by foot and in a wagon. The furnishings they'd brought with them would be carried up from the ship in a separate transport.

Lady Mackenzie had introduced them to Niall MacDonald, who was to accompany them on horseback. She explained that Mr. MacDonald had been dispatched from Balhaire to help them settle in. He appeared younger than Bernadette's twenty-nine years, and had a bad eye that wandered aimlessly as the other one looked directly at you.

Avaline's brutish fiancé did not appear to see them off, which Bernadette thought the height of uncivilized behavior. But his mother was there, and the lady was quite warm in her smiles and well wishes for them. "You will see some of our loveliest views on the road to Killeaven," she assured them. "The glen is lush this time of year." She took Avaline's hand in hers. "Miss Kent, please do forgive my son's absence this morning. Something has come up at Arrandale, our smaller estate, and where he currently resides. It required his immediate attention and he regretted deeply that he had to depart early this morning."

Bernadette turned her head so no one would see her roll her eyes.

"Oh. I see," Avaline said. But she clearly didn't see, as her cheeks were coloring with uncertainty.

Lady Mackenzie noticed it, too and said quickly, "But he means to call straightaway, just as soon as you're settled." She smiled reassuringly.

Bernadette thought the lady's smile was lacking something. Conviction, perhaps.

They piled into the coach—Lord Kent going first, as was his habit. The coach lacked sufficient springs and swayed badly as each one climbed in. Bernadette sat next to Avaline, across from her parents, as they set off for the four-mile journey to Killeaven in the company of several armed men.

"Why are they armed?" Avaline asked, looking out the window.

"Hmm?" her father asked, distracted. He'd already been at the bottle. "Mackenzie sent them." He shrugged, stifled a belch, then said, "Now then, girl, you'll marry Mackenzie in three weeks' time."

Avaline gasped and looked to her mother, who, as usual, remained silent. "So soon?"

"Yes, so *soon*," he said, mocking her. "Your mother and I can't stay on forever."

Avaline gasped again. "You mean to *leave* me?"

"Avaline, for heaven's sake," Lord Kent said with exasperation, and turned to his wife. "You have raised a simpleton, madam. Will you not say something?"

Lady Kent clearly didn't want to say anything, but she began hesitantly, "That—that is what your father—"

"Something useful!" Lord Kent spat, and turned his burgeoning rage to Bernadette.

"Ah...you will be married with your own house," Bernadette said quickly. "It wouldn't do for you to spend the first weeks or months of your married life with your parents, would it?" She glanced at Lady Kent, hoping for help, but Lady Kent had dropped her gaze to her lap, her confidence demolished years before Bernadette had come along.

"That's better," Lord Kent said. "Stop *weeping*, Avaline," he said, sounding resigned to it, and with a loud sigh, hunched down in his seat and propped his foot on the bench next to Bernadette. He turned his gaze to the window and closed his eyes.

Bernadette put her hand on Avaline's knee and squeezed tightly. She knew, after six years in the family's employ, that nothing undermined Avaline worse in the eyes of her unforgiving father than her tears.

Avaline didn't stop weeping, but she did manage to stifle the sound of it.

Bernadette turned her attention to the window, too, unwilling to talk to any of them any more than was absolutely necessary. As she watched the landscape slowly rolling along, she noticed a trio of riders. They were at a distance, but they had come to a halt, and the men on the horses were watching the coach. As the coach turned east with the road, the riders began to follow at a parallel for at least a half hour, at which point, they turned into the woods and disappeared.

The coach began to slow, and they started down a hill, the road curving slowly to the floor of the glen. Bernadette could see the house on the banks of a river, backed up to a hill. She counted twelve chimneys—the house was not small. It rather reminded her of Highfield, her family's home and where she'd happily grown up. Unfortunately, Highfield was not a happy place for her now.

"See, Avaline?" Bernadette whispered, leaning across her to point. "This will be your house."

"What?" Lord Kent said, waking from his nap. He rubbed his face as he sat up.

"It's Killeaven, is it?" Avaline asked. She had long since ceased her tears, but her face was swollen and splotchy.

"It is," Bernadette said.

They wended their way down and onto a drive that

was overgrown, the shrubs and trees untended. "Is it empty?" Avaline asked.

"Of course it is," her father said impatiently. "Do you think we would move furnishings into another man's house? The Somerleds have departed for greener pastures." He chuckled. "Chased out like the traitors they were, I've heard told," he added as the coach rolled to a halt. "Now, let me see what I have bought." He opened the coach door and leaped to the ground. He didn't bother to help anyone out, but let the carriage man do it. But the carriage man was apparently so unaccustomed to the job that he fairly flung them out of the coach.

In the drive, Lady Kent slipped her arm through Avaline's and held her close—for her own comfort or that of her daughter's, Bernadette couldn't guess. They followed behind Lord Kent as he marched forward to the door, threw it open and disappeared inside. Niall MacDonald was just behind them.

Bernadette paused as the Kents entered and looked up at the house. She noticed some pocks in the stone facade. The windows looked rather new to her, but the door was weathered and shrubbery growing wild. It was a curious mix of neglect and new. She started for the door, looking at the land around the house, and noticed, with a start, the three riders again. They were on a hill overlooking Killeaven, watching.

She hurried after the others.

She found them all in the foyer, looking around. The foyer was very grand, two stories tall, with a double staircase curving up like two sides of a human heart,

meeting in a wide corridor above. At their feet there
were marble tiles with some rather curious gashes and
marks. The walls were stone here, too, and Bernadette
noticed the same pocks as outside.

Mr. MacDonald stood with his hands clasped behind his back as Lord Kent marched about, opening
and slamming doors.

"What are these marks?" Bernadette inquired curiously, touching one of the pocks with her fingers.

Mr. MacDonald glanced at the wall. "Left by mus-
ket fire, then."

"Muskets!" Bernadette repeated, sure that he had
meant another word entirely.

He fixed his good eye on her and said, "There was
quite a fight for Killeaven, there was."

A *fight*? Bernadette looked around again, noticed
the pocks everywhere in this grand entry and tried
to imagine men firing guns at one another in such a
grand home.

"Miss Holly!" Lord Kent shouted from some interior room.

Bernadette went in the direction of his voice and
found him and his wife and daughter in what she assumed was a dining hall. "We'll need a mason to see
to these things," he said, pointing to plaster molding
overhead, which was crumbling in one corner.

She didn't understand why he was telling her and
looked curiously at him.

His gray brows floated upward. "Well? Make note,
make note!" he demanded, and walked on.

But she had nothing with which to make a note.

She followed his lordship, and in the next room, he pointed out more things that, presumably, she was to make a note of, uncaring that she had nothing with which to write his wishes, and apparently expecting her to commit it all to memory.

When he'd toured the house he said, "MacDonald has assured me the furnishings will arrive this afternoon. Go, go, now, busy yourselves," he said, waving his hands at the ladies in a sweeping motion. "Where is my brother? Has the second coach not come along?" He marched out of the room.

Bernadette waited until she was certain he was gone before looking back at Lady Kent and Avaline. "So much to do," she said, smiling a little. "At least we'll have something to occupy us."

Neither Kent woman looked convinced of that.

The furniture did indeed arrive that afternoon, on a caravan of carts and wagons. The servants who had the misfortune of being dragged to Scotland scampered about, with the Kent butler, Renard, directing things to be placed here and there. It quickly became apparent that even with all they'd brought, filling the hold in the Mackenzie ship with beds and cupboards and settees, there was not enough to furnish this large house. Three bedrooms sat empty, as well as a sitting and a morning room.

In the evening, before a cold meal was to be served, Lord Kent called Bernadette to him in the library. Its shelves still sported some of the books of the previous owners. There was no sign of muskets in this room.

"Make a list of all we need, then send it to Balhaire," he said without greeting.

"Yes, my lord. To someone's attention in particular?"

"Naturally, to someone's attention. The laird there." He perched one hip on the desk and folded his arms across his chest. "Now, listen to me, Bernadette. You'll have to do the thinking for Avaline."

"Pardon? I don't—"

"She's a child," he said bluntly. "She can't possibly run a house this large, and her mother has been an utterly incompetent teacher." He leaned forward, reached for a bottle and poured brandy into a glass. "*You* need to prepare her for this marriage."

Bernadette swayed backward. "I can't take the place of her mother."

"You've been doing it these last few years," he said. "And you have experience in this…inexperience," he said, flicking his wrist at her. "I doubt her mother can recall a blessed thing about her wedding night."

Bernadette's face began to warm. She was very uncomfortable with the directions of this conversation.

"Come now, I don't say it to demean you," he said impatiently, trying to read her thoughts. "I say it to point out that you know more than you think. Teach her how to present herself to her husband. Teach her how to please a man." He tossed the brandy down his throat.

"My lord!" Bernadette protested.

"Don't grow missish on me," he snapped. "She must please him, Bernadette. Do you understand me? As much as I am loath to admit it, I need those bloody Mackenzies to look after my property here. I want to expand my holdings, and I want access to the sea. Why should they have all the trade? If I fail to have them fully on board with me, I will not make these gains in a pleasant way, do you understand me? I am trusting you to ensure that little lamb knows to open her legs and do her duty."

Bernadette gasped.

He clucked his tongue at her. "Don't pretend you are a tender virgin. It was your own actions that put you in this position, was it not? You have benefited greatly from my employment of you when no one else would have you, and for *that*, you owe me your allegiance and your obedience. Do I need to say more?"

Bernadette couldn't even speak. She thought herself beyond being shocked by anything that happened in the Kent household, but he had shocked her.

"Good. Now go and make sure her mother hasn't frightened her half to death. And send Renard to me— surely we've brought some decent wine."

Bernadette nodded again, fearing that if she spoke, she would say something to put her position in serious jeopardy. She was shaking with indignation as she walked out of the library.

It had been eight years since she and Albert Whitman had eloped, but sometimes it felt as if it was yesterday. So desperately in love, so determined to be free of her father's rules for her. They'd managed nearly a week of blissful union, had made it to Gretna Green, had married. They were on their way to his parents' home when her father's men found them and dragged the two of them back to Highfield.

Bernadette had mistakenly believed that as she and Albert had legally married, and had lain together as husband and wife, that there was nothing her father could do. Oh, how she'd underestimated him—the marriage was quickly annulled, and Albert was quickly impressed onto a merchant ship. There was no hope for him—he was not a seaman, and was, either by accident or design, lost at sea several months later.

She had learned a bitter, heart-rending lesson—a father would go to great lengths to undo something his daughter had done against his express wishes. A vicar could be bribed or threatened to annul a marriage. Men could be paid to impress a young man in his prime and put him on a ship bound for India. A woman could watch her reputation and good name be utterly destroyed by her own actions, and a father's invisible shackles could tighten around her even more.

After that spectacular fall from grace, everyone in and around Highfield knew what had happened. No one would even look at her on the street. Her friends fell away, and even her own sister had avoided her for fear of guilt by association.

No one seemed to know about the baby she'd lost, however. No, that was her family's secret. Her father would have sooner died than have anyone know his daughter had carried a child of that union.

"Bernadette! There you are."

She hadn't seen Avaline, who appeared almost from air and grabbed her hand. "I don't like it here," she whispered as she glanced over her shoulder at Mr. Mac-

Donald, who was standing in the entry. "There is nothing here, nothing nearby."

"I'm sure there is," Bernadette said. "I beg your pardon, Mr. MacDonald, but there is a village nearby, is there not?"

"No' any longer," he said.

"Not any longer? What does that mean, precisely?"

"I mean to say the English forces…" He paused. "Removed it."

Removed it. "Ah…thank you, sir." Bernadette glanced at Avaline. "It's all right, darling—Balhaire is very near. Come and help me remember the things your father wants done, will you?" she asked, and pulled Avaline into a sitting room. Lady Kent was within, staring out the window, her arms wrapped tightly about her.

"What things?" Avaline asked.

"Pardon?" Lady Kent asked, turning about.

"I was reminding Avaline that there were several things his lordship wanted done, and asked that she help me remember them all," Bernadette responded. "We must make this place pleasing for your fiancé," she said to Avaline.

"Don't call him that," Avaline said.

"But that's what he is. The betrothal has been made."

"I don't want the betrothal!" Avaline said, jerking her hand free of Bernadette's. "He is *ghastly*."

She was a petulant child, only a moment away from stomping her foot. "That's enough, Avaline!" Bernadette said sternly. *"Enough."*

Lady Kent gaped at Bernadette, shocked by her tone.

Bernadette groaned. "I beg your pardon, but you both know as well as I that there is nothing to be done for this engagement."

Mother and daughter exchanged a look.

"This is what you were born to," Bernadette said to Avaline. "To make your father rich and prosperous by furthering his connections. You can't pretend it isn't so or believe that petulance will change it."

Avaline began to cry. So did her mother. They were like two kittens, mewling over spilled milk.

"For God's sake, will you stop?" Bernadette pleaded. "Best you meet your fate head-on than like a tiny little hare afraid of her own shadow. He will respect you more if you don't cower."

"Oh dear," Lady Kent said. "She's right, darling."

That surprised Bernadette. She watched as Lady Kent shakily swept the tears from her cheeks. "She's quite right, really. I've cowered all my life and you know very well what that has gained me. If you are to make this marriage bearable, you must find your footing."

Avaline's eyes widened with surprise at this unexpected bit of advice from her mother. "But how?" she asked plaintively. "What am I to do?"

Lady Kent and her daughter both looked to Bernadette for the answer to that.

Good Lord, they were the two most hapless women she had ever known. Bernadette sighed. "You must prepare to meet him a second time and make him welcome. We'll start there."

Avaline nodded obediently.

Bernadette smiled encouragingly, but privately, she could think of nothing worse than having to meet that cold-hearted man a second time and pretend to welcome him. She'd known men like him, men who thought themselves so superior that civility was not necessary. Her first instinct had been visceral, and her humor when he was near quite deplorable. She would give a special thanks to heaven tonight that she was not the one who would have to spend the rest of her days in misery with him.

Poor Avaline.

CHAPTER FOUR

HE FIRST NOTICES her at the Mackenzie feill, *an annual rite of celebration where Mackenzies and friends come from far and wide for games, dancing and song. She is wearing an* arasaid *plaid that leaves her ankles bare, and a* stiom, *the ribbon around her head that denotes she is not married. She is dancing with her friends, holding her skirt out and turning this way and that, kicking her heels and rising up on her toes and down again. She is laughing, her expression one of pure joy, and Rabbie feels a tiny tug in his heart that he's never felt before. The lass intrigues him.*

He moves, wanting to be closer. He catches her eye, and she smiles prettily at him, and that alone compels him to walk up to her and offer his hand.

She looks at his hand, then at him. "Do you mean to dance, then?"

He nods, curiously incapable of speech in that moment. Her soft brown eyes mesmerize him, make him think of the color of the hills in the morning light.

"Then you must ask, Mackenzie," she teases him.

"W-will you dance, then?"

She laughs at his stammering and slips her hand into his. "Aye, lad. I will."

They dance...all night. And for the first time in his twenty-seven years, Rabbie thinks seriously of marriage.

RABBIE'S MOTHER PUT her foot down with him, as if he was a lad instead of a man in his thirty-fifth year. As if he was still swaddled. "You will go and pay her a call," she said firmly, her eyes blazing with irritation.

"She will no' care if I call or no'," he said dismissively.

"*I* care," she snapped. "That you are not attached to her, that you do not care for her, is no excuse for poor manners. She is your fiancée now and you will treat her with the respect she is due."

Rabbie laughed at that. "What respect is she due, *Maither*? She is seventeen, scarcely out of the nursery. She is a *Sassenach*." She was pale and docile and hadn't lived, not like he had. She had no experience beyond her own English parlor. She trembled when he was near—or when anyone was near, for that matter. He couldn't imagine what he would even say to the lass, much less how he might inhabit the same house as her.

His mother sighed wearily at his pessimism. She sat next to him on the settee, where Rabbie had dropped like a naughty child when he'd been summoned. She put her hand on his knee and said, "My darling son, I'm so very sorry about Seona—"

Rabbie instantly vaulted to his feet. "Donna say her name."

"I *will* say it. She's gone, Rabbie. You can't live your life waiting for a ghost."

He shot his mother a warning look. "You think I wait for Seona to appear by sorcery? I saw her house. I saw where blood had spilled, where fires had burned," he said, his gut clenching at the mere mention of it. "I'm no' a dull man—I understand what happened. I'm no' waiting for a *ghost*." He strode to the window to avoid his mother's gaze and to bite down his anger.

In his mind's eye, he could see the house where Seona had lived with her family and a father who had abetted the Jacobites. A father who had sent his sons to join the forces marching to England to restore Charlie Stuart to the throne. They'd been slaughtered on the field at Culloden, and her father was hanged from an old tree on the shores of Lochcarron, so that any Highlander gliding past on a boat could see him, could see what vengeance the English had wrought on those who took Prince Charlie's cause.

But Seona? Her sister, her mother? No one knew what had become of them. Their home had been ransacked, the servants gone, the livestock stolen or shot. There was no one left, no one who could say what had happened to them. The only ones to survive the carnage were Seona's niece and nephew; two wee bairns who'd been sent to stay with a clan member when the news came the English were sweeping through the Highlands. There was no one else, no other MacBee living in these hills any longer. And judging by the devastation done to the MacBee home, a man could only imagine the worst—every night, in his dreams, he imagined it.

"If you're not waiting for a ghost, then what are you

waiting for?" his mother persisted as Rabbie tried once again to erase the image of the forsaken household.

Death. Every day, he waited for it. Perhaps in death he'd know what had become of the woman he'd loved. In death, there would be relief from this useless life he was living. From the searing guilt he bore every single day for having been unable to save her.

"And while you wait for whatever it is that will ease you, that poor English girl has been bartered like a fine ewe and has come all this way to a strange land, to marry a man she scarcely knows. A man who is older than her by more than fifteen years, and who is bigger than her in every way. Of *course* she is frightened. The least you might do is put her at ease."

Rabbie slowly turned, fixing his gaze on his mother. "You are verra protective of a lass you scarcely know, are you no'?"

His mother's vexation was apparent in the dip of her brows. "I *was* that lass once, Rabbie Mackenzie. I was a sheep, just like her, bartered to your father. I know what she must be enduring just now, and I have compassion for her. Just as I have compassion for you, darling— this isn't what either of you hoped for, but it is what has come. If only you could find some compassion in your own heart for her, you might find a way to accept it."

Rabbie didn't know how to explain to his mother that words like *compassion* and *hope* were far beyond his capacity to fathom. He was merely existing, moving from one day to the next, contemplating his own death with alarming regularity.

His mother was accustomed to his surliness, however, and she didn't wait for his answer, but turned and walked out the door of her sitting room, pausing just at the threshold. "Catriona will accompany you."

"Cat!"

"Yes, *Cat*," she said. "Your sister will be helpful in making Miss Kent feel comfortable and soothing any ruffled feathers."

"Ruffled feathers," he scoffed.

"Yes, Rabbie. Ruffled feathers. You have treated Miss Kent very ill."

Rabbie shook his head.

"She's a sweet girl. If you allowed yourself to stop thinking of your own hurts, you might be pleasantly surprised by her."

Once again, his mother didn't wait for him to say curtly that he couldn't possibly be surprised by the likes of her, and quit the room.

Rabbie turned back to the window and stared blankly ahead. His mother's words floated somewhere above him. His mind saw nothing but darkness.

WHEN RABBIE EMERGED in the bailey, having prepared himself as best he could to call on his fiancée, Catriona was already there, waiting impatiently for him. She was dressed properly, which was to say like a *Sassenach*. Highlanders were now banned by law from wearing plaid. His father had taken that edict to mean they should dress as the English would dress in all things. His father had softened with age, an old man with a bad leg who wanted no trouble from the redcoats that appeared from time to time at their door.

Catriona had a jaunty hat on her head, with a feather that shot off one side like an arrow's quill. It was a hat that their sister-in-law, Daisy, had given Catriona when she and Cailean had come to Balhaire after brokering the marriage offer between the Mackenzies and the Kents.

Rabbie paused next to her mount and looked up at her hat. "That is ridiculous."

"How verra kind," she said saucily. "Should I inquire as to what has made you so bloody cross today, then?"

"The same that makes me cross every day—life," he said, and hauled himself up onto the back of his horse. He gave his sister a sidelong glance. "I didna mean to wound your tender feelings," he said, gesturing to her hat. "You know verra well what I meant by it, aye?"

"No, Rabbie, I donna know what you meant. I never know what you mean. *No* one knows what you mean anymore." She was the second woman today to want no more words from him.

She wheeled her horse about and spurred it on, but then immediately drew up as two riders came in through the bailey gates. Seated behind each rider was a child.

"Who is it?" Rabbie asked as the riders turned to the right.

"You donna recognize them, then?" Catriona asked. Rabbie shook his head. "That is Fiona and Ualan Mac-Leod."

The names were familiar to Rabbie, but it took him a moment to recall the children of Seona's sister, Gavina

MacBee MacLeod. The last he'd seen them they were bairns, Fiona having only learned to walk, and Ualan still toddling about on fat wee legs.

"Why are they here, then? Are they no' in the care of a relative?"

Catriona looked at him. "Aye, the elderly cousin of a MacBee, I think. She's passed."

Rabbie's gaze followed the riders with the children as they disappeared into the stables. "Who has them now?"

"No one," Catriona said. "There are no MacBees or MacLeods left in these hills, are there? Aye, they've brought them to Balhaire for safe harbor until someone decides what's to be done with them."

Rabbie jerked his gaze to his sister. "Why was I no' told of it?"

Catriona snorted. "Look at you, lad. Do you think any of us would add to your burden?" She sent her horse to a trot.

Rabbie looked back to where the riders had gone, but there was no sign of them. He reluctantly followed after Catriona.

The ride to Killeaven was quicker than by coach, which plodded along on old, seldom-used roads. Catriona and Rabbie rode through the forest on trails well known to them from having spent their childhood exploring the land around them. They splashed across a shallow river, then trotted up a glen, through a meadow. At the old *Na Cùileagan* cairn, they turned west and cantered across the open field where the Killeaven cattle and sheep had once grazed—but they were all gone, seized by the English and sold at market.

As they trotted into the drive—newly graveled— Rabbie noted the new windows and the repair to two chimneys. The weathered front door of the house swung open. Lord Kent, in the company of Lord Ramsey, strode out to greet them. Both men were dressed for riding. Behind them was Niall MacDonald. Slight and taciturn, he'd proven himself to be a keen observer. He was good at what he did for the Mackenzies—which consisted primarily of keeping his eyes and ears open and reporting back to the laird.

"There you are, Mackenzie," Kent said. "I'd expected you well before now."

His voice was slightly admonishing, and Rabbie resisted the urge to shrug. Not that Kent would have noticed—his gaze was on Catriona.

"I beg your pardon, we've been detained," Rabbie lied. He swung off his horse to help down Catriona, but she'd leaped off her mount before he could reach her. "May I introduce my sister, Miss Catriona Mackenzie," Rabbie said. "She was away when you arrived."

"Miss Mackenzie," Lord Kent said, bowing his head, and then introducing his brother. "Now then, Mackenzie. We would like to be about the business of stocking sheep here. We'll need a market."

"Glasgow," Rabbie said instantly.

Kent frowned. "Glasgow is too far, isn't it? I'd need drovers and such. I had in mind buying from Highlanders, such as yourself."

Rabbie's pulse quickened a beat or two. Kent thought

he might help himself to what sheep they'd managed to keep, did he? "Our flocks have been decimated," he said as evenly as he could. "Sheep and cattle alike."

"We will eventually want to add cattle, naturally," Kent said, as if Rabbie hadn't spoken. If he understood how the Highland herds had been decimated, he was either unconcerned or obtuse. "But for now, we want to be about the business of sheep."

Of course they did. Wool was a lucrative business.

"You have sheep there at Balhaire, do you not?" he asked, squinting curiously, as if he'd expected Rabbie to offer them up.

He might have said something foolish, but Catriona slipped her hand into the crook of his elbow and smiled sweetly at him. Her eyes, however, were full of warning. "Aye," Rabbie said slowly. "But none for sale. They'll be lambing soon." That was a lie, but he gambled that Kent didn't know one end of a sheep from the other.

"Well. Perhaps we'll have a word with your father," he said, exchanging a look with his brother. "We're on our way to Balhaire now, as it happens."

Rabbie could well imagine his father selling off half their flock so as not to "make trouble," and said quickly, "You ought to call on the Buchanans" as casually as he might as he removed his gloves. "They've a flock they might cull."

Behind Kent, Rabbie noticed the look of surprise on Niall's face.

"The Buchanans," Lord Kent repeated, sounding uncertain.

"Aye, the Buchanans. You'll find them at Marraig, near the sea. Follow the road west. Mr. MacDonald knows where."

Lord Kent looked back at his escort, whose expression had fallen back into stoicism, then at Rabbie. "How far?"

"Seven miles at most."

"We'll be met with hospitality, or a gun?"

Rabbie smiled. "This is the Highlands, my lord." He let that statement linger, let Kent imagine what he would for a moment or two, and indeed, he and his brother exchanged another brief, but wary, look. "Aye, you'll be met with hospitality, you will. But were I you, I'd have a man or two with me."

Lord Kent nodded and gestured to his brother. "Assemble some of the men, then."

He turned back to Rabbie. "Very well, we will call on the Buchanans. You'll find your fiancée with the women." He began striding for the stables, his business with Rabbie done.

Rabbie watched him go, trailed by his brother. Niall paused briefly before following them.

"Anything?" Rabbie asked in Gaelic.

"Only that the food is not to their liking," Niall responded in kind.

"They'll like it well enough, come winter," Catriona said as she passed both men on her way to the door.

"The Buchanan sheep suffered the ovine plague," Niall reminded Rabbie.

Rabbie gave Niall the closest thing to a smile he'd managed in weeks. "Aye, lad, that I know."

"They've come round, they have," Niall said.

"Who?"

"The Buchanans. I've seen them twice up on the hill behind Killeaven."

"Aye, any clans remaining will come to have a look, will they no'?"

Niall shrugged. "It was odd, it was. They sit there, watching."

There was no trust between the Buchanans and the Mackenzies. Rabbie couldn't guess what they were about, but he'd reckon their interest wasn't a neighborly one.

By the time he caught up to Catriona, the butler had already met her. The man wore a freshly powdered wig and his shoes had been polished to a very high sheen. Perhaps he thought the king meant to call today.

"Welcome," the butler said, and showed them into the salon just beyond the entry. It smelled rather dank, Rabbie thought, even though the windows were open. Dry rot, he presumed, and supposed that would be his burden once he took the wee bird to wife.

"Have you a calling card I might present to her ladyship?" the butler asked.

Rabbie glared at him. A *calling* card? The lass was fortunate he'd come at all.

"I beg your pardon, but we donna make use of calling cards here," Catriona said. "If you would be so kind, then, to tell her that Mr. Rabbie Mackenzie and Miss Catriona Mackenzie have come?"

"He knows who we are," Rabbie said gruffly.

"Yes, of course," the man said, ignoring Rabbie entirely as he hurried off in little staccato steps.

"A calling card," Rabbie muttered.

"They're English, then," Catriona said. "They have their ways, and we have ours, aye? Donna be so sour, Rabbie."

He might have argued with her, but they were both startled by a lot of clomping overhead and looked to the ceiling. It sounded as if a herd of cattle had been aroused. One of them—the calf, he presumed—ran from one end of the room to the other, and back again.

Moments later, they arrived in a threesome—Lady Kent and her lookalike daughter, and the maid, who barely spared him a glance as she entered, but then smiled prettily at Catriona before moving briskly to stand on the other side of the room apart from the rest.

Rabbie watched her, frowning. What made this woman so arrogant? She should have curtsied to him, as he was her superior in every way. He was so distracted by her conceit that he failed to introduce his sister or greet his fiancée.

"My brother has forgotten his manners, aye?" Catriona said. "I am his sister, Catriona Mackenzie. I was away when you arrived, tending to our aunt. She's rather ill."

"Oh. I am very sorry to hear it," Miss Kent said. "Umm…" She glanced across the room at the maid, who gave her a tiny, almost imperceptible nod. "May I introduce my mother, Lady Kent?"

Lady Kent curtsied and mumbled something unintelligible to Rabbie. Catriona returned the greeting quite loudly, as if she thought the woman was deaf. Then Miss Kent slid her palms down her side and said, "Good afternoon, Mr. Mackenzie" without looking directly at him.

"Aye, good afternoon."

"Will you please sit?" she asked.

"Thank you," Catriona said, and plunked herself down on a settee. Rabbie didn't move from his position near the hearth.

"Might I offer you something to drink?" Miss Kent asked in a manner that suggested she'd been rehearsing the question, and looked nervously to Rabbie.

"No. Thank you."

"Have you any ale?" Catriona asked. "I'm a wee bit dry after our ride."

Miss Kent looked startled by Catriona's request. "Ah…" She glanced to the butler, who nodded and walked out in that same eager manner as before.

The maid was now leaning against a sill at the open window, gazing out, as if there was no one else in the room but her. "Oh, I beg your pardon, sir," Miss Kent said, having noticed the direction of Rabbie's gaze. "M-may I introduce Miss Bernadette Holly? She is my lady's maid."

Miss Bernadette Holly pushed herself away from the sill and sank into what could only be termed a very lazy curtsy.

"Aye, we've met," he said dismissively.

"You *have*?" Miss Kent exclaimed.

"In the Balhaire kitchen," he said, at the very same moment the maid said, "No."

Miss Kent looked at her lady's maid, her brows rising higher.

"What I mean to say is that we were not formally introduced," Miss Holly said. "Our paths crossed in the kitchen, that's all."

One of Rabbie's brows rose above the other. Was she openly contradicting him, this lady's maid?

"Oh, dear, of course, the kitchen," Miss Kent said. "That was…well, it was an unfortunate oversight."

He didn't know what Miss Kent thought was an oversight and he didn't care. He kept staring at the maid, this Miss Holly, wondering how she kept her employ with her supercilious ways. She leaned against the sill once more and folded her arms across her body, returning his gaze with one that seemed almost impatient.

"Do you ride, Miss Kent?" Catriona suddenly interjected, heading off anything Rabbie might have said about the maid.

"Oh, I, ah… I am a poor rider," the bird said, and glanced uncertainly at Miss Bernadette Holly, who once again gave her an almost imperceptible nod, as if giving her permission to continue. Rabbie glared at her.

"There is much to see in these hills, views you'd no' see in England, aye? Perhaps you would join Rabbie and I one afternoon?" Catriona suggested.

Again, Miss Kent looked to Miss Holly. This time, she raised her dark brows, and Miss Kent spoke instantly. "Yes, thank you."

What was this, was the bird the maid's bloody puppet? Even the girl's utterly useless mother kept glancing nervously and fretfully at Miss Holly.

Miss Holly smiled a little at Miss Kent, and Miss Kent suddenly smiled, too, as if she'd just remembered an amusing jest. And then she blushed, as if she were embarrassed by the jest. *Diah*, she was more a child than a woman grown. Rabbie shifted restlessly and caught Catriona's eye. She gave him a very meaningful and slightly heated look.

He suppressed a sigh of tedium and looked at the bird again. The color in her cheeks was very high.

The butler returned with Catriona's ale, at which point Miss Kent took a seat beside Catriona.

"How do you find Killeaven?" Rabbie asked, making some effort, he thought, although his voice was flat and emotionless, no doubt because he didn't care what she thought of Killeaven.

"It's…well, it's bigger than I anticipated," Miss Kent said, and again looked to Miss Holly. "I suppose…that is to say, perhaps we might make improvements to it?"

Was she asking him? "Pardon?"

Miss Kent looked in his direction—but at his feet. "Perhaps we might make some improvements to the house and the grounds."

He didn't care what she did to Killeaven. Burn it down for all he cared. "I donna really care."

That earned him another heated look from his sister. "What my brother means is that it is up to you, Miss Kent. This is your house to do as you please, aye?"

He hadn't meant that at all.

"Would you like to see it?" Miss Kent asked suddenly. She was not speaking to Rabbie, but to Catriona.

Catriona gulped down a bit of ale and said, "I should like it verra much, I would." She stood.

Miss Kent and her mother rose almost as one. The three of them walked out of the room, Miss Kent suddenly jabbering. At the door, Catriona glanced back and motioned with her head for Rabbie to come along. He ignored her. He didn't care about this house. What he cared about was Catriona's unfinished ale. He walked to the settee and the small table where she'd set it down, picked it up and drained it. He put the empty glass down, folded his arms and turned to Miss Holly.

She was glaring at him.

"Aye, what, then?" he asked impatiently. She shook her head, as if the burden of explaining what, exactly, was too great. "You are a peculiar one," Rabbie said irritably.

She watched him in silence.

"Tell me, then, is your charge capable of rational thought? Or must you do all of it for her?"

"I beg your pardon," she said indignantly. "I don't do any thinking for her."

"No? Why, then, does she look to you before she answers any question put to her?"

"She is anxious," Miss Holly said instantly. "And eager to impress you."

He snorted. "Well, that's no' possible."

"Is it likewise not possible for you to make her feel the least bit welcome?"

He jerked his head up at that bit of insolence. "You dare to instruct me, lass?" he asked incredulously.

"Someone ought to," she said pertly.

In that moment, Rabbie felt something besides anger or despair—he felt stunned. He'd never in his life been addressed by a servant in such a manner. He didn't know what game she was playing with him, but it was an unwinnable one. He casually moved to where she stood, standing close, towering over her. She was pretty in an exotic way, he decided. Her skin was flawless. Her lips were full and the color of new plums. And her brows, dark and full, were dipped into an annoying vee shape above those pretty hazel eyes sparkling with ire. "A wee bit of advice, lass," he said, voice low as he took in the slight upturn of her nose and the strand of hair that had come undone and now draped across her smooth, creamy décolletage. "Donna think to shame me. It will no' work. For one, I donna care what that wee mouse thinks of me, aye? For another, there is little anyone can do to me that's no' already been done, and been done worse."

One her dark brows lifted in a manner that reminded him of a woman hearing a tale she did not believe.

"You donna care for me, then," he allowed. "I donna care for you, either. But I will marry that lass, and if you continue on as you have in my presence, I will put you out on your lovely arse and pack you back to bloody old England. Do you understand me?" He was confident that would do it—that would make her quake in her festive little slippers.

But the maid surprised him with a smirk; she seemed almost amused by his threat. "Neither should you think to threaten me, sir. For there is little you can do to me that has not already been done, and been done worse." She gave him a bit of a triumphant look and stepped around him, walking out of the room and leaving the faint scent of her perfume in her wake.

What did that mean? What might have possibly been done to that privileged little butterfly? She was naive—she had no notion of the cruelty of life, not like he did.

But her lack of fear and her conceit would not leave him. He was still brooding about it when the women returned, at which point he picked up his gloves and held out his arm to Catriona. "We'll take our leave, aye? Lady Kent, Miss Kent, you and your family are invited to dine at Balhaire this Friday evening if it suits," he said formally.

The mouse smiled with surprise.

"Your lady's maid as well," he added awkwardly and, at least to him, surprisingly.

The mouse smiled as if she hadn't a brain in her head.

"We might discuss the details of the wedding, aye?" Catriona added. "Our customs are a wee bit different."

"Oh. Yes, we should…we would like that very much, wouldn't we, Mamma?" the mouse asked uncertainly.

"Yes, thank you," the mother said, and returned her daughter's anxious smile.

"Aye, verra well." Rabbie was suddenly eager to be gone. "Cat?" He began striding for the door.

They walked out of the house, Miss Kent and Lady Kent trailing behind, calling their goodbyes and thank-yous. Rabbie mounted his horse and looked back at the house, and imagined those hazel eyes shooting daggers at him from behind one of the new windows.

CHAPTER FIVE

AVALINE'S FORCED SMILE faded away the moment the door was closed to the departing Mackenzies. "He scarcely spoke to me at all," she said to Bernadette.

"You scarcely spoke to him, either, dearest," Bernadette said.

"I know, I *know*, but I don't know what to say to him," she said plaintively as they returned to the salon. "What am I to say to someone who is so aloof? It's desperately difficult to even *smile* at him. He's so…unappealing," she said, shuddering.

Bernadette didn't think his appearance was unappealing on closer inspection. He had good looks behind that unpleasant mien—a strong jaw, thick lashes that framed his stormy blue eyes, a regal, straight nose. He was quite obviously brimming with vitality, given his size and apparent strength. It was the blaze in his eyes that she found so disquieting, and the dark circles beneath them.

"Now you are invited to dine with him, so you must be prepared to converse with him," Bernadette advised.

Avaline snorted at that statement as she walked to the windows and gazed out at the vast landscape of nothing but meadow and hill. "It's useless," she said. "He won't respond."

"If he doesn't have the courtesy to make proper conversation with you, then perhaps you might draw it out of him by engaging him as we discussed."

Avaline glanced over her shoulder. "What questions?"

"I can't give you specific ones," Bernadette said. "You must allow the conversation to guide you."

Avaline turned from the window, looking confused. "Meaning?"

"Just…*questions*, Avaline," Bernadette said impatiently. "Any entry that will give him leave to talk about himself. You might ask where he attended school. Did he have tutors, what is the name of his dog, does he enjoy hunting or riding."

"What if he doesn't enjoy riding or hunting?"

Bernadette's patience was hanging by a tiny thread. She realized this was a difficult situation for Avaline, but could the girl not construct a few logical thoughts in her head? Did she truly have no sense of how to make conversation with a gentleman? "The point, darling, is to simply ask questions to promote conversation. Ask if he had a favorite governess, if takes his meals at Balhaire or his home, what is his favorite activity— *questions*."

"Yes, I see," Avaline said quickly, always eager to please, whether she knew how or not.

Bernadette sighed. She sat on the arm of the settee, her hands braced against her knees. "Like this," she said, softening her voice and, hopefully, any outward sign of her growing frustration. "You might ask him 'Do you often sail with your brother?' And he might answer you completely, or say something quite curt, as he is wont to do, such as *no*. Then what do you say?"

Avaline shook her head.

"You say something like 'I had my first voyage here, and I found it quite pleasing, although I took a bit seasick when we were in open waters. Have you ever experienced it?'"

Avaline blinked. "No, I was quite all right during the voyage, but Mamma took ill."

"Avaline!" Bernadette cried.

"I mean, yes, *yes*, I understand."

She understood nothing. Bernadette stood up and crossed the room to her charge. She put her hands on Avaline's shoulders. "Avaline—you really *must* be prepared. I can't always be there to help you."

"What?" Avaline exclaimed, her eyes widening. "Of course you will! You'll be beside me Friday evening to help me—"

"I don't think I should go," Bernadette said. "You rely on me far too much, and in this, you really must make your own way—"

"Bernadette!" Avaline grabbed Bernadette's hands from her shoulder and held them tightly in hers. "I can't *possibly* bear an entire meal without you! I *need* you!" She leaned forward and whispered, "You are my only hope. You know my mother is no help, my father doesn't care—"

"But I can't—"

Avaline suddenly let go of Bernadette's hands. "You must attend! I insist!"

"Avaline—"

"I *insist*," she said again, quite sternly, and much to Bernadette's great surprise.

"Well then," Bernadette said. It was high time Avaline stood up for something she wanted, even if that something was not what Bernadette desired in the least. "Naturally, I will do as you bid me."

Avaline looked slightly stunned by her victory. She sniffed. She twirled a curl at her nape. "I only insist because I need you."

"I understand."

"Otherwise I would not insist."

"As you said," Bernadette agreed.

"It's just that—"

"Not another word of apology," Bernadette said, smiling. "You are allowed to speak your mind."

Avaline released a long breath. "I feel as if my mind is always wrong," she said morosely. "Thank you. I mean that truly, Bernadette."

She didn't have to say it. Bernadette knew that Avaline loved her, and more than what was reasonable to love a servant of her household.

BERNADETTE, AVALINE AND Lady Kent spent the better part of Friday afternoon preparing Avaline for the evening, and Bernadette thought their efforts were rewarded— Avaline looked like a princess in her butter-yellow gown and stomacher. Bernadette had put up Avaline's golden hair in a tower that made her look taller than she was and had adorned it with tiny gold leaves. She couldn't fathom how Mackenzie might look at his fiancée and not be at least a bit smitten with her.

Avaline's preparations left precious little time for Bernadette to dress herself. She chose the gown of scarlet she'd worn to a Christmas feast two years past. There was no time to dress her hair, and she bound it simply at her nape. She looked quite plain in comparison to her charge.

At least she didn't look as plain as Lady Kent, who had, for reasons that escaped Bernadette, chosen a drab brown gown that made her pale, slight frame look even smaller. Perhaps she meant to fade into a wall, for she'd dressed perfectly for it. Lady Kent often reminded Bernadette of a leaf scudding across the courtyard at Highfield— without substance and in a permanent tremble whenever her husband was about.

Bernadette was taller than both women and larger in frame, and she did not tremble in the presence of men, for which she owed her father grim thanks. He'd been a tyrant, not unlike Lord Kent in his way, and Bernadette had learned at an early age that weakness was to be exploited, and therefore, it was far better to stand tall and proud than to cower.

She thought it only through the grace of her grandfather and Albert that she hadn't learned to despise all men. Her grandfather, God rest his soul, had been the kindest person she'd ever known. He would take her and her sister for long walks around Highfield, would invite them to his little house on the estate's grounds and make them mince pies and sing songs to them. She had loved him so, had mourned him deeply when he'd died from an ague in his seventy-second year.

And, of course, Albert, the son of a shop merchant. Albert had wanted to study law, and he'd worked in his father's dry goods shop until such time he could afford the schooling. He was bright and curious, thoughtful and tender with Bernadette, and he'd never said a cross word to her.

Albert and Grandpappa had taught Bernadette that there were men in this world who loved and cherished those in their lives. They were good, decent and loving men, both of them gone now, survived by men like Lord Kent and her father.

No, men didn't intimidate her. No one intimidated her. She was an island unto herself, an untouchable, damaged bit of flotsam in a vast sea. Occasionally, she bumped into this ship or that buoy, but she would always spin away and continued on with her solo journey through this life.

It was past time to depart when Lady Kent and Avaline made their way downstairs to join his lordship and Bernadette. Lord Kent reeked of wine. He was impatient and made cross by the wait. He'd dressed in formal clothing and a newly styled and powdered wig. His shirt was trimmed in lace that dripped from his coat sleeves, and his neck cloth was tied so ornately it was small wonder he hadn't choked himself in the process.

With one leg cast out, his hand on a staff that he carried for effect, he surveyed the three women before him and frowned slightly. "It will do, I suppose," he said, and gestured for them to carry on, out the door. "Make haste, make haste, we'll be tardy as it is."

The ladies were ushered into the coach, and Kent put himself on a horse. Lord Ramsey was not attending this evening. According to Bernadette's friend Charles, a footman, Ramsey had fallen into his cups far sooner than his brother and was too sodding drunk to travel. Charles was fond of Bernadette and often sought her out to regale her with news of the household. In fact, two months ago, it was Charles who told her that she would be sent to Scotland as the lady's maid of Avaline.

"To Scotland," she'd repeated disbelievingly. "Leave England?"

"You've not heard?" Charles asked, clearly exuberant in having the news before she did. "Miss Avaline is to marry one of the Highland brutes."

Of course she'd known that Avaline was to marry a man from the Highlands, but Bernadette hadn't, until that moment, imagined he was actually *from* the Highlands. She'd rather imagined a lord of some sort, with lands there, someone civilized, for everyone had heard that the Highlanders were brutal, traitorous people, and it had taken the English army to rout them.

"It's surely temporary," Bernadette said, thinking aloud. "I'll be meant to settle her."

But Charles, who had attended Lord Kent and Lady Chatwick when she and her husband had come to broker the marriage, shook his head. "You are to stay with her, as am I. As are a few more," Charles confided. "He told the lady he'd not leave his only daughter in the hands of such primitive people."

Wasn't Lady Chatwick herself married to one of those primitive people? "And what did the lady say?" Bernadette asked.

"She said it was a kind thing he did to think so tenderly of his daughter, but that he could trust she would be well cared for."

"There, you see?" Bernadette had said, walking away from Charles. "It's only temporary."

It was not, as it turned out, temporary. Lord Kent meant for her to stay on here with Avaline. Bernadette's father meant for her to do the same. While she did not relish the thought of being banished to Scotland, she did realize that the farther she was from either of those men, the better.

The Kent party loaded into the coach, and it lurched forward, starting on the tortuous journey of four miles. Bernadette would have preferred to walk. In the last few days, she'd taken to walking the many paths around Killeaven. It was beautiful scenery and physically invigorating—and she'd yet to meet another person. She felt herself growing stronger, too, going farther afield every day.

She wasn't entirely sure of how to walk to Balhaire, but she would have liked to try. It was a fine evening, and surely it couldn't be any more taxing on the body than this coach. Or perhaps they might have gone on horseback? She honestly didn't know if Lady Kent had ever been on the back of a horse, but Bernadette was a passable rider, as was Avaline. Unfortunately, his lordship did not think it proper for ladies to travel by horseback, not until they'd birthed all the children they were meant to have.

He had many odious opinions.

When Bernadette was certain she couldn't bear the ride another moment, the coach reached the village on the outskirts of Balhaire and began to move up the high road. The fortress looked so foreboding as they approached it, as unwelcoming as its son.

In the bailey, three stray dogs trotted over to have a sniff of them all, and two men who looked equally astray were on hand to greet them. The unsmiling Frang wordlessly showed them to a room near the great hall, where the Mackenzies were waiting.

Bernadette was surprised to see Avaline's fiancé dressed in a plaid blanket that fell just above his knees. He wore thick wool socks and shoes with it, a waistcoat and coat over it. It was such a peculiar dress, but it was, Bernadette had to admit, rather enticing, particularly as she could see just how muscular and long his legs were. She wondered if Avaline had noticed the same.

The room where they'd gathered was smaller and more intimate than any of the other rooms Bernadette had seen on her first visit to Balhaire. The walls had been covered with tapestries to ward off the chill that seemed to permeate the castle, but the effect was stifling, and Bernadette felt a little as if the walls were closing in on her. She stood near the door, where at least there was a bit of air.

Lord Kent herded his daughter and his wife forward to greet their hosts. Lord and Lady Mackenzie, their sons, their daughter, Miss Catriona Mackenzie, and another daughter they'd not yet met, Mrs. Vivienne Mackenzie. Lord Kent gestured absently to Bernadette when those introductions had been made. "Miss Holly, our daughter's maid," he said.

Bernadette curtsied.

"Welcome, all," Mrs. Vivienne Mackenzie said in a lovely, melodic voice. "There are more of us, aye? My husband has gone to bring our bairns to say good-night—" She hadn't even finished her thought when five children burst into the room and raced for their mother and their grandparents. The oldest, a girl, looked to be thirteen or fourteen years old. And the youngest, a boy, perhaps eight years of age. The children were raucous and gay, and they caused Bernadette's heart to squeeze painfully. Children, especially young children, always had that effect on her—they reminded her of her own loss. A loss so wretched that even after all these years, she could not escape its clutches at the most inopportune times. Even now, she felt flushed and had to look down at her feet to regain her balance.

The children were talking all at once, eager to be seen, eager to know their guests. Bernadette could well imagine that Lord Kent was nearly beside himself— he did not believe in mixing children with adults. She watched the children wiggle and sway about on their feet, unable to keep still. One boy carried something in his pocket that caused it to bulge, and Bernadette felt a smile softening her face. She would never know the pleasure of having a child that age. She would never feel the pride in watching one grow. When she'd lost her child, she'd almost died. She'd survived, but her ability to bear children had not.

When the children had received kisses from their family, Mrs. Mackenzie sent them out with a maid, and Bernadette happened to look up from them and realized with a start that Avaline's fiancé was watching her. She felt as if she'd been caught in a private moment, and awkwardly rubbed her nape, unnerved at having been caught in the act of admiring children. She turned her back to him and walked to a small table in a corner, where she pretended to closely examine what she could only imagine were some sort of artifacts.

A moment later, his deep voice rumbled behind her. "I thought you fearless, yet here you stand, cowering in the corner."

Ah, how lucky for her! The beast had followed her. Bernadette had managed to trap herself in the corner, and couldn't escape him without causing a scene. His presence felt too large, too powerful, and she shifted closer to the wall. "I'm not cowering. I'm admiring these artifacts. What are they, some sort of ancient weapon?"

He leaned across her body, the arm of his coat brushing lightly against her bare forearm as he picked one up. He held it up to her. "This is a rock. One that my nephew has collected."

Artifacts! She gave the rock a disapproving look as if it had deliberately misled her. Her cheeks bloomed with embarrassment. "I should have paid closer attention to my archeology lessons." She wished he would move, step aside. He stood so close that she could feel the power and bad humor radiating from him.

Of course he didn't move, as that would have been the polite, civilized thing to do. He kept his gaze locked on hers as he returned the rock to its place, and he looked entirely suspicious of her. What did he think, she had come here for nefarious reasons? The idea almost made her laugh.

"If you donna stand apart from fear, then given our previous conversation, I might only surmise you believe yourself superior to a few Scots." He waited for her to deny it.

Bernadette smiled slowly. "The only Scot I believe myself superior to is *you*, Mr. Mackenzie."

One corner of his mouth turned up. "I would expect no different of the *Sassenach*."

"Of what?"

The dark smile spread across his lips. "English," he said.

"If being English means that I believe in civility and manners, then yes, I suppose you should expect it of me."

His smirk deepened. "I advised you no' to attempt to shame me, Miss Holly."

"And I advised you not to try to intimidate me."

"You advised me no' to threaten you, lass."

He would quibble with her now? He could quibble with Avaline all that he liked, but not with her. There was a limit to what Bernadette would do to help this marital union, and speaking to him beyond what was absolutely necessary exceeded that limit. She thought about advising him of that, but decided that she would do best to keep her mouth shut and remove herself before she said something untoward. "Please excuse me." She stepped around him and walked into the center of the room.

"Miss Holly, will you join us for wine?" Lady Mackenzie asked, spotting her.

"No, thank you," Bernadette said politely.

"Rabbie, darling, will you?"

Rabbie. That was the first that Bernadette had heard his given name said out loud. Funny, but he didn't seem like a *Rabbie* to her. That name belonged to someone congenial and hospitable. He was more like a Hades. Yes, that suited him. *Hades Mackenzie, the rudest man in the Scottish Highlands.*

"Aye," he responded to his mother, and accepted the glass of wine Frang held out to him. Bernadette nudged Avaline and whispered she should speak to her fiancé. Whether Avaline took her advice, Bernadette didn't know, because she walked away, putting as many people and as much space between her and that ogre as she could.

In doing so, she quite literally bumped into Captain Mackenzie.

"I beg your pardon, Captain!" she said, alarmed that she had inadvertently stepped on the man's foot as she'd glanced over her shoulder to see where the ogre was now.

He caught her elbow and steadied her. "Good evening, Miss Holly," he said pleasantly.

"I'm rather surprised to see you here tonight. I thought you'd be at sea by now."

"Aye, as did I. Alas, our ship needs a wee bit of repair. I'll be a landlubber for a time." His eyes twinkled with his smile.

Bernadette was again struck by how different these brothers were in mien.

"You've met my sisters, have you no'?" he asked.

"I have, indeed."

"You are acquainted with every Mackenzie of Balhaire, then," he said with a chuckle.

Unfortunately.

He suddenly leaned forward and whispered, "Have you a verdict on Miss Kent's fiancé? Does he suit her, then?"

Bernadette could feel herself coloring. What was she supposed to say to that? "Ah…well," she said, and paused to clear her throat. "It's all so very new, isn't it? I suspect they will take some time learning about each other."

Captain Mackenzie blinked. He slowly cocked his head to one side, his gaze shrewd, and smiled very slowly. "Aye, then, you donna esteem him." Bernadette opened her mouth to deny it, but he waved his hand. "Donna deny it, lass—it's plain."

"I scarcely know him. I've not made any judgment."

He chuckled at that bold lie, sipped his wine, then put the glass aside. "Donna believe everything you see, Miss Holly. My brother is a wee bit hardened, that he is. But he's suffered a great loss and has no' come easily back to the living. On my word, the lad is a good man beneath the hurt."

A loss? *Hurt?* She tried to imagine what sort of loss might make a man so unregenerate, but couldn't think of a single thing. She'd lost her husband and her baby, and *she* wasn't so hardened. What possibly could have happened to him?

"Ah, there is Frang," Captain Mackenzie said. "We'll dine, now, aye?" He stepped away.

Bernadette was still trying to make sense of what the captain had said when Lady Mackenzie arranged them all for the promenade into the dining room. Naturally, Bernadette brought up the rear. She was seated next to Mrs. Vivienne Mackenzie with Avaline across from her. Next to Avaline sat the man who had suffered such an incomprehensible loss, apparently, as to have made him entirely contemptible.

As the meal was served, everyone was laughing and talking at once. Bernadette was especially enjoying the meal—it was the first decent thing she'd had to eat since arriving in Scotland, and it was delicious. A soup thick with chunks of fish, a pie bursting with savory meat and potatoes. The cook Mr. MacDonald had found for Killeaven didn't know how to prepare food like this, apparently, for everything she'd made thus far had tasted bland and, at times, even bitter.

Bernadette made small talk with Mrs. Vivienne Mackenzie, who told her about her children, including their names, and their traits. Bernadette politely answered the questions Mrs. Mackenzie put to her. How long had she been in the Kent employ? *Nearly seven years*. How did she find Scotland? *Quite beautiful*.

Lady Mackenzie and Lady Kent were engaged in a discussion of the wedding ceremony and the celebrations around it. Lady Mackenzie was quite animated in her descriptions of Scottish wedding customs. "No, you actually jump *over* the broom" Bernadette overheard her say to Lady Kent.

There was a lull in the chatter between Bernadette and Mrs. Mackenzie when the latter's husband caught her attention and she turned away.

Bernadette glanced across the table at Avaline. She looked unhappy. Bernadette very surreptitiously nodded in the direction of her fiancé. Avaline glanced at the man, then haltingly inquired if Mackenzie had received his education at a university.

"Aye," he said.

That was all he said—nothing more, no explanation of when or where or anything else to put Avaline at ease, the lout.

Avaline pushed a bit food around her plate, then said suddenly, "Which university?"

He paused in his eating. "Does it matter to you, then?"

He asked it in a way that sounded as if he was somehow offended, and Avaline's eyes widened. "No! No, of course not."

"Of course it does," his mother said kindly to Avaline, having caught that part of the conversation as well. "Rabbie attended St. Andrews, just as his brothers did before him."

Avaline nodded and gave Lady Mackenzie a faint smile of gratitude. She picked up her fork, took a small bite of food, then put down the fork. "Did you have a favorite governess?"

For heaven's sake. Bernadette hadn't meant Avaline to *ask* that question, but had used it merely as an example to spur Avaline's own thinking of how she might engage this man.

Her fiancé put down his fork, too, and turned his head to her, so that he might pierce her better with his cold glare. "We didna have a *governess*," he said, his gaze straying to Bernadette. "It is no' the way of the Highlands."

Avaline dropped her gaze to her plate.

The beast glanced across the table to Bernadette, as if he knew she was the one to have put the thought in Avaline's head. Well she hadn't meant for Avaline to take her so literally. "Then what *is* the way of the Highlands?" Bernadette asked pertly.

"Pardon?" he asked, clearly not anticipating a response from her.

"If you were not minded by a governess, then how were you raised? What is the way of the Highlands? A nursemaid? I had a nursemaid until I was eight years old."

"We were raised by wolves," he said. "Is that no' what is said of Highlanders in England?"

The conversation at the table slowly died away, and now everyone was listening. Bernadette smiled sweetly. "I wouldn't know what is said of Highlanders in England, sir. We rarely speak of them."

Captain Mackenzie laughed.

Bernadette glanced at Avaline, silently willing the girl not to shake with uneasiness sitting next to him.

Down the table, Lord Kent's voice rose with the unmistakable hoarseness of too much drink. "Enough of nursemaids and Highlanders and whatnot. Tell me now, laird, how does your trade fare? I might as well inquire, as it will all be in the family soon enough." He laughed.

Miss Catriona Mackenzie, seated next to her father and across from Lord Kent, choked on a sip of wine, coughing uncontrollably for a moment.

"Well enough," the laird said quietly, and leaned to one side to rub his daughter's back.

"Aye, well enough when we avoid the excise men," Rabbie Mackenzie said, and chuckled darkly.

That remark was met with stunned silence by them all. Bernadette didn't know what he meant, really, but his family seemed mortified.

Lord Kent seemed intrigued.

Suddenly, Captain Mackenzie laughed, and loudly, too. "My brother means to divert us," he said jovially. "He is master at it, so much so that we donna know when he teases us."

Bernadette did not miss the look that flowed between brothers, but Captain Mackenzie continued on. "I am reminded of an occasion we sailed to Norway, Rabbie. You recall it, aye?"

"I'll no' forget it," his brother said.

The captain said, "We sailed into a squall, we did, the seas so high we were pitched about like a bairn's toy. A few barrels of ale became unlashed and washed over the side with a toss of a mighty wave."

Bernadette's stomach lurched a tiny bit, the memory still fresh in her legs and chest of roiling seas.

"What a tragedy for you all to lose your *ale*," Lord Kent scoffed.

"Aye, but it was," the captain agreed with much congeniality, politely ignoring his lordship's tone. "Rabbie and I didna have the heart to tell our crew of the loss, no' with two days at sea ahead of us, aye? When the seas calmed, and the men looked about for their drink, I said to Rabbie, 'We'll be mutinied, mark me.'"

Lord Mackenzie smiled, amused by that.

"Rabbie said, 'No' on my watch, *braither.*' When I asked what he meant to do, then, he said he didna know, aye? But he'd think of something."

"Oh, aye, he'd think of something, would he?" Catriona said laughingly.

"What happened?" Avaline asked eagerly, held rapt by the captain's tale.

"He gathered the lads round, and told them a fantastic yarn of the sea serpent who stole their ale." Captain Mackenzie leaned forward and said in a low voice, "Now the lads, they've been a sea for a long time, they have, and they donna believe in sea monsters. But Rabbie was so convincing in his telling of it that more than one began to crowd to the middle of the main deck, fearing one of the serpent's arms would appear to pull them into the sea along with their drink." He laughed and settled back in his chair. "They didna fret about their ale, no' after that tale. My brother spoke with such confidence they couldna help but believe him."

Bernadette wondered after an entire ship of men who would fall prey to such a ridiculous tale. And yet, across from her sat a pretty, cake-headed girl, eyes wide with delight as she listened to Captain Mackenzie. Fortunately, Avaline seemed to have forgotten all about the ogre sitting next to her.

And yet it hardly mattered that Avaline's attention had been diverted, for the ogre appeared quite content to be forgotten. He sat back in his seat, his expression unreadable as everyone around him laughed at that ridiculous story. But his hand was curled into a tight fist against the table, and Bernadette had the distinct impression he was holding himself in check. From what? Was he angry? Did he dislike his brother's amusing tale?

"Shall we retire to the sitting room?" Lady Mackenzie asked, and stood.

The ogre stood, and, rather miraculously, he held Avaline's chair out so that she might rise. Avaline didn't seem to notice the polite gesture at all—her gaze was on Captain Mackenzie and she hurried to his side to ask him something about the story he'd just told as they began to make their way out of the small dining room.

Once again, Bernadette followed behind the rest of them, only this time, she had company. Rabbie Mackenzie fell in beside her, his hands clasped at his back. He said nothing, and certainly neither did Bernadette. She was aware of how much his body dwarfed hers. She felt unusually small next to him, and imagined how helpless Avaline would feel beside him. She tried not to picture their wedding night, but it was impossible once the thought had crowded into her head—Bernadette could see him, tall and broad and erect...

Goodness, but she imagined that in very vivid detail, and carefully rubbed her neck, trying to erase the heat that suddenly crawled into her skin.

The room in which they'd gathered was another sitting room, with two settees and a few armchairs, and a few spare dogs eager to greet everyone who entered the room.

At the far end of the room was a harpsichord. Bernadette sighed softly to herself. She knew where this was headed. They would have the obligatory demonstration of Avaline's "abilities." Avaline was terrified of performing before others, and frankly, Bernadette was terrified for her. She had little real talent for it, and the harder she tried, the worse she sang. It was a cruel fact that women of Avaline's birthright were expected to excel in all things domestic—in managing their household, in needlework, in art and song. She was also expected to demonstrate how pleasingly accommodating she was by showing an eagerness to perform at the mere invitation. And woe to the woman who did not excel at singing, for she couldn't escape her duty to display her so-called wares.

Bernadette's talent was in playing the harpsichord. She, too, had been born to this perch in life...but she'd fallen from it.

"Here then, allow my daughter to regale us with a song," Lord Kent said almost instantly, without any regard for his daughter's feelings on the matter, or her lack of talent. He was well aware how it frightened Avaline to stand before anyone and sing—the good Lord knew it had been a source of contention between them many times before this particular evening.

"Miss Holly, you will accompany her," his lordship decreed.

All heads swiveled about to where Bernadette stood just inside the door, the ogre at her side. She bristled at the command, could feel the heat of shame flood her cheeks. As if she were a trained monkey like the one she'd once seen in a London market.

"Go on, then," Mr. Mackenzie said. "Donna draw this out any more than is necessary."

"You have nothing to fear in that regard," she muttered, and walked to the front of the room—for Avaline's sake, *always for Avaline's sake*—wiping her palms on the sides of her gown as she went. She sat on the bench before the harpsichord, glanced up at an ashen Avaline and whispered, "Look above their heads, not at them. Pretend no one is here, pretend it is a music lesson."

Avaline nodded stiffly.

Bernadette began to play. Avaline began to warble. She held her hands clasped tightly at her waist, her nerves making her sing sharp to the music. At last, the poor girl finished the song to tepid applause. The ladies, Bernadette noticed, were shifting restlessly in their seats. And in the back of the room, standing exactly where she'd left him, stood Rabbie Mackenzie.

His head was down, his arms folded, his expression one of pure tedium.

But the song was done, and Avaline moved immediately to sit, as did Bernadette, but Lord Kent, slouching in his chair, his eyes half-open after the amount he'd drunk, waved her back. "Again, Avaline. Perhaps something a bit livelier that won't put us all asleep."

Avaline's shoulders tensed. She turned to Bernadette, her eyes blank now, her soul having retreated to that place of hiding. Bernadette managed a smile for the poor girl. "The song of summer," she said softly. "The one you like."

Avaline nodded. As she moved to take her place next to the pianoforte, and Bernadette played the first few chords, she looked up to see if Avaline was ready, and noticed, from the corner of her eye, that Avaline's fiancé had exited the room. How impossibly rude he was! It made her so angry that she hit a wrong chord, startling Avaline. "I beg your pardon," Bernadette said, and began again.

This time, when the song mercifully ended, it was Captain Mackenzie who rose to see Avaline to a seat, complimenting her on her singing as he did.

The evening dragged on from there. Bernadette stood near a bookcase, pretending to examine the few titles they had there, impatient for the evening to come to an end. She was trying desperately not to listen to Lady Kent and Avaline attempt to converse with the Mackenzie women about the blasted wedding.

At long last, his lordship rose, signaling to his party.

They could at last quit this horrible place and return to Killeaven.

None of the Mackenzies entreated them to stay, but eagerly followed them out like so many puppies—with the notable exception of Avaline's fiancé, of course—and called good-night as they climbed into the coach. Even his lordship took a seat inside the coach, having instructed a man to tether his horse to the back of it. As soon as they rolled out of the bailey, he turned a furious glare to Avaline. "You are a *stupid*, vapid girl!" he said heatedly. "You have no knowledge of how to woo a man! What am I to do if he cries off? What will I do with you then?"

"I beg your pardon, Father, but I tried—"

"You asked after his favorite governess!" her father shouted at her, spittle coming out of his mouth with the force of his voice. "Haven't you the *slightest* notion how to bat your eyes? And *you*," he said, swinging his gaze around to Bernadette.

"Me?"

"Yes, you! You're a wily woman, Bernadette. Can you not teach her to be less…vapid?" he exclaimed, flicking his wrist in the direction of his daughter. "Can you not teach her how to lure a man to her instead of cleaving the line and letting him sink away?"

"The man is entirely disagreeable—"

His lordship surged forward with such ferocity that his wig was very nearly left behind. "I don't care if he is Satan himself. The marriage has been agreed to and by God, if he cries off because of *her*," he said, jabbing his finger in the direction of Avaline, "I will take it out of her hide."

Avaline began to cry.

Her father fell back against the squabs and sighed heavily, as if he bore the weight of the world on his shoulders. "What have I done to deserve this?" he said to the ceiling. "What sin have I committed that you give me a miserable wife without the ability to give me a son, and a stupid twit for a daughter?"

Needless to say, by the time the old coach had bounced and plodded and bumbled along to Killeaven, the entire Kent family was in tears.

If Bernadette had been presented with a knife during that drive, she would have gladly plunged it into her own neck, just to escape them all.

CHAPTER SIX

AVALINE WAS FINALLY ALONE. She was never alone; there was always someone about to tell her what to do, what to say, how to behave.

It had been a very long day and a draining evening at Balhaire. Her eyes and her face were swollen from sobbing, and her mother's attempt at making a compress had only angered her. She'd sent her mother from the room, had locked the door behind her.

Now, Avaline had no tears left in her. What she had was a hatred of her father that burned so intently she felt ashamed and concerned God would strike her dead for it. She hated how her father treated her, but she hated worse how she sobbed when he said such awful things to her. She was quite determined not to, but she could never seem to help herself.

What she told him was true—she *had* done her best this evening. She had tried to engage that awful man as Bernadette said, had tried to be pleasant and pretty and quiet. Nothing worked. What was she to do? He stared at her with those dark, cold eyes. His jaw seemed perpetually clinched. He rarely spoke to her at all, and when he did, every word was biting. He hated her. Which was perfectly all right as far as Avaline was concerned, because she hated him, too, hated the very sight of him.

And the singing! Avaline groaned at the humiliation she had suffered. Couldn't her father hear with his own ears that she wasn't good enough to hold entire salons captive? He blamed her for her lack of talent and had once accused her of intentionally singing poorly only to vex him. What on earth would possess her to humiliate herself before others merely to annoy her father?

Avaline rolled onto her side and stared at the window, left open to admit a cool breeze. She couldn't see beyond it, but she imagined she could hear the sea from here. It was probably only a night breeze rustling the treetops, but she wanted to imagine the sea.

She thought about running away. She thought about stowing aboard Captain Mackenzie's ship. She pictured him now, with his kind smile, his hair so prettily streaked by endless days on the vast sea. He was so completely appealing! One night, as they sailed up the coast to the Highlands, Avaline had been too restless and too warm in the cabin she'd shared with Bernadette, and had waited until Bernadette was asleep before venturing onto the deck.

She'd been gazing up at the stars, so brilliant that they felt within reach. The captain had been surprised to stumble upon her there. "You must be cold, aye?" he asked in that lilting voice of his, and shrugged out of his coat and draped it around her shoulders. Then he pointed out some of the stars to her—Orion, Sirius and Polaris. He told her he'd been sailing since he was a "wee lad" and once he'd begun, he'd never left the sea. "Aye, I love it as if it was a bairn," he'd said. "It changes every day."

Avaline wanted to be somewhere that changed every day. She wanted to talk about stars and clouds and sea swells. She wanted to love something so fiercely that she couldn't leave it. She wanted to look into the captain's clear blue eyes and see him smile, and never, ever, think of his awful, wretched brother again.

She rolled onto her back and wondered what Captain Mackenzie would do if he found an English woman hiding on his ship. Perhaps even in his cabin, as no one would think to look for her there. Would he return her to father? Or would he take her in his arms and kiss her and promise her a life of adventure? Wouldn't that be very romantic?

Why couldn't it have been him, the man who knew the names of stars and always had a smile for her? Why was it his awful brother? Why, God, why?

Avaline wished she could confess her true feelings to Bernadette about Captain Mackenzie, but that was impossible—Bernadette would force her to forget Captain Mackenzie. She would dog Avaline, and she would know when Avaline was thinking of him. Bernadette always seemed to recognize what Avaline would do before Avaline realized it herself.

She sighed wearily, feeling quite heavy of heart for her seventeen years. She could feel sleep creeping into her body, pushing her down into unconsciousness, and as she drifted away, she imagined sneaking onboard the Mackenzie ship, imagined what the captain's private quarters must look like, and how comforting it would be to have all his things around her. She imagined the moment Captain Mackenzie entered the quarters and found her there...

CHAPTER SEVEN

*THEY MEET EVERY afternoon and walk along the cliff
above the cove, speaking of everything and nothing,
laughing at secret jokes. Their fingers are entwined
except in those moments when Rabbie leans down,
picks up a rock and hurls it out to sea. Sometimes,
he carries her on his back so that the hem of her* arasaid *will not get wet. Sometimes, they go down to the
beach, and she picks up a stick and draws the shape
of a heart with their initials.*

*They mean to be married. They don't know when,
and they have kept this promise to each other a secret.
These are uncertain times—whispers of rebellion and
treason seem to slip through the hills on every breeze.*

*On a particularly cool afternoon, Rabbie returns
Seona to her family home and sees the horses there,
still saddled. Inside, he hears the voices of men. Seona's
mother, a large woman with a welcoming smile, appears,
but today she seems unusually fretful. As they walk past
the room where Seona's father and brothers are gathered, Rabbie sees the men who have come. Buchanan,
Dinwiddie, MacLeary. All of them Jacobites, all of them
known to conspire against the king. This is treacherous
ground, and Rabbie glances at Seona. She doesn't ap-*

*pear to notice the men. She is smiling, telling her mother
about the ship they spotted passing along the coast with
a flag of black and red. He doesn't know if Seona under-
stands what her father and brothers are about.*

THE FOLLOWING TWO days after that interminable dinner, with singing so atrocious that Rabbie wished he
was deaf, passed in a haze of restlessness. His thoughts
kept going back to that evening and the moments he'd
stood at the back of the music room, endeavoring—
and failing—to grasp how he might possibly make a
life with the lass.

Perhaps his father was right. Perhaps he ought to
put her in at Killeaven and leave her there.

That dinner was intended to establish harmony between two families that would, in a matter of days, be
forever tied by matrimony, but Rabbie couldn't bear the
thought of even bedding her. He'd escaped unnoticed
from the music room, and had gone in search of drink
stronger than wine.

His path had taken him to the kitchen. He'd heard
voices as he approached, and figured the servants were
cleaning up after the supper. He could hear Barabel's
deep voice instruct someone in Gaelic, "Have a care
with the plate, lass. We've precious few of them now."

He walked into the kitchen and just over the threshold, he froze. Barabel was instructing the MacLeod
children. The lass glanced up at him and smiled. The
lad scarcely made eye contact before turning back to
his task of drying pots.

"Aye, Mr. Mackenzie, may I help you?" Barabel asked in Gaelic.

"Whisky," he said, his voice rough with an emotion he hadn't even realized he was holding.

Barabel disappeared into the adjoining storeroom to fetch it.

No one said a word. The two children stared at him, and Rabbie stared back. He didn't know what to say to them, and at last, he spoke to them in Gaelic. Did they speak English? "I, ah... I knew your mother."

The lad looked up at that admission.

"I donna remember her," the girl announced in English. "Mrs. Maloney said I look very much like her. She was bonny and so am I."

"Aye, she was, as are you," Rabbie agreed. The lass—Fiona—must be five or six years old now. Ualan was nearly two when last Rabbie had seen him, and he guessed him to be seven or eight years now. "She loved you both," he said.

Fiona smiled. The lad didn't utter a word.

"I knew them all," Rabbie said, and was embarrassed to hear his voice crack. "I even knew the two of you."

Fiona's eyes widened. "You *did*? I donna remember you."

"You were a bairn, lass," he said to her in English. "You played here at Balhaire, aye?"

The children stared at him. Perhaps they didn't believe him. He began to perspire; he could feel a bead of it running down his back. As he gazed into those vaguely familiar faces, he could see Gavina and Seona's eyes in the children. He could see the lad's father in him, in his rust-colored hair, just like that of Donald MacLeod.

Barabel returned to the kitchen with a flagon. "Why do you stand idle?" she chastised the children as she handed Rabbie a flagon of whisky. "Finish your chores, the both of you," she commanded.

Rabbie had glanced once more at the children before leaving. He was disquieted by their presence. What was to happen to them? Perhaps he didn't want to know—to know would require some action on his part, at the very least, some thought or feeling. He couldn't summon the strength for it that evening.

He'd taken the flagon to the top of the fortress tower, and there he had crouched on the parapet, drinking to numb the hopelessness in him. He'd absently viewed the bailey below—quite a fall that would be—but he didn't think of jumping.

At least not that night.

No, he'd found himself instead thinking first of those orphaned children, and then of the woman with the dark hair and hazel eyes and deep red gown. Or rather, he'd thought of the way she'd glared at him. With disdain. As if she had the right to disdain *him*. Somehow, the maid and the children became tangled in his muddied thoughts. He was angry that she could possibly find fault with him when there were two children working in the scullery because of the English forces.

The cold eventually sent him inside, long after that haughty little *Sassenach* had left Balhaire, long after the candles had been extinguished and everyone had gone to bed. And then he'd tried to sleep.

It was impossible.

It puzzled him—how could a man desire sleep so utterly above all else, and yet be unable to achieve it? But between his perpetual anguish and the hazel eyes burning their disdain into his mind's eye, he'd slept very little. Frankly, he wasn't certain if he'd slept at all in the last two days.

And now had come the day he'd be forced to take the chit riding.

Why did women believe it such a bonny pastime to amble aimlessly about the countryside? Even when he was in good spirits he chafed at the futility of such exercise. And, naturally, his family distrusted him so completely that Catriona had once again been dispatched to chaperone him. She was leading the charge, and she determined a picnic was the thing. She'd asked Barabel to prepare a basket for them. A picnic!

"It's a bonny day," she'd said when Rabbie had complained. "She will like it."

Rabbie didn't *picnic*.

Aye, but he'd resigned himself to it. Even his father had lost patience with Rabbie's surly apathy, chastising him this morning for having left the room the other night without bidding their guests good-night.

Truthfully, Rabbie had lost patience with himself. It wasn't as if he enjoyed his state of mind, but it was beyond his ability to affect. He struggled to shepherd his thoughts in a brighter direction. He couldn't seem to move them at all. It was as if a boulder had been placed before him, and until he could push it away, he was destined to stand still. No matter what he did, no matter how he prayed or swore that this day would be different, he could not move that boulder of melancholy. It grew bigger and heavier every day.

And today was no different.

He was to meet Catriona on the road. She'd gone to call on their father's cousin, whom they called Auntie Griselda. Quite unfortunately, she was failing. Catriona was especially close to Zelda, and visited her every day. While he restlessly waited, his thoughts spinning, Rabbie had ridden to the cliff above the cove. Now, here he stood, his toes just over the edge.

The tide was out, and from his vantage point he could see how the color of the water below him changed from green to dark blue where it deepened. If he leaped, spread his arms, he would sail out far enough to land in that hole. If he weighted his pockets with rocks, he would sink so far below the surface they might never find him.

He would disappear, like Seona, never to be heard from again.

The task of picking up rocks seemed too complicated and tiring.

Rabbie sighed, then wondered after the time. It was morning yet, the sun not fully overhead. Catriona would be furious with him if he was late. Not that Rabbie cared. He almost welcomed her fury—it served to test the boundaries of his desolation. He longed for something that would force him to feel anything other than rage, or despair, or the worst—absolutely nothing.

His only saving grace, he supposed, was that he did not want to find that thing at the expense of his family. He had told himself that his sole task today, the one thing he *must* accomplish, was to ride with the English lass to Auchenard, a hunting lodge that belonged to Daisy's young son, Lord Chatwick. It had been entrusted to Rabbie to keep in good repair until Ellis had reached his majority. It was scenic, Catriona said. The girl would like it, Catriona said.

A wind suddenly gusted up from the cove, pushing him, lifting the hem of his cloak and his hair, which he hadn't bothered to put in a queue. Rabbie quickly stepped back from the edge, his heart pounding with the abrupt surprise of that gust. And yet, wasn't that what he'd wanted? For a gust of wind to topple him from this ledge?

He didn't want to think about it, not now, not with the task upon him, and turned away from the edge of the cliff. That's when he saw her. The maid with the penetrating hazel gaze.

She was standing down the path a few feet from him, from where she could plainly see him. How long had she been standing there? Had she understood he was contemplating the end?

His question appeared to be answered when she abruptly turned and hurried down the path, her gait awkward. It was a moment before he realized she was running from him. It disconcerted him almost as much as the idea she'd seen him at one of his worst moments.

Rabbie pivoted about and stalked to his horse, threw

himself on her back and galloped after the maid, catching up to her quickly.

She tried to step off the path when he rode up behind her and she stumbled, righting herself awkwardly. She whirled around, her hands fisted and her arms held at her rib cage, as if she thought she might be forced to fight him.

He reined the horse to a halt, staring at her in confusion. Surely she did not think he would physically assault her. "What are you about? Why are you here?"

"Why?" she repeated, sounding incredulous.

"Do you *spy* on me?"

She gaped at him. "I beg your pardon!" she said hotly. "Of *course* not! I was having a walk."

He glanced at her feet and noticed that beneath the hem of her gown, she was wearing thick, clumsy boots that must have been at least two sizes too large for her. "Why did you turn and run, then?"

She hesitated. She unclenched her fists and folded her arms. "I didn't…" She dropped her arms. "I won't dissemble," she said, lifting her chin. "If you must know, Mr. Mackenzie, I didn't want to speak to you."

If she believed he would be offended, she was very much mistaken. He didn't want to speak to her, either—the fewer words, the better.

But strangely, Rabbie did want to look at her. He was loath to acknowledge that she was quite appealing. *Quite* appealing. His gaze slid down her body, to those boots that were so incongruent with the woman who wore them.

"What?" she asked impatiently, and Rabbie realized he hadn't responded to her declaration she didn't want to speak to him.

"Your boots."

She glanced down. "Do you object to even my *boots*?"

He didn't object to anything. Quite the contrary—he couldn't possibly care.

She rolled her eyes when he didn't respond right away. "Of *course* you do. Are they too English for you?"

"I donna object—"

"You object to everything about me," she snapped. "You've made it quite obvious."

Rabbie was taken aback by her accusation. Surprised, really, and he'd not been truly surprised in a very long time. It felt odd in his head and chest, tingling as if an ague was settling in. "Because I donna allow you to challenge me doesna mean I object to you, lass."

"Oh?" she said, shifting her weight onto her hip. "Well, *I* object to *you*."

"Aye, you've been bloody well clear about it. A man can only wonder what has happened to a woman to have turned her into such a shrew."

She gasped, affronted.

"Aye, you heard me," he said. "A shrew. A harridan."

Her lovely eyes narrowed. "*You're* hardly a prize."

"I've no' said I am, have I? I donna understand your resentment, on my life I donna—you're no' the one I'm forced to wed."

She gave a shout of nearly hysterical laughter at that.

"Thank *God* I am not. But my friend *is* forced to marry you, and you have treated her very ill!"

"That again," he said with a flick of his wrist. "Another rebuke of my manners."

"A rebuke of your *lack* of them," she said angrily. "I happen to care very much for Avaline, and that she must wed a brute who is so utterly indifferent to her is not to be born."

Rabbie didn't care to be called a brute and felt his temper rising. "I've no' touched your precious charge, and I am no brute. You're a wee fool if you believe that because a man and woman are bartered into matrimony, affection must accompany it."

She hesitated at that statement. "I don't believe that at all. But I do believe civility must accompany it."

"Civility," he said acidly. "Was it civility, then, that the English showed the men of these hills? Is *that* where you have learned it?"

Her eyes narrowed and from a distance of a few feet, he could almost feel the sparks coming out of them. She moved toward him, and Rabbie wondered if she indeed meant to strike him. "*I* am not to blame for what happened here, Mr. Mackenzie, and neither is Avaline. I don't *know* what has happened here, other than the king's forces put down an attempt at treason, as well they should have."

"Is *that* what you believe?" he asked, disbelieving.

"Have you seen any of us don a red coat?" she exclaimed, casting her arms wide. "Can you not, in that black heart of yours, perhaps try and understand how difficult this is for Avaline?"

"For *her*?" he roared. "I canna abide the lass, Miss Holly. There is naugh' to recommend her. She is a bairn—"

"You can't possibly know what she is, given that you scarcely address her at all. She is very kind—"

"She is cowardly," he snapped.

The maid's skin was turning pink. "She means well," she said through gritted teeth.

"She doesna know what she means," he returned. "She is a lamb, a lass scarcely out of her governess's lead."

She gasped at the implication of that. "At least she is trying!" she shouted at him. "That is more than can be said of you!"

He was furious now, but it was a different sort of fury than he'd felt in the last year. It was not the feeling of hopelessness that pervaded each and every day—this was a feeling of righteous indignation. "How is it that a servant of a baron's household may speak as she pleases? Is there no one to muzzle you?"

He saw the rage flash in her eyes. She pointed a finger at him. "Don't follow me," she said, her voice shaking. "I don't want the company of your ilk—I don't want to speak to you, I don't want to *see* you." She whipped around and began to stride away, her gait clumsy in boots too big, her arms swinging.

And just like that, Rabbie's rage turned into a strange swell of amusement. She looked perfectly ridiculous, striding along as she was, her arms flailing, her hair bouncing out of its pins and those boots clumping against the path.

He nudged his horse to walk beside her. She refused to look at him and kept her gaze fixed straight ahead. "Come, now, Miss Holly," he said impatiently. "You canna avoid seeing me, can you? I am to Killeaven now. You may ride—"

"No!"

"Donna be so bloody stubborn—"

"Stubborn! I'm protecting myself from *you*."

"You donna honestly believe the things that are said of Highlanders, do you? Are the lot of the *Sassenach* daft?"

She stopped so abruptly that he had to yank his horse's head hard to the right to keep from walking into her. "I don't know what is said of Highlanders, Mr. Mackenzie. When I said I was protecting myself from you, I meant I was protecting myself from the violence I very much want to inflict on you at the moment. I am asking kindly if you will please ride on and leave me be."

"Suit yourself, woman. I donna care what you do." He reined his horse and rode on, not bothering to look back.

THE MAID HAD clearly taken a long route to Killeaven, for she'd just come on to the drive when Rabbie and Catriona arrived. As they rode in behind her, she stopped walking, turned around after a bit of hesitation and smiled at Catriona.

She did not look at him.

"Feasgar math," Catriona said, hopping off her horse. She looked at Bernadette curiously, her gaze falling to the boots.

"Welcome, Miss Mackenzie," she said, still ignoring him.

"Are your feet as big as that?" Catriona asked, clearly baffled.

The maid lifted her chin slightly. "I find my shoes are too delicate for the hill walking here. One of the footmen was kind enough to lend me a pair."

"Pity, that. We had a cobbler in Balhaire, but he's gone now."

"Thank you, but these are quite all right. I'll inform Miss Kent you've come."

She spoke stiffly and formally—much more civilly than she'd spoken to Rabbie. Which was ironic, wasn't it, seeing as how she placed such importance on *civility.*

"Please, come in," she said, marching ahead.

Before she reached the door, the butler appeared, calling for a stable hand, and then briskly instructed him to saddle a horse for Miss Kent. When that bit of business had been done, he bowed and said, "May I show you to the salon? Miss Kent shall be down momentarily."

"I won't wait long," Rabbie warned his sister in Gaelic.

"Uist," Catriona said, silencing him.

They followed the butler inside. Miss Holly followed them, too, her boots clomping across the marble floor. She stepped just inside the room and stood near the door, her hands at her back. A thick strand of dark hair had come completely undone and draped her collarbone. Rabbie glanced sidelong at that long length of hair and imagined how it would feel between his fingers. Soft and silken, he imagined.

She seemed to notice the hair, too, and tried, unsuccessfully, to tuck the hair behind her ear. It fell over her collarbone again. That action, no matter how slight, was so innately feminine, and on some level, so endearing, that Rabbie felt a madness rise up in him, equal parts lust, anger, and perplexity.

He did not want to feel that madness in him. He wanted to walk out of this room and disappear into the vastness of the landscape. He wanted to be as far from this woman as he could be, but today's task made that impossible. So he paced before the hearth, impatiently slapping his gloves against his bare hand.

"You appear entirely mad to all who might reside here," Catriona said in Gaelic. "At least put the gloves away."

She was right—he looked as if he might explode into bits at any moment. He clasped his hands and his gloves tightly behind his back and continued pacing.

Catriona turned her attention to the maid, shaking her head as she helped herself to a seat on the settee. She frowned at the boots, and Miss Holly once again attempted to tuck that tress of hair behind her ear. "What is your age, Miss Holly?" Catriona suddenly asked.

"Pardon?"

"Your age," Catriona said again. She could be too direct in her speech at times, a trait she'd inherited from Auntie Zelda.

Miss Holly was clearly taken aback. "Ah…nine and twenty," she said.

Catriona laughed. "An old maid, are you? A spinster, put on the shelf."

"Cat," Rabbie said in Gaelic. "At least one of us must mind our manners."

"I beg your pardon, I shouldna have said, aye?" she said to Miss Holly. "I laugh because we are the same age, we are, and that is what has been said of me," she reported cheerfully.

"Far worse has been said of me," Miss Holly admitted, and glanced away from them both. She didn't sound indignant, but rather seemed to be correcting Catriona's view of her.

"What do you mean, then?" Catriona asked.

"You've said enough, Cat," Rabbie said in Gaelic. "Leave the woman be. She is not our concern."

Catriona smiled at Miss Holly. "My brother reminds me that I must learn to speak before I think. So you've no' married, Miss Holly?" she asked, ignoring Rabbie's advice.

Miss Holly swallowed. "Ah…no."

It was curious, the way she answered this question. Rabbie couldn't say if she was embarrassed that she was not married, or if she was perhaps not telling the truth.

"You?" she asked of Catriona.

"Oh, no," Catriona said, and strolled to the sideboard to have a look at the bottles there.

Rabbie knew, perhaps better than anyone, as he and Catriona had always been rather close, that Catriona's marital status was a source of anguish for her. She was a strong, independent woman…but she wanted a family. She had learned to hide her disappointment behind bravado.

"I'm like my Auntie Zelda, aye?" Catriona said, as if being unmarried scarcely bothered her at all. "Auntie Zelda never married and all her life, she has come and gone as she pleased." Catriona glanced up at Bernadette. "I like that I might live as I please. I've heard that in England a woman doesna have that freedom."

"I'm not… I don't know," Miss Holly said. She tried to tuck the hair behind her ear again, and again it fell.

"Even if I desired to marry, there is scarcely a lad about, is there?" Catriona continued. She turned from the sideboard and said, "All of them scattered now, are they no'?"

"Scattered?" Miss Holly repeated curiously.

Catriona's attention snapped to the maid. "Aye, scattered," she said. A wee bit of bitterness had crept into her voice. "Surely you know this."

"Know what?"

"She doesna know," Rabbie said impatiently. It was astounding to him that what had been done to the Highlands of Scotland could remain unknown to anyone. "Leave it be, Cat. She will no' care."

"She *ought* to know," Catriona said to him in Gaelic. "Every one of them ought to know what they did." She turned back to Miss Holly and said, in English, "You've heard of the slaughter at Culloden Moor, have you no'? The English forces slaughtered Stuart rebels and pillaged the hills."

"Pillaged!" Miss Holly seemed surprised by Catriona's choice of words.

"Aye, pillaged. Hamlets emptied, people gone missing."

"I didn't…" Miss Holly hesitated, frowning. "I had heard of the fighting, naturally, but I wasn't aware—"

"Good afternoon."

Miss Kent had arrived and stepped tentatively into the salon. She was dressed in a green riding habit and matching green hat.

"Aye, good afternoon, Miss Kent," said Catriona.

Miss Kent smiled, then glanced nervously at Rabbie. He nodded. "Aye, then," he said. "Let's be about it. I'll see to the mounts." He strode to the door, passing his fiancée without a word as he stepped out of the room.

It seemed several minutes before the ladies followed him out onto the drive. The Mackenzie horses had been brought round, and another from the Kent stables— horses bought for a song from some Highlander in desperate need of funds, Rabbie guessed—and a lad from the stable was on hand to help Miss Kent mount her horse. It took more than one effort, for the horse was tall and Miss Kent was small and obviously inexperienced.

Rabbie glanced at the maid. She was not dressed for riding, he realized. "You're no' attending your mistress?"

She shook her head, but kept her gaze straight ahead, still refusing to look at him.

Rabbie, however, glared at her. "I didna think you allowed your little sparrow out of your sight, then."

She looked at him then, her hazel gaze full of loathing. "Oh, I rarely do. But this time, I can't bear the company."

Rabbie stepped closer to her, so close that he could see the flecks of brown in her eyes, a barely noticeable smear of dirt across one cheek, a sprinkle of freckles across her slender nose. "You think yourself clever, lass. You still seem to believe you might chasten me into behavior you deem appropriate."

"I think that's impossible."

"It's impossible, aye. A word of advice, then—I wouldna risk my displeasure."

One of her fine, dark brows rose skeptically above the other.

His gaze flicked over her again, lingering a moment on her mouth. The feeling of madness rose up in him again, and he walked away, his cloak flying out behind him. He tossed himself up on his horse and wheeled it around, then said rather gruffly, "Aye, we go now."

His sister and Miss Kent dutifully trotted behind him. Thank God for it, for Rabbie didn't know what he might have done had they not. His thoughts were more jumbled than usual, and he felt incapable of conversation or rational thought for a few moments. He was aware of an unsettling curiosity brewing in him. That woman was like a book—as if he'd opened one with the certainty it would be dull, but then finding something compelling enough to make him want to turn the page.

That he wanted to turn that page was perhaps the most unsettling idea to have entered his thoughts in a very long while.

CHAPTER EIGHT

BERNADETTE SPENT THE afternoon tidying things—herself, her room—and she even made an attempt to tidy Avaline's. But she'd been chased away by the chambermaid, who took umbrage with her efforts.

With no tasks to occupy her, Bernadette wandered aimlessly about the grounds. She spoke to Niall MacDonald, who had come to speak to Lord Kent and was now on his way to parts unknown.

"You're leaving?" Bernadette said, perhaps a bit plaintively, thinking that she might have someone to talk to.

"Aye, that I am. I've work elsewhere." He'd tipped his hat, and turned his horse about, intending to ride on. But he paused and glanced back at her. "Have a care in the hills, Miss Holly."

"What do you mean?"

"There is bad blood between the Scots and the English," he said. "Bad blood between some clans, as well. Mind you have a care." And with that cryptic warning, he rode on.

Bernadette hardly gave it another thought. She had yet to see another living soul on her morning walks, other than the least friendly Scot of all, Mr. Mackenzie.

Without Mr. MacDonald to divert her, Bernadette tried to read. Yet she hardly saw a word—her thoughts were racing, her mind on that hard-hearted man and the things he'd said to her today. He cared for no one but himself, was the worst sort of person.

And yet, that uncivilized man seemed wholly different from the one who had stood on the cliff. She'd known instantly who it was when she'd stumbled across him—his was a foreboding presence, even at a distance. She'd paused, confused as to what he was doing there, and made uneasy by how uncomfortably close he stood to the edge. She'd been struck with the sick feeling that he might fall. Or worse—jump.

He'd obviously known how close to the edge he was, but still, Bernadette had fought a gut instinct to call out, to warn him that he stood too close. She might have done so, too, had he not suddenly stepped back from the edge.

And then, of course, he'd seen her there, and she'd panicked.

It was so strange, she thought now, with the luxury of a few hours alone to gather her thoughts. There had been something dark and desperate about him up on that cliff. Something that made her skin crawl even now. And something that made her feel an uncomfortable, unwanted twinge of compassion.

When Bernadette at last conceded that reading was a futile endeavor, she took to restlessly roaming the house. Unfortunately, she could hear Lord Kent haranguing his wife, which made her feel sick. So she took another long walk, Mr. MacDonald's warnings notwithstanding.

It seemed as if she was walking miles and miles every day now, anything to escape the tension at Killeaven. But there were only so many miles she could walk before hunger or dark skies or a fear of becoming hopelessly lost drove her back. Today, she returned with pangs of hunger, and was walking up the drive when she heard horses approaching. She glanced over her shoulder and noticed one horse was far in front of the others. It was obviously Mackenzie, racing as if the devil chased him. Behind him, Avaline's and Miss Mackenzie's horses trotted companionably along.

Naturally, Mackenzie galloped right past her, the horse's speed kicking up the hem of her gown. Bernadette coughed, waving the dust of the road from her face, then continued on, reaching the front drive at the same time Avaline and Miss Mackenzie reached it. They were nattering away with each other and called out a friendly greeting to her.

In the drive, Avaline's fiancé did not bother to come down from his mount, not even to help his fiancée from hers. He looked on insouciantly as the stable hand appeared to assist Avaline. The poor girl stumbled when her feet touched the ground, no doubt a result of being unaccustomed to riding for such a long period of time.

"Thank you," she said to Miss Mackenzie. "It has been a pleasure. You must thank your cook for the bannock cakes. They were delicious."

"Aye, you must come to Balhaire and thank her yourself."

"I will. Very soon," Avaline said.

"We'll look forward to it, then," said Miss Mackenzie.

Her brother reined his horse about. "We best ride on," he said, and glanced at Avaline. "Good day, then." He glanced at Bernadette, his eyes raking over her before he turned his back and rode on.

"Yes, thank you," Avaline said, but he'd already sent his horse to trot.

Miss Mackenzie, Bernadette noticed, watched her brother move with murderous intent in her eyes, but then sighed and shook her head. "He must seem wretched to you, aye?"

"What? No!" Avaline said at the same time Bernadette muttered, *"Entirely,"* and received a look of mortification from Avaline.

"Aye, as he does to us all," Miss Mackenzie agreed. "He's no' always been so…"

Rude? Churlish? Tactless?

"Wounded," she uttered.

Wounded. That was the second sibling of his to allude to some deep wound, and yet, Bernadette glanced down so no one would see her skepticism. She couldn't imagine what could have happened to make him unbearable at every turn.

"One day perhaps I might explain it," Miss Mackenzie said. But she sounded uncertain, no doubt owing to the reality that there was no explaining such insolent behavior.

"Cat!" her brother called over his shoulder.

Miss Mackenzie gathered her reins, then paused

and looked at Avaline. "He's really no' a bad man, he's no'," she said softly, and then spurred her horse to catch her brother.

"Then he has fooled us both," Bernadette muttered.

Miss Mackenzie quickly caught up to her brother, and when she did, she slowed her mount and reached her hand for him. Much to Bernadette's surprise, he took his sister's hand, his gloved hand closing protectively around it. There was something quite tender about it, something that reminded her of that strange twinge of compassion she'd felt for him earlier today.

Or maybe it was hunger she felt. She turned away from them, and from her complicated feelings, and said to Avaline, "Well then! How was your day?" And then she saw Avaline's face. "Oh, dear," she murmured.

Tears streaked Avaline's cheeks. Her skin had gone pale and her fists were curled tightly at her sides.

"Avaline!" Bernadette said with alarm.

"He is the most awful, wretched, *unbearable* man," she said, so angry that her voice shook. "I hate him."

"Oh, darling—"

"I *hate* him," she said again, and whirled around and ran into the house.

AVALINE WOULD NOT come out of her room for the remainder of the day and refused her supper.

"What will we do?" her mother fretted to Bernadette.

"Nothing," Bernadette said gravely. "She won't starve herself to death, madam. She will, eventually, come out of her room."

Her mother did not look convinced of that and tried,

unsuccessfully, on two more occasions to convince her daughter to open the door.

Bernadette did not press Avaline, but she brooded about the girl's situation. She decided at last that the only thing to be done for her was to appeal to Lord Kent.

She realized, as soon as she was admitted to his study, that perhaps that was not a very good idea.

His lordship and his brother were well into their cups, arguing over a chess game.

"I beg your pardon, I won't interrupt," Bernadette said.

"You are most welcome," Lord Kent said jovially, motioning for her to come forward. "I am of good cheer, for I am winning. But if you wish to speak to Edward, you will be disappointed. He is foul when he is losing."

"You will do us both a service if you shut your bloody mouth," Lord Ramsey groused, and his brother laughed.

"What is it, Bernadette? What brings you into this den of bad gaming?" his lordship asked, and gestured for her to pour more whisky.

She picked up the bottle and poured into their glasses. "I wish to speak to you about Avaline."

Her father didn't look up. "What is it now?"

She put aside the bottle. "My lord… I beseech you to consider that she does not esteem Mr. Mackenzie."

Lord Kent laughed at that and leaned back in his chair. "Then perhaps she has more sense than I thought," he said. "No one esteems him, do they? He's a bloody miserable man."

Bernadette was astounded. She was prepared to present her case to convince his lordship. "He is," she said, seizing the moment. "And Avaline is very unhappy."

"Yes, well," he said, turning his attention to the chessboard once more, "what would you have me do about it?"

"Revoke the marriage agreement," she said quickly. "Allow Avaline to return to England. I am certain Mackenzie will not care a whit. We can say that you found him entirely unsuitable so that her reputation won't suffer."

Lord Kent exchanged a look with his brother, who snickered darkly as he shook his head. His lordship was not so amused; he slowly turned his head. His gaze pierced Bernadette's. "You'd like me to renege on our agreement," he said flatly.

Bernadette swallowed. She nodded—that was precisely what she wanted.

There was a change in Lord Kent's expression—his features seemed to turn harder. "I thought you more clever than that, Bernadette. What *possible* reason would I have to go back on the agreement?"

What reason? Was his daughter's happiness not reason enough? Could he not understand how heartbroken his own flesh and blood had been made by this betrothal? "Avaline is *inconsolable*—" she began.

"Inconsolable?" he repeated loudly. "She'd be inconsolable if she lost a bloody slipper."

Bernadette bristled at how he reduced his daughter's

tears to nothing more than a tantrum. "My lord, please believe me when I tell you she is *desperately* unhappy."

"I don't care!" he shouted, and slammed his fist down onto the table so hard that he knocked the chess pieces over.

"Bloody hell, look what you've done!" Lord Ramsey exclaimed irritably.

Lord Kent surged to his feet, and his face, twisted with anger, only inches from hers. "There will be no revocation, Miss Holly. Avaline will marry that bloody savage whether she wants to or not. She will give him an heir, she will secure this land for her family. Do you understand?"

No, Bernadette didn't understand, she would never understand, but found herself unable to speak when he loomed over her as he was.

"She best stop her constant complaints," he said, pointing a bony finger at her. "I need that land that lies between Killeaven and Balhaire, and I need the Mackenzies to help me obtain it. That's our access to the sea, do you understand? I will not have this arrangement fall apart because I have a weak, missish daughter who is unwilling to do her duty."

Bernadette was shocked. While it was true she'd never seen any hint of affection flow from Lord Kent to his daughter, he was her father nonetheless. How could he be so uncaring?

Lord Kent shifted closer, his finger still pointing at her. "*Never* ask me this again," he said, his voice menacing. "Never *speak* to me of this again, am I quite clear? If you cannot ready her for the wedding, then she will suffer in her marriage, and I care *not*."

Bernadette gaped in disbelief. She'd believed her father was rather unique in his heartlessness, but clearly he was not the only man who would treat his daughter as nothing more than a piece of property, no better than a horse to be traded, without the slightest twinge of conscience.

His message delivered, Lord Kent fell into his chair and drank his whisky. "I'll say this for these savages— they distill a fine whisky," he said, and tossed the contents down his throat.

"Walk on, girl," said Lord Ramsey, waving her away, and then offering his glass to his brother to be refilled.

Bernadette couldn't wait to be free of that room. She turned about and strode quickly to the door. She had not yet made her escape when Lord Kent stopped her. "Bernadette!"

She reluctantly turned back.

"Do not disappoint me in this. If you cannot bring that girl around, I will send you back to your father. You'll not like that, will you?" He smirked, fully aware what that would mean for her. Bernadette's father would just as soon send her to a convent than keep her under his roof.

She turned away from Lord Kent before she said something she would sorely regret.

How ironic, she thought as she fled the study. She thought she'd despised Avaline's Scotsman, but her disgust for him came nowhere near what she was feeling for his lordship at the moment.

BERNADETTE SPENT A sleepless night, her mind whirling with ideas. She was determined to find a way out of this for Avaline. She decided she didn't care if Lord Kent sent her back to Highfield—life under her father's roof couldn't be any worse than Kent's employ. She was indignant, enraged, and felt so impotent that Avaline was the sacrificial lamb.

After a lot of tossing and turning, an idea did occur to her. It wouldn't be easy, but if Avaline cried off from her engagement—publicly, and for good reason—there was nothing her father could do. He would be angry with her, certainly—but he could not force her to marry Mackenzie if her grievance was made public—not legally, not morally. His power over his daughter existed in the privacy of this family's affairs.

Convincing Avaline would be the hard part. She was an obedient and fearful young woman. But Bernadette was determined, if for no other reason than to best Lord Kent and his grand plans that so callously disregarded the well-being of his only child.

Or, perhaps it was far more personal than she was willing to admit, even to herself. The anger in Bernadette for what had happened to her still burned. Her father's disregard for her feelings had been almost as painful as losing the baby she'd carried. Her father had said such vile things, had called her such horrible names, had said she was a whore, selling her body to any man who would pay.

Bernadette's only crime had been to fall in love with the son of a shopkeeper. Unfortunately, that occupation was not what her father had in mind. Her father had become rich from making iron, and he saw Bernadette and her sister, Nan, as his entry into a higher level of society—not an inferior one. Bernadette's crime was eloping with the man she wanted to spend her life with. And after they were caught and Albert disappeared, Bernadette's ultimate crime had been discovering that she'd carried Albert's child. Her bastard child, really, since her father had forced the annulment of her marriage.

The pregnancy did not soften her father's heart; if anything it only gave him more reason to despise Bernadette. She'd been made a pariah, even among her own family, and then she'd lost the baby, and had almost lost her own life.

Her feelings has been disregarded, but Bernadette was determined that Avaline's feelings would be heard and properly addressed.

The next morning, she walked into Avaline's room without knocking. The girl was buried under a mound of coverlet and linens, and when Bernadette shook her leg, her head popped up from between a pair of pillows. She blinked the sleep away, then glared at Bernadette. "Go away. I don't want to see anyone." She fell facedown into the pillows.

"You've had an entire evening of self-pity, darling. Now is the time we must think what to do," Bernadette said, and walked across the room to throw the windows open wide.

Avaline slowly pushed up. "Do?"

"Yes, *do*," Bernadette said, and returned to the bed. "Your effort to be pleasing and courteous has not worked to garner any affection from…him," she said. "Everything we've done thus far has only made you unhappy."

"*He* makes me unhappy, and there is nothing to be done for it!" Avaline buried her face in the pillow again.

"Avaline," Bernadette said. "Listen to me. You hate him, you said so yourself. There is nothing we've seen thus far that recommends him in any way, isn't that so?"

Avaline snorted. *"Nothing,"* she agreed.

"So…if he is truly reprehensible to you, you might still cry off the engagement."

Avaline slowly turned to look at Bernadette, her eyes filled with skepticism. "Father would *never* allow it—"

"Your father cannot legally force you into a marriage you don't want…particularly if Mackenzie did something that everyone would see as unacceptable."

"What do you mean?"

"I don't really know," Bernadette admitted. "But I think we should go to Balhaire today and call on him. The more time we are in his company, the better the chances are that he will do or say something so egregious, that no one can deny you have reason to end your engagement. There is a caveat, however—you must end it publicly."

"Publicly," Avaline repeated cautiously, and sat up. "But I thought perhaps I might make him a gift."

Honestly, sometimes Bernadette wondered if the girl had been born without a full complement of brains. She drew a steadying breath so she would not shout her question and asked, "Why would you give him a gift, dearest? He's done nothing to deserve it, has he? That makes no sense."

"I don't know," Avaline said. "Perhaps I've gone about it wrong. Perhaps I've been too timid. You've told me more than once I'm too timid, Bernadette."

Patience, Lord, please grant me patience. "But this is a bit different, isn't it? I want us to find an opportunity that would give you reason to cry off. Do you see?"

Avaline shook her head. "I don't see how I might."

"Because I am confident—*entirely* confident—that we can discover something about him so objectionable that you would be well justified to end the engagement. But we can't possibly know what that is if we avoid him. We must go to Balhaire and engage him."

"I'll take a gift, then," Avaline said.

"Why?" Bernadette demanded again. "What possible good can come of it?"

Avaline shrugged.

Bernadette bit her tongue to keep herself from accusing Avaline of being the most cake-headed person she'd ever met. "What will you give him?" she asked skeptically.

"I don't know," Avaline admitted. "But I'll think of something." She drew her knees up to her chest and absently picked at a loose thread on the coverlet. "I *would* very much like to see Catriona again. I rather like her."

"That's no reason—"

"I've thought quite a lot about it, Bernadette," Avaline said primly, interrupting her. "I've gone about it all wrong, I am certain of it. I want to try again."

Well, then. Bernadette supposed she ought to be encouraged that Avaline had actually come to this conclusion all on her own, but she could only think she was woefully naive and impossible. "If that is your wish," she said, forcing herself to sound as pleasant as she possibly could in spite of her great frustration.

"It is," Avaline said.

"It won't work," Bernadette said, unable to help herself.

Avaline shrugged again. "Perhaps not. At least I will know I tried everything within my power to do as my father wished."

That was the thing that made Bernadette groan. She sank down onto the edge of the bed. "What about what *you* wish, Avaline? What about *you*?"

Avaline gave her a tremulous smile. "Really, Bernadette, you know the answer to that. It doesn't matter what I wish. It never has." She stood up from the bed and walked to her bureau. She opened it, looked through the few things there and then held up a lace handkerchief to Bernadette. "I'll embroider his initials on this."

Bernadette looked at the delicate thing and imagined it in the hands of a brute. "It's made of lace. He won't care for it."

"Perhaps not. But it's the thought that counts, isn't it?"

"In any situation but this," Bernadette said bluntly.

Avaline looked at her curiously. "Why are you so cross?" she asked curiously. "You've always said a good woman's first instincts should always lean toward compassion and kindness."

The question set Bernadette back on her heels. She *did* always say things like that to Avaline. And for the first time since seeing the dark eyes of this particular Scot, Bernadette wondered why her instincts had leaned so far the other way. Oh, but it was obvious, wasn't it? He was cold and cruel, and…and he was much like Bernadette's father that was what.

Except that he wasn't, really.

Today, she had sensed that Mackenzie's was a different sort of darkness than her father's.

"I'll find some thread," she said, and went out, mulling that over.

CHAPTER NINE

THEY FEEL AS if they are rebels, hiding away at Auche-nard as they are, lying in bed, their legs laced with each other and in spite of the bitter cold in a lodge with empty hearths, both of them slick with the sweat of having made wild love.

Seona twirls a bit of Rabbie's hair around her finger, then traces a line down his chest. He catches her hand and kisses it, too spent to have another go. He wants to marry this lass, to make her his wife, to live at Arrandale and begin a family. But they won't until her brothers return from Inverness, where they are part of the Jacobite army that has seized, and now hold, that stronghold.

"I donna want to wait any longer," he tells her. "I want to wed you now, Seona. What we do here is immoral."

She strokes his cheek and smiles sadly. "You know very well my father will no' allow it before my brothers have returned, Rabbie Mackenzie."

"Have you any word of them?" he asks, and kisses her breast.

"No. My father says Lord Cumberland is advancing, and they are needed to hold Inverness." She shrugs and

nuzzles his neck. "I donna want to speak of it now...do you?" She nibbles his ear.

Rabbie doesn't want to speak of it, either, but he is filled with foreboding.

CAILEAN MACKENZIE, RABBIE'S oldest brother, was laird of Arrandale, the estate just up the loch from Balhaire. He'd built his house with his own hands. But as stately as it was, it was nearly uninhabited, save for its current resident, Rabbie, accompanied by the ghost of Seona's memory, and Mr. and Mrs. Brock, an elderly couple who had survived the dispersal of the MacAulay clan. They had a cottage down on the shore of Lochcarron, only yards from Arrandale, and kept the house and grounds and animals and cooked for Rabbie when he was about. Their living was so quiet that Rabbie scarcely noticed them.

About a mile from Arrandale was Auchenard, the hunting lodge that Daisy—Lady Chatwick before she'd married Cailean—held in stead for her son, young Lord Chatwick. It sat empty now, as it had for many years. Since the rebellion had been put down, Daisy did not feel safe bringing her viscount son so far into the Scottish Highlands, fearing retribution for what had happened at the fields of Culloden. Someday, when Ellis was of age, he would come again. But for now, Rabbie saw after it. For the time being, they resided at Chatwick Hall in northern England, a grand place by the sound of it, where Ellis was being properly educated to be an English viscount.

Rabbie missed his brother and Daisy, he did, but

the solitude at Arrandale suited him. He felt useless otherwise. He wasn't even a help to his own father. Though his father's leg bothered him very much, he was still the head of a clan, still had responsibilities to their extended family, although that family had been diminished. Rabbie couldn't seem to summon the wherewithal to help his father in the ongoing affairs of Balhaire. Everything seemed so bloody pointless.

Catriona, whose future seemed as bleak to Rabbie as his own, had begun to handle more of their father's dealings and, in notable contrast to Rabbie, without complaint. Her willingness to help where she could shamed him. They were born of the same parents, had shared the same upbringing. How could her heart stay as strong as it had, still beating, still capable of feeling, when his heart had turned so hard?

He thought of all this one day as he rattled around the estate, with nothing to occupy him but his thoughts. He was restless again, and decided to go to Balhaire. He found Mrs. Brock and told her not to leave supper for him. He also decided, as it was a fine, clear day, that he'd take one of the boats. It had been a very long time since he'd been on the water. One of the Balhaire dogs had followed him home two days ago, and eagerly leaped in the small boat and settled at the stern like a captain.

Rabbie pushed the boat away from the shore, then stepped in, found the oars and began to row.

The loch was still this afternoon, the rowing easy work. He glided past the point where they'd hanged Seona's father, past the point the traitor Murray had led English soldiers to shore so that they could sneak inland to attack Killeaven and Marraig.

When Rabbie reached the place where the loch met the sea, the water turned a bit rougher. The rowing became work, and the dog came to its feet, as if on guard for any impediment in their path. Rabbie kept up his pace. His muscles burned to the point that he could scarcely feel his arms, but he did not let up. He wanted the burn to spread through every limb. He wanted to burn up completely.

He reached their cove without disintegrating into flames, however. The dog leaped from the boat, choosing to swim to shore. Perhaps it feared Rabbie would row it out to sea. He got out of the boat and sank into water above his knees. It was icy cold and filled his boots, and still, he didn't care. If his body wouldn't burn, perhaps it would freeze. He dragged the boat to shore and paused, looking up at the cliff. *His* cliff. It looked higher from here, which gave him a slight shiver. That might have been the result of the frigid water in his boots, but he couldn't be certain.

With the boat secure, Rabbie began the half-mile walk from the shore to Balhaire, up a gradual slope, through a forest and then onto the high road, past shuttered houses and shops, past clan members who lifted their hands in half-hearted greetings.

When he reached the bailey, he realized something was happening. He was so accustomed to the bailey being empty now, but he could hear voices. And laughter.

He was met by a pair of dogs, who lifted their snouts to be petted. He obliged them for a moment, then ventured on and walked toward the sound of the voices. He went round the corner and found, to his surprise, his brother and sisters, and Vivienne's children and husband, on the green. Fiona and Ualan were out as well, but standing apart from the others. Fiona was pulling grass from the green. Ualan watched the others intently.

But it was not the children that added to Rabbie's great consternation. It was the presence of Miss Holly and Miss Kent. They were bowling.

Bowling.

He hadn't seen anyone bowl on this green in years. He remembered when his father had brought them the kit from France, the balls polished to a high sheen, and he and his siblings had climbed over each other to touch them. For many years of his childhood, members of the Mackenzie clan would gather on the green on Saturday evenings, to dine and drink and play games such as this. Those times were long gone, and it made him sentimental to see his family at the sport now. His nieces and nephews were delighted; they were laughing and shrieking, running back and forth to examine each ball bowled.

It was strange to see Miss Holly and Miss Kent among them. Had he forgotten they were calling at Balhaire? He couldn't remember any mention of it. He watched them for a moment, unnoticed. His fiancée was laughing at something Aulay had said, and pretended to collapse with laughter into his shoulder. Aulay, laughing, too, caught her and righted her, then let her go with a smile.

It was Miss Holly's turn to bowl. She enlisted the

help of several of the children to instruct her, then bent down in something of a curtsy, and rolled her ball. It wobbled down the path she'd sent it and knocked a blue cone out of its way. That was met by cheering from the rest of them, his nieces and nephews jumping wildly about.

He hesitantly walked toward them.

Fiona MacLeod was the first to see him. She waved, as if they were dear old friends. She began to skip toward him. Her brother didn't move, but his gaze locked on Rabbie's. That lad seemed to carry an invisible weight on his shoulders.

"Rabbie!" Vivienne said, noticing Fiona skipping in his direction. Suddenly, his nieces and nephews began to shout "Uncle Rabbie!" and soon, they had raced ahead of Fiona to throw their arms around his legs, laughing.

Fiona stopped, watching the other children with curiosity.

"Look at the lot of you, aye?" Rabbie said as he tousled the hair of several of them, then gestured for Fiona to join in the fray. She didn't move. "Bowlers now, are you?"

"Uncle Rabbie, will you play?" asked his oldest niece, Maira. She had big blue eyes, like his Auntie Zelda.

"He'll no' play," said Bruce. The lad was old enough to remember a boisterous uncle who would carry him on his shoulders and toss him in the loch on hot summer days. Rabbie remembered that uncle, too—he'd been lost somewhere along the way. He stroked Maira's cheek and managed the best smile he could.

"Maira, *leannan*, he canna join the play in the middle of the game," Vivienne said, and put her hands on her daughter's shoulders. "Go now, it's your turn."

As Maira scampered back to the green, the other children, remembering the game, ran after her. Fiona had turned back, too, and was once again at her brother's side. Vivienne rose up and kissed Rabbie's cheek.

"What is this, then?" he asked, lazily returning her kiss.

"What do you think, lad? A game."

"Aye, a game we've no' played in years."

"We've naugh' else to entertain your fiancée, do we?"

He looked at Miss Kent. It didn't appear she'd noticed him…but her saucy maid had. She was wearing a pale blue gown, and for once, her hair was put up properly, so that he had a complete view of her long, slender neck. She was also smiling, as he had rarely seen her do, and it was…charming.

Rabbie looked away from the smile to the MacLeod children again. "Why do they no' play?" he asked, motioning with his head in their direction.

"I donna know," Vivienne said thoughtfully. "It's the lad, really—he's a wee bit shy."

"What's to become of them, then?" Rabbie asked.

Vivienne did not look at him. She turned her attention to the green and said, "We are endeavoring to find a relative or a family friend who might take them in."

She knew as well as Rabbie did that there was no relative to be found.

"The vicar said he recalls a Mr. Tawley, who was as close as a brother to Donald MacLeod. He has sent a man to deliver a message to him."

"They'll no' remain here, at Balhaire?" Rabbie asked.

Vivienne smiled at him. "Silly lad. They need parents, aye? They need a hearth and someone to tuck them into bed at night."

Of course they did.

"Aye, but it's a bonny day, is it no'?" Vivienne asked, and brushed hair from his forehead. "We mean to walk down to the cove. You will join us—"

"No."

Vivienne clucked her tongue at him. "Aye, you will. You canna have your lass here and no' acknowledge her, Rabbie."

"She is no' my lass and I didna invite her."

"No one did. She doesna need an invitation now, does she? Within a matter of days, she'll be family."

Rabbie winced at that blatant reminder. "I must marry her, Vivi, aye? But I'll no' be forced into entertaining her."

"Oh, Rabbie, really—"

"Oh. Mr. Mackenzie! You've come!"

Rabbie groaned, closed his eyes a moment, then turned about to face his fiancée. She was approaching him cautiously, as if she expected him to lash out at her. Why was she so cautious? He hadn't shouted at her—he hadn't shown her anything but apathy thus far.

"I'm… I thought I wouldn't see you."

Rabbie could not determine if, by that remark, she meant she had rejoiced in the hope of not seeing him, or had hoped that she might.

"Feasgar math," he said, and clasped his hands behind him and gave her a curt nod. "I wasna expecting you," he said.

"Oh, ah…yes, I know," she said. She looked to Rabbie as if she wanted desperately to wring her hands, but was struggling to keep from it. Her keeper was walking toward them now, laughing at something Catriona had said.

"I'm…happy you have come," she said. She didn't sound particularly happy. She sounded afraid. "I've brought you a gift!"

"A gift," he repeated. Why in God's name had she done that?

She withdrew a small package from her pocket and held it out to him.

"What is it?" he asked, making no move to take it.

Miss Holly had arrived at her side, no doubt, to direct this wee woman.

"Open it, and you'll see."

Rabbie had no desire to take a gift from her or even know what it was. But he could feel their eyes on him, could almost feel the expectation flowing from his brother and sisters, and made himself take it. He undid the bit of twine and unfolded the vellum. Inside was a lacy handkerchief, and he was suddenly and jarringly reminded of the time Seona had given him a gift, wrapped similarly. Her gift had been a brooch to pin to his plaid sash, a replica of a broadsword topped with the Highland thistle.

This was a lace handkerchief. A ladies' handkerchief, he was certain, although he knew that of late, English men dripped in lace. He picked it up between finger and thumb and held it out for all to see.

"I embroidered your initials," she said, pointing. "See? There, in the corner."

He could see the tiny letters. *R* and *M*, unsteadily applied, the *R* slightly larger than the *M*. He looked at the lass. "What am I to do with this, then?"

She blinked. Twice. "It's a gift," she repeated, as if that should answer any outstanding questions he might have about it.

The gift embarrassed him, and he hastily shoved it into a pocket. Did this ridiculous creature honestly believe he had any use at all for a *lace* handkerchief? "Thank you."

"Rabbie," Catriona muttered. She'd put a protective arm around the chit. "Miss Kent has gone to some effort, aye?"

What effort? He himself might have sewn initials onto a handkerchief. He looked at the woman he was to marry in less than a fortnight. "You are too…" *Absurd, that was what.* "Kind," he said, and forced a slim smile. And then quickly looked away. Unfortunately, his gaze happened to land on Miss Holly. What was that, a wee smirk on her lips? He had the distinct impression she was amused by his discomfort.

"Come back to the game, Miss Kent," Aulay suggested. "We're almost to the end, aye?" Aulay offered his arm and Miss Kent put her hand on it, smiling once again as he led her back to the green.

Always the diplomat, his brother.

That left two sisters to glare at him and one English-woman to smirk. Bloody fine day it was, indeed.

"What is the matter with you?" Vivienne asked in Gaelic. "She made it for you. And don't dare say you don't care. I know you're unhappy, Rabbie, we're *all* of us unhappy. But we can't simply lay down and die."

"Why not?" he asked.

Her glare deepened. "If you mean to be this cruel, you should tell Father you will not wed her and spare us all the agony." She turned and flounced away, Catriona hurrying to keep up with her.

That left Rabbie with the smug English flower. He sighed. "Go on, then—no doubt you want to impress your bad opinion on me."

"Me? I'm merely an observer," she said, and flashed a bit of a smirk. "Although I'm quite certain that if I knew what your sister said, I would agree completely." Her smile broadened, and ended in a pair of very appealing dimples in her cheeks. She glanced down to his boots and buckskins. "Did you swim here?"

He sighed. "I tried. Go on, back to your game, Miss Holly."

"Rabbie, lad, come on, then!" Aulay called out to him.

God help him, not Aulay, too. Rabbie shook his head.

Aulay began striding forward. "We're to the cove, we are. A walk with the children. You'll join us."

"No—"

Aulay's grin was not exactly a sunny one. He clapped Rabbie on the shoulder, squeezing painfully. "I wasna asking, lad. We'll have a walk with the children, and you'll take the opportunity to acquaint yourself with our guests." He squeezed once more, only harder, and then turned away. "Shall we walk?" he called to the others.

The children, naturally, were thrilled with the idea, and with shrieks of glee began to race each other toward the bailey gates, the dogs on their heels, galloping alongside them, tails high in the air. Rabbie looked around for Ualan and Fiona, and saw them following Barabel's broad behind in through a door to the kitchen. There was something that chafed about that, those two children being put to work. But then again, he supposed they could not be left to run wild, without supervision.

"Come along then, Rabbie!" Catriona called, gaining his attention once more.

There was no escaping it. In spite of his melancholy and his increasing unwillingness to play this courtship game, a part of him really did understand that he had to make some effort. His siblings would not believe him if he told them that he desired to do so more than they could wish it...but Rabbie couldn't summon the pluck necessary to say it.

He watched as Aulay rounded them all up and began to walk with Catriona and Miss Kent, followed by Miss Holly. The children ran ahead of them all, only the youngest of Vivienne's riding atop his father's shoulders as Vivienne walked beside them.

Rabbie followed last, his mind blank.

The group's progress was slower than he could tolerate, however, and he ended up passing Vivienne and Marcas. Soon, he was walking behind Aulay and the ladies, listening idly to their conversation. Miss Kent was speaking of the stars, he thought, reciting those used to navigate, with Aulay correcting her pronunciation a time or two.

Miss Holly asked about the repairs Aulay was making to the ship, which prompted his brother to mention the new navigational equipment they'd acquired at a dear expense.

"An octant?" Miss Holly asked brightly, rousing Rabbie from the lethargy of his thoughts. How could she possibly know that?

"Exactly so, Miss Holly," Aulay said, sounding surprised. "How do you know of it, then?"

"Oh, I read about it." She said it breezily, as if it was common for a woman who laid out her mistress's gowns and put up her hair to read about navigation tools.

"You read about it," Rabbie said skeptically.

She glanced dismissively over her shoulder at him. "Lord Kent has an impressive library." She quickened her step to catch up to Aulay. "I understand it's remarkable in its design," she said. "Quite an improvement over the sextant."

"Aye, that it is," Aulay said. "It can be used for celestial navigation in both day and night, then, and the accuracy of direction is vastly improved."

She beamed with a smile, obviously proud of herself for knowing it.

Rabbie studied her with suspicion. He glanced at

her charge, wondering if she'd read anything like it, but Miss Kent wasn't listening at all. She and Catriona had their heads close together and were speaking in low tones.

They had reached the shore now, and the children began to scour the coastline for interesting finds, their parents trailing lazily behind. Miss Kent and Catriona wandered farther afield, still engrossed in their conversation about God knew what. Aulay, naturally, had wandered over to Rabbie's boat to have a look. Since they were wee lads, Rabbie could not remember an instance in which Aulay was interested in anything other than boats and the sea.

The sea had never lured Rabbie, even then. He recalled a particularly bad voyage as a lad with his father at the helm. A fierce storm had given him a bout of seasickness so severe that Rabbie could hazily recall some question of his recovery. Part of his sickness, he suspected, had been his abject fear of being capsized. Since that voyage, there was something about the sea's vastness and the ferocious strength of it that had intimidated him into keeping his feet firmly on terra firma for the most part.

What Rabbie had enjoyed as a lad and as a young man was soldiering and feats of strength. His father, and his father's father before him, and his Uncle Jock, God rest his soul, had made a name by training Highland guards.

What had begun as an effort to protect what was theirs in a land where loyalties and alliances were constantly changing had grown into a formidable strength for the Mackenzies. Rabbie's father and Uncle Jock had trained men who had gone on to serve in the crown's forces. For the young men of their clan, the option was an appealing one, as their keep was paid and there was money to send home. Rabbie had liked the work of training, had relished challenging his body to stronger and stronger feats. He might have joined the soldiers in joining the king's army, might have led a regiment into battle for the king, had the Jacobites not begun their rebellion.

It was not the rebellion itself that that had attracted him, but the questions the rebellion had raised. Was the true king of England and Scotland sitting on the throne? An argument could be made that the Stuarts had a more legitimate claim than the Hanoverians, from whom King George had descended. Was the taxation the crown imposed fair? Rabbie didn't know the answer to that, but he knew that before the union of Scotland and England, his family had not resorted to piracy. It had become necessary when they couldn't recoup the costs of bringing goods to Scotland after the taxes and excise had been levied, and their people couldn't afford the goods because of the tax burden.

Nevertheless, the Mackenzies had remained neutral and had believed their neutrality would keep them out of the fray. Bloody hell if it had—their livelihood had been damaged and his own life threatened, all because they were Highlanders. Rabbie could not serve a king who had sent the murderous Lord Cumberland and his forces into the Highlands as he had.

Aye, everything had changed after that. *Everything*.

Rabbie sat on a rock. He kept his gaze on the children, and only happened to see Miss Holly when she wandered along the water's edge, squatting down every few steps, picking up this or that and examining it before tossing it down again. Maybe she'd read about seashells, too. Maybe she had superior knowledge of the tides, thanks to Lord Kent's impressive library. It was incredible that she had chosen *navigation* to wile away a few hours.

He stood from his rock, clasped his hands behind his back and moved lazily in her direction. "On the hunt for artifacts, are you?" he asked as he reached her.

She glanced up at him, squinting into the sun. "No. Just rocks." She smiled pertly. She rose up and brushed her hands free of sand.

"How is it that a maid, bound to nothing more than laying out her mistress's petticoats, should know about navigation, then?"

A brow lifted. "I told you. I read it. Is that so unusual?"

"Aye, I'd say it is. It doesna fit with that of a servant."

"Neither does being a *shrew* or a *harridan*." She gave him a meaningful look, then dipped down to pick up a shell. "It might astound you to know that there are women in this world who seek to improve their mind."

She was right—everything about her was unusual. Who spoke in such a way? "Who is your father?" he asked curiously.

The question seemed to startle her, which Rabbie found even more curious.

"Why do you ask? Do you intend to complain of me?"

"I've no' thought of it," he said. "Perhaps I should."

"I don't care if you do," she said, a little too forcefully.

"How is that you've come to attend Miss Kent? You're too educated, aye? A lass does no' possess that sort of education and confidence without an eye toward an advantageous match. So why, then, have you no' married?"

Now her eyes narrowed in a manner that almost made him regret the question. "Why haven't *you*?"

A fair question, he supposed, but one that hit him squarely in the gut. "There are times when life doesna unfurl as one might have hoped."

"Exactly," she said, and dropped the shell. She looked away from him and rubbed her nape. Her cheeks were blooming, which he thought odd. She had not struck him as a person who was easily flustered. "I know that life for Avaline has not unfurled as *she* hoped."

Avaline. He thought of her so little that he'd almost forgotten her name.

"Look at her now," she said, nodding in the direction of his fiancée.

Rabbie didn't want to look away from Miss Holly's profile. There was something maddening about her, but there was also something quite captivating, too. Particularly because she was English and yet did not employ towering hair or a powdered face to make herself attractive as so many of them did. She seemed quite at ease in plain frocks and hairdressings and her tongue wagging freely.

Even more startling was that Rabbie was noticing these things at all.

"She is happy with your sister. She's rather fond of her."

Rabbie had to shake off the admiration of Miss Holly to glance in the direction of Miss Kent. "A pity she's no' to marry Cat, then," he said.

When he looked back at Miss Holly, she was frowning. As she was wont to do. Particularly in his direction.

"She's really quite...different once you know her," she said, clearly searching for the right word. "She is diverting. And sweet. And very accommodating to those she cares about."

"She'd make a fine governess, then."

Miss Holly snapped her gaze to him. "She'll make a good *wife*. What more can a man ask?"

So much more than that, Rabbie thought. A man could ask to love his wife. To want to be with her at every turn. Was that too much to ask?

Miss Holly suddenly gasped. "Look!" she said, dipping down. "It's a farthing." She picked up the object and held it in her hand. Rabbie leaned over, peering at it.

"Aye, that it is."

"Where do you suppose it's come from?"

"*Och*, any number of men, aye? This is a ship's cove. Seaman, their families—all of them walk through here at low tide."

She turned it over in her hand. She was smiling, delighted with her find. "It's good luck," she said.

"It's no'," he said.

She slipped it into her pocket. "You are curiously determined to see gloom in everything."

"On the contrary—I see the truth in everything."

She studied him, assessing him. He noticed the flecks of brown and green in her eyes, the dark lashes that framed them.

"Aye, come on, then!" Aulay called to them. Rabbie glanced away from her eyes. Aulay was waving to them, gesturing to the path. The tide was coming in and the beach would soon disappear. Catriona and Miss Kent were still in a tête-à-tête, already walking up the path. Vivienne and her family were halfway up the hill and into the forest, along with Fiona and Ualan. Miss Holly quickly started after them, as if she feared the tide would swallow her before she reached the path. Or perhaps she feared she'd be left alone with him. But as Rabbie followed her, she suddenly exclaimed and turned around, running back toward the sea, lifting her skirts to keep the hem from the sand. When she reached the edge of the water, she put her hand in the pocket of her gown, then hurled something into the water. The farthing.

She ran back, slowing as she neared him, working to catch her breath.

"You threw the farthing into the sea," he said.

"I did," she said breathlessly. "I made a wish."

"I donna know this custom, throwing good coin away."

"It's not a custom," she said, and began to walk. "But as there is no wishing well about, it seemed the next best thing."

"What folly, tossing coins into the sea. It'd be better use to you in your pocket, aye?"

"There's nothing wrong with believing in a bit of magic, Mr. Mackenzie!" she called over her shoulder.

There was something completely wrong with believing in folly. He hastened to keep step with her and fell in beside her. "Well, then? What did you wish?"

She laughed with surprise, and the sound of it shot down his spine. "You are mad to ask! To reveal my wish is to ruin it."

"That's the superstition of fishwives," he said, feeling annoyed that she would waste the money and allow her obviously superior feminine mind to believe in such farce. "You're a fool to believe it."

"Now I may add *fool* to the list of attributes you've given me. Shrew, harridan, fool... I'm astonished I've not been rounded up by the authorities and put on a ship back to England. How can you be so sure of your beliefs? Have you ever tried wishing for something?"

"Aye, lass, I've wished," he said with a snort. "I've wished for things you'd no' understand." He noticed a fuzzy curl of hair behind her ear. He wanted to touch it, to tuck it up into the rest of her hair.

"Miss Kent will agree with my putting hope above despair and wishing," she said breezily, ignoring him. "I'll save my breath for her."

"Aye, she will, because she knows nothing of the world and of how people struggle for farthings."

"Well," Miss Holly said, dipping down to avoid the bough of a tree. "She is very young yet—"

"She is scarcely out of the nursery. She hasna the

proper knowledge of the world and how bloody cruel it can be." He said it without thinking, had allowed his grousing to tumble off his tongue. He hadn't even realized what he said until Miss Holly suddenly stopped on the path ahead of him and twisted around, startling him. She was standing very close to him, and this time he noticed the faint fan of lines in the corners of her eyes. Laugh lines, his mother called them. When had she laughed? What amused her? He wanted to see her laugh.

She certainly wasn't doing so now—she folded her arms and glared at him. "I beg your pardon, Mr. Mackenzie, but I think you enjoy your cozy mantle of pity. You wrap it around you like a winter cloak."

His brows rose slightly. He supposed he ought to take offense, but Miss Holly was drumming her fingers against her arm, a habit he'd noticed in her before. What he had not noticed was how long and delicate her fingers were, and he was seized, utterly seized, with the idea of touching them to his lips. They were like an exotic fruit he'd never tasted.

"You spend each day in search of it!" she insisted.

He took her hand, pulling it away from her arm to hold in his palm.

She looked at her hand, then at him. "Won't you at least *attempt* to find some good in your situation? Or do you intend to march to the altar with that dour look and a world of woe on your shoulders?"

Rabbie was listening to her with only one ear. Even so, he scarcely heard her, as his heart had begun to beat wildly in his chest. He slowly lifted her hand and kissed her palm.

Miss Holly gasped as if she'd been stung and yanked her hand free of his. "What is the matter with you?"

"*Diah*, I donna know," he said with unabashed honesty, and suddenly reached for her, one hand on her waist, the other to the side of her head. And he kissed her. Aye, he kissed her. He knew only that the urge to do so had filled him so violently and swiftly that he couldn't stop himself.

Miss Holly pushed against him, but Rabbie slipped his tongue into her mouth and met hers, and it was so sweet, and so soft, and so bloody arousing that he was shocked by it. It was a bolt of lightning striking him from above and lighting him up. He hadn't felt this spark in so long, had assumed he would never feel it again, and yet here it was, reverberating through his body, causing his parched soul to thirst for more, and proving to him that he was alive. He was *alive*.

He did not want to let go. He knew, vaguely, that his family was just ahead of them on the path, and still, he could not make himself let go. Especially not when Miss Holly, for all her blustering and condescension to him, opened her mouth and kissed him back. This was not the startled kiss of an innocent lass—her lips eagerly pressed against his as her body pressed against his chest and groin. Her hands were clinging to his arms and her tongue was moving with his. Miss Holly was kissing him as hard as he was kissing her.

And then she made a soft, but unmistakable sound of pleasure in the back of her throat that exploded in his head. Suddenly everything was raining down on him—desire, greed—and just as suddenly, she shoved against him with all her might. She was strong, too, because he stumbled backward. She gasped for air and moved away from him, dragging the back of her hand across her mouth. "Are you *mad*?" she whispered.

Rabbie thought about that a moment. "Aye."

She looked frantically to the group ahead, but they had disappeared on the path. No one had noticed them kissing like two lovers. She turned back to him, staring wildly at him. Her hand was shaking. "You are to marry my friend!"

"Your charge," he amended.

"No, Mr. Mackenzie, she is my *friend*. I am incensed for her! Yes, she is young and inexperienced, but she is hopeful and she wants to make you a good wife."

"Why are you the one to defend her thoughts? Why does she no' speak for herself?"

Miss Holly blinked. "She's shy!" she blustered.

"Uist," he said. She was ruining this moment, ruining that kiss. "I think there is more to your interest in her marriage than you will admit, aye? But donna scold me, lass—I'm a grown man."

She gasped. "That does not give you the right to crush a young woman's heart!"

She said it so vehemently that he wondered briefly, curiously, if she was speaking of Miss Kent at all. He put his hand on her shoulder and dipped down to look her directly in the eye. "It was a wee kiss, no' a declaration of love. Donna make more of it than there is."

"*That* was more than a wee kiss!"

"Was it? Then I will bow to your superior under-standing of kissing, aye? No doubt you read about it in Lord Kent's impressive library. No doubt you'll correct me now," he said, and spread his arms wide, indicating he was ready to be addressed.

"I am speaking the truth! Why do you object to it?"

He pressed a hand to her neck, and spoke earnestly. "I object to the fact that you speak about things you canna possibly understand. I didna seek to wed your little lamb, aye? I wouldna wed at all, were it no' for my duty to my family. Donna speak to me of what is right and wrong. You canna possibly know what that is in this land."

She stared at him. Her gaze slowly drifted to his mouth, stirring the embers in him. Some of the fight seemed to have gone out of her and, rather subdued, she said, "I know quite a lot more than you think I do, sir. And I know that if you gave Avaline only half a chance, you could very well be pleasantly surprised. Have you no regard for *her* situation? Can you not see how difficult this is for her? Can you not imagine how kissing me would hurt her?"

He removed his hand from her neck. "Your righteousness comes several moments too late, does it no'?"

Her lush mouth gaped at the implication of what he was saying. Her hazel eyes narrowed. "Yes, it does," she agreed. "You are…" Now her voice was shaking as she tried to find the correct word. "You are *wretched*, Rabbie Mackenzie."

"Ah, wretched." He couldn't help but chuckle at

that. He'd been called far worse in his thirty some-odd years. He pulled the lace handkerchief from his pocket and handed it to her.

She stared down at it. "Why are you giving this to me?"

"You've a wee bit of sand on your face, aye?" he said, gesturing to her cheek. "Keep it. It means far more to you than it ever will to me." He stepped around her and began to walk up the path, leaving her there.

But he heard her mutter under her breath.

The others were waiting for them as they emerged from the forest. Miss Kent's gaze swept right past Rabbie and went to her lady's maid. "We're invited to dine, Bernadette," she said brightly.

"Oh, no, I—" Miss Holly glanced around at all of them, standing there, watching her. "We must reach Killeaven before nightfall."

"But we might stay until—"

Miss Holly grabbed the lass's hand and squeezed it. "I promised your mother I'd have you home, Avaline," she said earnestly. "We *must* go."

Miss Kent seemed unconvinced, but some unspoken understanding passed between the two women, because she nodded once and mumbled, "Yes, of course, we must."

Miss Holly linked her arm in Miss Kent's, and they resumed their walk up the road. Miss Holly's cheeks were flushed and her hair, he noticed, was a bit mussed on the side of her head where he'd held her.

Rabbie started up, too, but became aware of a pair

of eyes on him and turned back. Those eyes belonged to Catriona.

"Aye, what?" he asked, holding his hand out to her, indicating she should come along.

"What are you about?" she asked slyly.

"Naugh' more than making it through each day and the next," he answered truthfully.

Catriona clucked his tongue at him. "I donna know what to make of you any more, Rabbie."'

Aye, he didn't know what to make of himself. Especially not after that forbidden kiss.

CHAPTER TEN

IN HINDSIGHT, AVALINE supposed the gift of the handkerchief was rather silly of her. Bernadette was right—he didn't care for the lace, no matter that she had embroidered his initials on it. She'd thought he might think it sweet, might put it in a special place and from time to time in the course of their marriage, he would take it out and admire it, smile softly and remember the innocence of his fiancée before they'd wed.

It was quite clear that man was incapable of reflection or sentiment.

Well, at least she'd tried, as she'd told Bernadette she would, which was more than could be said for him. But really, quite honestly, since God was listening—Avaline assumed He was, as the Reverend Nokum was forever warning them that God Saw All—but if He was listening now, she would confess that the handkerchief had really been an excuse to ride to Balhaire. Even though she really disliked riding. Even though she was fearful of her fiancé. And not for the reasons Bernadette had suggested. Avaline had no intention of crying off. But she'd thought—hoped—her fiancé would appreciate her efforts, and if he did not, well…

There was Captain Mackenzie.

Oh, what a *glorious* day it had been, even when her fiancé had appeared, which Avaline had at first feared would ruin everything. Bernadette was so kind to occupy him so that Avaline might enjoy the company of Catriona.

What an unexpected friendship she'd found with Catriona! Once Avaline had become accustomed to the way Catriona voiced aloud every thought she was thinking, and was not, as Avaline had first supposed, judging her, she'd seen a sunny side to Catriona that she really very much liked.

But it was Captain Mackenzie who had carried the day for her.

Aulay. His name was Aulay. She had not been invited to call him that, naturally, but she adored his name. It was quite different and it suited him, for *he* was different than any man she'd ever known. He was so...*divine*. Handsome, which was the first thing she'd noticed about him. And so very kind, and *attentive*. He'd taught her the names of the stars and how to bowl properly, and he'd asked after her family, and about her home in England. He was *so* much more appealing than his brother!

Ah, but to that... Catriona had told her the most distressingly sad story about Mr. Mackenzie that Avaline had ever heard. Now she at least understood why he seemed so very angry. At least she thought she did, based on what Catriona had said...but then again, Catriona had said a *lot*, and Avaline couldn't be entirely certain she'd caught every detail.

Nevertheless, Catriona had explained that Mr.

Mackenzie's last fiancée—well, she wasn't certain if she was, indeed, a *fiancée*—had been lost in the aftermath of the rebellion. And Mr. Mackenzie—*Rabbie*—didn't know what had happened to her. She had just… disappeared.

Naturally, this distressed the poor man. Naturally, he was resentful of Avaline, for she was not the fiancée he'd chosen.

The story was so desperately mournful that Avaline was resolved to try harder to please him. She really didn't want to leave, not now that she'd decided she would be quite at home at Killeaven with her father and mother far from her. Bernadette would be with her, and really, did she need anyone else? She would get along very well here, and now that she knew the tragedy her poor husband-to-be had suffered, perhaps she might help him.

Avaline lay back against the pillows and closed her eyes. She imagined bringing the poor man back from the brink of complete despair. It would take an effort from her—she would need to see to all his needs, and engage him so as to take his mind off his loss. She imagined, as she pictured the lovely home she would create for him, how he would come to love her. She imagined how he would gaze at her with great affection and gratitude. He would one day realize that without her, he might very well have fallen into a melancholy so deep he could not recover. She'd heard of that happening. They put people who were quite sad into madhouses, didn't they?

Avaline lay her hands on her belly and imagined

how his family would thank her, would look upon her not unlike a saint, for all of their efforts had been for naught until she'd come and married him had humbly taken up the responsibility of being a wife to such a desperately sad man, and they would whisper to each other, when she was not present, "oh, how grateful we are for Avaline." His father, the laird, would write long letters to her father detailing how invaluable she has been in saving their despondent son, and her father— her *father*—would bow before her and say he'd been so very wrong about her all along.

Avaline rolled onto her side. And if, for some reason, that did not come to pass, there was always Aulay.

CHAPTER ELEVEN

BERNADETTE FELT UNCHARACTERISTICALLY FRAUGHT. She was frantic to hide the offending handkerchief, frantic to *do* something to erase the great mistake she'd made.

Such a horrible, awful mistake at Balhaire today... made so much worse by the knowledge that she'd felt that kiss down to her toes, had felt it simmering in her groin and in her veins. It was a kiss full of undeniable, stark desire, and she had been swept along with it, had forgotten herself so completely that she had scarcely been able to claw her way back to her senses.

And now she felt wild with guilt and fear that somehow Avaline would discover it. She hadn't felt things spiraling out of control so quickly since...well, since her father's men had caught her and Albert in that tiny little inn.

She shuddered at that memory—how humiliating it had been to be startled by men bursting into their room, and for them to find her in her chemise, and Albert, dear God, in nothing but his drawers.

In a peculiar way, this felt even worse than that. When those men had come, Bernadette knew that she and Albert had only hurt themselves. But in this, she had harmed Avaline. Not that Avaline knew it—but if she ever learned of it, it would ruin them.

Bernadette hid Avaline's handkerchief in a drawer beneath several of her things where no one would find it. She walked a circle around her small room, her hands locked behind her head, trying desperately to think rationally.

How had that kiss happened? One moment she'd been standing there, and the next her hand was in his much larger one, and she should have pulled it free, but she'd liked the way her hand felt in his. And then she'd been stunned by the touch of his lips to the palm of her hand and the way it had sent a thousand shocks of light through her. He'd done it so casually, so easily, and the sensation of it had lingered like a burn on the surface of her skin for several moments after he'd let go of her hand.

And then he'd *kissed* her. He'd kissed her *ardently*, like a man who was not afraid for her to know that he wanted all of her. She'd pushed him, because she'd not *agreed* to it, she'd not invited it, had not encouraged it...

But part of her had agreed, obviously. Part of her had not resisted him because there was something so raw and darkly masculine about him, and that kiss had been so...stirring. So astonishingly *stirring*.

Bernadette sat heavily on a stool at her vanity, her head in the palm of her hand. "What have I done?" she whispered. To have taken such a risk for a few moments of pleasure! And yet that kiss had startled her awake—

it had been so long since she'd known the pleasure of a man's touch.

She knew what Mackenzie had wanted of her. She knew what she'd wanted of him. She'd wanted the touch of a madman.

Until her common sense had taken hold and shook her into seeing what she was doing, and then, she'd felt a surge of panic and guilt and horror so great that she'd thought for a moment she might be sick with it.

She felt sick yet.

Bernadette lifted her head and looked at herself in the looking glass. What was she to do? Should she tell Avaline? *She couldn't!* Avaline would be heartbroken, might even collapse with grief as her constitution was not particularly strong. Worse, she probably wouldn't even understand at first that with her confession, Bernadette would have to leave her employ. Avaline would be angry and heartbroken, but at the same time, she would be lost without Bernadette.

Or, perhaps, Avaline would not be the least heartbroken. It was entirely possible that she would be so angry about the dissolution of trust between them that she would banish Bernadette to Highfield before Lord Kent could even think of it.

No, she couldn't tell Avaline—not now. Maybe someday, but not now. But what Bernadette *could* do, what she *must* do, was convince Avaline to cry off. That was the only solution for them both.

BERNADETTE BROACHED THE subject at breakfast the next morning. Avaline had slept late, and as a result, she and Bernadette were the only two in the dining room. When Renard left them to carry dishes to the kitchen, Bernadette cleared her throat and said, "Avaline, dearest, there is something I'd like to say."

Avaline looked up from her toast points. "Yes?"

A swell of nerves rose up in Bernadette. Avaline looked so young and trusting this morning, with the tail of her hair draped prettily over her shoulder. "Goodness, but you look positively ill, Bernadette. What's wrong? Does your breakfast not agree with you?"

"No, I'm very well." She hadn't eaten anything but a bite or two of toast. "I've been thinking of how we might entice Mr. Mackenzie to say something that will give you reason to cry off."

Avaline said nothing. She steadily held Bernadette's gaze.

"I've come to the conclusion that it's all really very simple. He cannot *abide* the English—"

"No?" Avaline asked, looking a bit surprised.

"No," Bernadette said carefully. Was it not obvious to her? "Because of what happened between Scotland and England."

"Oh, yes, of course, that's all so very sad, isn't it?" she asked, and idly toyed with her toast. "But surely he doesn't hold *all* the English people responsible." She suddenly looked up. "How do you know his feelings? Did he tell you?"

Bernadette felt a slight burn in her chest. "Well, I—"

Avaline gasped. "Of course! Catriona told you, too, didn't she?"

"Told me what?"

"About his first fiancée," Avaline said, and pulled a very sad face.

What in blazes was she nattering about? "What do you mean his first fiancée?"

"I can't recall her name, precisely. Something like Showna, I think."

Bernadette shook her head. "I haven't the slightest idea what you are talking about."

"No?" Avaline said, seeming surprised again. "Oh dear, it is the most tragic story of all, Bernadette!" she said eagerly. "He was very much in love with her, and they planned to be married, just as soon as her brothers returned from the rebellion. But her brothers didn't return, for they were killed in a *terrible* battle. And then, of course, it wouldn't do to marry, not with her family in mourning. But in the meantime, someone whispered that Mr. Mackenzie had sympathized with the rebels, and his father put him on a ship straightaway to Norway, or else they might have put him on trial."

"Who?" Bernadette asked, still not following.

"The English soldiers!" Avaline exclaimed, as if Bernadette should have known that. "They would have tried him for *treason*." She leaned across the table and whispered, "But *that's* not even the worst of it. When he came back from exile—I say exile, for it can scarcely be named anything less than that, can it? When he came back, there was no sign of her *or* her family. They were all gone. Can you believe it?"

No, Bernadette couldn't believe it—she was certain that Avaline had misheard or misinterpreted something. "Gone," Bernadette repeated. "Gone where?"

"That's just it—*no one* knows." She settled back in her chair and picked up a toast point. "Oh!" she said, remembering something. "And they hanged her father."

Bernadette recoiled. "*Hanged* him?"

"Very near Arrandale. Catriona says he rows past it when he comes by loch to Balhaire."

Bernadette stared at Avaline as she took a bite of her toast. Could this tale possibly be true? It would certainly explain his utter disdain of all things English. Good God, she'd accused him of wearing the mantle of pity! Bernadette closed her eyes and pressed her fingertips to them a moment. She slowly opened them and asked, "Are you certain, Avaline?"

"Well, I'm entirely sure this is what Catriona told me." She spread jam over her toast. "Now that I know what a cruel hand life has dealt him, I couldn't *possibly* cry off."

Bernadette was so confused! Such a tragic story should have strengthened Avaline's resolve to end the engagement. Surely she didn't want to begin a marriage with a man who still mourned his first love? She studied Avaline. "Have you changed your mind about him?" she asked, sounding as incredulous as she felt.

"No!" Avaline said adamantly. "I should not like to be his wife." She suddenly put down her toast and her knife. "But there is nothing to be done for it now, and it occurs to me that perhaps I might help him. Perhaps I might find a way to bring a smile to his face once more, do you suppose?"

No, Bernadette didn't suppose. "I don't..." She shifted anxiously. "I'm not entirely certain what could put a smile on the man's face who has suffered such a tragedy."

"Mmm," Avaline said, nodding. "But I must try, mustn't I? His family would be ever so grateful if I was able to help, I should think."

"No, you mustn't try," Bernadette said, and the feeling of panic began to creep up on her. "He might *never* recover—"

"Oh, Bernadette, I know you mean well," Avaline said. "But how could I desert him? How could I be the *second* fiancée he would lose?"

"But on the other hand, you are tethering yourself to a man who despises the English and loved another woman. It's hardly fair for *you*, dearest."

"Oh, I know, I *know*," she said, nodding in agreement. "How I wish that I would not be forced to wed that man, but my hands are tied, are they not? I really don't know what else I might do." She stood up and deposited her linen napkin on the table next to her plate. "I promised my mother I would come to her sitting room to talk about the wedding. I never knew how many details there are! The customs here are quite different. I'm to have a sixpence in my shoe, can you imagine? Will you join us?"

Bernadette forced a smile that she hoped hid the anxiety she was feeling at the moment. "Perhaps after my morning walk?" she suggested.

"Oh, dear, you *do* like all that walking, don't you? Walk all you like," she said with an airy wave of her hand. "But you mustn't forget your hat this time, Bernadette. You've too many new freckles," she said as she went out of the room.

Bernadette touched her face when Avaline disappeared through the door. "I do?" she muttered to herself.

A half hour later, having assured herself she had not freckled inappropriately, Bernadette pulled on her heavy boots and went for her walk. She scarcely saw any of the scenery she'd come to appreciate, because her body was still recalling that kiss. It had haunted her all night and was still rumbling about in her, causing her skin to tingle when she recalled it, her heart to flutter.

And now her head was full of questions about the story Avaline had told her. Was it true? Surely Avaline had gotten parts of it wrong—or rather, Bernadette hoped that she had.

But what if it *was* true, any part, or all of it? And Bernadette had so eagerly made assumptions about his demeanor. She didn't like to think what that said of her. She didn't want to think that she'd failed to give a man she scarcely knew the courtesy of doubt. That was precisely the sort of thing that had had harmed her through the years, when people who really didn't know her at all were so quick to judge. Had she done the same to him?

She paused on the path when she reached the small bluff that led down to the beach and squatted to pick some of the wildflowers that had sprouted. She stood up, opened her palm and let the breeze carry them off. They fluttered to the beach, disappearing from sight.

Had the girl really disappeared? How horrifying that must have been for him. Bernadette knew how unanswered questions of where someone had gone could torment a person until she no longer knew herself, because it had happened to her. One moment, she was lying in bed with Albert, giggling at some silly thing he'd said to her. And the next moment, he was gone, dragged away by two men while a third threw her clothes at her and commanded her to "make herself decent."

Bernadette never saw Albert again.

She'd gone for months without knowing what had happened to him. Her father had been without remorse or conscience, and had refused to answer any of her entreaties or pleas for information about Albert. She kept expecting Albert to appear, to try and reach her in some way.

Her aunt, her father's sister, had finally taken pity on Bernadette and freed her from her private prison. There were no details as to how it had happened. "A storm, an accident, I really can't say what," her aunt had said, clearly distressed.

After the shock of it, and the grief, Bernadette had not wanted to believe the worst about her father...but she'd never looked at him the same. She could never keep the doubts about him from creeping into her mind.

The feeling was entirely mutual. Her father despised her so much for what she'd done that she couldn't be entirely sure she wouldn't be the next person lost at sea.

Knowing Albert's fate had not eased her pain at all—if anything, she'd felt responsible for his demise.

She'd imagined his death—still did, at times—over and over, torturing her through many sleepless nights. She convinced herself she should have understood how deep and vicious her father's vengeance would run, that she should have understood he was a man who would not be crossed.

She should never have eloped. It had cost her everything. *Everything*.

She couldn't allow herself to think of it, lest she would cry for the thousandth time, so she wiped her palms on her skirts and turned to carry on—but was startled by the sight of a man and a horse on the path ahead of her.

There was something vaguely familiar about him, but Bernadette was too startled to think why. He didn't move until she did, then spurred his horse forward and began to move toward her.

The hair on the back of Bernadette's neck rose, and she glanced over her shoulder, assessing how far it was to Killeaven from here, Mr. MacDonald's warning entering her thoughts. She thought she might be closer to Balhaire, but she wasn't certain of it and tried frantically to work out which way to run as the man neared her.

He slowed as he approached and doffed his hat. His hair was wild and unkempt, his face unshaven, his clothes unwashed. He brazenly eyed her, making her feel queasy. *"Madainn mhath."*

"Ah…good morning," she said. Her voice was shaking. "Lost?"

"Not at all," Bernadette said, willing the tremor out of her voice.

He could see her fear, Bernadette was certain of it, because of the way he smirked. "Aye, good, then. A bonny thing like you would no' want to be lost round here."

"I am not lost," she insisted.

He reseated his hat and set his horse to walk again. But he continued to smirk as he and his horse ambled by. When he passed, he looked back at her, his gaze moving up and down her body.

Bernadette whirled about and walked as fast as she could in her ill-fitting boots in the opposite direction.

She must have stumbled on for another quarter of an hour or more, her heart pounding, and constantly looked over her shoulder. She wasn't thinking of Albert anymore, or of Mackenzie, or anything other than putting distance between herself and that man, so she was startled nearly out of her boots for the second time that morning when she climbed the path near the cove, and saw Mackenzie on the cliff, standing so desperately close to the edge again.

Just like the first time she'd seen him there, it seemed a private moment. But he stood so *close*, and now that she knew the source of his despair, she couldn't bear it—there was something quite ominous about standing on the edge as he was. "Sir!" she shouted into the wind, surprising herself. "Mr. Mackenzie!"

He seemed almost in a trance as he slowly turned his head. When he saw her, he stepped back and ran a hand through his hair. He wore no hat, or a neck cloth, for that matter. He wore only a lawn shirt whose tail billowed over his pantaloons, and a cloak thrown over them. He looked bedraggled.

"Again?" he said gruffly when she climbed up the path toward him. "Do you no' have something you ought to be doing for your mistress rather than spying on me?"

"I wasn't spying," she said breathlessly. "I like to walk by the sea in the mornings." Except this morning, which had had been very disconcerting thus far. She peered at him curiously, seeking any sign of his intentions in his expression and finding none.

Her study of him displeased him—his frown deepened. "Why do you look at me like that?"

"Pardon?"

"As if you've never met me."

"I don't...was I?" she sputtered.

"What, then," he said impatiently, and gestured for her to speak. "Say your piece."

Here was her opportunity to make amends. She clasped her hands at her waist and thought quickly how to apologize to him. "I, ah, I don't quite know how to say..."

He muttered disapprovingly in his native tongue and began to walk up the hill.

"I owe you an apology!" she called after him.

He stopped walking. He stood with his back to her for a moment, then slowly turned around. "An apology," he said, his voice dripping with skepticism. "Do you fret about a wee kiss? *Och*, I told you, it was no' a—"

"Yes, I know, not a declaration of love, you were quite clear," she said, now as impatient as he.

"Then *what*?" he exclaimed, throwing his arms wide.

"I owe you an apology for remarking that you wore pity like a mantle," she said.

He seemed not to understand at first, but then his face darkened, and his eyes narrowed. One hand closed into a fist at his side and he took several steps toward her. "Bloody hell, lass, do you think I care a *whit* what you say of me? I donna wear pity, no—I wear indifference. I wear it like a bloody second skin."

He was angry! And when he looked at her with the fury he did now, she didn't completely trust him not to toss her off the cliff. She unthinkingly took a step backward.

Mackenzie clucked his tongue at her. "For the love of God, donna shake now in those bloody awful boots, aye? I've told you, I'm no brute."

"I don't think you are." She was allowing his size and the fact that she'd already encountered one strange man today to intimidate her, and she squared her shoulders.

"Aye, you think it," he scoffed.

"I don't! Especially not since I…" Lord help her, she was wading into dangerous waters. "I mean to say, and I'm saying it very poorly, I admit, but I want to say that I understand your…demeanor, as I've heard of your tragic misfortune."

He stilled. His gaze went cold and locked on hers. "What misfortune is that?"

"I, ah, I understand that Avaline is not your first fiancée."

Now the color drained from his face. And still he didn't move, didn't look away. She could almost feel the rage building in him and half expected to see him begin to shake and erupt at any moment.

She should not have mentioned it. It was obviously very painful, and she should not have said it. She, of *all* people, should have known not to speak of it! "I beg your pardon, I've spoken out of turn."

"Aye, you have."

"But I…" She rubbed her ear lobe, searching for the right words. "I judged you unfairly, and for that, I must apologize."

"What do you know of it?" he snapped.

"Just that you went to Norway and when you returned, she was gone."

"How do you know this?"

"Your sister mentioned it to Avaline—"

He interrupted her with a string of Gaelic that sounded as if might have been quite profane. He turned partially away from her, his hands on his hips, staring toward the sea.

"She meant no harm," Bernadette hastened to say. "I'm sure she explained it to Avaline so that she might understand why…" She caught herself before she said something she ought not to say. She wondered briefly if there was still time to turn and run down the path.

"Why I've been an arse," he flatly finished for her.

"Well… I would never say it in quite that way, but yes," Bernadette said with a wince.

"And now you've heard my sister's interpretation of my life, and you've turned it into some romantic nonsense and offer me your pity."

"Not my pity. I never said that."

His face darkened. "You know nothing, Miss Holly. You donna know what happened in these Highlands. What do you think, that I returned from Norway and Seona had simply…what? Walked away?"

"I suppose I assumed she and her family moved away," Bernadette said uncertainly.

"From their home? To where? For what reason? To do what?" he asked, his arm sweeping long toward the sea.

This had gone well beyond her good and apparently misguided intentions. She'd meant only to apologize, but this was uncomfortable. How could she possibly know what had happened to his fiancée? "Perhaps they'd lost their livelihood," she said, guessing now. It was as if her tutor was putting questions to her. *Which country invaded France and why?* "Perhaps to the colonies," she added as an afterthought. Hadn't there been a lot of emigration of late? She was certain she'd read that somewhere.

Mackenzie's gaze raked over her, from the top of her head to her boots. "You're a wee *Sassenach* with no understanding of this world. Naive. Artless."

She bristled at the characterization. He made her sound as foolish as Avaline. "That is not true—"

He suddenly thrust out his hand to her. "Come," he commanded.

"What?" Bernadette looked at his hand. "Where?"

"You'll see soon enough."

She didn't like this. Something felt wrong to her. And she was still reeling from the terrible wrong she'd committed yesterday—not to mention her botched apology today. She shook her head. "I can't."

He took a step closer to her. "You're a fearless lass, you are. Will you allow fear to stop you now?"

She felt oddly complimented by that. And like a smitten girl, her misgivings were alarmingly brushed aside. Bernadette nodded. She put her hand in his outstretched palm. He closed his fingers around hers and tightened his grip as he pulled her along behind him, up the hill, to where his horse was grazing in a copse of trees.

He grabbed the horse's bridle and pulled it out of the trees.

"How will we—*oh*!" she said with alarm, because without warning, he put his hands on her waist and lifted her up, dropping her down on the front of his saddle. "Sir!" she protested, but he'd already swung up behind her and had thrown his arm around her waist.

Bernadette made another small cry of alarm and tried to sit straight, tried not to touch him.

"For God's sake, donna alarm the mount."

"I should not be *riding* with you!" she protested. "It's too familiar!"

"What will you do, then, plod along behind me in those boots? Settle back so that I might see."

She had no intention of doing that, but he spurred the horse to a trot, and she was bounced back against him as he reined the horse about and headed away from the sea and Killeaven.

"Where are we going?" she demanded.

He didn't respond, naturally, as that would have been the polite thing to do.

He held her steady as the horse began to canter. They rode in silence for what she guessed was a quarter of an hour. Everything she thought to say sounded flippant in her mind, or flew out of her head a moment after it appeared, as she was so acutely aware of his body against her back, of the strength and breadth and firmness of his body relative to hers, that she could scarcely think of anything else. There was not a soft spot on the man—he was all hard planes and sharp bends.

Her head filled with unwanted images of him with a Scottish woman. Had their love been as intensely felt and as passionate as it had been with her and Albert? Had it been a union of souls, as she'd felt with Albert? Or had theirs been a marriage arranged, the woman a mere acquaintance to him?

Eventually, the horse veered onto a path that went into the woods. They seemed to be going a great distance, and Bernadette's nerves began to ratchet up. "I'll be missed if I'm gone long," she warned him.

"We are near," he said, unconcerned.

Bernadette tried not to think of Avaline waiting for her. She tried not to think about the warmth of him at her back. She tried to focus on the scenery around her, but all she could see was trees and all she could think was how exquisite was the agony of having a man of his vitality so near to her.

They began to move up out of the trees and over a hill, and when they crested it, Bernadette spotted a house in the glen below. They were too far away for her to see many details, but she could see that part of the roof had burned. "Where are we?"

He responded by spurring his horse to a faster pace. She clung to the arm he'd anchored around her waist as the horse careered down the hill and into what once had been a front lawn. The door of the house was standing open. She could see into the interior, could see sunlight streaming in where the roof had given away.

Mackenzie reined the horse to a halt, then swung down, lifted her off the horse and put her on her feet. His jaw was clenched, but his expression was shuttered. "Come," he said, and walked on, his stride long and determined.

Bernadette took a breath and felt great apprehension. It was as if she was walking into a place she ought not to see, to a memory that didn't include her. She very reluctantly followed him to the door.

She was surprised to see a few furnishings still within when she stepped inside. A table, broken in half, lay on its side. An armchair was turned upside down and was missing two legs. A small stool had been tossed into a corner, and a wooden chandelier lay in ruin where it had fallen. The room was covered in leaves and debris that had come in through the hole in the ceiling.

Bernadette did not need to be told who had lived in this modest house, but nonetheless, Mackenzie said, "This is where Seona lived."

He walked across the main room, kicking a tree branch out of his path on his way to the broken windows that provided a view of the glen. Bernadette slowly followed him, taking it all in. There were marks on the wall here, too, she noted, the same as those at Killeaven—the evidence that swords and guns had been used in this house.

Near a door leading into another room was a large brown stain. She stared down at it, uncertain what it was.

"Blood," Mackenzie said.

She glanced up; he'd turned from the window, was watching her study the stain, his expression blank.

"Aye, it's blood."

Blood? But it was such a big stain, spreading across half the floor. And there was another stain across the room. Pools of blood, a swath of it, too, as if someone had been dragged…

Bernadette felt sick to her stomach. She swallowed down a sharp swell of nausea. His fiancée had not merely boarded a ship bound for America as she'd imagined, her portmanteau in hand, perhaps a smart new cloak for the journey. Something awful had happened here, and the tragedy was curling in Bernadette's belly. She unthinkingly reached out, trying to find the wall to steady her.

"Easy," Mackenzie said softly. He was suddenly beside her, taking her hand, then his arm went around her back as he pulled her into his side before her knees buckled beneath her. "Come outside," he said, and led her out of the house.

Bernadette felt clammy and cold, and worse, so

very sad. She must have been shivering, as Mackenzie shrugged out of his coat and put it around her. She buried her face in it, ashamed to have lost her composure. The cloak spelled of spice and horse. A man's scent.

"Sit," he said, and helped her to sit on a bench outside the home and sat next to her.

She wanted to tell him she understood his devastation, that she knew something about how deep and how soul-searing that sort of loss could go. But she couldn't speak, and groped for his hand, squeezing it.

"Are you all right?" he asked, sounding a bit alarmed.

She shook her head and glanced up at him. All that coldness she'd seen in his eyes wasn't the disdain she'd been so certain of—it was pain. She should have recognized it, she should have seen what had once been in her, was *still* in her. Bernadette wanted to convey all these things to him, to apologize again for having judged him, to tell him she understood more than he could ever know, but she was lost in an emotional storm.

She touched his face.

He flinched.

She slid her arm around his neck and pulled him to her and his coat fell away from her shoulders. "I'm so very sorry for your loss," she said. She meant only to hug him, but as she drew him closer, Bernadette was kissing him. Softly. Tenderly. With all the grief she was feeling for them both.

He shifted as if he meant to pull away, but he didn't. He sat stiffly, and allowed her to kiss him, allowed her to press closer, to stroke his hair. But then he touched her, his hand on her arm, sliding down to her hip. And Bernadette was sinking into him, teasing him with her tongue.

He sighed and moved his mouth to her neck. Bernadette came completely undone—everything in her ignited, tiny flames flaring under her skin where he touched her. She shifted closer, sank her fingers into his hair, her body filled with anticipation. It had been a very long time since she'd felt so full of need, to be held, to be loved. That need was roaring inside, and she felt...*panicky*. She realized what she was doing, and hysteria began to rise up in her. She suddenly swayed away from him and gasped for breath.

He instantly stood up, took several steps away from the bench, his hands laced behind his head.

"I beg your pardon," she said instantly. God, *what* was she thinking? She stood, too, and clasped her arms tightly across her middle. "I should not have… I meant only…" She shook her head—excuses were unnecessary and insulting. She tried to put herself in his shoes once again. "Was it only her and her brothers?" she asked, her voice damnably weak.

"Her mother. Two sisters. Her brothers didna return from Culloden." He made a sound of disgust and shook his head. "And still we all believed that would be the end of it. But it wasna the end, it was only the beginning, aye? They hanged her father."

"It's the worst sort of tragedy."

His gaze was fixed on something in the distance. "Everyone fled afterward. The MacBees, all of them, fled the Highlands. Her sister's children were wee bairns then—Fiona no' a year old. They sent them to a distant cousin for safekeeping. They never saw their family again." He looked back at her, his dark eyes full of anger. "Perhaps now you understand why I'm no' pleased to marry an English lass with no sense in her head, aye?" he said, fluttering his fingers at his head. "Why it galls me to have to do it."

Bernadette wanted to defend Avaline, but how could she? He was right—Avaline could never cope with the magnitude of this tragedy. She was too soft, too sheltered. She didn't even know the full truth about Bernadette— how could she ever understand the grief that raged in her would-be husband?

"I shouldna have brought you here," he said.

"No, you should have. I've been so wrong—"

"Aye, now you know," he said brusquely. He picked up his coat and donned it. "Come. I'll return you to Killeaven." He strode away from her, not looking back to see if she followed, clearly eager to be gone from this morbid reminder.

He tossed her up onto his horse as he had before, then put himself behind her.

They rode back in the same manner they'd ventured out—in complete silence, the only sound the horse's labored breathing. Or maybe that was her own harsh breathing, for Bernadette couldn't shake the vision of that house from her mind, could not keep her thoughts from filling in the images of what must have taken place there, could not stop thinking of the way his mouth and hands felt on her.

When they reached the turn to Killeaven, she asked

him to stop. "I'll walk from here." Her fear of running across the stranger she'd encountered earlier this morning notwithstanding, she couldn't allow anyone to see her riding with him.

Mackenzie didn't question it and helped her down. He glanced at the sky, and the gray clouds that were beginning to slide in from the sea. "You best be quick, aye?" he said, emotionless.

Bernadette knew the look he wore now. She could almost feel it, it was so familiar to her—he was still numbed by tragedy. "I will," she assured him, and began to walk briskly away. To wish good day to a man who likely had not had one in some time seemed ridiculous to her, and she wanted nothing more than to flee now, to try and understand why she'd kissed him in that moment, to try and understand what she was doing to Avaline. But she didn't understand, and she couldn't walk fast enough away from her crime. She began to run, laboring up a hill in her boots. She reached a point in the road that turned to the east, and she paused to catch her breath. She glanced back.

Mackenzie was still atop his horse where she'd left him, watching her. He slowly turned his horse about and rode on.

Bernadette arrived at Killeaven a few minutes later. Her feet ached and her hair had lost a few pins along the way.

"What has happened to you?" Charles asked when he opened the door to her, concerned.

"I went for a walk," she said, brushing past him

to enter the house. She felt cold, and hugged herself. "Where is Miss Kent?"

"With her mother in the lady's sitting room. Are you unwell?"

"No, I'm… It's a bit cold, that's all." She hurried away from him before he saw that she was lying.

She paused in her room to remove the boots and tuck her hair into place, then hurried to Lady Kent's sitting room. She knocked softly, heard the voice bidding her to enter. When Bernadette stepped in, her heart skipped—Avaline was dressed in a sumptuous gown of pale blue silk. A maid was on the floor at her feet, pinning the hem.

Avaline smiled brilliantly. "Isn't it beautiful?" she asked, and held out her arms. "This is to be my wedding dress."

Bernadette's heart began to race. "Oh."

"Don't you like it?"

"What? Yes, of course I do. It's beautiful," Bernadette said, and privately willed herself to get hold of her emotions.

"Mamma had it commissioned before we left," Avaline said, looking down, admiring her gown. "It was a surprise!"

Lady Kent was beaming at her daughter. "She will be the loveliest of brides. The banns will be posted on the morrow."

The marriage banns! That made it seem so inescapable, so permanent!

"We'll have the wedding in a fortnight," Lady Kent said, and clasped her hands together at her throat, admiring the gown. It was as if she'd forgotten all about the wretched circumstances of this wedding or her fear that her daughter was marrying a Highlander.

"So soon?" Bernadette asked weakly. Her heart was now beating so soundly that she had to sit down.

"What's wrong, Bernadette?" Avaline asked, frowning with concern. "You look unwell."

"No. No, I—I went for a walk."

Avaline clucked her tongue at her. "You've been walking far too much. It can't possibly be good for you. What do you think?" she asked, holding up a pair of white silk gloves. "These? Or these?" she asked, and held up a pair of blue silk gloves.

Bernadette forced herself to smile. "The blue," she said. She had to say something. She had to stop this insanity. "Avaline…you're certain of this wedding, are you?"

She noticed the look that passed between mother and daughter before Avaline said, "I'm certain that I have no choice. And therefore, I best be about it."

"You can end it," Bernadette said, her voice shaking. "You can always refuse it."

"I beg your pardon!" Lady Kent said. "She cannot!"

Avaline turned her back to Bernadette. "I would that I could, dearest, I do. But I can't, and I think you must accept that I can't, Bernadette."

Bernadette wasn't accepting anything just yet.

CHAPTER TWELVE

IT'S BEGUN TO RAIN, *a storm rising up so quickly that they
are caught without shelter. Rabbie grabs Seona's hand
and she laughs as he runs with her, tugging her along
to the hillside and a small cave he knows is there. The
two of them can scarcely fit inside, but they huddle together, watching the rain come down with a ferocity
that startles Rabbie. It feels almost as if God is angry
at the Highlands for their rebellion and is attempting
to wash them away.*

*Seona lays her head on his shoulder, her hand on
his thigh. "I could remain here forever, I could. Only
you and me, Rabbie."*

*"You'd be hungry, aye? You'd send me out to hunt
for you."*

*"And to bring ale," she says, and laughs softly. But
her laugh seems a wee bit forced, and he wonders if she
is truly all right, as she insists she is. He knows she wor-
ries about the fate of her brothers—they'd not returned
from Inverness or Culloden. No one has seen them.*

*She glances up at him, her soft brown eyes lumi-
nous in the dark of the storm. "How long will you be
away, then?"*

Rabbie doesn't want to talk about his departure at

the end of the week. He doesn't want to be reminded of the heated argument he had with his father this very morning. He doesn't want to go. "I donna know, lass. No' long, I hope."

"I hope, too, Rabbie. I canna do without you. God help me, I can no'."

"Ah, mo ghraidh, I canna do without you, either." It's true—when he thinks of leaving her, he feels an ache in his chest so profound that a part of him fears perhaps his heart is failing. He closes his eyes, for he finds it difficult to look into her eyes when he knows he must leave her. He kisses her, his hands gliding over her body, memorizing every curve. He should know them all by now, he should know every inch, and still, he fears he will forget something. He presses her down onto the soft earth while the rain falls with relentless force, washing out the world beyond the cave.

THEY CAME TO BALHAIRE, all of them—Lord and Lady Kent, Lord Ramsey, the girl and her maid. They'd come at the behest of Rabbie's mother, who was determined to celebrate the posting of the banns. The stoic Niall MacDonald accompanied them, and reported to Rabbie, Aulay, Catriona and their father that Kent desperately wanted to acquire the land that lay between Balhaire and Killeaven, the same stretch of land rumor had it the Buchanans were eying. The Buchanans were no friends of the Mackenzies.

That strategic stretch of land provided access to the sea and belonged to the MacGregor clan. Their numbers had been decimated in the last few years, but a few remained, their situation as dire as anyone in the Highlands. Kent had been to call on Laird MacGregor, an old man with no hearing, a feeble heart and a dire need for money.

The four Mackenzies scarcely discussed this news. There was no need—they all understood what that meant. Kent wanted to explore trade. Specifically, Kent no doubt meant to compete with the Mackenzies—as would the Buchanans, if they ever managed to obtain that bit of land, or strike an agreement with whoever owned it—and then export wool shorn from the sheep that Kent intended to seed through these hills. Given the lay of the land, the Mackenzies would be hard-pressed to compete. They couldn't farm as many sheep as someone at Killeaven, or on the Buchanan lands, might. Their advantage was keeping that bit of land in the family, so to speak—in other words, to marry into the Kents.

In his old room at Balhaire, Rabbie dressed in a plaid for the evening. Wearing the plaid was a punishable offense, but he didn't care. Let them punish him—they'd taken everything from him, but he would keep what tatters of his Highland pride remained, and that was a plaid.

He looked dispassionately at himself in the looking glass. His hair was in a neat queue, his coat, cleaned and pressed. He wore a swath of plaid across his waistcoat, too, the clan emblem pinned to it. He looked like a proud Highlander…but even he could see the dark circles beneath his eyes, the gray dullness in his gaze. He was blackened, inside and out. The ashes of what was once his spirit inhabited him now.

Miss Holly had seen the blackness in him. He kept recalling the expression on her face when she'd walked in to the MacBee house and had realized she was standing on spilled blood. He'd thought she would faint, and he'd move to catch her before she fell onto the bare stone floor. When she opened her eyes, he saw the way she looked at him. She'd looked at him with pity, and it had scraped across his heart.

He'd felt the pity when she'd kissed him, too. So unexpected, that kiss, and so bloody tender that his insides had warbled and turned into wee butterflies. He tried not to think of that kiss now, or the way her lips, warm and wet, had moved with careless abandon over his. Or the way her fingers had touched his chin, or her arm had gone around his neck, the feel of it unnervingly arousing, disturbingly comforting. He tried not to think of how her breasts had felt pressed against his side or how hard it had been not to touch her, to *really* touch her.

In truth, that kiss had been surprisingly erotic, and his body had reacted accordingly, every nerve resonating with desire.

In hindsight, it was all wretchedly disconcerting to him. Rabbie had lost his heart, but not his mind. A man did not like to be kissed with pity. There was scarcely anything worse than that—except, perhaps, the fact that he'd been so physically aroused in the place Seona had likely died. *That* had filled him with a terrible sense of betrayal that he could not banish.

Rabbie did not want to see Miss Holly tonight. He did not want to be reminded of how he'd fallen, in her eyes, from his stature as a strong Highlander. He didn't want to see any of that bloody English lot, no—but *especially* not her.

There was a knock on his door. "Come," he said.

The door swung open and his brother walked in wearing his captain's garb—a black coat and black pantaloons. He'd combed his hair into a neat queue, had tied it with a black ribbon. Rabbie had always considered Aulay the comeliest of the Mackenzie brothers, and in this suit of clothing, he could very well imagine the number of lassies who would swoon tonight.

Aulay stopped in his tracks when he saw what Rabbie was wearing.

"You donna approve," Rabbie said, unconcerned.

"You surprise me, lad, but I donna disapprove. I think you're bloody brave."

Rabbie snorted as Aulay walked deeper into the room. "Because I wear the plaid in my father's house? That's hardly brave."

"No' only because of the plaid—but because you've agreed to this marriage."

This was the first Aulay had mentioned Rabbie's doom. Cailean had spoken to Rabbie about it when last he'd been at Balhaire—his oldest brother had openly struggled with his desire that Rabbie help the family, and his more brotherly instinct to protect his youngest brother. But Aulay? He'd not spoken of it at all until this very moment.

"I didna agree as much as I was pushed into a corner," Rabbie reminded him.

Aulay nodded. "I canna imagine how bloody well difficult it must be."

"That it is," Rabbie agreed, and looked curiously at his brother. "What would you have done in my shoes?"

Aulay shrugged. "I donna know. I'll never know, will I? My own fate is no' entirely of my choosing, either. The trade is all we've left, and if I donna sail, who will?" He smiled wryly. "As your fate was set for you, so was mine set for me, lad. The difference between us is that I donna despair for my future. But if I didna have the sea?" He shook his head. "I donna know."

That was the truth of it—two brothers bound by duty to the family, one of them happy with the path, the other wretchedly unhappy. Rabbie sighed wearily. It seemed he was always sighing, as if he carried the weight of this clan on his back. He turned back to the looking glass to straighten his neck cloth.

Aulay walked to the window and looked out. "You do this for all Mackenzies, and God thank you for it. I believe Seona would have understood."

Rabbie's head came round at that. No one ever mentioned her to him. No doubt because when they did, he reacted much like he did now—his tongue suddenly felt thick in his mouth and he couldn't quite find the words to speak.

Aulay turned from the window and locked his gaze on Rabbie. "Aye, she would have, lad. Think about that—you know better than anyone that she did all that she could to save her family, aye? She is the one who sent the bairns to safety. She would expect the same of you, she would."

The mass of guilt and grief swelled in Rabbie's chest, pressing against his ribs, making him feel almost as if he couldn't breathe. Would she approve? Would she want him to go through with this marriage to save his family? Would she have done the same?

"Let her go, laddie," Aulay said quietly.

Rabbie shook his head.

Aulay walked to where Rabbie stood and placed his hand on his shoulder. "God rest her soul, but Seona is gone, aye? You canna bring her back. You canna change what happened. You canna stop living. She'd want you to live, she would, you know that is true. It's time you let her go and stop mourning. If you want a wee bit of her, acquaint yourself with her niece and nephew."

Rabbie opened his mouth, but no words came out.

"I canna bear to watch you live the rest of your life in misery and guilt, lad. Miss Kent is a pretty little lass, and with time, she'll make you a good wife. You could verra well enjoy the union, if only you will allow."

Rabbie wanted to argue that it was too late, that his misery had been sealed for him the day they'd arrived back at Balhaire and his father had met him at the cove with such abject sorrow on his face that Rabbie's gut still churned when he thought of it.

Aulay patted Rabbie's cheek. "Think on it. Now come," he said, smiling. "The bloody *Sassenach* have invaded."

THE ENGLISH HAD arrived in their finery, seemingly oblivious to the looks of hostility as they swanned through the great hall on their way to the dais, and ignored the dogs that had come forward to sniff them.

There was a bit of ceremony as the so-called happy couple was presented, and Rabbie stood before his clan, the lass's tiny hand in his. There was a smattering of polite applause, but nothing like the days of old when the applause would have been thunderous, the good wishes called up to them ribald, the smiles on the faces of the people quite genuine in their happiness for a union that would benefit the Mackenzie clan.

His clan endured it scarcely better than he.

The feasting began after that, and Miss Kent retreated to the safety of her mother's side. Her father and equally odious uncle fell quickly into their cups as they seemed to do at every opportunity. Catriona began to whisper in Miss Kent's ear again, no doubt explaining now how Rabbie's dislike of peas had stemmed from an unfortunate incident when he was six years old. He knew his sister, and he knew she would leave no tale untold, especially not with a new, impressionable audience. He'd not bothered to chastise Catriona for revealing his deepest pain to Miss Kent—he couldn't even summon the energy to be angry about it.

Rabbie's mother kept glancing away from the dais, to where the remains of their clan were seated, her expression a beseeching one. She could beseech all she liked, but the Mackenzies who had survived the worst spring of their lives would never accept these *Sassenach*, not after so much pain and loss. Aye, they would accept that he was forced to marry one of them, but call Miss Kent their own? Never.

Miss Holly sat next to Niall MacDonald, several seats away from Rabbie. She kept her hands folded in her lap, her back straight, her gaze fixed on something above the heads of the clan. Rabbie tried not to look at her. He tried harder not to conjure up that kiss, but he wasn't strong enough to fight it.

Aye, she was a bonny woman. She'd put her hair up in a fashionable way that drew his attention to the spot just behind her ear that he'd kissed. She wore a gown of dark green, the stomacher cinched so tightly that her breasts seemed to spill like cream from her bodice. *Diah*, but Rabbie didn't want to notice her, didn't want to think of her, and yet, he was still a man, and he could not deny that some part of him, apparently still very much alive, had been awakened by her.

He still burned with the humiliation that she'd kissed him out of pity, with the indignation that she was English, with the impatience that she thought she could possibly understand what he'd endured. But he was also consumed with a need he'd not felt in a very long time. He'd buried that need so deeply that he'd hardly recognized it at first. But it had seen light, and he could feel it blooming in him.

The meal had been served, and the musicians had begun to play. Aulay invited Miss Kent to dance with him, and several others stood up to dance as well. The clan was beginning to disregard the *Sassenach* on the dais and enjoy the evening. "We've needed this," his mother said proudly into Rabbie's ear. "Do you see, darling? We've all needed something to celebrate, something to look forward to."

He couldn't disagree. These gatherings had once happened with great frequency. Now, the moments and reasons for celebration were quite rare.

Again, Rabbie's gaze strayed down the dais to Miss Holly, who was watching the dancing. She reminded him of a prim-and-proper English governess who'd been relegated to the wall to watch the dancing instead of participate. He couldn't bear it any longer—he stood from his chair, swiped up his tankard of ale and walked down the dais. He kicked back a chair next to her and sat heavily, clapping his tankard onto the tabletop. He didn't look at her at first, but stared blindly at the dancers. After a long moment, he turned his head and admired her regal profile. Naturally, she had not looked at him, either—they were the both of them fighting it, then.

"Enjoying the evening, are you?" he asked.

She glanced at him sidelong. "Not particularly. You?"

"No' at all," he said, and turned his attention back to the dancing.

"You've come dressed as a Scot," she said, her voice full of curiosity.

"I *am* a bloody Scot."

He picked up his tankard, and as he was drinking, Miss Holly said, "She doesn't want to marry you, you know."

He slowly lowered his tankard. "You're no' even a wee bit bashful, are you?"

"Should I be? I didn't think you appreciated that trait."

He tilted his head to one side. "Allow me to explain

something to you, Miss Holly. It's a wee bit too late for your mistress's doubts."

"Is it?" she asked, and looked at him directly. He noticed how dark her lashes were against her light hazel eyes. Bonny eyes, she had. Quite bonny. "And yet, you have doubts, too."

He sighed impatiently. What was the point of speaking of upcoming wedding now? "No, I donna have doubts. Again, it's too late for them."

"You dissemble, Mr. Mackenzie. You could scarcely hold her hand."

He was already regretting this. He moved as if he meant to stand, but she said, "You might give her reason to cry off."

Now Rabbie looked at her sternly. "What nonsense are you speaking, then? The banns have been posted. The bloody wheels are in motion. Give her reason to cry off?" He gave a rueful bark of laughter.

"You'd not be the first couple to fail to arrive at an altar after posting the banns." She twisted in her seat to face him. "You *could* give her reason to cry off."

Rabbie frowned at her. He swiped up his ale and drank healthily, then slammed it back down. "If the lass doesna want to wed, then I'll do the damned crying off."

"No!" she whispered hotly, and glanced around them to see if anyone noticed them. "You can't possibly!"

"Aye, I *can*." Could he? No, of course not. He was resigned to his duty. He'd given his father his word. This conversation was nonsense.

"If *you* cry off, she'd be ruined in England."

It took a moment for Rabbie to understand her meaning, and when he did, he felt a swell of anger in him so raw that he could scarcely contain his contempt for her.

She calmly returned his gaze, clearly prepared for his contempt. "I know you must think very ill of me in this moment, but you cannot fault me for speaking the truth. Miss Kent came to Scotland to marry a Highlander, everyone knows it," she said, speaking quickly, as if she understood she had only moments before he lost his composure completely. "If she is rejected and sent back to England, she will be ruined. No one will want to make a match with a woman who was not deemed good enough by a Scotsman, do you see?"

"No' deemed good enough by a bloody savage, is that it?"

"I didn't say *I* believe it is so."

His anger swelled. He suddenly surged forward in his seat, his face only inches from hers. "Do you believe for even a moment that I give a damn what happens to that cake-headed lass?"

Miss Holly did not back away, and steadily held his gaze. "Yes. I do."

He glared at her. His eyes moved to her lips and he felt that unwanted stirring again. And for that, he despised her.

"I know you're not as hard-hearted as that—"

"You donna know a bloody thing about me," he said, and sank back in his chair, looking away from her.

"She's young and innocent, and I don't believe for a moment that you would ruin her life out of spite because *yours* was ruined. I think you are many things, sir, but I don't think you are cruelly spiteful. I also know that if she was to cry off...none of the Mackenzies could blame you for failing your end of the agreement."

The anger in him twisted. *Failing* his agreement? He wanted to put his fist through a wall. Toss a table across the room. "So I should spare the English lass because the English did no' spare me, is that it, then?"

"Yes," she said firmly.

Rabbie hated her, hated her reasoning, hated everything about this great room. He drummed his fingers against the table. His attention drifted to Miss Kent, who was laughing gaily as she tried some of the steps of the Scotch reel Aulay was attempting to teach her.

As much as he couldn't bear to admit it, Miss Holly was right. Avaline Kent was a child with no understanding or even awareness of the resentment that simmered in this room. She was utterly blind to the faces of his clan. And she was nothing to him. God knew she was nothing to him. But he couldn't ruin her to have his revenge—it would be akin to kicking an unsuspecting wee hare off a cliff.

There was something else Miss Holly had said that rang true—if Miss Kent was the one to end the engagement, his father could not blame him. There was still the matter of the need to join forces with the Kents—or somehow blunt the rise of the Buchanans in the Highlands— but Rabbie was so unhappy, he found himself actually considering her preposterous suggestion. He groaned, rubbed his face. "What do I have to do, then?"

We'd like to send you two free books,

similar to the one you are enjoying now, from the Harlequin® Historical series. Your two books have a combined cover price of over $10 retail, but they are yours to keep absolutely FREE! We'll even send you 2 wonderful surprise gifts. You can't lose!

LAURA MARTIN

Heiress on the Run

LOUISE ALLEN

Surrender to the Marquess

His defiant lady

REMEMBER: Your Free Merchandise, consisting of **2 Free Books** and **2 Free Gifts**, is worth over $20 retail! No purchase is necessary, so please send for your Free Merchandise today.

Get TWO FREE GIFTS!

We'll also send you 2 wonderful FREE GIFTS (worth about $10 retail), in addition to your 2 Free books!

Visit us at:
www.ReaderService.com

Books received may not be as shown.

YOUR FREE MERCHANDISE INCLUDES...

2 FREE Books **AND** 2 FREE Mystery Gifts

FREE MERCHANDISE VOUCHER

2 FREE
BOOKS
and
2 FREE
GIFTS

Please send my Free Merchandise, consisting of
2 Free Books and **2 Free Mystery Gifts**.
I understand that I am under no obligation to buy
anything, as explained on the back of this card.

246/349 HDL GLUP

Please Print

FIRST NAME

LAST NAME

ADDRESS

APT.#   CITY

STATE/PROV.   ZIP/POSTAL CODE

NO PURCHASE NECESSARY!

FP-517-FM17

▲ If offer card is missing write to: Reader Service, P.O. Box 1341, Buffalo, NY 14240-8531 or visit www.ReaderService.com ▲

BUSINESS REPLY MAIL
FIRST-CLASS MAIL   PERMIT NO.717   BUFFALO, NY

POSTAGE WILL BE PAID BY ADDRESSEE

READER SERVICE
PO BOX 1341
BUFFALO NY 14240-8571

NO POSTAGE
NECESSARY
IF MAILED
IN THE
UNITED STATES

"Give her a reason, any reason."

"Aye, and what is that? I am no' practiced in the art of making lassies cry off their engagement." He looked at Miss Holly for the answer. The color in her cheeks was high, the blush of a rose in fair skin. He gripped his hand into a fist to keep his desire in check and looked away.

"Tell her you mean to take a mistress as soon as you are wed."

"No," he said instantly. "I would no'. No one would believe it."

"The only person who must believe it is Avaline. Don't be so proud, sir—do you want to marry her?"

He could feel the storm of rage in him, swirling about, ready to blow the roof off this fortress.

"Be quite plain about it and don't give in to her tears or trembling chin," she said. "Avaline cries rather easily."

He snorted. "There is no danger of my giving in to anything." He suddenly stood, needing to be away from the blush of Miss Holly's skin. But he glanced down at her before he walked away, trying to understand her. "I wonder how it is that a woman employed to see after an innocent lass can be so cunning in her deceit of her."

Miss Holly's color deepened. Her expression changed, and he had the impression he'd hurt her. "You said it yourself," she said softly. "She is too artless. She is doing this out of a sense of duty with no notion of the anguish it might cause her for years to come."

Rabbie didn't want to marry that little chit, no. But

he did not like to be painted as the swine who would ruin her life, either. He walked away, off the dais, and stepped into the middle of the dancing to relieve Aulay and stand up with his fiancée.

"Ah, here he is," Aulay said, and looked, Rabbie thought, gratefully relieved of the duty. He handed Miss Kent to Rabbie. "Thank you, Avaline," he said, and bowed.

Avaline?

"The pleasure was mine, Aulay," she said, smiling sweetly.

Her smile faded the moment Aulay disappeared into the crowd.

"A reel, is it?" Rabbie asked, and began to dance, spinning her around, avoiding any conversation. Thankfully, the dance ended very soon after he'd relieved Aulay. He clasped her hand in his. "A word," he said crisply.

"Oh." She glanced over her shoulder toward the dais.

"Donna look so frightened," he said gruffly. "I will no' eat you." He moved his hand to the small of her back to her hurry her along, and led her out of the great hall.

He escorted her down the corridor to the family salon. The hearth was lit, but there was no one within. He guided her in, and instantly dropped his hand. The moment he did, Miss Kent scurried to the middle of the room, and turned to face him. She was clutching one side of her gown and shaking like a leaf. *Diah*, she was a mouse. He leaned back against the closed door and folded his arms across his chest, studying her. She looked scarcely older than his niece, Maira. She *was* scarcely older than his niece. "We are to be married," he said stiffly.

Her brows rose as if this was somehow news. "Yes," she agreed. Her grip of her gown tightened.

"We ought to establish some rules, aye?"

"Rules?" she repeated, and now her brow furrowed in confusion.

"Aye. You will keep Killeaven in the manner the wife of a nobleman ought to keep it."

She began to nod with great enthusiasm. "Of course. I know how—my mother has taught me."

"I will keep Arrandale."

Once again, her brow furrowed with confusion. "I don't understand."

"You donna understand," he repeated, and pushed away from the door, walking toward her, his arms folded tightly across him. "Then I will make it plain, Miss Kent—"

"Avaline," she said softly. "Miss Kent sounds so formal, doesn't it? Please, mightn't you call me Avaline?"

"I will make it plain, *Avaline*," he bit out. "I will keep Arrandale for my mistress."

Avaline blanched. Her jaw slowly dropped open as the words sank into her wee cake-head, and she clutched her hands together now, the knuckles white with the exertion of it. She was still trembling and staring at him with eyes as wide as tea saucers.

"You ought to know it," he said gruffly.

"I, ah…" She swallowed. She looked wildly about, as if she was seeking an escape. The lass was utterly shocked and Rabbie felt a twinge of guilt for it. He didn't mean to harm her. He'd fully expected she would tell him she wouldn't stand for that arrangement.

"Aye, what then?" he asked impatiently. "Does this displease you?"

Avaline slowly shook her head, which was not what Rabbie expected.

"Of course it displeases you," he said, annoyed that she didn't understand what her role was in this. "You may tell your father what I've said, I donna care."

"That—that is not necessary," she said carefully.

Had she lost her bloody mind? "Aye, it *is*," he insisted.

"No, really," she said. "This news is not…it's not completely unexpected."

Now it was Rabbie's turn to look shocked. He felt almost a brotherly duty to explain to this chit that it *was* unexpected, and she really ought to expect the exact opposite of him. She ought to expect fidelity above all else. What in God's name was wrong with the English?

"If that's what you desire, then as your wife—your *future* wife—I will do what I must."

"*Diah*, Avaline," he said, and sighed with resignation for what seemed the hundredth time that day. "You should end this engagement for it. I donna care if you do, do you understand? You should no' accept such rules."

"Oh, you mustn't worry over it, Mr. Mackenzie. Or may I call you Rabbie? You may trust me. That is one of my best attributes, really—I am quite loyal and I can be trusted."

She was making this difficult. "Verra well. If that is your wish," he said. He moved away from her, eager to be gone.

"What's her name?"

He paused. He turned back. "Pardon?"

"Your mistress. Have I met her?"

He stared at her, unable to comprehend this conversation. "No," he said, and opened the door. "Go back, then," he said, gesturing for her to precede him. "Run back to your ma."

She hesitated, clearly debating it. But at last she moved and walked out of the salon.

He escorted her back to the great hall, at which point she scurried away from him to her mother's side. She sat on the dais and pressed a hand to her heart as if she'd sprinted all the way from Killeaven.

It was ridiculous to have believed, if only for a few hopeful moments, there was a way to escape his fate. He should never have listened to Miss Holly, damn her.

Rabbie turned away from the great hall. He'd had his fill of this so-called celebration and began to stride for the corridor that would lead up to the family's private rooms. But as he neared the staircase, he saw Miss Holly in the shadows, standing by an open window.

He came to an abrupt halt. He looked around them, searching for her companion.

"There is no one here," she said, reading his thoughts. She placed her hands on the windowsill and leaned out, breathing deeply of the night air.

Rabbie's frustration boiled over; he grabbed her by

the shoulder and whirled her around. "Your *advice*," he said bitterly, "was for naugh'."

"What?" She gaped at him with surprise. "But surely—"

"Why did you kiss me?" he blurted, suddenly unconcerned with his fiancée.

Miss Holly stared.

"Why?" he demanded. "Did you desire me, lass? Or did you *pity* me?"

"It wasn't *pity*—"

Rabbie caught her head between his hands and kissed her, pushing her up against the wall. It was not the tender kiss she had given him, but one blistering with desire. He nipped at her bottom lip, swept his tongue inside her mouth, moved his lips across hers as he titled her head so that he could kiss her more thoroughly.

She gave a soft whimper—either from pleasure or pain, he wasn't certain—but it was enough to arouse the beast in him, and it pressed against his ribs and his heart. He in turn pressed his body against hers, his arousal against her belly.

Miss Holly could have ended it. She could have kicked him, hit him, any number of things to make him stop. But her arms slid up his chest and around his neck, and she pressed right back into him. *Diah*, everything about this woman was unexpected and difficult.

He slid a palm down her arm, to her hand, his fingers tangling with hers before slipping his hand to her waist and around to her hip, squeezing it, pushing her harder into his body. There was fire in his groin, the flames on the verge of surging out of him and engulfing the air around them. He felt hot in his plaid and wanted to rip it from his body. He wanted to put this woman on her back here and now. He had not felt such raging want...*ever*.

He'd never felt it like this.

Miss Holly fanned those flames. She cupped his face, she stroked his hair. He dropped his hand to her bosom, caressing it with his knuckles, then dug his fingers into her cleavage, pushing deeper, until he was able to free her breast from the low décolletage, and she arched her back, lifting herself to him. He took the tip of her breast in between his thumb and forefinger, rolling it. Miss Holly gasped, jerked her head away from his kiss and looked wildly around them. "What—"

No, it was too late for her to protest. He didn't allow her to finish, and with one hand around her waist, he easily lifted her off her feet, twirled her about and pushed her deeper into the shadows, into a space between the stairs and the wall. He moved himself down her body, brazenly taking her breast into his mouth, nibbling at the peak, lashing across it with his tongue.

Miss Holly's breathing turned quick and shallow. She pressed the back of her head against the wall and closed her eyes as she dug her fingers into his shoulders.

Rabbie's desire had ratcheted to the end of his tether. He was as hard as granite, his cock pulsing with need. It was as if someone had flung open the gates of all the emotions he'd kept caged, and they were stampeding out of him, chewing up the earth, the wall, and the woman before him.

When she slid her leg between his and pressed into his erection, he could bear it no more—it was either end it now, or have all of her. He forced himself to lift his head. He gulped for air as he pinned her to the wall with arms on either side of her and glared down at her like a fire-breathing dragon. "Donna pity me. *Never* pity me."

With that, he spun around and stalked away, dragging the back of his hand across his mouth, his jaw clenched against the sheer agony of no satisfaction. He didn't look back at Bernadette Holly because he *was* that hard-hearted.

And she would never question it again.

CHAPTER THIRTEEN

SHE WAS IN LOVE.

Avaline had received not the slightest encouragement from Aulay, but she understood that because he was such a gentleman, he would never do something as dishonorable as that to his brother's fiancée. She'd not received any encouragement from him…but she'd tried with all her might to give him every indication of her interest. She'd sat next to him tonight, had positioned herself in such a way that she was certain he could gaze at her bosom at his leisure. Whether or not he took advantage of her seating, she didn't know, because she also strove to demonstrate how demure she was.

She'd danced with him, too, and she could say without reservation that Aulay was a far superior dancer to anyone with whom she'd ever been partnered. He was quite light on his feet and was very good in his instruction to her. And oh, how he made her laugh as they dined, teasing Catriona about the silly things she'd done when she was a girl!

Avaline was so in love that she could almost, *almost* forget the horrible thing Rabbie had said to her.

A mistress!

What a wretched, cheerless, harsh man he was! Avaline didn't believe for a moment that he meant to take a mistress—she didn't believe he even had one, quite honestly—for Catriona had told her he'd shown not the slightest interest in any woman since his fiancée disappeared. Why did he say it, then? She didn't know and she didn't care.

She thought again of dancing with Aulay and smiled.

Catriona had likewise confessed that Aulay had never seriously pursued an acquaintance with any woman of which she was aware. "Perhaps he has a mistress in every port," she'd whispered, her eyes dancing devilishly at the look of shock on Avaline's face.

Well, of course, Avaline had been shocked. No one ever spoke so boldly around her. But she was not entirely naive, and she didn't believe that of Aulay. Perhaps he'd never felt a particular esteem for anyone because he was waiting for the right woman to come along. She'd heard of love stories like that. Mr. Kessler, their elderly neighbor at Bothing, once told her that he'd not married until he was well into his thirties, because he'd been waiting for Mrs. Kessler to appear. Perhaps all this time Aulay had been waiting for her and never knew it.

Avaline stifled a giggle with her pillow.

She'd danced with Aulay twice, and her mother had told her that was quite enough, that everyone would wonder why she danced so often with the brother of her fiancé and would assume there was bad business there. Avaline didn't argue with her mother, but she suspected they'd all understand why she did—because Rabbie Mackenzie was haughty and cold and there wasn't a woman in all of Scotland who would want to dance with him. Certainly not her. She'd been very disappointed when he'd cut in on her dancing with Aulay.

Oh, Aulay—he was everything she'd ever wished for, the perfect man who would make a perfect husband. Her belly filled with butterflies just thinking about him.

She thought of Bernadette, sitting at the far end of the dais, staring off into space. Bernadette had not been herself these last few days. Scotland didn't seem to agree with her. She seemed quite tense and rather too tart when she spoke to Avaline. Perhaps she was unhappy that Avaline was to marry and she would never marry. Oh, how she wished Bernadette could experience such happiness! Avaline knew that Bernadette had once tried to elope. Or perhaps she had eloped? She really couldn't recall the details of it now, and Bernadette had never spoken about it, of course, because that would be terribly inappropriate. But Avaline's mother had confided that no one could offer for Bernadette now—she'd been irreparably ruined by whatever it was she'd done. It was really all very sad, because Avaline loved Bernadette, and she wanted her to know such sheer happiness as she felt in herself tonight.

She wished Aulay would irreparably ruin her. There it was, her truest, most secret desire, a shocking wish, and Avaline didn't care! She wished Aulay would ruin her as Bernadette had been ruined, and then, Avaline would not have to marry that odious brother of his. She moaned with despair at the thought of marrying him and rolled onto her back.

Her thoughts drifted back to Rabbie. What a silly man he was, thinking he could convince her to end their engagement. It would take more than a mistress to end it. Frankly, the only way this engagement could be ended is if one of them was to die. Avaline was simply too frightened to risk her father's displeasure, and too determined not to leave Aulay behind in the Highlands.

She wished *Rabbie* would end their engagement, and then she'd—

Avaline suddenly gasped and sat up, staring into the dark of her room. A thought occurred to her—if she could seduce Aulay into ruining her, then Aulay would have to marry her! Of course there would be quite a lot of commotion and hurt feelings surrounding it, and Rabbie would be *very* angry…but he wouldn't be forced to marry her. *Aulay* would. Her father would still have his alliance with the Mackenzies, and Rabbie could go and hide away at Arrandale for all she cared and leave them all in peace.

Avaline stacked her hands over her heart and pressed against her rapidly beating heart. *Could that really happen?* She didn't know the first thing about seduction. Bernadette would know—she'd obviously seduced a man to elope with her. *Yes*. She would ask Bernadette to teach her.

But Bernadette would be suspicious, and Avaline had to be very careful not to give anything away. She thought hard about that…and then it suddenly struck her—she would simply explain to Bernadette that Rabbie had threatened to keep a mistress, and then implore her to teach her how to seduce her husband so that he would not take a lover.

This was brilliant. Avaline could scarcely believe she'd thought of it all on her own! But she didn't have very long—she would be standing at the altar with the wrong Mackenzie brother if she didn't act quickly.

She lowered herself down onto her pillow and tried to sleep, but it was useless. Her thoughts danced with the image of Aulay Mackenzie ruining her.

CHAPTER FOURTEEN

SOMEWHERE IN THE last several days, Bernadette had abandoned all morals and decency and had given in to the raw desires of her flesh.

She was distraught about it. Not because the kiss had happened—because she had been quite moved by it and yearned for more. *She wanted more.* But she was *not* that sort of woman, *she was not.*

Why, then, had her fall been so easy?

Bernadette donned a cloak and her boots, desperate to be out on her morning walk, to be out from under the same roof as Avaline, whom she'd betrayed more than once since they'd arrived in Scotland. She needed to breathe. To *think*.

Avaline had not yet come down for her breakfast, for which Bernadette was grateful. She had noticed that Avaline had been very quiet last night when they'd journeyed home, her gaze on a window too dark through which to see. While his lordship and his brother had drunkenly reviewed how vastly superior they were to their hosts in their thoughts and actions, or anyone for that matter, Bernadette fretted that Avaline somehow suspected what she and Mackenzie had done in that darkened hall. Was it even possible? Bernadette herself had stumbled into that hall in search of a retiring room. No, no, it was impossible Avaline could know—there'd been no one in that darkened corridor, no one but her and Mackenzie.

But Bernadette also knew that women had a strange intuition when it came to these things. Though Avaline had rarely revealed any intuition at all, it was entirely possible that in this, she might.

No matter what Avaline did or did not know, Bernadette was frantic to be away, to straighten her thoughts, to determine what she did from here. She was walking—nearly sprinting, really—to the door of Killeaven when she heard a sound above her and made the mistake of looking up.

"Good morning, Bernadette," Avaline said, and yawned. She stood at the top of the stairs in her dressing gown, and then glided down the stairs like a princess, her hand trailing the railing as she went. She looked ethereal, almost as if she was walking in a dream.

"Good morning," Bernadette said. God help her—did she sound as nervous as she felt?

"What are you about?" Avaline asked, eying her cloak.

"I, ah, I meant to have my morning walk."

"You and all that *walking*," Avaline said, sighing. "You'll have legs the size of a man's if you keep at it."

Bernadette smiled tightly. "I'll be along shortly to attend you—"

"Before you go," Avaline said casually, "I should like a word."

Bernadette's gut twisted. She felt a little fuzzy, as if she was about to sink to the ground. "Now?"

"Yes," Avaline said and continued her glide down the stairs to the ground floor. "Has Renard left any breakfast for me?" she asked as she carried on, past the pockmarked walls that had yet to repaired, down the hall to the dining room.

"Yes," Bernadette said, and suppressed a sigh as she followed Avaline. She desperately thought how she might explain herself, how to make Avaline understand that sometimes, forces beyond our control could compel a person to act out of character. She would use the moment to convince Avaline to cry off this engagement, to see the folly in it.

In the dining room, Avaline went to the sideboard and helped herself to some toast and fish. She yanked on the bell pull before heading to the table to sit.

Bernadette removed her cloak, but she didn't sit.

"The fish is cold," Avaline complained. "I prefer it warmed."

Renard appeared, carrying a tea service. "Good morning, Miss Kent," he said cheerfully. "Shall I pour?"

"Yes, please. Bernadette, would you care for tea?"

"No. Thank you," she said.

"I don't care for cold fish, Renard," Avaline said as the butler arranged the tea service around her.

"Yes, miss."

Avaline lazily buttered her toast as Renard removed the offending piece of fish and carried it away on the tray.

"What did you wish to speak to me about?" Bernadette asked after he'd gone.

Avaline suddenly smiled, and her cheeks flushed

pink. She put down her knife and the toast. "I need your help desperately, Bernadette. You must teach me how to seduce."

Bernadette didn't understand her at first. She thought perhaps Avaline was using the word incorrectly. "Seduce?"

"Yes," Avaline said. "I wish to seduce my fiancé."

Bernadette's breath left her a moment. She turned away from Avaline, and with a hand pressed against her abdomen, she walked a few feet, then turned back. "*Seduce* him? You do know what the means, don't you?"

"Of course I do," Avaline said, looking slightly perturbed. "I must fight for him, and if I'm to fight properly, I must know how, and I don't."

She wasn't making sense. "Fight for him," Bernadette repeated uncertainly. "Why must you?"

"Can you believe it, that wretched man has told me he means to keep a mistress after we are wed? But perhaps he won't if I know how to please him." She smiled sheepishly, then picked up her toast.

Bernadette wanted to walk to the window and fling it open and take great gulps of air before she fainted. She was overcome with waves of relief that Avaline had not discovered her betrayal, followed by waves of despair that Avaline believed that she ought to entice a man she'd not yet married who had told her he would prefer a mistress.

"If he said as much to you, that is grounds for ending your engagement, Avaline. No man should enter into matrimony with the idea that he does not intend

210   HARD-HEARTED HIGHLANDER

to honor his vows. No *woman* should enter into matrimony without complete confidence in his fidelity."

"Oh, I understand all that," Avaline said with an airy wave of her hand. "But I'm not going to end it, Bernadette. So… I must seduce him into desiring me before any other, and I need you to teach me."

"*I* can't teach you," Bernadette said, irked that Avaline thought she might.

Avaline glanced up from her toast, surprised. "Why ever not?"

"What do I know of seduction?" Bernadette said irritably. She had gone from guilt, to disbelief, to vexation all in the space of a minute. "I live my life looking after you." She was irrationally angry, she realized, because of that blasted kiss. Because she had felt desired, truly desired, and for once, she hadn't been a servant, and especially not one being ordered to teach a girl to seduce a man. That blasted Highlander had her at sixes and sevens and Avaline was so…so *stupid*, that she wanted to repair a marriage that hadn't yet begun! Could she not see how fraught with distrust and incompatibility her life would be?

Oh, but Bernadette was stupid, too, more so than her young charge, because she wanted that very man. She wanted him to make love to her, and God help her, she could imagine how volatile and passionate and exciting it would be.

"What's wrong?" Avaline asked, her brow furrowing with concern. "You don't look yourself."

"Pardon?" Bernadette asked, forcing herself out of her thoughts. "Nothing. It's just that I—I fear for you,

Avaline. I fear that you would enter a marriage for all of eternity on such unspeakable terms."

"I don't know why you're so upset. All men look elsewhere eventually, do they not?"

"That is not true," Bernadette said.

Avaline shrugged again and ate her toast, her eyes on Bernadette.

All right, then, she had to think calmly and act rationally. Bernadette clasped her hands behind her back, digging her fingernails into her palms to keep her thoughts focused. "I can't help you, Avaline. I don't know how to teach you to…attract him in that way."

Avaline sighed. "Very well," she said. "I suppose I must figure it out on my own." She lifted her teacup and sipped daintily.

"I'm going out," Bernadette said. She picked up her cloak.

"I think I'll go back to bed," Avaline said, and yawned. "I've not been sleeping well." She stood up, and with her tea in hand, she removed herself from the room. As she walked out the door, Renard appeared with the warmed fish. He looked at the empty table, then at Bernadette. She shrugged helplessly.

BERNADETTE MARCHED OUT across the Killeaven lawn and into the woods, then pausing where the woods gave way to moors to look for any strange passersby. Seeing none, she followed the well-worn path, but didn't take in the scenery today. When she reached the sea she debated turning right and walking in the direction of Balhaire, where she'd twice seen Mackenzie. Or she could turn left, away from him, as far from the trouble she'd created for herself as she could possibly get in one day. Her wish to escape Avaline and Mackenzie was pointless, however—how far would she get? And where would she end? One couldn't simply walk off into the hills unless one never wanted to be seen again.

She went right.

She trudged up the path, reaching the point she could see the top. He was there, as she'd somehow known he would be. As he'd somehow known she would be. The only difference today was that he wasn't standing at the very edge of the cliff. In fact, he was nowhere near it. He was standing by his horse, his back against a birch tree, clearly waiting for her.

Bernadette's heart began to race. Perhaps she was a bit mad. What else could explain it? This man had nothing to recommend him—he was a Highlander, a word synonymous with *savage* to some. He was a brooding, tortured figure who, frankly, wallowed in despair. And he was engaged to another woman.

And yet Bernadette looked at him now and felt nothing but that pressing desire. It felt almost as if he'd only just touched her instead of hours having passed.

He slowly pushed away from the tree. When she didn't move, he started toward her. He moved cautiously, as if he feared she might bolt.

"What are you doing here?" she demanded as he neared her, her anger once again flaring out of nothing and everything.

He tilted his head to one side and frowned lightly. "You know why I am here—I wait for you."

Bernadette's heart skipped, which made her anger soar. She did not want to be pleased by that! She did not want to desire him! There was no end to this infatuation that wouldn't hurt everyone involved, and yet she just stood there. "I don't know what you said to her, but you said it poorly," she said coldly. "Now she wants to seduce you!"

He laughed.

"It's not the least bit amusing," she snapped, and folded her arms across her body, holding herself tightly. "She doesn't know what she is doing, and really, neither do I. I've somehow taken leave of all my senses and allowed you to kiss me *three* times—"

"*Och*, I've kissed you twice, lass. You kissed me once—"

"Yes, all right, twice then," she said, the heat in her cheeks flaring. "But I am her *maid*, sir, and *this*," she said, gesturing wildly between them, "is nothing but disaster in the making!"

He reached out, brushed a bit of hair from her eye and said with quiet authority, "Calm yourself, Bernadette."

A drop of liquid silver slipped down her spine. He'd scarcely mentioned her at all, and had never said her given name. "Don't tell me to calm myself," she said, feeling slightly on the verge of hysteria. "And you've not been invited to address me by my given name! You do realize, don't you, that your brooding has made a mess of everything?"

He smiled slightly, and a bit lopsidedly, as he touched her chin. The brush of his fingers sizzled on her skin.

"You may call me Rabbie, aye? You're no' in England now. I've made a mess, have I? Of what, then? The very engagement *you* advised me to end?"

"You know very well what I mean," she said, pushing his hand away. "You're stubborn, and you're perpetually despondent, and offensively impolite, and you don't give the situation the consideration it so deserves—"

He suddenly grabbed her arms, pulled her forward and kissed her. It was a demanding kiss, a silencing kiss, and Bernadette responded to it, kissing him back.

But then she regained her senses and shoved against his chest. "What are you *doing*? Haven't we done enough?"

He stared at her, but his eyes were not dark and cold as she'd come to expect. Incredibly, there was a spark of amusement in them. He was *amused* by this predicament. For the first time since she'd met him, *this* is what amused him? "This must *stop*," she said, her voice shaking. "We just did it again! We betrayed Avaline for the fourth time!"

"Aye, as to that," he said easily, "I've an idea to end it."

Bernadette blinked. Her anger deflated. "You do?"

"I will explain to her that we Mackenzies are free traders. That ought to strike fear in her tender little heart, aye?"

"You're what?"

"Smugglers, lass."

Bernadette gaped at him. And then she burst into hysterical laughter.

Mackenzie didn't move as much as a muscle, but patiently waited for to stop her gales of laughter. "You can't possibly be serious! Who would believe such a thing?"

"You donna believe it?"

"Of course not! *Smugglers*." She laughed again. "It's absurd!"

"Is it?" he asked, his brows dipping. "Come, then, and I'll show you."

He turned back to his horse. Bernadette didn't move from where she'd rooted herself. "You're mad if you think I will ride with you again."

Mackenzie impatiently turned back. "*Och*, donna be stubborn."

"I won't. It's wrong—"

"Aye, you will," he said, and strode back to where she stood, grabbed her by the wrist before Bernadette realized what he was doing and tugged her along. "I'll have you see with your own bonny eyes so that you might convince your wee mistress that what I tell her is true."

Like he'd done the last time, Mackenzie tossed her up on his horse and swung up behind her before she'd even found her balance. This time, however, he didn't instruct her how to sit. He roughly pulled her back into his chest, anchoring her there in strong, possessive hold as he sent the horse trotting away from the sea.

And unlike last time, Bernadette complained of his treatment of her the entire way. "You can't simply throw a person on a horse like a bag of grain and carry her off," she said. "If there is something you wish to show me, you ought to invite me and receive my favorable reply. At least allow me to arrive wherever you mean to take me in the company of Avaline."

He did not respond to her, as was his infuriating habit, so Bernadette twisted about. "Have you nothing to say for yourself?"

"What I have to say is that you're nattering. You donna know what to do now that you've kissed me, and you're nattering." With one hand, he pushed her back around and anchored her again, this time much more tightly against him, so that she couldn't move and couldn't ignore his entire body pressed against hers.

"What is it that I must see?" she demanded. "Could you not have explained it to me? You don't seem to understand what a predicament I find myself in here— I'm being terribly disloyal and an abominable friend to Avaline."

"Aye, that you are."

She gasped. "But it's *your fault*," she pointed out.

"No' all my fault," he said, and bent his head, then whispered in her ear, "You must accept part of the blame, lass. You must allow that you like to be kissed, aye? Admit that you bloody well enjoyed that kiss as much as I did, and at the very least, admit that *you* kissed *me*."

"That…" Bernadette was so incensed that she could hardly find the words. "That is *not* true—"

"Aye, of course it is. You like it verra much, donna deny it. Look, then, here we are," he said, and pointed.

For a moment, Bernadette lost her ardent desire to argue with him. She saw the spires of the house above the treetops, then the house itself. It was a bucolic set-

ting, a country house tucked away on the shores of
the sea amid so many trees. It wasn't a terribly large
house, not even as big as Killeaven, but what it lacked
in size, it made up in charm. "What is it?" she asked.
"Where are we?"

"Arrandale. This is the home my brother Cailean
has built. He is laird here."

"Here? Where is here?"

Mackenzie chuckled and Bernadette felt it reverber-
ate in her. "*Here* is Arrandale. Aye, my brother is laird
of only this, but laird nonetheless."

They rode up a neatly manicured lawn, where he
reined the horse to a halt.

Bernadette slid down off the horse before he could
help her, stumbling a bit, determined to put some distance between the two of them. She slid her damp
palms down the sides of her gown and studied the
house. A small turret anchored it. The structure itself,
two stories, was long, with a wing that curved around
toward the gardens.

As she stood admiring it, the door opened and a
stout woman wearing an apron and holding a broom
stepped out. Mackenzie spoke to her in Gaelic, and
her gaze slid curiously to Bernadette before she disappeared back inside.

Bernadette moaned. She covered her face with her
hands a moment, then dropped them with a sigh. There
it was then, the end of her. That servant, or whoever she
was, would be wagging her tongue about the woman
who had appeared with Mackenzie. Her predicament
only grew worse by the moment.

"*Och*, now, donna fret about Mrs. Brock," Mackenzie said gruffly, and put his arm around her shoulders, steering her toward the end of the house. "She is loyal to me. She'll no' utter a word to anyone."

Bernadette shot him a look full of skepticism. She knew servants. She knew people. She knew, from painful personal experience, how inhabitants of the world over wanted to be the one to have news, to share something interesting with their friends. No matter anyone's good intentions, they *talked*. She shrugged free of his arm and moved away from his side.

"Will you sulk all day, then?"

"I will keep my distance. I will see whatever it is that has made you kidnap me, and then I will hie myself back to Killeaven and away from you."

"As you like," he said, and smiling, gestured grandly to the path.

They walked around the house and through the gardens, to a path that led down to the water's edge. This was not the sea, she realized, but what the Scots termed a loch and, given the distance they had ridden, one that fed into the sea.

Before they reached the water's edge, Mackenzie veered off the path and led her up a hill. In a thick stand of rowan trees, he stepped behind a large rock and dipped down. A bush—or what she'd thought was a bush—came tumbling out from behind that rock. Mackenzie stepped out from behind it and said, "Here, then."

Bernadette, curious now, stepped up behind the rock and saw a small opening into the side of the hill.

Mackenzie dipped down and disappeared inside. She stepped up to the opening and squatted down, bracing her arms on either side of it and peering inside, just scarcely making him out.

She heard the strike of a flint, which was followed by the flare of a wick or candle. He turned back to the opening and held out his hand to her. Bernadette did not hesitate—she was here, she wanted to see—and slipped her hand into his and stepped down, then followed him a few feet inside. When he lifted the lantern, she could see several crates stacked along an earthen wall.

"What is it?"

"French wine. Brandy. Tobacco. Tea. Some silk, I think."

When she looked up at him, he returned her gaze impassively. She turned her attention to the crates again. It seemed a strange place to store such things. "But why are they here?" she asked. "Why have you not stored them in your house?"

"The excise men might find them in one house or another, aye? They'll no' find them here."

They really *were* smugglers. "This is…unlawful," she said carefully. It was more than that—it was criminal.

"Aye," he agreed with a shrug.

Bernadette looked again at the crates, more than twenty in all, trying to understand what would compel men to risk so much. It was so dangerous! "Have you no care for your person?" she asked sincerely.

"I think you've guessed the answer by now."

"But this—"

"This is how we've kept our clan," he said. "It has been necessary."

"Necessary to go against the law?"

He shook his head. "You donna understand, Bernadette. When Scotland and England were unified, the crown used that opportunity to assess taxes on goods we'd long purchased at a fair price. Taxes so high that our people couldna afford life's necessities. Candles, wine, tea, tobacco," he said, gesturing with his hand to indicate a rather long list. "My father found a way to afford it for them. My brothers and I have carried on with it."

"By *smuggling*?" Bernadette said softly, suddenly alarmed that someone might overhear her.

"We prefer to call it free trading."

Her blood began to race. She wanted out of this small cave, away from the evidence of his crime. "What if you are caught?"

"What if I am?" he said with a shrug. "What have I to lose?"

She suddenly lurched for the door, now desperate to be away from the smuggled goods. She brushed past him and stumbled into sunlight, breathing in fresh air.

She heard him behind her, heard him replace the bush that hid the entrance to the cave. And then he was before her, peering at her with concern. "Are you ill?"

"No, I'm fine," she said. "A bit shocked."

He clucked his tongue at her. "You've no right to judge us, lass. You've no' lived the life we have, aye? You've no' watched entire hamlets disappear. You've no' watched the people of your clan pack their belongings and leave the Highlands because of fear or hunger. You've lived a life of leisure," he said, his voice tinged with disdain.

"You've no idea what sort of life I've led."

"I've an idea of it—my mother is English, aye?"

"And therefore, you know all there is to know of me. If you know all, then you must know that I've not lived a life of leisure. Far from it." She began to walk down the hill to return to the path.

Mackenzie followed her, and as they reached the path, he took hold of her hand. Bernadette did not try and remove it, because she liked how he held it, his fingers clasped firmly around hers. "What are you doing?"

"This way," he said, and turned away from the house, headed toward the loch.

"Where are we going?" She felt uneasy, her thoughts warring with her heart over all the things she ought to do in this moment and all the things she wanted to do. "I should return to Killeaven. I've been gone too long. I've seen too much."

"There is one more thing I'd have you see," he said, and hooked her hand into the crook of his arm to pull her closer. Again, Bernadette did not resist him. She liked the feel of him beside her.

He led her along the edge of the loch, down a well-worn path that rose up from the water's edge and climbed a small hill. At the top of the hill was a lone oak. It looked almost abandoned there, as if a forest had once stood around it and had deserted it. Mackenzie paused and looked up at the tree.

So did Bernadette. She knew, without a word passing between them, what it was about this tree that drew him. Strangely enough, she could almost feel the sorrow here, could almost picture a man hanging by his neck from the limb that stretched away from the other tree limbs toward the sea. She could well imagine how shockingly disheartening it must have been for the Highlanders to see the man hanging here, to understand what had become of those who had joined the rebellion against the king.

Mackenzie's expression was blank.

"Why do you come?" she asked.

"To remember. To no' forget."

"But it's…heartbreaking."

"Aye. Sorrow has become a way of life."

She could see the sorrow in his eyes, the lines of it in his face. Bernadette had lived with debilitating sorrow for a very long time. "It doesn't have to be so," she said quietly.

His eyes moved over her cheeks, her nose. Her lips. "What would you have me do, then? Forget? Convince myself it never happened? Or worse, that it didna matter?"

Those were questions she'd asked herself. Could she forget? No. Could she pick herself up and go on? She thought she had. "I would have you stop living in the grip of your grief. To live for the future and not what is gone."

He sighed wearily, as if he'd been so advised before, as if this suggestion were so obvious as to be tedious now. But Bernadette could not let her words hang between them now like the poor man who'd swung on this tree. "You're not the only man to have lost someone dear to you, or to have suffered a great tragedy, Mackenzie. These things have happened, but you survived them, and if you mean to honor those you lost, you must strive to live, mustn't you?"

"You think it is as easy as that, do you?"

"I know, from personal experience, that it is exceedingly difficult."

"Aye, and what experience is that?"

Bernadette didn't really care to tell him why, or anyone for that matter—but in this moment, standing under this tree, she wanted to assure this wounded man that he was not alone with the pain of his loss. "There is a reason I am a lady's maid instead of mistress of my own home. I am the daughter of a wealthy man, and I might have made a very good match. But I ruined my father's life, and he ruined mine."

She had Mackenzie's attention. He turned away from the tree to her. "How?"

He was examining her so closely that she could feel color flood her cheeks. She'd not spoken of her tragedy in so long and it felt thick in her throat. "I fell in love with a man my father did not want for me," she said stiffly. "We...eloped," she said, avoiding his gaze, and tried to swallow down her shame. "My father sent men after us, and they caught us a few days after we'd taken our vows." She looked sheepishly at him, and for once, he did not return an impassive gaze. He looked almost pained for her.

"You needna say more, Bernadette."

"We were, ah…we were at an inn in Penrith, very near the border of Scotland, when we were caught. Those men had bribed the innkeeper to divulge our presence. They burst into the room." She was shaking, and grabbed the skirt of her gown to keep from it.

"Donna say more, please," he begged her, and caressed her back.

But Bernadette couldn't stop. "They took Albert away." She was startled that after all this time the memory could still cause her voice to catch and her tears to well. She'd never told anyone other than her sister what happened to her and Albert at that inn. "They took him," she said again, her voice softer. "They impressed him onto a ship. I didn't know what had become of him, not until a few months later, when my aunt told me that he'd been lost at sea." Her voice quavered, and she tried, in vain, to swallow down her emotions.

He muttered something in Gaelic and shook his head. "He was lost at sea and I—" She caught a sob in her throat. "I never saw him or spoke to him again after that awful morning in Penrith. My father had our marriage annulled, and I was to pretend as if it had never happened. So you see, you are not the only to have suffered a devastating loss. My loss was just as deeply felt." She hastily wiped a single tear from beneath her eye. "We are more unlike than either of us knew. The difference between us is that I've refused to allow my grief to claim me for all eternity."

Mackenzie said nothing for a long moment.

Bernadette wanted to flee now that she'd said it, to

mourn Albert and the loss of their child again, in spite of all that she'd just said. Her tragedy had never left her. The pain had never really gone away. But she had somehow managed to get on with her life.

"Aye, *leannan*, you're right," he said. "I live in the grip of my grief. From the moment I realized Seona was gone, I resigned myself to the idea I'd never feel alive again. I didna want to feel alive again. I've wanted death, I have," he admitted.

Bernadette shook her head, disturbed by his admission.

"But in these last few days," he said, turning his gaze to her, "I've felt a wee bit of me sputter to life."

There was something different about his eyes, she realized. There was a light in them that had not been there before. "Have you?"

"Aye, I have," he said, and put his arm around her waist, drawing her closer. "I donna know how," he said, his gaze falling to her mouth. "I know only that I've been challenged in a way I've no' been challenged before, and it has caused my blood to rise."

The way he was looking at her now filled her with a potent desire. "Mine, too," she admitted.

He pulled her into his arms to kiss her. Sensual delirium quickly overtook Bernadette, pushing aside all rational thought. He lifted his hand to her face, touched his finger to the corner of her mouth as he kissed her. What she did was wrong, and every moment she remained in his arms, she harmed Avaline further, but Bernadette could not make herself stop. She couldn't fathom how much her body and her heart wanted his touch. She'd already fallen, had plummeted into that vat of desire, and had wrapped her hand around his wrist, holding tightly so that she wouldn't float away.

Somehow, they were on the ground beneath that tree of sorrow, and he pressed his body and the evidence of his desire against her. Something very deep and primal stirred inside of Bernadette, and as he cupped her breast, squeezing it, she ran her hands over his shoulders, up the hard, muscular planes of his chest. His tongue tangled with hers, his hands stroked her body, his fingers sought the hem of her gown.

A heavy sensation of pleasure, not unlike the feeling she imagined of being swept under by a tide, was rolling and spinning through her. Mackenzie's touch had submerged her into a pool of desire; she was sinking deeper, sinking well below the surface of her awareness and her morals.

He lifted his head, his breathing as uneven and hard as hers. His stormy gray eyes took her in, the intensity of his scrutiny searing, making her feel slightly feverish. Bernadette lost all sense—she was so desperate to touch him, to feel him, that she threw her arms around his neck and pulled him down to her, kissing him as ardently, as passionately, as he'd kissed her.

He made a sound of surprise, but he rolled with her, so now she was lying on top of him, his head firmly in her grasp. He caressed her as he kissed her, then rolled again, putting her on her back once more. He groped for her gown, dragging it up and slipping his hand beneath it, to the bare skin of her leg. Bernadette began to pant as his hand made a slow, torturous trek up her

leg, to the fleshy inside of her thigh, and then slid in between her legs. The tide of pleasure was quick to crash
through her as he stroked her. Bernadette responded
with the force of pent-up desire, harbored and subdued
for years, now breaking free.

Somehow, her hair came loose, tumbling down her
shoulders in unruly waves. She pressed shamelessly
against his hand, her core fluttering with the escalat-
ing tension. She nipped at his lips, kissed his neck,
his mouth, his cheek, racing toward that moment of
oblivion. When her release came, when she could no
longer keep her desires tethered to her, she cried out.

His breath was hot on her skin, his mouth wet on
her breast as a rolling sea of sensation rocked through
her, numbing Bernadette's thoughts to everything but
the feeling of his hands and his mouth and his breath
on her skin.

When she could at last open her eyes, he was staring
down at her. The storm still raged in his eyes, but it was
a different sort of storm than she'd seen in him before—
it was desire she saw raging in him now. "*Diah*, lass, go
from me now," he said gruffly, and rolled away from her.
"I want to touch you, all of you, feel myself inside you."

She wanted that, too, and it scared her. She clam-
bered to her feet, brushed the grass and leaves from
her gown, yanked at her stomacher, then twisted her
hair into a knot at her nape. He came to his feet, too,
and watched her trying to remove any sign of what
had just happened.

She realized what she was doing and slowly dropped
her hands. They stared at each other for one very long,

highly charged, but silent moment. "What are we doing?" Bernadette asked weakly.

"I donna rightly know," he admitted.

"You're to be wed next week."

He clenched his jaw but said nothing.

"We can't continue on like this," she said, her heart squeezing painfully. "God forgive me for what I've done, but I can't—I can't do this, Mackenzie." The regret was already stewing in her.

"Rabbie," he said quietly. "I am Rabbie."

Rabbie. She nodded, his name tumbling around in her head. Of course he was Rabbie to her now—they'd just shared a very intimate moment. Had he even heard what she'd said? "You don't understand—" she began, but he quickly interrupted her.

"Will you deny that there is something between us, then?" he asked. "Will you pretend that it doesna exist?"

"How can I?"

He grabbed her hand and held it between both of his. "You said it yourself, Bernadette, we are more alike than we know, aye? We deserve—"

"No," she said, pulling her hand free. "Don't say it. If I can't pretend this feeling between us doesn't exist, then *you* can't pretend this is you and me against the world, Rabbie. *You* can't pretend that there aren't others whose lives are affected by what we've done. You must agree—you *must* agree—that I can't see you again."

She was begging him, but Rabbie folded his arms implacably as he contemplated her. It felt to her as if a bit of sorcery had surrounded them, because she could feel an unnatural power between them, a current that seemed to lock them together beneath this tree.

This situation was impossible.

How could she experience all these feelings for *this* man, of all men? How could she betray Avaline so completely, over and over again?

"I have to leave," she said, and turned back to the path, striding along, her heart still hammering against her chest.

Rabbie followed her in silence, which had become their habit when confronted by their mutual desire. They rode in silence, too, Bernadette leaning forward, desperate not to touch him, afraid of what would become of her, of how she would crumble if she allowed herself to feel his body against hers. When they reached the cliff above the sea, Rabbie helped her to her feet. But he didn't let her go straightaway. He held her there, one hand on her arm, the other running roughly over the top of her head, the way you might caress a child. "I'll no' apologize for it," he said. "I've found a light in you, Bernadette, and I'll no' apologize."

"Then I will," she said, and moved around him and began to walk down the path.

Her heart was still hammering, but the cause of it now was not desire. It was regret. Ugly, distended regret for so many things, in so many ways, and it was consuming her with each step.

CHAPTER FIFTEEN

THE WINDS ARE against them, and it seems to take a day instead of a few hours before Aulay can change tack, sail the ship into the cove and anchor there. Rabbie lowers the rowboat and jumps into it like a man fleeing a walk on the plank. He has been gone from home for almost two years, living in the bleak cold of Bergen, rising every day with the hope that word would come from his father that it was safe to return home.

Rabbie brings two seamen with him, commands them to row. As he nears shore, he sees his father standing in the company of his oldest brother, Cailean. He is too eager, and before the boat can reach the shore, he leaps out of it and wades in, uncaring of the cold water in his boots. Madainn mhath! *He calls, waving his arm. He is grinning. His happiness has buoyed him—he feels no heavier than a feather. At long last, he is home. At long last, everything will be put to rights.*

But when he sees the look his father and brother exchange, sees how they come forward, walking like a pair of undertakers, his gut sinks. His first thought is his mother. Diah, *not his mother! He is so convinced something has befallen her that at first he can hardly absorb what they say...but then the words begin to sink*

*into his heart. It can't possibly be Seona, and yet, they
cruelly insist all the MacBees are gone. He doesn't believe them—if this is so, why did they not send word
to him months ago when they disappeared? "So you'd
no' come home, lad," his brother says. "So you'd no'
risk your life for a lost cause."*

*Rabbie shoves Cailean's hand from him and strides
away, his homecoming ruined by their false news. He
believes they haven't looked hard enough. He believes
she has left him some clue, that she would know he
would move heaven and earth to find her. When he
reaches the top of the cliff, he begins to run. It is
roughly two miles to her home, and he runs, his sea
legs causing him to stumble at first, then finding their
strength and pumping, carrying him faster. When he
reaches the house, he draws up with air burning in
his lungs and stares at the half-gone roof, the broken
windows, the door standing open.*

*He runs again, bursting into that house, calling for
Seona, even though somewhere inside him he knows
the truth. If he had any more doubt of it, the evidence
of carnage erases it. He collapses in grief onto the
floor and rails against God, against the* Sassenach, *but
mostly, against himself for ever having left her.*

*No one comes for him, no one tries to draw him
away. It is dusk by the time he picks himself up and
begins the long walk to Balhaire. He sees nothing as
he walks, his head full of the images of what must
have happened there. He wants desperately to believe
Seona escaped.*

But he knows. He knows that if she escaped, she

would have gone to Balhaire, she would be waiting
for him. His head can't fully accept it, not yet, but
his heart crumbles into dust. He can't bear the truth.
He will never bear the truth and the guilt that seems
to swallow him whole. Nothing will ever be the same
again, and Rabbie feels as if the curtain is being drawn
across his life.

HE RODE INTO the bailey as if he was being chased by
English soldiers, when in reality, he was being chased
by his own *diabhal*. He was possessed with a need
he'd not felt so intently, and without restraint, as he
did now. His body was still pulsing for a release he
could not reach.

He threw himself off his horse and handed the reins
to the young lad who'd lost his father to Culloden and
started for the entrance. But the sound of children playing distracted him, and he paused, turning toward the
green.

His nieces and nephews were there, and another
child, one so small that it took him a moment to realize
it was Georgina, Cailean and Daisy's bairn. He glanced
at the lad who held his horse. "My brother has come?"
He hadn't expected them so soon as this.

"Aye, this morning."

Rabbie changed course and walked to the green to
have a look at the wee little lass. He'd not seen her in
some time. She was what, perhaps three years, now,
maybe four? She had golden hair and pale green eyes,
like her mother. His niece Maira was minding the children, all of them racing about, and he noticed Fiona and

Ualan MacBee standing nearby. "It's Uncle Rabbie!" his nephew Bruce shouted, and like a heard of sheep, the other children raced toward him.

"Halt there," Rabbie said, but it was no use—they swarmed him, giggling and laughing as they did, knocking him to the ground...or perhaps Rabbie fell. He wanted to laugh with them as he used to do, but he couldn't. He *couldn't*. He rolled with them, tossing one and then the other, much to their delight, until he was able to stand again. He stared down at those smiling, upturned faces, their eyes and mouths and brows so sweet and carefree, showing no signs of despair or tragedy. Their day would come, but today, they were beautiful in their innocence.

"Are you sad today, uncle?" asked Nira, Vivienne's youngest daughter.

"No' today, lass. No' today. Who's this?" he asked, and picked up Georgina to kiss her cheek. Georgina screwed up her face and turned her head.

"I'm your uncle, lass, do you know me, then?"

"No," she said. "I want down."

"Come, on then," Maira said, reaching for Georgina. His nieces and nephews had already tired of him, and they had raced back to the green. Maira took Georgina by the hand and ran behind them.

Rabbie noticed Fiona had come forward, tentatively. He gestured for her to come to him. She ran forward, eager to be included. Rabbie caressed her head and thought of what Aulay had said—that he ought to acquaint himself with these two children. "A bonny lass you are, Fiona," he said. "You look so much like your mother, aye?"

"Do I?" She had Seona's eyes, he thought, and they were shining at him. Rabbie felt a peculiar whisper sweep through him, almost as if it was Seona looking at him now. Did she know that he'd pleasured another woman and had fiercely wanted to find his own pleasure in her?

"Do you know more about my mother?" Fiona asked. "Was her hair as long as mine?"

"Aye, as long as yours."

"Did she have a dog?"

"Two," he said, and the lass smiled with delight.

"What else?"

"I've an idea," he said. "We'll have a wee walk, we will, and I'll tell you all that I know of your mother and father. Where is your brother, then?"

Fiona pointed.

The lad hung back, separate from the rest of them, watching them all with hooded eyes. It struck Rabbie that he seemed uncertain of his place. He motioned him forward, and when Ualan reached him, Rabbie put his arm around his shoulders. *"Ciamar a tha thu?"* he asked.

"Verra well," Ualan muttered, and looked at his feet.

"Bonny day, is it no'?" Rabbie asked.

Ualan shrugged.

"Fiona and I mean to have a wee walk so that I might tell her what I recall about your parents, aye? Will you join us?"

Ualan nodded. He did not smile like his sister. His

dark eyes looked haunted. Bleak. Much the way Rabbie often felt inside, and it made him ache for the lad. For himself, as well. He tousled Ualan's hair. "It's all right, lad," Rabbie said, apropos of nothing, other than a kindred feeling of despair. "It's all right."

If Ualan wondered what, precisely, was all right, he did not inquire. Rabbie didn't know why he'd said it, for nothing would ever be all right for a wee lad who'd lost his family and now had a sister to look after. But something in him wanted this child to have a modicum of hope.

"Aye, then, let's have a walk," he said, and turned about and began to move.

Fiona skipped alongside him. Ualan took great strides, his head down, saying very little.

Rabbie proceeded to tell them all he could recall of Gavina MacLeod. He regretted that he couldn't recall more than he did, and that everything he said felt inadequate. He toyed with the thought of bringing them to Arrandale until some decision was made as to their future. But then he thought of how often he couldn't seem to keep the darkness from swallowing his thoughts, how often it led to drinking and brooding. They didn't deserve that.

They didn't deserve what had happened to them. They didn't deserve to be orphans.

He spent more than an hour with them, saying more than he guessed he might have said in the last year. He answered Fiona's many questions, surreptitiously watching Ualan for any sign of good humor. But then Ualan said they were expected in the kitchens, and carefully pocketed the sweetmeat Rabbie had bought them when they'd passed the inn.

He didn't like to think of them toiling in the kitchen. "And how do you find it there?" he asked as they headed up the high road.

"Barabel is teaching us to make cakes," Fiona said. "When I grow up, I shall make cakes. Barabel is teaching us *everything*."

"You'll no' remember it," Ualan said, saying more than he'd said in Rabbie's presence yet.

"I will!"

"You will no', Fiona. We are going to Inverness soon, and there will be no cakes there."

"I donna believe you!" she said.

"Inverness?" Rabbie asked, catching Fiona's hand before she struck her brother.

"Aye," Ualan said, and shifted his gaze to the ground again. "We're to go to Mr. and Mrs. Tawley. They knew our father," he muttered. They'd come to the bailey and the lad glanced away from Rabbie. "We must be gone now, sir. We're to work now."

"Aye, go on," Rabbie said.

Ualan began striding for the service door. Fiona's ire was forgotten, and she skipped behind him.

Rabbie watched them go until they had disappeared inside. He didn't like the sound of it, this distant Mr. Tawley.

He carried on into the great hall. It gave him no small amount of happiness to hear the sound of his oldest brother's laughter booming in the great hall. He walked inside and stood a moment, surveying the familial scene. It reminded him of a time when the Mackenzies had prospered, when they were all young and happy and had no fears for the future.

His parents were here, of course. Catriona was sitting on the dais table, her legs swinging underneath her. Vivienne as well, and Marcas, too, his arm around his wife's shoulders. Aulay was seated lazily at the end of the table, his boots propped on a chair, and Cailean and Daisy were eating from plates laden with food. Daisy's son Ellis, Lord Chatwick, had finished his plate and was sitting by Rabbie's father, and was the first to notice Rabbie.

"Uncle Rabbie!" he cried, and rose up. *Diah*, but the lad had grown, standing almost as tall as Rabbie. He bounced off the dais and hurried down the aisle to embrace Rabbie, his arms tight. He was as tall as a man, but as thin as a reed, and still very much a lad.

"*Feasgar mhath*, Ellis," he said, patting his back. "Look at you, then, you've grown a foot since last I saw you, aye?"

"Aye," Ellis said. He'd picked up a bit of Highlander talk through the years, although it always sounded strange to Rabbie's ear when spoken with an English accent. "I'll be seventeen years old next month," he proudly reported.

"As old as that?" Rabbie said, smiling. He walked with Ellis to the dais.

His beautiful sister-in-law rose from her seat, her smile warm, her eyes shining. "Rabbie!" she said, opening her arms to him as she came off the dais. "How very well you look!"

Rabbie kissed her cheek.

"Aye, that he does," Cailean agreed, following his wife. He embraced Rabbie, too, giving him a hearty shake before letting go. "It would seem the summer agrees with you. The last I saw you, I worried for your health, I did."

The last time they met, Cailean had brought the news of Avaline Kent's agreement to marry him. Rabbie had been a shell of himself then, nothing but bones and flesh waiting to die. He was struck with the sudden idea that today he was not waiting to die. That in fact, something else other than death had filled his thoughts.

"I wasna expecting you so soon," he said to Cailean.

"We'd no' risk missing your nuptials, lad," Cailean said, and grinned.

Rabbie joined the rest of his family on the dais and listened as Cailean filled them in on the events at Chatwick Hall. Daisy asked after the Mackenzies, listening intently as Aulay and Vivienne spoke about who had left Scotland, who had gone to Glasgow and Edinburgh to find work, and how their numbers continued to dwindle.

"Well, then," Cailean said, and turned to clap Rabbie on the shoulder. "You're to be wed."

Rabbie tried to muster a bit of enthusiasm for his observation, but it was pointless. He felt nothing but dread. "Aye."

"He doesna want to wed," Catriona offered.

"Cat, darling," Rabbie's mother said. "Do allow Rabbie to speak for himself."

"It's all right," Rabbie said with a lazy flick of his

wrist. "Let the lass say what she wants. It's hard for me to speak of it…but Cat excels at it."

Vivienne snickered, but Catriona glared at him. "Who *will* speak of it, then? You pretend as if it willna happen."

That seemed to surprise Cailean. "What's this? But you've agreed to it."

"Aye, aye, I've agreed," Rabbie said, sighing. "I will honor my word, donna doubt it." Except that he hadn't honored his word. He hadn't honored himself, his family, his word—*anything.* The knowledge made him feel cross, and he abruptly stood from the table and strode to the sideboard, where Frang had laid out a meal for Cailean and his family. He poured a generous serving of ale. When he turned around, he discovered that Cailean had followed him.

"Leave him be, Cailean," Catriona said lightly. "He's always foul of temper. He's like an old bailey cat, that lad. You'll see."

"*Diah,* Cat!" It was Vivienne's turn to chastise her sister. "Donna speak another word! It's none of your affair."

"None of my affair? Am I no' the one who must chaperone him every time he is to ride to Killeaven? On my word, it's a wee bit like pulling a large rock behind me, it is."

Rabbie shrugged. "It's true," he said lazily.

Cailean said quietly, "Let's have a walk, you and I."

"I poured the ale—" His brother gave him such a sharp look that Rabbie sighed again. He sipped from the tankard, then put it aside. "Aye, then, let's have it done."

"You needna sound as if I'm leading you to the gallows," Cailean muttered as they walked out of the great hall together.

"It feels a wee bit like it."

Cailean halted his march toward the front door. "*Diah*, Rabbie—you didna have to agree to the betrothal. If you donna want to marry the lass, then say it."

"I donna want to marry the lass, then," he said throwing his arms wide. "But I *must*. You know it as well as I do." He said those words to Cailean, knowing them to be true, but at the same moment, his heart was searching for any idea of how to end this engagement. His blood churned with the discomfort of being at odds with what his family needed of him and what he wanted. He shoved a hand through his unkempt hair and looked wildly about, avoiding Cailean's gaze. He wished he knew what to do, he wished he could think of a way to save them all without tethering himself for all his days.

Cailean was staring at him with concern.

"*Och*, donna look at me as if I am mad," Rabbie said. "What will become of Balhaire if I donna honor the agreement? We've *Sassenach* to the west and east of us now. We've no' enough men to keep Balhaire. Our trade is threatened, our land is unsuitable for herding large numbers and yet there are enough sheep to overrun our arable fields…" He shrugged morosely. "We'll be ruined if I donna go through with it." He waited for his brother's response, hoping, praying, that Cailean would miraculously offer him an out and say none of that was true.

But Cailean didn't say that. He said, "In the worst of circumstances, you could all come to Chatwick Hall, aye? There's room enough there for an army."

"All of us?" Rabbie asked uncertainly.

"The Mackenzies," Cailean said.

"Take our father from the Highlands? Our *children*?"

"If need be to survive," Cailean said. "That's more important than pride, is it no'?"

"No," Rabbie said flatly. He'd not be responsible for the Mackenzies leaving the Highlands like scores of Highlanders had already done. "It's too late for it. The banns have been posted. I'm to wed in four days, Cailean."

Cailean pressed his lips together and studied the floor a moment, idly scratching the head of a dog that had wandered in between them. "Is she so bad, then?" he asked softly. "She's no' plain. She's comely."

Rabbie shook his head. "It's no' the lass, Cailean. Aye, she's comely. She's far too young, she is...but it's no' her."

He didn't have to say more than that, because Cailean understood him. "We oft must lie with the devil to save our souls," he muttered, and began to walk, gesturing for Rabbie to follow him.

They walked out onto the bailey, where the children were still playing. Georgina, seeing her father, raced on her squat little legs for him. "Pappa, Pappa!" she cried gleefully, and Cailean's face shone with so much joy, so much pride.

Perhaps, Rabbie thought wistfully, he might have that. Perhaps that would be his consolation in this wretched affair. Sons and daughters to raise as Scots. Perhaps he'd bring Fiona and Ualan into their fold, too. He'd have a score of children to think about and keep his mind from his wife.

"We best take you to your Mamma, aye?" Cailean said to Georgina, kissing her cheek.

They returned to the great hall at a snail's pace, so that Georgina might walk, too, and stop to examine everything in her path. By the time they reached the hall, the family had dispersed. Frang had accompanied Daisy up to the rooms they would use while at Balhaire. Rabbie's sisters had left, and Aulay was speaking with their father about his next voyage. He planned to depart for Norway the day after the wedding. The ship's repairs had been made, and he was eager to be at sea.

"Rabbie, darling, I've sent a messenger round to Killeaven to invite the Kents for supper tomorrow," his mother said. "They'll want to greet Cailean and Daisy. But tonight, we'll dine with the Mackenzies only," she said, and patted his cheek. "One last time I might have my boy all to myself."

Rabbie snorted. "You'll have me more than you think, *Maither*."

THE NEXT DAY, Rabbie rode with Cailean, Daisy and Lord Chatwick to have a look at Arrandale and Auchenard. At Arrandale, Rabbie took Cailean down to the cave to see what goods they had.

Cailean examined the contents of the crates and was speaking of how they might sell it to Inverness or Glasgow, as there wasn't enough market in the Highlands now.

Rabbie tried to listen, but he was distracted. Just yesterday, he'd made up his mind to do what he must for his family. He'd made a conscious effort to remove any thoughts of giving Avaline Kent a reason to end their engagement. He'd spent a long night of restlessness, trying to rid his mind of Bernadette. But today, he and Cailean had walked up to the hanging tree, and all of Rabbie's pleading with himself was for naught— all he could think of was Bernadette, of what had happened between them here, on this hill. He recalled how he'd kissed her, and the way she'd responded to him, making him mad with want.

Perhaps he would make her his mistress, he mused idly. Perhaps he would bring her to Arrandale while his wife remained at Killeaven, just as he'd threatened to do. Oh, he had no hope that Bernadette would ever agree to it, but for now, the fantasy sustained him.

"Are you listening?" Cailean asked, cuffing him on the shoulder.

"De?" Rabbie said, startled out of his rumination.

"Have you heard a bloody word I've said, then?"

"Aye, of course," Rabbie said. "It's growing late. Let's carry on to Auchenard, aye?"

Cailean's eyes narrowed suspiciously, but he didn't argue and returned with Rabbie to the house.

Daisy was especially happy to see Auchenard, and praised Rabbie for keeping the garden she'd started eight years ago when she'd first come to the Highlands.

"Donna thank me," he said, leaning lazing against the ivy-covered arched entrance to the garden. "Mr. Brock has done it."

"It's beautiful," she said, turning slowly about. "You cannot imagine the state of disrepair when we arrived. Remember your dog, darling?" she said to Cailean.

"Aye. Fabienne was fine hunter, she was," Cailean said nostalgically. Like so many of their dogs, Fabienne had gone missing.

"I saw you kissing the laird here," Ellis said as he idly felt the petals of a rose. "I saw it from my window," he added, pointing to one above the garden.

Daisy laughed brightly, but her cheeks turned pink.

"Bloody good he didna see more than that," Cailean muttered.

"I mean to spend all my summers here when I'm of age," Ellis declared.

"Do you?" Daisy asked, and smiled indulgently at her son. "I hope that you do. Auchenard will always hold a special place in our hearts, will it not?"

Rabbie suspected Ellis would never return here, not really—only for a visit now and again. But Ellis was a viscount, and when he reached his majority, he would want what all English lords and ladies wanted—a proper society. Lassies in silk dresses. Drink and gaming.

No, he'd not return here.

"We never stalked the red stags," Ellis said to Cailean. "You promised."

"Aye, that I did," Cailean said, laughing. "And you've reminded me time and again, you have. We will, lad, we will. If you have a desire for something, you reach for it, aye? Your mother taught me that."

Daisy smiled so brilliantly at her husband that Rabbie felt a small tug in his chest. It was envy he felt. Pure, simple envy.

"It had to be taught, my darling husband."

He laughed and pulled her into his embrace. "You are right, *leannan*. Again."

The two of them laughed as if they shared a private jest about this, and then kissed.

Rabbie groaned at the sight of them. "Aye, all right, then," he said, and pushed away from the arch. "If you find all in order, we best return to Balhaire, aye? The Kents will arrive in a few hours."

Cailean and Ellis walked on, both of them curious about a broken windowpane Mr. Brock had yet to repair.

"Who all has come to Scotland?" Daisy asked curiously as she walked along with Rabbie behind them. "Miss Kent, naturally, and I assume her mother."

"Aye, her father, too," Rabbie said. "Her uncle, Lord Ramsey." He brushed a twig aside with the toe of his boot. "Her lady's maid, Miss Bernadette Holly, and a few servants."

"Bernadette Holly," Daisy repeated. "That name sounds very familiar, but I can't say why." Her eyes suddenly widened. "Yes, of course! She is the daughter of Mr. Theodore Holly," she said, and then turned her head and pulled on her earlobe. "She was involved in a bit of a scandal," she said lightly.

"Aye, so I've heard," Rabbie said.

"You know of the elopement?" Daisy asked.

He nodded.

"Ah. Poor thing. She must have loved him dearly to be compelled to elope. I recall there was some talk of a child, too, although who can say if that is true?"

A *child*? Rabbie managed to shrug and remain stoic, but that bit of news stunned him. She had a bastard child? Where was the child? He couldn't imagine she'd be here, attending the mouse, if she had a child...would she?

The idea of a child filled his thoughts on the return ride to Balhaire.

At Balhaire once again, Cailean went to speak to their father about his ideas for the smuggled cargo, and Rabbie retired to the rooms he used when at the castle. He lay on his bed, staring up at the fraying canopy. Something had shifted in him, he realized. His universe, so narrow and closed not two weeks ago, had tilted.

The difference was that he didn't feel the need to die. What was different was that he realized, with painful clarity, that he wanted what Cailean and Daisy shared. What Vivienne and Marcas shared. He wanted a wife he loved and children he adored. He still wanted all the things he'd assumed he'd have with Seona. He was only beginning to understand that those desires had not died with her, and that those desires were still alive in him—weak and neglected, but still alive.

Somehow, that idea that Bernadette might have a

child in the world somewhere had helped him to understand it. He was not appalled or put off by it, not in the least—he didn't know if it was even true. But it made him curious, made him think about having a child. He could imagine it, and it surprised him that he could, given how bleak his thoughts had been for so long. And yet, lying there, he could imagine being a father, a husband, a lover. He could imagine all those things that he thought were dead to him.

Unfortunately, he could not imagine those things with Avaline Kent, and the conflict in him raged.

When it came time for supper, Rabbie dressed in his plaid, uncaring who might object. And in fact, when he entered the great hall, Cailean's dark brow rose. But he said nothing.

There was quite a lot of commotion when the Kents arrived—it seemed that Lord Kent never grew weary of hearing himself speak, and particularly liked to start the moment he walked into a room. In they all trooped, Lady Kent in a drab gray gown, Miss Kent in blue. Lord Kent and his brother had already had a wee bit of whisky—they boasted of the fine stock they'd purchased from the Buchanans—and began firing questions to Rabbie's father about this or that.

Rabbie looked to the back of the hall, waiting for Bernadette to make her appearance. Drinks were poured, Lord Kent greeted Cailean like a long-lost brother.

Still, Bernadette did not come. A slight panic rose in Rabbie. He made his way to his fiancée, who was speaking quite gaily to Aulay.

"Feasgar math," Rabbie said, interrupting.

She made a sound of surprise. Her lashes fluttered nervously, and the color in her cheeks suddenly rose. "Good evening," she said, and curtsied. "I was just telling your brother that we almost lost a horse! Can you imagine?" she asked, and turned back to Aulay to continue her story.

When she had finished—it did seem to Rabbie to wind around the point a wee bit long—he said, "If I may, Miss Kent?"

"Please," Aulay said briskly, gesturing to Rabbie, and quickly walked away.

Miss Kent watched him go, then looked up at Rabbie. "Yes, sir?"

"You have come without your maid, aye?"

"Bernadette? Oh, yes, unfortunately. She's unwell."

Unwell? "What's wrong, then?"

"A headache, that's all. Oh, there is your sister! Will you excuse me? I should like to thank her for the wedding cup she sent me." She walked away to where her mother was standing with Vivienne and Aulay, leaving Rabbie to stand alone.

Bloody hell if she had a headache. Rabbie glared at the entrance to the great hall. She was avoiding him, and a rush of fury rose up in him so swiftly, he could scarcely contain it. He glanced at the mantel clock. He had an hour and a half before the supper would be served, and walked out the door without looking back or saying a word to anyone.

CHAPTER SIXTEEN

BERNADETTE WAS DETERMINED to tell Avaline the truth about what had happened between her and Rabbie. She fully expected to be turned out for it, and she was prepared for that—or as best she could be, realizing she'd have no choice but to retreat to Balhaire and hope for mercy there. But it hardly mattered if she was banished to wander the Highlands for the rest of her life—she couldn't live with herself after what she'd done. She couldn't watch Avaline stand at the altar with Rabbie and swear fidelity for the rest of her life, knowing she'd betrayed her. She couldn't listen to Avaline take her vows to marry him, knowing what she felt in her heart about him.

Bernadette was determined, but when she'd returned to Killeaven the afternoon of her tryst, Avaline was feverish with excitement. "Lady Chatwick and her husband have come," she said with great verve as she took Bernadette by the hand and pulled her into her room. "We are invited to dine tomorrow night! Should I wear this?" she asked, holding up a gold gown and embroidered stomacher. "Or this?" She next held up a blue mantua.

When Lady Chatwick—or more properly, Mrs.

Mackenzie—and her husband had called at Bothing with a proposal of marriage all those months ago, the woman had mesmerized Avaline. Bernadette had not had the pleasure of making the lady's acquaintance, but Avaline assured Bernadette several times over that Lady Chatwick was a beautiful woman full of grace and poise, and "wore a smile for everyone, down to the lowest stable boy. You should have seen her."

Avaline had been so enthralled with Mrs. Mackenzie that she'd not seemed to understand her father had agreed to marry her off to a Highlander she'd never met. She chose instead to think of all the ways Lady Chatwick was superior to any other woman she'd ever met and professed that she hoped one day to be just like her.

"They say Chatwick Hall is quite grand, but that Lady Chatwick prefers the smaller dowager house for her family, for it's very quaint and cozy," Avaline had declared after that initial meeting.

Bernadette wondered who *they* were. "I believe the correct address now is Mrs. Mackenzie," she'd patiently reminded her.

"Well, of course, that's correct *now*," Avaline had said. "But she's really a lady. She married for love, you know. She defied everyone."

Bernadette didn't know who everyone was, either, or if Avaline had heard the irony in praising Mrs. Mackenzie for marrying for love when she herself would have her marriage arranged for her by an unfeeling father.

Yesterday afternoon, as Avaline studied her gowns,

she'd said, "I wonder what clothes Lady Chatwick will wear this evening. Do you suppose she'll don plaid? She's always so stylishly dressed. My mother said her modiste is French and she uses only fabrics from Paris."

"Avaline, there is something I must tell you," Bernadette had said, uncaring what Lady Chatwick wore.

"What is it? Oh, I nearly forgot! Do you think you might arrange my hair as she wears it? She has long tresses pinned just so," Avaline said, using her own long hair to demonstrate.

"I will try—"

"Goodness that reminds me!" Avaline said suddenly. "Stay here, darling—I must mention something to Mamma before I forget it entirely." She'd skipped out of her room, leaving her gowns in the piles on the floor where she'd dropped them when she'd twirled to the mirror to have a look at her hair.

And so it had gone. On those rare moments Avaline and Bernadette were alone, Avaline chattered like a flock of starlings, her glowing admiration of Lady Chatwick uppermost in her thoughts, followed only by thoughts of the garland her mother wanted her to wear in her hair on the day of her wedding, and what she meant to do with the north sitting room, as her father had agreed she might have a bit of money to change things about at Killeaven.

Bernadette was miserable. It was impossible to take her aside and speak to her in confidence. And yet the clock was ticking, and Bernadette felt every stroke of it thrumming in her head.

The next day, when they were all to pile into that

awful coach bound for Balhaire and supper with the Mackenzies, Bernadette begged off. "I am unwell," she'd said to Lady Kent and Avaline.

"Unwell!" Lady Kent said, stepping back. "A contagion?"

"A rather excruciating headache, that's all." Bernadette pressed her fingers to her temples. It wasn't exactly a lie—she had a headache, which, she supposed, was to be expected when one did not eat or sleep.

"Oh, but you must come, Bernadette," Avaline complained. "You're much better at speaking to Mackenzie than I am."

That only served to make Bernadette feel worse. "Please, darling, go without me."

Avaline pouted.

"Of course you may stay behind," Lady Kent said. "Avaline, you can't rely on Bernadette to always speak to Mackenzie on your behalf."

Avaline complained, but it was decided—the Kents would go on to Balhaire without her.

When it came time for them to depart, Bernadette stood in the drive next to Charles and Renard as the coach pulled away with all the Kents stuffed inside of it. As he coach swayed and bumped down the drive, Charles said, "Well then, Miss Holly, what crime have you committed to be left behind?"

"I begged," Bernadette said, her gaze still on the coach.

Charles laughed. "Then you are free to join us. Fancy a game?" he asked.

Bernadette looked at him, then at Renard. "A game?"

"While the cat's away," Renard said, and looked her up and down. "If you have a purse, you may come to the servants dining hall at half past seven." He strode for the door but paused there and looked back. "We don't play parlor games, Miss Holly," he warned her. "Don't bother to come if you aren't prepared to lose." He disappeared inside.

"Is *this* what you all do when we are at Balhaire?" Bernadette asked Charles.

"What else is there?" Charles asked with a shrug. "There's nothing to divert us for miles and miles, except perhaps wondering what those two are about." He pointed up on the hill. Two riders were ambling by. "They come round to have a look several days a week. What can they possibly think to see?" he asked. Then to Bernadette he added, "Well then? Are you prepared to lose, Miss Holly?" He winked.

She shook her head. "I feel as if I've already lost and was banished to the farthest reaches of earth."

He chuckled and said, "Suit yourself, then." He turned on his heel and walked into the house, apparently eager to get to the gaming.

Bernadette stood a moment longer, watching the riders as they moved on, disappearing over the rise in the hill. The sight of them made her restless. She felt prickly in her own skin.

She returned to her room and tried to read from a book of poetry, but the language was too flowery and sweet and vexed her. She attempted to mend a gown she'd inadvertently torn, but her mind was elsewhere, and she took out more stitches than she made.

She at last she decided she would walk, and donned her boots.

A quarter of an hour later, Bernadette strode along a familiar path. Clouds were gathering, and it felt as if it might rain. She tried to clear her thoughts, but she couldn't keep from imagining that supper at Balhaire. She simply couldn't keep the memory of how he'd touched her from her mind. When she did think of it, her blood began to heat, and inevitably, she would feel ill with guilt and grief.

Since Albert had disappeared, Bernadette had not been so beguiled. Was there another word for what she was feeling? No, that was precisely the thing. He had lured her in somehow. How strange that at first she'd seen nothing but his cold demeanor. And then his pain. And the way he'd looked at her, then had touched her. It was stunning, really, for Bernadette had been so bloody careful since her humiliation. She had moved with great care through each day to avoid any situation that might give anyone pause, to keep talk of her to nothing. She'd gone full circle now, from the woman who never gave anyone reason to mention a breath of scandal, to one who had plunged headlong into it. She was tortured by what she'd done, and yet, she couldn't stop thinking of him, couldn't stop tamping down feelings about him that stubbornly rose to the surface.

It was as if she had no capacity to control her own thoughts or emotions.

She was, against all good judgment, smitten with that beast of a man. "Rabbie," he'd said, his gaze so earnest, the need for her to say his name so evident in his expression. "I am Rabbie."

Bernadette paused and closed her eyes a moment, recalling in vivid detail those moments under the hanging tree again…

And then quickly opened her eyes and walked on, furious with herself for having allowed her feelings to tumble so far down this path. Even in her wildest dreams, even if Avaline found reason to end this engagement, Bernadette couldn't be with Rabbie—she couldn't marry anyone, really, because when she'd lost her baby, she'd lost the ability to bear children. All this wishing and hoping and imagining were for naught. She was harming no one but herself.

"For heaven's sake," she muttered to herself. What was she doing? Why was she continuing to torment herself with these thoughts?

Rabbie would marry Avaline at the end of the week and Bernadette was a damned fool for having believed she could have stopped it. Moreover, she likely would be gone before any wedding could take place, banished to Highfield, where her father would surely beat her for what she'd done, if not worse.

When the path reached the sea, she turned right as she normally did. She wouldn't find Rabbie above the cove today, of course not. He would be at Balhaire with his family, all of them gathered to greet the Kents.

She trudged up the hill, her gaze on the sea. The darkest clouds were gathering in the distance, and the sea was turning rough. She'd have to turn about soon. She dipped her head to pull the hood of her cloak over her head, and when she glanced up, her heart leaped to her throat—Rabbie was standing on the cliff. More precisely, on the path directly in her line of sight.

And he looked rather perturbed.

What madness had brought him here, when he ought to be dining with his fiancée and their families? Bernadette was suddenly, inexplicably angry, and ran up the path to him, her chest heaving, her breath strangled with her ire. "Have you lost your mind?" she demanded hotly. "Why are you *here*?"

"You ought to be at Balhaire," he said irritably.

"No! I won't attend—"

"Why no'?"

"Oh, God, this is disastrous! What if someone comes looking for you? You shouldn't be here, Rabbie! Someone will see you—"

"I donna care if they do—"

"Yes, you do!" she retorted. "And if you don't, *I* certainly do! Please, for the love of God, go to Balhaire where you belong!"

"Tell me why you didna come," he demanded.

She was going to be sick. Bernadette could feel the bile rising up, mixing fear and guilt and pure elation that he'd come. She was thrilled and mortified—angry and confused that he was not with Avaline, but likewise relieved that he was not. What was she to do with him?

She stared at him. He was wearing the plaid the Scots had once worn, the hem of it lifting with each gust to reveal a powerful thigh. His weight shifted to one hip, his arms folded across his broad chest.

The mere sight of him was disturbingly arousing.

God in his heaven, she was as mad as he was.

"You've no' answered me, lass. Why will you no' attend?"

"You *know* why."

"No, I donna know why," he said gruffly, then dropped his arms and began to move down the path toward her.

"The better question is 'why are you here?' Avaline will be arriving at any moment."

"She's arrived."

"For God's sake, you are to be *wed*, you're to start a new life. This is absurd!"

"This is what you want," he said, nearly upon her. "As do I."

"I don't want this!" she insisted, but her words sounded false to her own ears. "You don't understand," she said, her voice trembling now. "I am standing on the edge of utter destruction, Rabbie. *You* stand on the edge of ruining a young woman's life. Is this…this *infatuation* worth that?" she asked pleadingly. "You need to be with her now! We both must rid ourselves of the madness that has gripped us!"

He put his hand on her elbow and drew her into him. He shoved his fingers into her hair, pulled her head back and kissed her hard.

Bernadette splintered.

She rose up on her toes and gripped his arms as she returned his kiss with a ferociousness that felt quite unlike her. He was suddenly holding her so tightly that she could feel the thud of his heart against her chest. "I want you, Bernadette," he whispered into her ear.

He roughly ran his palm over her hair while his gaze searched her face. "Aye, I do, I want you, and you want me. You betray your mistress. I betray a memory. We are both of us traitors, then, we are, but let's no' betray each other."

Her heart pulse was racing, her body craving him, her mind screaming its warning to her. "It's so *wrong.*"

"Aye," he agreed. "But the desire exists between us, and *Diah*, we'll neither of us rest until we've put an end to it."

"Go back to Balhaire and leave me be," she pleaded with him. "*That* will end it."

One corner of his mouth tipped up. "If only it would, I'd be gone a thousand times over. But you know as well as I it will no' do anything but fan the flames."

He was right. As much as Bernadette hated to admit it, he was right.

She pressed her hand against his chest. He covered it with his, and pulled it free, then stepped backward, tugging her along.

"What are you doing?"

He responded by turning to walk up the hill with her in tow. Bernadette let him lead her. Again. She had no power to resist him, the last of it having bled out of her when he kissed her.

He led her up the hill and into the trees near his horse. There was a small clearing there, and he let go of her hand, removed his cloak and spread it on the ground. He looked back at her and his eyes, which had once reminded her of storms, were full of hunger.

She couldn't believe she was going through with

this, but she stepped up to his cloak, unfastened the clasp of her own and let it slide from her body.

Rabbie drew her closer, helped her down onto his cloak.

Bernadette couldn't breathe—it was if the air had been snatched from her. *"Soirbh,"* he murmured. "Easy, *mo chridha*," he murmured and shifted his body over hers.

She smoothed hair back from his face and traced her fingers along his chin, feeling the stubble of his beard.

Rabbie lowered his head, freed her breast from the confines of the gown and took it in his mouth.

"I mean to tell her," Bernadette said breathlessly as his mouth and tongue teased her. She grasped his head, her fingers raking through his hair. "I can't bear to live with myself if I don't."

He didn't care or he didn't hear her. He rose up, his mouth on hers, one hand sweeping down her side, to her hip, then down her leg.

Bernadette turned her gaze to the patch of gray sky above them as he moved his lips over her chin, kissed the hollow of her throat, then down, to her breast again, as his hand slid higher up her leg.

Intensely physical sensations began to flow through her. She could feel his hardness, the strength of his legs surrounding hers. His kisses were deepening, turning wilder, and Bernadette's response was turning wild, too. She pressed her breasts against him and explored him with her hands, moving over thick arms, across a muscled back, down a trim waist, and around, to the front of his plaid, and the hardness of his erection.

He moaned when she touched him and lifted his head as if he meant to speak, but when he gazed down at her, his lashes fluttered, and he shook his head. *"Alainn,"* he muttered.

She didn't know what he said, but whatever it was, spoken in such intimate circumstances, caused a dam to burst in her, flooding every part of her with pleasure and desire and affection—intense, undeniable affection for him.

Rabbie kissed her neck as he slipped his arms behind her back and crushed her to him. *"Diah, leannan,"* he said.

He suddenly rolled onto his back, pulling Bernadette on top of him. She straddled his body, pulled her skirts free, then pushed his plaid up around his waist. She slid her hands over his legs. They were sinewy and hard, his skin dampened with perspiration. She wrapped her hands around his member and could feel his heartbeat beneath her hand, the steady, rapid rhythm of need.

She was terribly aroused and leaned down to kiss him as she moved her hand on him.

But Rabbie was too impatient. He put his arm around her and tossed her on her back, and moved between her legs. Something primal began to surge through Bernadette, ripping through her veins, drowning out all rational thought, submitting everything in her to the need to feel his body inside of hers.

Rabbie pressed the tip of his erection against her sex; she drew her leg up, locked her gaze with his, then reached between them and guided him into her body.

He slid agonizingly slow into her, his eyes piercing

hers until she closed them and allowed the exquisite sensation of his body to wash over her. He moved with deliberation, his hand caressing her thigh, then caressing the wet folds of her sex as he moved.

She was lost. She grabbed at his cloak, curling her fingers into twin fists as she struggled for patience, to not rush along but luxuriate in this. He buried his face in her hair, lengthening his stroke, his hand between their joined bodies, bringing her to a moment of crisis.

Bernadette choked on a cry of release. It rained down on her, the dust and fragments of her life, the bits and pieces of what had been a thick wall of desire.

His strokes took on a new urgency now. "Hold me," he whispered, and Bernadette slipped her arms around him, kissed his face, his neck, his forehead, as he rode his way to release inside her.

When she had floated down from the cloud of ecstasy they'd created in one another, she opened her eyes. The wind had picked up, and the clouds had moved closer to shore. And yet, bits of sunlight glittered through the tops of the trees, and it felt to Bernadette as if they were being showered by gold dust.

It had been magical.

But as their bodies cooled, and the sky grew darker, reality began to creep in. The moments of insanity had passed, and now Bernadette was caught again in a vise of deceit and betrayal so tight that she feared her chest might burst with it.

Rabbie rose and helped her to her feet. He helped her arrange herself in her gown, picked up her cloak and wrapped it around her.

She brushed a twig from his shoulder. "You can't return to Balhaire like this," she said, worried by the state of his appearance.

"Donna worry," he said, and kissed the top her of head. He picked up her cloak and put it around her shoulders, fastening the clasp. "Go home, now, *leannan*. It will rain soon and I'll no' have you caught in it."

Bernadette nodded. She fastened her cloak and pulled the hood over her head. "This doesn't change anything, Rabbie. It didn't end it."

He gave her a questioning look.

"You said we wouldn't rest until we'd put an end to this thing between us. But it hasn't ended for me. I can't feel all this…esteem for you and prepare Avaline to marry you."

He touched his fingers to her cheek.

"I don't know what to do," she pleaded with him.

"I would ease you if I could, *leannan*, but in this moment, I donna know what to do, either, aye? All I can do is promise you I will put it to rights."

She wanted to believe him. She desperately, ardently, wanted to believe him.

He cupped her face. "You donna know what you mean to me," he said. She nodded—he didn't know what he meant to her, either. And she feared they would never have the opportunity to know.

His abruptly pulled her to him and kissed her again. When he let her go, he said, "Make haste." He turned and walked quickly, his cloak billowing out behind him.

Bernadette waited until he'd gone, then started back

to Killeaven, her body still vibrating from their love-making. But the closer she got to Killeaven, the colder she grew. Guilt began to choke out the desire.

There was nothing to be done for it. She'd fallen like a star fell from the sky, fast and hard, disappearing into nothing.

She would tell Avaline tonight.

How fitting the rain should start to fall.

CHAPTER SEVENTEEN

AULAY MET RABBIE at the door of Balhaire.

"Where've you been, then?" he demanded as Rabbie wiped the rain from his shoulders.

Rabbie swallowed down a trifle of guilt. "I needed air," he said, and pushed past his brother. He feared Aulay would detect Bernadette's scent, so firmly set in his own nose. He feared the truth of where he'd been and what he'd been about could be read in his expression.

But Aulay caught his arm, wouldn't let him pass. "Bloody hell you needed air," he spat. "I know where you've been, lad. I know what you're about, aye?"

Rabbie was almost relieved to have been caught. He wanted to confess that he had feelings—*strong* feelings—for the first time in years. Old, brittle feelings he'd thought long dead were cracking their shells and opening to new life.

"Donna do it again, do you understand? I've kept that cake-headed lass long enough in your stead, and I will no' do it again. Bloody well tend to her yourself."

Rabbie nodded, having no desire to antagonize Aulay any more than he'd already done. At least his secret was safe for the time being, until he could think what to do.

He followed Aulay into the great hall, where both families were gathered.

"There he is, our boy!" Lord Kent said loudly, and stood, swaying a bit on his feet and sloshing a tankard in Rabbie's direction. "We thought perhaps you'd run away," he said jovially. "God knows I wanted to escape before I was wed," he added, and he and his brother laughed loudly.

Lady Kent sat quietly, her hands in her lap, her face blank.

"My apologies," Rabbie said. "There was a matter I'd left unattended." He couldn't help but notice the glower his father exchanged with his mother. They clearly did not care for the Kents. And they most assuredly did not care for Rabbie's behavior.

Miss Kent came to her feet and dipped a curtsy to him. "Good evening, Mr. Mackenzie." She glanced away, as if she couldn't bear to look at him, but then cast a sunny smile at Aulay.

Rabbie's father gestured for him to come forward, and Rabbie steadied himself. He walked to the dais and took a seat next to him.

"Where have you been?" his father asked curtly.

"I needed a wee bit of air," Rabbie said.

His father leveled a look at him that clearly relayed his doubts. "Donna disappear again."

Frang appeared, stepped behind the dais and whispered something in his mother's ear. "At last," she muttered and stood. "I beg your pardon, if I may? Supper is served." She smiled and gestured toward the table set in the middle of the great hall. As everyone turned toward the table, she passed Rabbie with a dark look.

The two families dined in the great hall. Rabbie sat across from Avaline, who was seated between Catriona and Ellis. When she wasn't whispering with Catriona, the two of them like a pair of wee thieves, Ellis engaged her with animated speech.

That suited Rabbie very well, for he was in no mood to speak with her. He could scarcely look at her—his heart and his thoughts were with Bernadette.

He couldn't fathom how everything had happened so quickly, or even why it had. She'd despised him at first, and he'd been annoyed by her arrogance. But something had changed. It had started as an ember, had flamed with the wind off the sea at the cliff. He and Bernadette had just caught fire, that was what.

Lord Kent startled him with a loud guffaw, and Rabbie glanced in his direction. He was a man enslaved to drink. Rabbie had yet to pass an evening in his acquaintance when he did not fall into his cups, and his brother was no better. He glanced down at his meal, scarcely touched, his appetite consumed with thoughts of making love to Bernadette.

"By the *by*," Lord Kent said loudly, and brought his whisky glass down on the table with a thud. He leaned forward to see down the table, and the tails of his lacy neck cloth dragged in the gravy on his plate. "With the help of my friend Buchanan, I've struck a bargain with the old man MacGregor. He's agreed to a fair price for the land between our estates, my lord. Who, then, will build me a ship?"

Rabbie glanced at his father, but the laird's expression was stoic. "What sort of ship would you like, then, my lord?"

"The same as you have," he said, waving a beefy hand. "I like what you do here, Mackenzie. I rather think I ought to do the same."

"What I do?" his father said, and smiled coldly. "Do you mean head a clan? Keep my people well fed and with occupation?"

"No, *no*," he said irritably. "The *trade*, sir. Seems like a good venture to me. Wool is a dear commodity, and I intend to sell it by the ship-full in England." He slapped his hand on the table and laughed loudly, as if the idea was so brilliant, so unique.

"Well, then, I donna know," his father said evenly. "The MacDonalds were shipbuilders," he said, nodding in Niall's direction. "Alas they've been chased off of Skye."

"Where'd they go?" Kent asked, leaning again, his neck cloth in the gravy again. "They can't have gone far." He looked at Niall.

"I canna rightly say," the young man said, and shrugged. "Glasgow?"

Lord Kent snorted. "I'll find someone who is willing to build me a ship, here, in the Highlands. You might even sail it, Mackenzie. You or one of your sons."

"Perhaps," his father said, and lifted his tot of whisky. "Frang, pour Lord Kent the Erbusaig whisky, aye? He's no' had the likes of it."

"Yes, yes, let's have some of that," Lord Kent said greedily.

Rabbie's father narrowed his eyes and fixed them menacingly on Kent. If Rabbie didn't know his father, he would fear for Kent's safety.

When the meal was done, the two families moved to the more intimate salon where Rabbie prayed his fiancée would not be commanded to sing. He was tormented enough as it was. Avaline had engaged Aulay in a corner. She was very animated, her countenance bright. Aulay looked as if he was fighting sleep.

He had to marry her. Was it not quite clear that he did? Kent had struck an agreement to buy the land that would give him access to the sea. At the very least, Rabbie had to marry the lass to control what Kent intended to do, or how the Buchanans meant to use him. If he was the man's son-in-law, the Mackenzies might manage to balance his desire to sell wool with their own trade, might keep his flocks to the barest minimum so as not to lose their own limited grazing fields.

Rabbie had no choice.

And yet, he couldn't stop thinking of Bernadette. He couldn't risk losing her.

He had to speak to Avaline. What he meant to do had no defendable justification and would threaten the welfare of his clan. Rabbie knew what he risked, but he couldn't help himself—he couldn't lose Bernadette, either, not after she'd brought him back from the brink. He walked across the room to his fiancée. "Miss Kent," he said, said, interrupting the tale with which she had cornered Aulay.

She started. "Yes?"

He held out his hand to her. "A word, please."

She looked at his hand, then at Aulay.

"Please," he said.

"Yes, of course," she said. But she made no effort to move.

"No' here," Rabbie said. "I would like a word in private."

"Oh." She glanced to her left. Rabbie followed her gaze. She was looking at her mother, who was watching them closely. "*Diah*, do you seek permission for everything that you do?" he muttered.

"What?" A blush rose in her cheeks. "I only... Where are we going?"

"Out of this room," he said, and held out his palm again.

She very reluctantly slipped her hand into it and allowed him to lead her out of the room. He announced they needed a word in private and would return momentarily.

"By all *means*," Lord Kent said, and laughed nastily.

If the man was not to be his future father-in-law, Rabbie might have put a fist in his gullet. He could scarcely contain his disgust.

He escorted Avaline to his father's study. She stepped inside and turned around to face him, her hands clasped tightly before her. She was anxious. She was always anxious in his company. How she must despise him—was he really so unsettling?

"I've something you ought to know," he said. *I made love to your maid. I didn't seek the attraction, but it has happened. I can't put her out of my mind for even a moment, even here and now.* "You ought to know that we Mackenzies are free traders."

She titled her head to one side. "Pardon?"

"Smugglers."

Her eyes widened. "*Oh.* I *see.*" She looked to the window, unblinking, and her hand went to her throat, fluttering there.

He rather doubted she saw anything at all. "You are aware, are you no', that smuggling is unlawful and immoral?"

"You mean to say that *you* smuggle," she said, and turned her gaze back to him. "But not *all* of Mackenzies engage in this...practice," she said carefully.

Was she referring to the entire clan? "No' my mother or sisters, no. But the rest of us, aye."

She nodded slowly, absorbing this information, then asked, "But Aulay doesn't smuggle...does he?"

Was she truly as ignorant as this? Rabbie peered at her, trying to understand how she could misinterpret anything he'd said. "He is the captain of the ship we use to bring the cargo here."

"Yes, but he doesn't actually... I mean... He doesn't..."

Why was she so concerned with Aulay? "Do you take my meaning, then, Avaline? You're to marry a smuggler."

She made a sound of alarm. And then she stared at him for a long moment, her lashes fluttering, her lips pursed as if she wanted to speak. "All right," she said at last.

All right? That's all she would say? "*Diah*, no, Avaline, it's no' all right, is it, then? Do you no' want a good reason to end this engagement? I am giving it to you." *On a bloody platter*, he wanted to add.

"No!" she said, and pressed a hand to her chest. "No, I *don't* want to end this engagement, not like this!" She spoke as if the idea was abhorrent to her.

Rabbie was astonished. She so clearly despised him—why would she not take what he was offering?

"*I* haven't smuggled anything. My conscience is clear. I see no reason to end our engagement."

She was entirely impossible to understand.

"May we go back now?" she asked.

"*No,*" he said. He tried to think how to explain this to her. "You do realize you will vow to honor and obey me for all the rest of your days in two days' time, do you no'?"

"Of course I do," she said softly.

He stepped closer. "You will be wed to a man who doesna want to be wed to you, Avaline. A man who is a free trader. And a Highlander. Are you certain that is what you want?"

She laughed nervously. "Well…no. Are you certain of it?"

"I donna want it at all," he answered truthfully.

"But the agreement has been made."

"Agreements can be broken," he said, but she was shaking her head.

"I understand," she said carefully. "But if I don't marry you as agreed, my father will return me to Bothing, and mine will not be a happy life, sir. At least here…at *least* I have Killeaven."

For the first time since meeting her, something clicked in Rabbie's head, and he thought he understood her—she was as trapped as he was. He clenched his jaw and nodded. His chest felt as if it was cracking open.

"May we please go back now?" she asked.

He nodded again, feeling suddenly incapable of speech. The lass practically ran for the door. She despised him, she feared him, and yet she was determined to wed him to escape life under Kent's thumb. Rabbie was not unsympathetic.

The world seemed impossibly unfair to him. He'd finally found the spark that ignited his will to live again...only to have it doused by Avaline's determination to escape her father.

He followed Avaline into the great room and watched how she hurried in the direction of his siblings, all of them gathered near the hearth. But before Avaline could reach them, Ellis intercepted her.

Rabbie spent the rest of the evening in a haze of disbelief, anger and longing. It seemed an eternity before Lord Kent agreed it was time for them to depart, but not without first exacting a promise that the Mackenzies would dine at Killeaven on the morrow. His mother agreed, Rabbie suspected, just so the Kents would go.

"We've not much time left, have we?" Kent said jovially. "Another supper, a wedding and a feast, and then, we shall leave our daughter in your care and return to England," he explained to Rabbie's mother.

"So soon," she said mildly as she handed Lady Kent her cloak.

"I am needed at Bothing. It's an estate of great standing, you see. Quite larger than anything you would have experienced in the Highlands."

"Naturally," Rabbie's mother said. "Then by all means, you should make haste."

When they had poured themselves into the coach and it had lumbered away, the Mackenzies wearily retreated to the family salon.

"Impossible people," his mother said. "And we must dine with them again on the morrow! I've never in my *life* done so much celebrating of a nuptial!"

"I knew Old MacGregor would sell the land, I did," Rabbie's father said as he caned his way to a seat and sat, stretching out his bad leg.

"Aye, but Kent doesna have a ship," Cailean pointed out.

"No, but Kent has money, and a lot of it, he does. He'll buy a ship, and then fill it with Highlanders looking for work. We canna stop it." He glanced at Rabbie. "And you, Rabbie. Have you anything to say?"

Startled, Rabbie looked around him. "Me?"

"Do you mean to go through with it?" his father asked bluntly.

Rabbie knew a moment in which he thought he would speak the truth and say no. But he said, "Aye, as I've said."

"Aye, you've said…but it is verra clear that your heart doesna want it."

They were all watching him, and Rabbie had that

uncomfortable feeling that his family had discussed this without him, much as they had his melancholy. They knew him better than anyone, and they would know if he deceived them now. He looked around him, at their faces. "My heart doesna want it, no," he admitted.

"Then donna—" his father began, but his mother interrupted him.

"Then don't *what*, Arran?" she demanded. "It's too *late*. It's all too late! The banns have been posted. We have set this marriage in motion, and to end it now would be *ruinous* to that young woman!"

"Why must we care about her?" Aulay grumbled.

"Because she is helpless in this, Aulay. Because we will live on, but her life will be ruined—"

"I mean to wed, *Maither*," Rabbie said, aware that his father was shrewdly watching him. "I am no' happy with her, no, but I will find a way."

His mother's face fell. She sank onto a chair. "Oh, Rabbie. This is our fault, your father and I—we should never have asked this of you. No, it's even worse than that—it's *my* fault," she said, pressing both hands to her bosom. "I thought—I *hoped*—that this young woman would bring you back to us, pull you back from such despair."

How could she have believed that Avaline Kent would ever make up for the loss of Seona? And now she was to make up for the loss of Bernadette as well? Rabbie swallowed down his bitterness. "Donna blame yourself, *Maither*. I should no' have agreed, then," he said, and turned away, unable to look at them all now. Unable to bear their pity. Determined that no one would see how his heart was beginning to shatter.

CHAPTER EIGHTEEN

AVALINE DID NOT wake Bernadette as she'd promised when they returned to Killeaven. She didn't want company tonight, fearful that any conversation would cause her to forget all the things she wanted to remember about Aulay.

As she dressed for bed and brushed her hair, she reviewed everything Aulay had said. Every smile. Every glance in her direction. She was utterly convinced that he esteemed her in the same manner she esteemed him. She was also utterly convinced that the only reason he hadn't told her so was out of the respect he felt for his brother and, of course, the untenable situation in which they found themselves. Aulay was a gentleman and a loyal brother and a moral man. It would not do to declare his adoration of the woman his brother was supposed to wed in only two days' time.

In fact, when they were standing in the corner, away from all the ears and prying eyes, Avaline had glanced over her shoulder at the others and said, "Oh, Aulay, how I wish we could surprise them all."

"Surprise who, then?" Aulay had asked her.

"Our families," Avaline said and gave him a knowing look to convey she understood his dilemma. "I should very much like to *surprise* them, wouldn't you?"

Aulay sipped from the wine he was holding as he considered her. "Surprise them how?"

She looked him directly in the eye and said, "With a wedding they never expected."

Aulay smiled and idly looked away as he nodded. "Is there something in particular you have in mind?"

"Yes, actually," she said as saucily as she knew how, and leaned in to tell him…but at that very inopportune moment, who should appear but her betrothed. His appearance had been unfortunate indeed, and she'd been quite perturbed by it. He hadn't even had the common courtesy of allowing her and Aulay to finish their conversation. And she'd lost her opportunity to sit beside Aulay at the dining table because of that wretched Lord Chatwick.

She knew Lord Chatwick requested that *he* be seated next to her—she'd overheard the butler tell a footman. What bother that boy was, whether he wished to believe it or not. She didn't care that he'd soon be seventeen as he'd pointed out to her. She *was* seventeen, and she had to point out to *him* that clearly made her superior in age and in life. But the boy was so obtuse he didn't seem to understand at all, because he followed that with inviting her to Chatwick Hall.

"It's one of the largest homes in all of northern England," he'd boasted, as if she wasn't aware.

"I *know*," Avaline said pointedly.

"Do you enjoy riding?" he continued eagerly. "We

have a stable full of horses. Or perhaps you prefer archery? We have everything at Chatwick Hall."

"I enjoy *all* those things," she assured him, as if he was a child. She tried to turn her attention back to Catriona, but Chatwick kept interrupting. He could teach her to shoot, he said, or to hunt, he said. He said his Pappa taught him to hunt, and he'd nodded at Mr. Cailean Mackenzie, who was most certainly *not* Lord Chatwick's father, everyone knew that, and then he'd mentioned they had the best hunting dogs in all of England.

Did he really think she cared a whit about dogs? When she married Aulay, she would have to insist that dogs did not roam the house freely as they did at Balhaire. It seemed she was forever bumping into one, or nearly tripping over another. There were far too many of them, and they touched their wet snouts to her fine gowns, and she didn't care for it at all.

But never mind Chatwick. They were all to dine again on the morrow, here at Killeaven, and she had to find a way to speak to Aulay of her feelings, as she was running out of time. She was certain she could convince him that everything was really perfectly aligned for them. The wedding was set, and Avaline believed it hardly mattered if one Mackenzie married in the place of another. The posting of the banns was really just for show, wasn't it? And if not, there was surely something that could be done for it. Her father always said that everyone had their price.

Avaline drifted to sleep with the image of meeting Aulay Mackenzie at the altar.

She was awakened early the next morning by Bernadette, who shook her awake. Avaline blinked the sleep
from her eyes then looked up, and almost gasped with
surprise. Bernadette looked truly *awful*. "Good Lord,
you really are unwell," she said.

"What?" Bernadette asked. She touched her face.
"I didn't sleep well."

Well, Avaline had slept like a baby and she stretched
her arms high overhead. "What time is it?"

"Eight o'clock."

"Eight!" Avaline exclaimed, and meant to complain.

But Bernadette said, "I must speak with you, Avaline."

"Yes, all right, but at breakfast," Avaline said, and
rolled onto her side, intending to return to sleep.

Bernadette put her hand on Avaline's hip. "It really
must be now," she said, sounding a wee bit hoarse.

Avaline groaned. There was nothing she hated worse
than conversations in the morning. "Very well," she
said irritably, and pushed herself upright. She pulled
her braid over her shoulder, drew her knees up to her
chest and wrapped her arms around them. "Well? What
is it?"

Bernadette didn't answer straightaway. She began
to pace. Her hair was unkempt, Avaline noticed, as if
she'd slept with it loose. She had never seen Bernadette
like this, had never seen her with a hair out of place.
Bernadette was always so…confident. In appearance,
in word and in deed.

She suddenly stopped pacing and fixed her gaze on
Avaline. "Well, I can think of no way to soften it, so

I'll just say it. Mr. Mackenzie and I have…we have…"
Her chin trembled, and Bernadette pressed her fingertips to her cheeks.

"What have you and Mr. Mackenzie done? Argued?"

"Kissed," Bernadette said tightly.

It took a moment for Avaline to fully grasp that.
What did that *mean*, precisely? A peck on the cheek?
Or a *kiss*? "Pardon?"

"We have kissed," Bernadette said again. A blush
was creeping up her neck.

And still Avaline didn't understand. *"Why?"* she
asked, truly astounded. She couldn't imagine why anyone would kiss that man if it wasn't necessary, not
even his own mother.

The questions seemed to confuse Bernadette. She
pushed her hair back from her face. "I'm really not
sure," she said softly and, amazingly, tears filled her
eyes.

Avaline's eyes widened with surprise. Bernadette
never wept. Avaline leaned forward. "Do you…do you
esteem him? I thought you despised him."

"I don't despise him…" She winced. "That's not
true, I did despise him in the beginning. But mostly
I didn't want to see you wed such a cheerless, hard-
hearted man."

"So why then did you *kiss* him?" Avaline asked, terribly confused. "Was it part of a scheme to save me?"
she asked hopefully, although she couldn't see what
sort of scheme would require Bernadette to *kiss* him.

"No, God, no," Bernadette said quickly. "It just

happened, Avaline. I can't really even say how. And it happened more than once. It happened—" a tear slid down her cheek "—in a manner I can't even describe to you."

Avaline blinked. She was very curious to know what manner could not be described.

"It's horrible, I know," Bernadette said. "Somehow, we, ah…well I, came to esteem him in a way that defies all logic—"

"Do you *love* him?" Avaline exclaimed, shocked and horrified for Bernadette.

"No!" Bernadette quickly insisted. But she didn't look as if that was true. She looked as if she was trying *not* to love him.

Bernadette fell to her knees beside Avaline's bed, and clasped her hands before her as if she was praying. "I know what I've done is the height of betrayal, and for that, I offer you my sincerest apologies. If I could take it back, I would, but I can't. I don't know what possessed me, other than I was swept away by sentiments I've never experienced quite like this." She bowed her head over her hands, hiding her face from Avaline.

Avaline stared down at her dark head. This was brilliant. It was the answer to her prayers! "Oh, dear, you mustn't upset yourself," she said, and put her hand on Bernadette's head. She wouldn't have to worry about that wretched man now—she would give him to Bernadette!

"It's too late. I'm beside myself with grief," Bernadette said tearfully.

"Well, of course you are," Avaline said soothingly. "No doubt you saw a kiss from even him as your only opportunity for passion."

Bernadette stilled. She lifted her head. "I don't think—"

"Were I in your shoes, I'm sure I'd have been tempted as well," Avaline said soothingly.

Bernadette's brows dipped into a dubious vee. "You would?"

"You mustn't give it another thought, Bernadette. I completely understand how you must have needed the attention, and I forgive you." Avaline felt a bit like a saint. Of course, Bernadette would never have any chance at happiness, and Avaline could hardly blame her for stealing a bit of hers. Not that she'd stolen anything from her at all, really.

Bernadette dropped her head again. "I am *so sorry*, Avaline."

"There is no need for apology," she said. "It's not as if I've found any rapport with him, after all."

Bernadette sniffed. She slowly pushed herself to her feet. She looked much older and…and ill when she wept. "I'll gather my things."

"Why?" Avaline asked, confused again.

Bernadette frowned again. "Avaline—you must dismiss me. You must send me home to Highfield."

"I beg your pardon! I won't hear of it!" Avaline exclaimed. She didn't intend to live in the Highlands by herself, for God's sake.

"But…"

Avaline shook her head, and slid off her bed. "You

won't leave me, Bernadette," she said as she made her way to the dressing table. It occurred to her that she ought to admonish Bernadette in some way, and glanced back, pointed at her and said, "But never do that again. All right, then, we've had our talk. I'd like to be alone now."

Bernadette stared at Avaline. Clearly, she was astounded by how forgiving Avaline was to her. And she ought to be, for kissing Mackenzie was badly done, *very* badly done. In any other circumstance, Avaline would have been quite cross and would have gone to her father to tell him of the betrayal. But she was astonishingly grateful for Bernadette's wretched behavior. She just had to think of how to best use it to her advantage.

Bernadette was walking to the door, still sniffling.

"Bernadette? You'll be at supper this evening with the Mackenzies, won't you?" Avaline asked.

"The Mackenzies are coming *here*?"

"Yes, all of them. You'll dine with us this evening," she said. It was not a question.

"Do you think that wise, given what I just told you?" Bernadette asked.

Avaline sighed and turned around to Bernadette. "I want you to be there. I might need you."

Bernadette grimaced. "If you like."

Avaline smiled. "Don't look so despondent, dearest. It should be a very interesting evening. Very well, that's all."

Bernadette went out.

Avaline smiled at her reflection. She didn't know

how she was going to manage it, but Bernadette kissing Mr. Mackenzie was the opening she needed to wed Aulay.

Avaline couldn't wait for tonight.

CHAPTER NINETEEN

BERNADETTE HARDLY HAD a moment to understand what had happened in that extraordinary meeting with Avaline this morning, much less do anything about it, because Lord Kent wouldn't allow it. He was in a very foul mood and kept bellowing at them all to do this and bring that.

They were all gathered round him now in the dining room, sitting or standing nervously as he had his luncheon. Bernadette had tried to avoid this meeting, but he'd commanded her to come, and frankly, she feared what Avaline would say if anyone questioned about her absence. *I don't rightly know. Perhaps she has gone off to kiss my fiancé again, although she promised she would not.*

Bernadette stood at the sideboard next to Charles, who had the unpleasant task of serving his lordship.

"I, for one, will be quite relieved when this interminable wedding is over and we might leave this godforsaken place and return to Bothing!" Lord Kent snapped through a mouthful of potatoes in response to Avaline's question as to whether the wedding breakfast should include fish or beef.

"I don't like to think of you leaving," Avaline said

with a bit of a girlish mewl in her voice. Bernadette didn't know why she said it—it was a sentiment she knew not to be true, and moreover, it earned Avaline a tongue-lashing.

"Do *not* induce me to fury, Avaline! If there is one thing which I cannot abide, it is your constant complaint!"

"My constant—"

"Not a word!" he bellowed, pointing a menacing fork at her. "It will not do to attend your wedding with a fat lip!"

Naturally, Avaline fled the room in tears. Lord Kent dabbed at his perspiring forehead with his napkin. His wife didn't move as much as a finger, and neither did Bernadette. That didn't stop his lordship from curling his lip and saying nastily to his wife, "You have succeeded, madam, in rearing a bloody dandelion for a daughter! I don't know why I ever dared to expect more from you—look at you, sitting there like a lump of clay.

"And *you*," he said, turning his head to level a look at Bernadette. "I have taken you into my home to do what she failed to do," he said, pointing at his wife. "And what have you done? Nothing! You're as useless as the others! For God's sake, do something about Avaline's face before our guests arrive. I won't have it swollen from her bloody tears." He suddenly pushed back from the table and threw his napkin to the ground. "I've had all I can abide." He stalked out of the room, shouting at the heavens to tell him what he'd ever done to deserve being saddled with the most useless women in all of England.

Lady Kent waited until she heard the sound of a door being slammed firmly shut, then she hurried from the room, too, her head down, her face pale.

Bernadette looked at Charles, who'd stood stoically at the sideboard as his lordship had railed. "He's in a mood," Charles muttered as he picked up his lord-ship's plate.

"Too much drink," Bernadette said. She pushed away from the sideboard and took her leave as well.

She didn't go to see about Avaline's face, however— she couldn't face her again, not yet. She was still reeling. It was almost like a dream—Bernadette had admitted something so awful, so unforgivable, and Avaline had seemed not to care at all. A strong sense of foreboding was pressing down on her now, making her feel slightly panicked.

Something wasn't right. Something about the way Avaline had taken the news was not right.

Bernadette ducked into the unfinished morning room and quietly shut the door. She stood with her back to a wall, holding herself, her eyes closed, and thought of the way Rabbie had held her, the way he'd looked at her, and the emotion, the relief and the ado-ration swimming in his eyes. She pictured him at the altar with Avaline. How could she bear to hear him swear to honor Avaline and be faithful to her? It was not to be born.

Bernadette ached with yearning for him. She turned and put her cheek to the wall, sliding her hand up the paneling, and closed her eyes. She thought she'd borne the worst this life had offered her, but she was beginning to fear she'd not yet begun to know pain. She would be forced to wait on Avaline after she was sleeping in Rabbie's bed. She would be forced to listen to Avaline as she shared their most intimate details. She would see a baby grow in Avaline's belly, and she could say nothing, *do* nothing, for even the slightest glance would betray her agony and her impossible feelings for Avaline's husband.

"I can't remain here," she said aloud, and opened her eyes. There was nothing to be done for it—she had to leave. At once. She would not stay here and watch their marriage unfold and be tormented at every turn. If Avaline didn't have sense enough to turn her out, then she would resign her post and return to Highfield, no matter how difficult that would be. Whatever her father dealt out to her would surely be less painful than remaining here to suffer.

She pushed away from the wall, smoothed her gown and tucked up a tress of her hair. Tomorrow, then. She would see her way through this interminable supper, would pack her few things and resign her post first thing in the morning.

SOMEHOW, BERNADETTE MANAGED to make it through the rest of the day in spite of the disorderly jumble of competing thoughts in her head. She repaired the hem on the gown Avaline was excited to wear this evening, which she'd thrust on Bernadette as if they'd never spoken this morning. She chattered about the wedding, and the wedding cup they would drink from, and the fish that would be served at the wedding breakfast. From all outward appearances, it seemed as if she was now looking forward to this wedding. Maybe she'd changed her opinion of Rabbie, too. Maybe she'd seen the same things in him that Bernadette had seen.

When the hem was prepared, Bernadette helped Lady Kent prepare place names for the wedding breakfast seating. By some miracle, the stroke of Bernadette's quill was strong and steady. Remarkable, given that she almost blindly wrote each name, her mind's eye filled with images of Rabbie.

She bathed and washed her hair, then dressed for dinner. She wore a pale silver mantua and stomacher, intricately embroidered with gold thread, and a trail of rosebuds sewn into the stomacher and around the edge of the sleeves. It was Bernadette's best gown, the one she reserved for special occasions. She had meant to wear it to Avaline's wedding, but now she wanted Rabbie to remember her in this gown when he thought of her in the weeks and months and years to come…if he remembered her at all. She winced at the thought, but it was entirely possible that with time, Rabbie would come to love Avaline, and Bernadette would be forgotten except perhaps in those moments when he happened to walk out on the cliff.

A knock at her door was followed by Charles's deep voice. "The Mackenzies have come."

Bernadette took one last look at herself. At least she didn't appear as haunted as she felt. She drew a deep breath, then made her way downstairs.

The Mackenzies had come on horseback. Catriona was the first one to alight, and explained that her sister and her husband would not be attending this evening, as one of their children had turned ill. Lord Mackenzie was quite dashing on a horse, Bernadette thought, and she could see the sort of figure he must have presented to Lady Mackenzie all those years ago. Lady Mackenzie and Mrs. Cailean Mackenzie wore cloaks with hoods that covered their hair, and looked remarkably fresh after the ride. Cailean and Aulay Mackenzie, and Lord Chatwick, followed. Behind them was Rabbie.

He was not wearing the plaid today, but had dressed in evening attire she might see on an English gentleman. His neck cloth was tied with precision, his waistcoat plain, but clearly made of superior fabric. His hair was neatly combed and tied in a queue. In her eyes, he was the most handsome among them. A truly stunning, full figure of a man. But Bernadette almost preferred the rough-hewn side of him.

His gaze met hers for a single, sizzling moment as he dismounted. She feared he would speak to her, and she would collapse with grief, but then he turned his head and moved forward to greet the Kents.

Lord Kent had apparently spent the afternoon in his study with his whisky, for his wig was slightly askew and his neck cloth tied crookedly, and he was talking loudly about the lack of good servants in the Highlands, wondering aloud if the Mackenzies fared any better, then invited them inside.

As the gentlemen stood back to allow the ladies to precede them, Rabbie glanced at Bernadette. *"Feasgar math,"* he said lightly…but his eyes were boring through hers.

Bernadette could not bear to be so close to him and not touch him. Her only defense was to pretend as if nothing had happened between them. She inclined her head and curtsied. "Good evening, sir."

"Oh, Miss Holly!" Lady Mackenzie said, halting her progress toward the door. "You've not had the pleasure of meeting my oldest son and his wife," she said, and introduced her to Mr. Cailean Mackenzie and his wife.

"How do you do," Bernadette said, greeting them. Mrs. Cailean Mackenzie smiled warmly and spoke to Bernadette about Scotland. While Bernadette somehow managed to answer her polite questions, she noticed from the corner of her eye that Avaline was standing with Aulay, and she observed how quickly her smile faded when Rabbie approached her. Bernadette's anxiety began to soar. None of it made sense—Avaline had been so bloody cheerful about the wedding this afternoon, and now she looked as if she'd just realized who she'd be marrying and found him wanting.

The party meandered into the main salon, Bernadette the last to enter. She stood to one side, wishing she could disappear and trying hopelessly not to stare at Rabbie. Lord Kent was prattling about something to do with the cook, his voice loud and grating. What in blazes had happened with the cook? Whatever it was, he seemed obsessed with it.

Bernadette's head began to ache. She touched her fingers to her temple, her thoughts and feelings roaring in her head. Nothing was making sense to her. Everything felt upside down.

The women arranged themselves on the settees, and

the men took up positions about the room. Lord Chatwick was the only one of the gentlemen to sit, finding a seat next to Avaline on the settee.

Did she imagine it, or did everyone seem unusually tense? Bernadette glanced again at Rabbie. He was speaking quietly to his brother's wife, and suddenly, both of them glanced at Bernadette. She quickly averted her gaze.

In that moment, Charles appeared before her. He handed her a glass of wine and said quietly, "The cook is leaving."

Bernadette's eyes widened. "I beg your pardon?"

He nodded, his gaze sliding to Lord Kent before walking away.

Bernadette turned her head, meaning to get Lady Kent's attention, but Rabbie was moving casually toward her. She panicked. She looked about for an escape and, finding none, she unthinkingly curtsied again.

"You greet me so formally," he said.

"I, ah…" She glanced nervously at Avaline, but she was engaged in conversation with Catriona and Aulay. "I don't think I should greet you at all."

Bernadette couldn't help herself—she looked at him then. She could see his regard for her, could feel it, and it made her sick with despair. Who would ever look at her like that again? Who would look past what had happened to her and see her for who she was? Would Rabbie still hold her in such high regard if he knew everything about her? If he knew that she couldn't bear children? She would never know—there would never be a reason to admit such a dark truth to him.

"Perhaps no', but I canna abide being in the same room with you and no' speaking to you, aye? I've thought of naugh' but you, Bernadette," he muttered. "I canna sleep, I canna eat."

"Neither can I," she whispered, and looked away from him. "But we've made everything so much worse."

"Worse? No, Bernadette—you've given me hope, you have."

"Don't say it," she begged him. "It's impossible." She caught sight of Renard returning to the room. He walked directly to Lord Kent, who was holding forth about something, and bent down to whisper in his ear. "I told Avaline about us," she whispered.

"Pardon?" Rabbie said, a little louder.

Bernadette was frantic—they would notice, they would all see, they would understand what she and Rabbie had done. She moved, meaning to step away, but Rabbie caught her elbow and pulled her around, moving her to the hearth. He pointed at the cornice above the mantel, and said, quite loudly, "This piece was handcrafted by Mr. Abernathy."

Bernadette shifted her gaze upward.

"Why?" he demanded under his breath.

"I told you—I couldn't live with myself knowing I'd betrayed her so."

He glanced over his shoulder. "And?" he asked impatiently.

"And…she didn't care," Bernadette said, and looked at him then. "She intends to—"

"Miss Holly! Miss Holly, come away from there at once and come with me!" Lord Kent said loudly.

Bernadette's heart lurched—her first thought was that he'd discovered what she and Rabbie had done. She whirled around, but Lord Kent was stalking out of the room, and Renard gestured for her to follow. She and Rabbie exchanged a look, and then she hurried from the room, following his lordship to the kitchen.

Mrs. MacInerny, the hired cook, had removed her apron and was wrapping her cloak about her.

"Where in God's name do you think *you're* going?" Lord Kent railed at her as Renard and Bernadette crowded in behind him.

Mrs. MacInerny responded quite heatedly in Gaelic, with a finger shaking directed at his lordship that so startled Bernadette, she gasped. The woman then turned about and stomped out of the kitchen. A moment later, they heard the kitchen's exterior door slam.

A girl, hardly taller than the kitchen table, stood clutching a pot and looking terrified.

Lord Kent swung around to Bernadette. "You'll have to finish the slop she was making."

"Me?" Bernadette cried. "I don't know how—"

"I don't care, you'll learn!" he said hotly. "I will *not* be made a fool of before the likes of these Highland thieves! Finish the meal." He moved to depart so abruptly and with so little balance that he almost collided with Renard. "Move aside!" he barked, and stormed out of the kitchen.

Bernadette looked helplessly at Renard. "I'm no cook! I don't have the slightest notion how to do it!"

"Do what you can. You're the only hope we have," he said, and went after Lord Kent.

Bernadette couldn't catch her breath. She was wheezing with panic. She looked down at her beautiful gown and winced. Then she remembered the girl and looked up. "What is your name?"

"Ina." The girl was shaking.

"Do you know how to cook?" Bernadette asked, the desperation clear in her voice.

"A wee bit, aye," Ina said.

"Heaven help us, then, Ina," Bernadette said, and picked up the apron Mrs. MacInerny had discarded and put it on. "You'll have to teach me what you know, because I know even less than a wee bit."

If there was one saving grace, it was that Mrs. MacInerny had mentioned to Ina that the lamb and potatoes were very nearly done roasting before she'd had her argument with Renard about the meal and had thrown her apron to the ground and fled. But the bread had not yet finished baking and the soup was something of a mystery. Bernadette and Ina couldn't even determine what sort of soup it was supposed to be. They added ingredients, but the taste changed little. Ina was in the midst of finishing a pie, and called out suggestions to Bernadette as she worked.

Bernadette was frantic. She couldn't say how much time had passed, but it seemed as if hours were ticking by. Her anxiety was made worse by the fact that Renard seemed to appear every few minutes, demanding to know when the meal could be served. No wonder Mrs. MacInerny had quit.

On his fourth or fifth appearance, Bernadette said irritably, "I'll come and find you when it's done, Renard, but your constant presence isn't helping in the least!"

"They are restless. They've all gone out into the gardens, and Lord Kent is drunk."

"He's *always* drunk," she curtly reminded him. "I'm doing the best I can," she pleaded. "I think we are close. Let me come to you, please."

Renard blew out his cheeks, then nodded. "You will find me on the terrace," he said. "Make haste, Miss Holly!"

"What does he think, that I'm at my leisure?" she asked when his back had disappeared through the door. She added salt to the soup, then tasted it. "Dear God, it's awful," she said, as Ina removed the bread from the oven. "But I think it's at least edible. Come, come," she said, gesturing for the girl to come forward.

Ina tasted the soup. She frowned a little. "Aye, 'tis edible," she agreed half-heartedly.

"Thank God," Bernadette said, and removed the apron. "I'll fetch Renard. Keep it warm, Ina!" She went out the kitchen door, knowing that the path around the edge of the house to the terrace was quicker than going through the house.

She rounded the corner, practically at a run, but was brought up short to almost stumbling by the sight of the backside of Avaline's dress at the next corner of the house. Avaline was standing in the hedgerow, and Bernadette could hear her pleading with someone, although Bernadette couldn't make out what she was saying. Was she speaking to Rabbie? Her heart clenched, and she slowly moved forward, expecting to find Avaline berating him about kissing Bernadette. She slowed, uncertain what she ought to do. But as she neared them, she saw it was Aulay. His arms were crossed implacably across his chest. Whatever Avaline had said had clearly displeased him.

Bernadette stepped forward, meaning to announce herself, but Avaline suddenly threw her arms around Aulay's neck and kissed him, full on the mouth. Aulay made a sound of alarm at the same time Bernadette gasped. His hands found Avaline's waist and he roughly set her back. "What in bloody hell is the matter with you?" he shouted.

Avaline never had a chance to answer, as Lord Kent came stumbling onto that scene, roaring at his daughter, his face red with rage. He must have seen them from the other walk.

His drunken shouting brought everyone else. Aulay moved away from Avaline, his expression quite angry, and Avaline began to sob. Lord Kent began to berate Aulay, who shouted at him in return, then he turned his shouting to Gaelic when his brothers appeared, all the while gesturing at Avaline. They looked at him, then at Avaline. Rabbie stared at his fiancée, his expression stoic.

Then Lord Kent grabbed Avaline by the arm and yanked her away from Aulay. Avaline screamed as he tried to drag her in the direction of the terrace. Bernadette didn't think—she ran forward to help Avaline, but Rabbie reached Avaline first. He grabbed Lord Kent's arm and jerked it away from Avaline, then pushed him back against the wall with one hand. "You'll keep your hands from her," he said calmly. Lord Kent was so drunk he stumbled and fell sideways, righting himself just before he might have sprawled on the ground.

Lord Ramsey, as drunk as his brother, tried to engage Rabbie with a swing of his arm, but Cailean Mackenzie swatted him back like a fly.

"Miss Kent," Lord Chatwick said, pushing in between the older men. He reached for Avaline, presumably to help her, to soothe her, but she pushed away his outstretched hand and ran to her mother's arms, burying her face in her mother's shoulder. Lady Kent quickly ushered her down the walk, disappearing around the corner from Bernadette's view. Aulay followed, still ranting in Gaelic. Cailean followed, as did Lord Mackenzie. Rabbie put his hand firmly on his mother's elbow and spoke to Catriona, and they, too, disappeared around the corner and down the path Bernadette could not see. As Lord Kent realized he was being deserted at the corner of the house, his head came up, and he was suddenly bellowing, chasing after them.

Bernadette was so stunned by what had just happened that she stood momentarily rooted to her place on the path. But then she heard voices rise again and ran after the others, rounding the corner and darting to the French doors of the salon, where she slipped inside, unnoticed.

It was pandemonium in that room, everyone shouting at one another in English and in Gaelic. Charles and Renard looked as if they'd been backed into a corner and stared with shock at them all.

"You will be hanged for defaming my daughter!" Lord Kent shouted at Aulay. "I challenge you, sir!"

Aulay rolled his eyes. "I didna defame her," he said hotly. "She's a barmy lass! You saw with your own two eyes that she kissed *me*, aye?"

Lady Kent gasped. "She did *not*!" she cried and looked at Avaline.

Avaline did not deny it. Incredibly, she tried to defend it. "I did because we esteem each other—"

"*Och, uist*, Miss Kent!" Aulay spat. "No' another foolish word from you. *You* may believe you esteem me, but I donna esteem you, do you ken?" he said, ignoring Avaline's weeping. "I've given you no cause to believe it. I am more than twice your age! I'm the captain of a ship and I'm at sea more than I am on land. You've created a fairy tale in your foolish head," he said, gesturing to his own head. "*Mi Diah*, you are *betrothed to my brother*."

"I don't *want* to be betrothed to him! I want to be betrothed to you!"

"Oh, dear God," Bernadette whispered. Suddenly, all her feelings of foreboding made sense. Aulay was right—Avaline had created a fairy tale, and now, a debacle. She had done the worst possible thing she could have. It was astounding, really, that Avaline could be so bloody obtuse. Bernadette looked at Rabbie. His gaze met hers, and from across the room, she saw the barest bit of relief glance his features. She felt that same relief—she would *not* see them married, not now. She would not be forced to live in agony tending his wife.

She would not have to resign or flee or any number of things she thought she were possible.

"You must have given her reason to believe her feelings were returned!" Lord Kent accused Aulay. "No one is so daft as to create esteem where none exists."

"I've no' said a word of encouragement," Aulay said. "Ask her."

Lord Kent looked at his daughter. She was still weeping. Bernadette's heart went out to her—she looked utterly heartbroken.

When she did not offer any explanation, Lord Kent sneered at her. "You stupid, *stupid* clown," he said. "You've ruined *everything*."

"No!"

Lady Kent's voice was so unexpected that everyone stared at her with surprise. She was glaring at her husband. "*You* are the stupid clown, Raymond!" she said hotly. "You have used your daughter very ill, indeed. You've gone against her *express* wishes and have forced her into an untenable match."

Rabbie sighed to the ceiling.

"I won't stand for it a moment longer. Not one moment longer!" Lady Kent said loudly.

Lord Kent was so stunned that he was, for once, quite speechless.

Lord Mackenzie was not. He was leaning heavily on his cane, and yet he still seemed the most authoritative figure in the room. "Given the turn of events, there will be no wedding, aye? We'll take our leave now, we will. Aulay, Cailean…go and bring the horses round."

Cailean gestured for Lord Chatwick to follow, which

he did, reluctantly. He could not tear his eyes away from Avaline, nearly bumping into a chair in his distraction.

"Margot," Lord Mackenzie said softly.

"Yes," Lady Mackenzie said. She walked to where Avaline had now collapsed onto her side on the settee. She seemed to debate whether or not to disturb her, then finally looked at Lady Kent. "You have my sympathies," she said, then looked back at Catriona and Mrs. Mackenzie, nodding at the pair of them. They quit the room with her, their gazes politely averted from Avaline and Lady Kent.

Lord Kent was panting now, the exertion of his anger having exhausted him. He sank onto a settee across from Avaline, next to his brother, who had been the first to find a seat in all the commotion.

Rabbie walked to where Avaline was laying and squatted down beside her. "My apologies, lass, if you found this union wanting. I think it is better for us this way, aye?"

She nodded mutely.

Rabbie stood up. He looked at Bernadette for a moment. She tried to understand his expression, but it was useless. It had all been too shocking. He exited the room with his father.

Their guests gone and the wedding called off, the Kents were spent. Lady Kent sank down onto the settee beside her daughter. Lord Ramsey poured himself two whiskies, but remarkably, Lord Kent shook his head to the one he was offered. He seemed as downtrodden as Bernadette had ever seen him. He pushed himself off the settee and moved to the door with heavy steps. With some effort, he lifted his arm and pulled off his wig, letting it hang from his hand as he made his way out.

Avaline watched him a moment, then sat up. "Pappa—"

Lord Kent threw up his hand, still holding the wig. "I can't bear to even look at you now. Do not complete my utter destruction by *speaking*," he said, and disappeared through the door.

Lady Kent whispered to her daughter, and the two of them stood, leaning against each other, and walked slowly from the room.

Only Lord Ramsey remained in addition to Bernadette, Renard and Charles. Lord Ramsey sipped his whisky, then looked up at Bernadette. "What has happened to our supper?"

She wished she knew how to tie a noose so that she could hang this buffoon from the rafters. What had happened to his supper, indeed? What had just happened to all their lives?

CHAPTER TWENTY

THERE WAS AN air of celebration and liberation in the Mackenzie household that night as they gathered to dine on ham and bread, all of them famished after the calamity at Killeaven. Their concerns over the Mac-Gregor land notwithstanding, they were, all of them, relieved.

Aulay told them of the extraordinary meeting in the garden, how Avaline, unbeknownst to him, had believed there was something unstated between them, and believed it equally felt by him as well.

"It's my fault, it is," Rabbie said. "I left her too often in your company, Aulay. I couldna bear it otherwise."

"Aye, 'tis your fault," Aulay agreed, but then shook his head. "But I canna fault you, lad. She was bloody impossible, that one."

"Be kind, Aulay," Rabbie's mother said. "She is young yet. I feel quite bad for her, really, for she'll have a very uncertain future now. If word were ever to reach certain societies in England about the disaster that occurred at Killeaven tonight, she might never wed."

"How would anyone in England ever know of it?" Catriona asked.

Rabbie's father snorted. "I'd no' put it past Ramsey. Or a servant."

"They will hear of it," Daisy said sagely. "Everyone knew she came to the Highlands to marry and it will not go unnoticed that she didn't. People will sort out why."

They all fell silent a moment.

"What of Killeaven now?" Cailean asked of no one in particular. "He has negotiated for the MacGregor land. What will he do now, then?"

"Niall has said the Buchanans have kept a close eye on Killeaven. I suspect they might put a son forth to offer, aye?" Rabbie said. "It would put them in direct competition for grazing land with us, would it no', and with a wee bit of help from Kent, they'll put a ship to sea."

"Oh, dear," said his mother. "That does not bode well for us."

"No," the laird agreed. "We'll manage, we will. Mackenzies have survived the worst of times, have we no'?"

Rabbie wished he could be as confident as his father was in that belief.

"Rabbie?" his mother said. "We've not inquired after you, darling. How are you, given all that's happened this evening?"

"Relieved," he said.

"As are we all," Aulay muttered.

Rabbie couldn't say more than that, not yet. But in truth, he was elated. A great burden had been lifted from him, and he'd not realized just how heavy that weight had been until he'd been freed of it.

"How did she ever believe that *Aulay*, of all people, held her in some esteem?" Catriona asked, shaking her head.

"What do you mean, then, of *all* people," Aulay asked laughingly. "*Och*, I donna know, lass. She's as barmy as a bird."

"Well, I'm relieved for you, Rabbie," Daisy said. "I should hate to think of you attached to that family. To think they've employed someone of Miss Holly's reputation to attend her. There is something quite pedestrian about them."

"Miss Holly?" Cailean asked, confused.

Aulay, Rabbie noticed, was peering at him.

"Oh, pay me no mind," Daisy said, and waved her hand. "She was involved in a bit of scandal a few years ago. It was a long time ago—I should not have mentioned it."

"Good riddance to the *Sassenach*," Catriona said, and lifted her glass. "To the Mackenzies. To our good health, to Balhaire."

"To the Mackenzies!" they all said in unison, lifting their glasses in toast.

They fell into conversation about how soon Aulay might sail, how soon before Cailean, Daisy, Ellis and wee Georgina would return to Chatwick Hall.

Avaline Kent would be erased from their memory in the coming weeks, and they would congratulate themselves on somehow having avoided that wretched union. They would determine a new path to save their clan and deal with the Buchanans, perhaps a harder one when it was all said and done, but the laird was right—their lives would go on.

But Rabbie? He had only one thought: Bernadette.

AT DAWN THE following day, Rabbie left Balhaire. He intended to return to Arrandale, to think about what he would do about Bernadette now that the wedding had ended, but at the last moment, he turned toward the sea, drawn by a feeling. At the cliff—*his* cliff, where he'd contemplated leaping to his death only a fortnight ago—he sat under an oak and waited.

The sun continued its steady rise, and he had no idea how much time had passed. Long enough that his belly growled with hunger. Long enough that he removed his cloak, the sun's warmth making itself known. Rabbie was about to concede his intuition had been wrong, and stood up and brushed off his clothing. That's when he saw her. She was walking up the path, her head down, her arms swinging, her stride long, the clomping sound of her too-large boots reaching him.

She suddenly paused midstride and looked up, almost as if she'd sensed him there. They stared at each other across that distance, and it felt to him as if a river of understanding flowed between them—relief. Joy. *Desire.*

And then she was running toward him. He ran, too, catching her up in his arms, burying his face in her neck, breathing in her scent, kissing her. He set her down, cupped her head in his hands. "Come. We'll talk at Arrandale, aye?"

For once, she didn't argue. She slipped her hand into his, and ran up the path with him.

He pushed his horse to run hard, and they arrived at Arrandale in half the time it should have taken. He helped Bernadette down from the mount.

"Your servants," she said, uncertainly.

"They'll be gone from their morning chores, to Auchenard now. They'll no' return before the afternoon," he said, and with his hand on the small of her back, he hurried her inside.

Inside, Bernadette looked around her with an expression of someone who expected to find an unwelcome surprise.

"Are you all right, *leannan*?" he asked. "No harm has come to you, aye?"

"What?" She shifted her gaze from the furnishings to him. "No, no harm," she said. "I'm fine."

Except that she didn't look fine. She looked as stunned as she'd appeared last night.

He tossed his cloak onto a chair. "And Avaline? How does she fare?"

Bernadette winced and shook her head. "It's chaos at Killeaven. His lordship has gone to call on a man he calls Buchanan, and has inquired after a caretaker for the property. He and Lord Ramsey mean to take their leave straightaway, as soon as they find passage. He's so angry, Rabbie."

"What of Avaline and her mother?"

She shook her head. "He refuses to accompany them back to England. He swears he can't bear the sight of them and has told them they might rot at Killeaven for all he cares. They are, of course, frantic, as they have no idea how they will return to England and are frightened of staying on without the least bit of protection."

Rabbie could well imagine how intimidating the prospect would seem to the two Kent women, particularly with no friendly faces around them. Neither of them possessed the fortitude necessary to live in the Highlands. "Aulay will see them to England," he said.

Bernadette's bonny eyes rounded. "Aulay!"

"Aye, Aulay. He intends to sail in two days as it is, returning my brother and his family to England. Cailean and Daisy will see Lady Kent and Avaline safely home."

"He would be so kind after all that has happened?" Bernadette said. "What *did* happen, Rabbie? Avaline wouldn't speak of it. She's scarcely stopped weeping since last night."

"I donna know, really," Rabbie said. "Aulay said she had a fanciful notion that he esteemed her."

"Foolish, *foolish* girl!" Bernadette said, and fisted her hands, knocking them against her legs in frustration. "Now what will become of her? I tried to warn her, I begged her to cry off—"

"It's my fault," Rabbie said brusquely. "I wouldna give her the attention as I ought to have done. But I'd no' fret over her future, were I you. I rather suspect she'll have more Scottish suitors. Killeaven is valuable property."

"No," Bernadette said. "They're all going home and they won't come back, I swear it. Avaline is too humiliated." She ran her hand over her head, resting it on the crown a moment, then dropped it. She looked as if her thoughts had taken her out of this room.

"And what of you, Bernadette?" he asked quietly. "What will become of you?"

She jerked her gaze to him when he asked, and a shot of uneasiness sluiced through Rabbie. "I'm to stay behind until a caretaker can be arranged and installed."

That sliver of uneasiness began to rush like a river. "And then what?" he asked, his voice damnably weak.

"I suppose I am to return to my parents in Highfield."

He shifted closer to her. "I wouldna like to see you go," he said. "God has shined His light upon me and I donna want to lose you." He reached for her, drawing her into his arms. "I *canna* lose you, Bernadette," he said, and lowered his head to kiss her. The moment their lips touched, a violent turmoil of desire rose up in him so strong that it felt as if he might disintegrate with it. His arms slid around her back and he held her tightly to him. The kiss was urgent, and Bernadette clung to his neck, almost as if she feared he would step away if she let go.

There was no inhibition between them now—their want had been laid bare. Rabbie would not have believed it possible to feel this way again, but this desire for her pulsed in him like a living, breathing thing.

He lifted his head, impulsively kissed the palm of her hand that she'd pressed against his face, then roughly took her head in his hands and gazed at her. "Where did you come from? How did you appear on my cliff?" It was a rhetorical question, but it mystified him how this woman, this *Sassenach*, might have presented herself when he needed her most. He grabbed her up, lifted her off her feet and kissed her, then walked with her to the settee, falling onto it with her. He pressed his lips against her cheek, her eyes, and her mouth again. "I've fought my desire for you, I have, but I'm powerless against it."

"As am I," she admitted, and dipped her tongue into his mouth, and sent a wave of prurience crashing through him, pushing him into the deep of absolute desire.

He shifted onto his back, pulling Bernadette on top of him, his hands on her body, his lips on her mouth, on her face, her ears and neck. He was intoxicated with her soft lips, the weight of her breasts, the curve of her hip. The bedlam of the last twenty-four hours fell away—Rabbie was only aware of Bernadette, of her scent, of the feel of her hair beneath his fingers, of the smoothness of her skin.

He had to have her out of the gown. He rose up, his fingers working on the fasteners of her gown, then the stomacher, until he could reach the strings of the stay.

As he worked to disrobe her, she fumbled with his neck cloth, pulling it free, and undid the buttons of his waistcoat. In a flurry of movements, his chest was bared to her, and her breasts to him. He took them in his hands, and Bernadette gasped softly, then dropped her head back with a sigh of longing.

This beautiful woman before him who longed to be touched was an elixir to Rabbie. She was a salve to his mortally wounded soul and he couldn't imagine anyone else, not even Seona, being the person he needed at this moment in his life. Only her.

He twisted again, this time standing up with her. With her gown dragging behind her, he began to move her across the salon and down the corridor to his room. He put her on her back on his bed and crawled over her, taking her breast in his mouth.

Purely male instinct was guiding him now, his hands and his body moving without his conscious thought, his body striving to feel every bit of her, his desire to give her pleasure overwhelming him.

She was growing impatient—she undid the buttons of his pantaloons, pushing them down his hips, then taking him in hand, stroking him. Any splinters of reason that had remained in his thoughts tumbled away. He pushed up, bracing himself above her with his arms, and stared down at her. *Diah*, but she was arresting in her beauty. Had she been so beautiful the first moment he'd laid eyes on her? Because there was no woman on earth who could possibly compare to her now. He couldn't look away from her body, ferociously aroused by her stark femininity.

She watched him take her in, her expression full of tenderness and another emotion that shone bright. That emotion felt like love. Rabbie could *feel* her loving him, and the crack in the shell around his heart widened.

He took her hand and laced his fingers through hers, curling his around her hand. *"Mo maise,"* he said. *My beauty*.

Bernadette's smile made his heart ache with it. She lifted up to him to kiss him. Her arms went around

his neck and she pressed her breasts against him, and
Rabbie could feel himself untangling, as if his heart
and lungs and limbs had been pulled into a knot with
every trial over the last few years and were finally,
at long last, letting go. He pressed the tip of his body
against her. His pulse was beating too fast, his heart
pounding too hard. He moved to her breasts, his hand
floating down her side and across her belly, then down
again, between their bodies, stroking her as he slowly
pushed into her.

Bernadette growled and arched her neck as he entered her. She was warm and wet, her body welcoming. Rabbie began to move, straining to hold back and
take his time, but his restraint was rapidly eroding as
need built in him. It had been years since he'd felt such
desire. He'd forgotten what it was to feel alive, to feel
his body erupt into flames.

Bernadette was moving against him, her body rising to meet his, urging him to move harder and faster.
Her hands gripped at him, clutching him, holding on
to him. He was so hard, so hot and moving in her
with such force that he had the fleeting thought he
might harm her in his eagerness. But Bernadette kept
pressing back, kept digging her fingers into his hips,
pushing him deeper inside her. She was panting, near-
ing her climax, and he covered her mouth in a kiss as
he thrust powerfully into her. She cried out nonetheless, her body shuddering against his, and the waves
of pleasure crashed over Rabbie, submerging him in
carnal bliss.

He collapsed beside her, completely spent. Her

breathing was as ravaged as his, and a few moments passed before he became aware of her fingers in his hair, and then sliding along his spine.

Rabbie lifted himself up. Her eyes had gone soft, the color of autumn leaves. He thought of how it would be to wake to her each morning, to walk with her along the loch. To give her children, to grow old with her.

"What is it?" she asked, and casually brushed his hair from his forehead.

He shook his head, his heart still affected by their lovemaking, his mind still swimming in images he'd not allowed himself to see until this very moment.

She kissed the corner of his mouth, then pushed herself up to sitting. Her hair had come undone from the braid. When had that happened? He put his hand on her back, caressing her skin as she braided her hair with swift efficiency. When she was done, she smiled at him over her shoulder, her gaze full of contentment, a woman well pleasured. "What are you thinking?" she asked, her smile turning playful.

That she was so artless in her beauty. That she was the sort of woman he could spend his life with. *"Mo nighean dubh,"* he said. *My dark-haired lass.*

She gave him a sultry smile as she pushed the bed linens off her legs. "I haven't the slightest idea what you mean," she said. She reached for a plaid at the end of his bed and wrapped it around her shoulders, then moved as if to stand.

"No," he said, and put his hand on her arm. "Stay here, with me."

She smiled and laid next to him, her back to his

chest. He slipped his arm around her middle and held her tight.

"Imagine how it could be," he said into her fragrant hair. "You and I. The two of us."

"The two of us?" she murmured.

"Aye. The two of us, *leannan*. Imagine it—waking to each other each new morn, filling this house with children, the future of the Highlands—"

She stiffened. And then abruptly sat up and pulled the plaid tighter.

Rabbie was startled by her reaction. "What have I said, then?" he asked. "Am I wrong? Now that the betrothal is ended, is it no' true that we—"

"What are you saying?" she said frantically, and stood up from the bed.

Rabbie rose up on his elbow, confused by the sudden change in her. "You know verra well. What I meant when I brought you into my bed, aye? We can be one now."

"No!" she exclaimed, shaking her head. "How can you think it? Of *course* we can't, Rabbie."

He was confused by her reaction. "Why no'? I am no longer betrothed and you—"

"I am still a lady's maid to the woman who was your fiancée."

He couldn't understand her. "*Diah*, Bernadette, I am offering for you hand. I want to marry you, aye?"

Her eyes widened with alarm. "*No,*" she said frantically.

The tender emotions he'd been experiencing began

to disappear. "Why in bloody hell no'?" he demanded, coming to his feet.

"We scarcely know each other!"

"We donna?" he asked, gesturing to the bed, to his nakedness.

She flushed. She avoided his gaze by stooping down to gather her clothing. "I mean that we've not spent sufficient time in one another's company—"

"I donna care. I know that I've no' felt as strongly for someone as I do for you, Bernadette."

She looked at him sharply. "What of Seona?"

The words startled him. "She's gone," he said. "You said I should no' live in the past. And this," he said, pointing to her, "is no' the same as that was, Bernadette. You are a verra different woman and I am a different man than I was then. I've fallen in love with you, *mo chridhe*."

Her eyes filled with myriad emotions. Shock and tenderness, and something else, something that made him think of fear. She looked as if she wanted to speak, but then pressed her lips together as she dipped down to pick up the last of her clothing. She dropped the plaid and quickly began to dress.

Rabbie watched her, uncertain as to what was happening between them. What had he misunderstood? Had he been the only one in that bed? "What is the matter?" he asked, a little frantic himself now.

"Everything!" She tossed his pantaloons at him. "You can't say those things to me," she said, her voice rough with emotion. "Your engagement to Avaline has just ended in the most spectacular fashion—"

"What has that to do with it?" he asked with frustration as he thrust one leg and then the other into his pantaloons.

"I am her friend!" she cried.

"*Och,*" he said, and grabbed up his shirt. "You are no' her friend, Bernadette. You are her servant—"

"And her friend! Do you see? There is a so much you don't *understand*, so much you don't know," she said, and caught what sounded like a sob in her throat as she fumbled with the fastenings of her stomacher.

Rabbie reached out to help her. She tried to move away but he clucked his tongue at her and did up the last hooks of her stomacher. She donned her gown as quickly as she could, tears slipping down her cheeks. He reached for her again, but she said, "*Don't.* Please, I beg of you, don't." She turned away from him.

He stood helplessly, trying to comprehend what was happening. "What is it, *leannan*?" he begged her. "What has you in tears?"

"I have to leave," she said shortly. Her voice sounded as if she was determined to go, but her eyes, when she looked back at him... Her eyes said differently.

He strode forward and wrapped his arms around her in a strong embrace. She tried to resist it at first, but when he wouldn't let go of her, she sagged against him and began to cry. Fat tears that wet his chest. "Ah, *mo chridhe*, what has you wrought?" he asked, cupping her head, resting his chin lightly on top of her head as he held her. "I'll no' have you so sad, aye? Tell me."

She shook her head and slowly lifted her head, leaning back from him. "I can't... I'm wrong for you, Rabbie. I wish I was the one, you've no idea how I wish it. But I'm wrong for you—you need a Scots woman."

"I need *you*," he argued.

More tears fell. She put her hands up between them, placed them against his bare chest, then pushed against him. Hard. His arms fell away from her, and she stepped back. She picked up her boots and clutched them to her chest like a shield. "No one brought you back but you. I'm sorry, I am truly so very sorry, but I am leaving for England when arrangements have been made for Killeaven, and there is nothing you can stay that will dissuade me from it."

The words she spoke were harsh to his ears, but they did not match the tears sliding down her cheeks.

"No," he said, and he meant it. She would not leave for England. He didn't know how he'd prevent it, but he would. His heart began to pound in his chest with trepidation. He couldn't allow this to happen. Not now, not after he'd found something to live for.

But as he moved to reach for her again, Bernadette shook her head and fled the room, and he could hear the slap of her bare feet on the stone floor as she hurried down the corridor. A moment later, he heard the front door shut.

Rabbie stood precisely where she'd left him, utterly stunned. He didn't understand what had happened. He was wounded, he was angry…but more than anything else, he didn't believe her. He'd seen the way she'd looked at him, had felt the way she'd responded to him, and he didn't believe there was nothing that could change her mind.

Aye, but he was angry with her at the moment. He didn't know what held her back—was it her child? He'd not thought of it until this moment, but if that was what had made her refuse him, he'd go and fetch the bairn himself. If he had to fight for her and what existed between them, so be it, he would, without hesitation.

He *would* fight for her, too. He'd been robbed of the opportunity to fight for a woman he'd once cared for and he'd not be robbed again. He'd not *lose* again.

But he had to unearth the reason for her trouble and change her mind.

RABBIE NUMBLY WANDERED about Arrandale, wanting an occupation, his mind racing, his thoughts so scattered that he couldn't seem to concentrate on any one task. He was confused by what had happened—how could a woman make love as she had then turn so coldly against him? It made him heartsick with doubt. His thoughts had begun to turn dark, and he was relieved when he heard riders on the lawn, relieved to have a diversion.

He walked outside and found Cailean, Daisy and Ellis coming down from their mounts.

Cailean glanced at Rabbie's plaid. "Do you want them to hang you, lad?" he asked jovially.

"I donna care if they do," Rabbie said with a shrug. "What brings you to Arrandale?"

"We've come to see after your welfare, darling," Daisy said, and rose up on her toes to kiss his cheek.

"My welfare," Rabbie repeated. He didn't think it

was wise to mention that it had been shattered this morning by the tears of a *Sassenach*.

"Well, yes," she said as she adjusted her hat. "Yesterday must have been rather an ordeal for you."

"Yesterday was a release from my chains," he said.

Daisy smiled, but young Ellis frowned mightily at his remark. "It wasn't Miss Kent's fault," he said. "It's her father who is to blame."

"Aye, that he is," Rabbie agreed, and motioned for them to come inside.

"Ellis is right," Daisy said as she removed her gloves in his great room. "I do worry for Miss Kent."

"I understand that Kent and his brother mean to depart immediately, without his wife and daughter," Rabbie said. "I offered that perhaps you'd see Lady Kent and Avaline safely to England, aye?"

"Oh," Daisy said, and glanced at her husband. "Who has said they are to leave?" she asked curiously.

Rabbie had spoken without thought—he'd given a bit of his secret away, and turned to the sideboard, hoping no one noticed his flush. "Miss Holly," he said. "She came round to inquire on their behalf."

"Aye, we will," Cailean said. "I'll send Niall around on the morrow to offer."

"I have thought quite a lot about her," Daisy said quite casually.

"Who?" Cailean asked.

"Miss Holly."

Rabbie turned around from the sideboard. "Aye, and why is that?" he asked carefully, his gaze on the window, afraid that he might reveal himself yet.

"Oh, I don't know," Daisy said. "I suppose I was rather unkind about her yesterday, but in thinking about it, I've recalled the talk about her elopement."

Rabbie was not surprised. He guessed that news had spread through northern England when it happened. Certainly that would have happened in the Highlands had she been a Scot.

"They say she and her new husband were caught by her father's men right after they supposedly took their vows. The marriage was annulled straightaway," Daisy said softly, her gaze on Ellis as he wandered about the room. "How awful that must have been for her."

"Aye," Cailean agreed.

Ellis moved away from them, apparently uninterested in the gossip. With his hands at his back, he wandered to the far end of the great room to examine a claymore Cailean had placed on a wall when he'd built Arrandale. It had belonged to their grandfather.

"You said there was a bairn," Rabbie said, his gaze fixed on Ellis. He couldn't look at Daisy, couldn't let her see the rush of emotions that were suddenly churning in him. "What happened to it?"

"I don't know," Daisy said. "Her father is very wealthy, you know. He makes iron. I remember there was some speculation…"

"Look, Pappa," Ellis said, standing next to the claymore. "It's as tall as me."

"Aye, that belonged to our *seanair*, our grandfather," Cailean said, and walked across the room to have a look with Ellis.

"What speculation?" Rabbie asked Daisy. "That she

abandoned it?" It was the only thing that made sense to him, the only reason she might be in Scotland with a young mistress instead of with her child.

"No…that she lost it," Daisy whispered.

Rabbie's gut plummeted.

"Mamma, you must come and look!" Ellis said excitedly.

"What is it, a sword?" Daisy asked, moving in that direction.

Rabbie remained rooted. He was filled with sorrow for Bernadette. He could understand why she'd not told him this part of her story, too. Was that it, then, the thing that kept her from agreeing that they ought to be together? Did she have some macabre need to be near the bairn's grave? He realized that he didn't care what scandals she'd been involved in. He didn't care if she'd loved before. It hurt him that she'd lost a bairn, but it didn't change his opinion of her in the least. After all that he'd endured, there was nothing Bernadette could do or say or admit to him now that would persuade him against loving her.

Nothing.

CHAPTER TWENTY-ONE

AVALINE HAD CRIED until she couldn't possibly shed another tear.

Her father and uncle had departed Killeaven two days after the disaster of her declaring her love to Aulay. She shuddered every time she thought of it. What a fool she'd been! And oh, how she hated Aulay now; hated him with the strength of a thousand suns.

She'd been so certain that he returned her affections! Wasn't he always at her side? Had he not smiled and complimented her? And then to so cruelly and openly deny her! To allow her lips to touch his then to react as if he'd been bitten by an asp! Twice her age, he'd said, as if that had any bearing. A ship's captain, he'd said, as if she was not allowed on the sea alongside him.

Yes, Avaline, despised Aulay Mackenzie and Scotland and Killeaven. To think she'd once thought this decrepit pile of rocks could be her home!

She couldn't wait to leave this place.

How she would leave this place was another question entirely.

That question was answered, apparently, when Mr. MacDonald arrived from Balhaire and asked for an audience with Avaline and her mother. "Mr. Cailean

Mackenzie has asked me to invite you to sail with him and Mrs. Mackenzie to England. He has asked me to say that he will see you safely home, then."

"Sail," Avaline said. "On whose ship?"

"The Mackenzie ship," Mr. MacDonald said.

"No!" Avaline said instantly, and looked at her mother, incredulous that anyone would suggest such a thing after all she'd been through.

But her mother did not look at her. Her mother said calmly, "Thank you, Mr. MacDonald. When shall we depart?"

Avaline gasped with outrage. *"No!"* she shouted. "How can you even think of it, Mamma? You *know* who captains that ship! You saw what he did to me!"

"I also know we have no other means home," her mother snapped. "When should we be ready to depart, Mr. MacDonald?" she stubbornly demanded.

And so it was set—Avaline would be forced to board that devil's ship. They had two days to prepare.

Bernadette was desperate to help Avaline, but Avaline didn't want her help. She might have kept Bernadette's wretched secret, but she was really rather cross with her. Bernadette had been so distracted by her own affair that she hadn't been there to help Avaline when she needed her most. If her lady's maid had been paying closer attention to her, perhaps Avaline would have confided in her. Perhaps Bernadette might have stopped her from making a horrid mistake.

But she hadn't, and at present, Avaline could scarcely stand the sight of her, either. She left her packing to Bernadette and quit her rooms so she'd not have to look at her at all.

Two DAYS LATER, with as many of their belongings gathered as they could carry, Avaline and her mother set off for Balhaire.

Bernadette looked rather tearful as she hugged Avaline's mother goodbye.

She turned to Avaline, and while Avaline leaned forward so that Bernadette could put her arms about her, she refused to look her in the eye.

"Godspeed, darling," Bernadette said.

"Thank you," Avaline said coolly, and turned away from her, stepping into the coach.

She couldn't look at Bernadette then, but she did glance out the window as the coach began to roll forward, and saw Bernadette standing there, watching her, her expression full of sorrow. Avaline had felt tears burning in her eyes. Fortunately, none were shed, as she'd spent them all.

At Balhaire, they were directed straightaway to the cove. They boarded the ship without any greeting whatsoever from the captain, for which Avaline was thankful. They were shown to their cabin and Avaline swore to herself she'd not leave it, she'd hide away here like a stowaway until they reached England's shores.

Unfortunately, that night, the seas grew rough and her mother grew ill. Avaline could not bear all the retching and gathered her cloak about her. "Are you certain there is nothing I can do for you?" she asked, even though her hand was already on the door latch.

Her mother responded by retching again into the bucket.

With a shiver, Avaline hurried out.

She kept near the forecastle, away from the aft castle, where the captain's quarters were located. There were seamen roaming about, and Avaline put herself near the railing, as to keep out of their path and not invite any conversation. She stood facing the sea, staring out over the rolling waves, at the faint swath of moonlight the sometimes broke through the clouds.

"You ought not to be about."

Avaline closed her eyes and prayed for forbearance, then turned around to face Lord Chatwick. "Are you *following* me?"

"No," he said, and lifted his chin, where a few hairs had sprouted. This, she'd noted in the course of that very long meal she'd endure in his company at Balhaire. "I was having a bit of a stroll and happened to see you here. You should be in your cabin. It's not safe to be about in the dark. No one would know if you fell overboard."

"I won't fall overboard, and you are not my father," Avaline said haughtily.

"No, but I am the one seeing you safely to England," he said with great authority.

As if he could see her safely anywhere. He was taller than her by a very few inches and as thin as a sapling. He couldn't protect her from as much as a headwind.

"Fine," she snapped. "I prefer the company of my mother retching into a bucket than a boy scarcely out of his mother's arms." She stepped around him and marched on.

Naturally, Lord Chatwick fell in beside her. "You'd

not speak to me in that manner if I had reached my majority. Perhaps you are unaware of all that comes with my title."

"I hardly care."

"You are not in a position to be rude, Miss Kent."

She rolled her eyes and tried to hurry her step, but Lord Chatwick kept pace with her.

"I will be a great man one day, and you will regret treating me ill."

"I will regret nothing," Avaline said sharply.

"Nothing?" he asked.

Avaline's stomach dipped. They had reached the door to her cabin. She glared at the young man. "I beg you, my lord—please leave me be. I know you hold me in some esteem, but I do not return it." She went in through the door and shut it firmly, then sighed with relief. She would *not* leave her cabin, not for a moment. She'd not have that young and boastful pup following after her.

Her fierce resolve in this decision was shattered like fine crystal not two days later when her mother explained to her they would be traveling on to Chatwick Hall with the Mackenzies for a time.

"But *why*?" Avaline demanded. "I want to go home!"

"Yes, well, your father does not want you home, not as yet. He is quite well bruised from your behavior. And Mrs. Mackenzie has very graciously offered us a place to reside until such time cooler heads prevail."

Avaline felt as if her entire world had collapsed in on her. Only a few short weeks ago, she was to be married. Now she was a pariah, forced to live under the roof of a boy who thought himself superior to her in every way. And worse, he had witnessed her complete humiliation. She would never survive it. *Never.*

CHAPTER TWENTY-TWO

EVERYONE HAD LEFT KILLEAVEN, save Charles and Bernadette, two stable hands and Ina, who had stayed on to help with the cooking and cleaning. They had very little to occupy them now that the furnishings had been moved and the horses sold or returned to the seller. Niall MacDonald had come round and told them a ship would arrive in a day or so and ferry them back to England. "A MacDonald ship," he'd said. "Cousins of mine, then."

All they had left to do was wait.

Bernadette moved like the dead through each day, wandering listlessly from room to room. She could think of little else other than Rabbie, of how he'd felt inside her, of how she'd felt when he'd held her. She thought of the things he said, of how his words had spilled into her heart. She loved him, and realizing that she did made it all the more painful. She wished she could turn back time. She wished she'd never taken a walk that day and seen him standing on the edge of the cliff.

What was he doing since she'd fled Arrandale? Did he mourn her? Hate her? Every sound, every jangle of a horse's bridle, she thought was him. Part of her hoped he would come to her. Part of her hoped she never saw him again so she'd be spared the agony. All of her wished she could lie down and sleep for all eternity, and wake up with no memory of what had happened here.

Two days after Lady Kent and Avaline had departed, she heard a horse on the drive and her heart skipped. She was certain it was Rabbie—who else could it be? There was no one left to come to Killeaven. She threw aside the linens she was packing away in a trunk and ran to the door, her heart thudding with relief and anxiety at once. She threw open the door—

It was not Rabbie who had come up the drive, but two men, one of whom she'd seen before, on the path by the sea. Their coats were caked with the dirt of the road, their uncombed hair tied in queues. They came down off their mounts and sauntered forward, taking in the house and peering curiously at her.

Bernadette was relieved when she felt Charles at her back. "Yes, my lords?" he said, stepping around her as he walked out to greet them.

"Who might you be, then?" one of them asked.

"Charles Farrington, sir. I am the caretaker here."

"No' for long, lad. No' for long," the other one said, and chuckled darkly as he walked past Charles, brushed past Bernadette and carried on into the house, as if he was master here.

"I beg your pardon," Charles said gruffly to the other man, who appeared twenty years older than the first. "Who are you?

"Bhaltair Buchanan," he said, and bowed with an

exaggerated flourish before rising up. His gaze raked over Charles. "You're a wee bit lean for a caretaker in these parts if you ask me."

"I didn't ask you," Charles said.

The man grinned, showing the absence of a pair of teeth, then fixed his gaze on Bernadette. "Well, then, here you are, lass. No' lost at all." He deliberately moved his eyes down her body to her slippers and back up again, as Bernadette worked to suppress a strong shiver of revulsion.

He grinned again, then walked on, following the other man inside.

"What does he mean, 'you're not lost'?" Charles asked gruffly.

"I met him on the path by the sea one day," Bernadette said. "I thought he was only passing by."

"No," Charles said. "These are the men that ride up on the hill to have a look at Killeaven. Let's see what they're about."

Bernadette and Charles followed the two men inside, then stood stiffly by as the two of them roamed about the house as if they were owners here, remarking to each other in Gaelic as they pointed at this and that. When they had apparently satisfied themselves with the tour, they returned to the foyer.

Bhaltair Buchanan paused, and his eyes drifted to Bernadette. "Are you part and parcel of the property, then?"

Charles immediately moved forward to stand in front of Bernadette. "We take our leave in four days, sir," he said. "You may have entry then."

The man's gap-toothed smile was cold. He nodded at the younger one, who opened the front door. "We'll come back when we please and toss out any rubbish that remains, aye?" His gaze slid to Bernadette again. "Or find a new use for it…if Mackenzie hasna done it first."

Bernadette's heart climbed to her throat.

"Good day," Charles said briskly, and gestured for them to carry on outside.

He followed them out on to the path, standing before the door with his legs braced apart until the men had disappeared from view. Only then did he turn back to Bernadette. "I don't trust them."

"No," she said. She was shaking, she realized.

"We should send to Balhaire for help," he said, his expression stern. "I don't trust them and we have no means of protecting ourselves. You know how they feel about Englishmen here." He walked into the house, calling for Ina. When she appeared, he said, "Fetch me one of the stable boys. Tell them to be ready to ride."

"No, wait," Bernadette said. "You're right, we should send for help. But I'll go."

Charles hesitated.

"At least the Mackenzies know who I am. They won't know a stable hand and they'd not give him an audience with the laird."

"You're right," Charles said, nodding. "Then go. Take one of the stable boys with you and make haste. None of your meandering walks."

"No, of course not," she agreed, and went in search of her boots.

She and the young stable boy arrived at Balhaire a little more than an hour later. She walked up the high road and into the bailey, and pushed through a gathering of dogs wanting a good sniff of her boots. She went to the massive entry door and used the door knocker several times before it finally opened.

Frang, the dour butler, stared down his nose at her. "Aye?"

"Good afternoon," she said.

Frang did not respond.

"I've come with an important message for Lady Mackenzie. Will you please announce me?"

"The lady is away from Balhaire," he said.

Bernadette felt a tiny tic of panic. "What of Miss Mackenzie?" she asked.

"Aye, gone too," Frang said.

Bernadette swallowed down her pride. "Please, sir, is there someone I might speak to? It's really rather important—"

"No. None of them here, aye?"

"Bernadette?"

She twisted around, surprised by the sound of Rabbie's voice. And then she was overwhelmed by it, relieved and grateful and wanting nothing more than to collapse in his arms.

He frowned with concern. "What's wrong?" he asked. "Has something happened, then?"

"Yes, something…" She swallowed.

"Come," he said, and put his hand to her back, ushering her past Frang and into a sitting room. "Sit," he commanded her. He strode to the sideboard, poured a glass of water and returned with it, sitting next to her as he handed her the glass. His presence next to her kicked up the dust of her feelings, still so raw, and they began to eddy in her. Desire. Want. *Love.* All of them mixing together and making her reel.

He laid his hand on hers and said, "Take a breath, *leannan*, then tell me what has happened."

The feel of his hand on hers was more comforting than she had a right to expect. "Two men came," she explained. "Bhaltair Buchanan and another one. They said they would return and throw out any rubbish that remained."

Rabbie nodded.

"They—they were rather menacing, and Charles, the footman, thought we ought to ask for help, because we both had the sense they mean bad business. If help can be spared, that is." She swallowed. "I'd not ask, I wouldn't bother you at all after what…" After what she'd said to him, words that still burned in her gullet. "But we've no protection for ourselves, and we are English…"

"Bloody bastards, the lot of them. Aye, stay here," he said. He stood abruptly and walked out of the receiving room.

Bernadette waited. She drank the water, put the glass aside and stood, too restless to sit. She began to pace before a narrow window. Her palms were damp, and she rubbed then along her sides. Her heart felt erratic, as if it couldn't beat quite fast enough, but then again, it was beating so fast that it felt uncomfortable in her chest, and she wondered if perhaps her heart, made so heavy in these last few days, was giving way.

A few moments later Rabbie swept into the room. "Niall MacDonald will take two men to Killeaven and remain there until the household sails," he said.

"Thank you," she said with a rush of gratitude and reassurance.

"You are welcome here, Bernadette. You will be safe—"

"No, thank you," she said quickly. She couldn't bear it. "I am needed at Killeaven."

"Then I'll take you back," he said.

God in heaven, she couldn't bear that any better. She couldn't ride with him and feel him at her back, his arm around her middle, and hold her emotions in check. She would break apart into pieces. "Thank you. But I'll walk."

Rabbie frowned. He moved closer. "I know why you have put this distance between us, I do," he said. "I know the truth about you, *leannan*, and I donna care."

She felt the blood drain from her face. "Pardon?" No, he couldn't possibly know all of it, and Bernadette began to shake her head.

"Donna hide from me, lass."

"I don't know what you think you know—"

"Daisy recalled your name," he said quietly.

Her body felt as if it was floating, even though she still stood before him. Surely he hadn't heard everything. "I told you that I eloped—"

"I know there was a bairn, Bernadette."

The mention of her lost baby caused Bernadette's

knees to suddenly wobble. She grabbed on to the back of a chair to steady herself, and he caught her arm, leaning over her.

"My deepest condolences, lass. I canna bear to think of your pain."

Her pain. He had no idea how deep her pain was. Bernadette hadn't thought of that night in so long. She'd struggled to put the horror behind her, but at a single mention, it all came smashing through her windows, the force of her memories startling her.

It had been a beautiful summer night, the lawn lit by so many bright stars. She'd been seven months along in her pregnancy. As her belly had grown, so had her father's hatred of her. He'd once adored her, had called her his princess. But he'd never forgiven her elopement or the child growing in her. He'd worked hard for his wealth and had set his sights on substantial social connections, and in his eyes, Bernadette had ruined all he'd worked so hard to achieve.

That night, at the top of the stairs, as he'd gone up to bed and she'd gone down for water, he'd said she disgusted him, and Bernadette...*oh, how it hurt to think of it*.

She put both hands on the back of the chair, fearful that her knees would give away.

"Bernadette?" Rabbie asked, but it seemed as if he was at some distance.

Her father had looked at her with such venom in his eyes and voice and had said, "You disgust me," and Bernadette, who had kept her mouth shut and had accepted his vitriol against her all those months, could bear it no more. She'd said, "And your utter lack of regard for your own grandchild disgusts me."

What had possessed her? Why that night, what that remark?

To this day, Bernadette didn't know how it had happened—had she been standing so close to the top of the stairs? Or had he pushed her? What she remembered was that her father had reacted harshly and instantly, backhanding her across her mouth. She didn't remember the fall at all, only coming to at the bottom of the stairs, the pain in her belly already pressing against her spine and her heart.

She'd started bleeding an hour or so later. The midwife was called. The pain became unbearable and in the throes of it, she'd heard the midwife tell someone that the baby must come out. But it had been too early, and Bernadette had begged them not to take her baby, but her words were only a strangled cry.

What followed was excruciating. Someone inserted something cold and metallic into her that was so painful her heart had fluttered almost dead. She'd felt as if she was being ripped apart, as if someone had plunged daggers into her womb to tear her open.

And then had come that distant, faint voice, saying the baby was dead. How could her baby be dead? They'd said her baby was dead, and Bernadette had found her voice. She'd screamed.

She didn't remember more than that. Apparently, she'd bled so profusely that she'd almost died herself. When she came to, she would wish she'd died.

It was a boy, her mother had said. *A boy.*

"Bernadette, for the love of God," Rabbie said. She felt his hands on her shoulders, pulling her up. Somehow, she had sunk down onto her haunches behind that chair, still clinging to it.

Rabbie helped her around to the chair then squatted in front of her. "Is that why you ran from me? Did you think I'd turn against you if I knew?"

"I ran because I ruined your marriage. And I would ruin your life."

Rabbie stroked her cheek with his knuckle. "You couldna ruin me, *leannan*. I've told you—you've resurrected me, then."

Bernadette began to shake. She shook with the memory of her loss, with the repression of it. She shook with the desire for this man, and she shook knowing that she could never saddle him with all what had happened. She hadn't admitted everything to him... she hadn't really admitted everything to herself. She'd known since that happened that she couldn't bear children, but until this moment, she hadn't admitted to herself that it mattered. God, how it mattered. "Please, Rabbie... Please don't do this. Just let me be."

He might have argued with her, but there was a knock on the door, and as Rabbie rose to his feet, Frang entered. "The mounts are ready," he announced.

THEY ARRIVED AT KILLEAVEN, four men and Bernadette, three of the men with bedrolls and muskets. Charles came out to meet them and speak to Rabbie.

Bernadette made her way inside and sat heavily in

the salon, staring at nothing. She felt empty. Her heart felt as if it had turned to dust.

Charles and Rabbie came inside eventually; Charles said he would take the men to the stables and see that they had a place to sleep. He left Rabbie standing at the salon door.

Bernadette forced herself to stand on numb legs. This was it, then. They would say fare-thee-well until the end of time. Her heart had turned to dust, but there were still bits and pieces of it clinging to life, apparently, because she couldn't look at him without feeling agony. "How I wish you would go," she said. "I can't bear it."

"Bernadette, listen to me," Rabbie said, and moved into the room. "Come with me, now. I donna care about your past, none of it. You'll find no judgment in me, I swear it."

"You don't know what you are saying, Rabbie—"

"Aye, I do—"

"No, you *don't*," she said angrily, her voice suddenly strong. "You don't know all of it!"

"Then for God's sake, *tell* me."

"Will you make me relive it? Is that the only way I can force you to leave me in peace?"

Now he looked confused. Alarmed. "*Diah*, relive what?"

"I'll tell you," she said, her vision blurring with her tears. "Prepare yourself for it, for it is not possible for you to repair it or overlook it."

"*Say* it," he said impatiently.

"I can never bear children, Rabbie. Did you hear

me? *Never*. I can't give you sons. I can't fill your house with children. I am *worthless*." She pressed her hands to her abdomen and bent over, squeezing her eyes shut against the rash of hot tears that threatened to fall.

"Bernadette—"

"When I lost that child, I lost the ability to bear children. I will spare you the horrifying details of it, but you must know that I am worthless to you." She looked up.

"That doesna make you worthless—"

"Of course it does," she said bitterly. "Don't be a fool, Rabbie—you will want heirs. Just go, will you?"

Rabbie didn't move. He stood rooted, staring at her, his expression incredulous and confused. Or perhaps it was revulsion she saw in him. Well, then, so be it. If she could change the truth, she would give all that she had to do it, but she couldn't. "Please, I am begging you—just go." She felt ill, felt like she might faint, and she turned away from him, moving unevenly to the window.

"Verra well," he said, his voice so low she could scarcely hear him. She heard him quit the room, heard his footfalls on the stone floor, heard the door open and shut.

Apparently, Rabbie couldn't forgive everything. Bernadette turned around, hoping that she'd somehow misheard, hoping that he was still standing before her. But he was gone.

She bolted for her room and the window, bracing against it, watching him ride down the road, away from her, his horse at a gallop. He was *racing* away from her. He couldn't wait to be as far from her as he possibly could, and she didn't blame him.

She turned from the sight of his departure and threw herself on her bed as sobs racked her body. She loved Rabbie Mackenzie. Against all odds, she'd found someone to love again, and her father was right, she'd destroyed everything.

CHAPTER TWENTY-THREE

RABBIE'S GRIP OF the reins had been so tight that his fingers ached. He stretched them out, then closed them, then stretched them again as he walked to the edge of the cliff.

He stood there, his hands on his waist, his mind a chaotic brew as he tried to grasp the implications of what Bernadette had told him. She was ruined for any gentleman—he could well imagine how quickly the fops and dandies in England would shun her. Most Scots would shun her, too.

In all honesty, her news had given him some pause, as well—it was one thing to accept the woman you loved had given birth to another man's bairn. It was quite another to know the woman you loved couldn't give you one. But nevertheless, Rabbie had heard her news and had seen her in a different light. His good opinion of her had not changed—if anything, it had made his heart ache for her.

He understood her loss. He realized that the whole of her tragedy had been as great as his, and yet, she'd managed the consequences with grace.

Hers was a sobering story, and while Rabbie was grateful to her for telling him the truth, he could not deny it had affected his earlier optimism and hope that after long last, there might be happiness for him. Because in these last days, when he'd thought of Bernadette, he'd thought of family. He'd thought of sons and daughters, of a raucous household like the one in which he'd been raised. That dream had faded somewhat.

He glanced down at the cove below. The sea was calm, and from this high above it, the water appeared to be gently lapping the shore. It was, and always had been, a safe harbor.

A safe harbor.

Rabbie suddenly realized what he had to do. He stepped away from the edge, returned to his horse and rode for Balhaire.

When he reached the bailey, he handed the horse over to a stable hand and strode into the castle. He did not go to the great hall, but went directly to the kitchen.

Fiona and Ualan were there, all right. Ualan was at a small table near the window, polishing silver. Fiona was seated on a stool, her ankles crossed and her feet swinging above the ground. She was humming as she carefully cut potatoes.

"Aye, sir?" Barabel asked, wiping her hands on her apron.

Rabbie should have been more attentive to these children, but his own pain and guilt had kept him from it. From quite a lot of life, he realized, and he was suddenly ashamed of it. He wanted to discard the hurt, toss it aside like a worn bit of plaid. He looked at the MacLeod children and thought of how desperately they needed someone. As Vivienne had said, someone to look over them, to tuck them in at night.

"Can I do something for you?" Barabel asked in Gaelic.

Both children looked up then. Fiona gasped with delight. "Did you bring us sweetmeats?"

"Uist," Barabel said, scolding the lass into silence.

"Beg your pardon, but I'd like a word with Fiona and Ualan," Rabbie said.

Fiona didn't wait for permission; she hopped off the stool. Ualan looked concerned. Rabbie motioned for them to come, and Ualan put his cloth down and followed Fiona as she hopped to where Rabbie stood.

Rabbie took them out into the corridor for a bit of privacy, and there, he stared down at their upturned faces, debating how to say what he wanted to convey.

He squatted before them, so that he could look them in the eye. He spoke to them in Gaelic. "We've something in common, did you know it? When you lost your parents, I lost my fiancée. I was to marry your Aunt Seona. Had they not gone away, we would be a family now."

"We *would*?" Fiona asked. "Where did Aunt Seona go?"

"They *died*," Ualan muttered to his sister in Gaelic. "They didn't go away."

Rabbie swallowed. "Aye, they died," he softly agreed. He swallowed again, hard. What he was thinking was utter madness. He'd only just come out of the dark—how could he possibly be thinking what was in his heart? And yet, Rabbie blurted it all the same. "I've been thinking… we might have a family yet, the three of us."

Fiona's eyes widened with surprise and she looked at her brother.

"What I mean," Rabbie said, pausing to draw a breath, "is that you might come to live with me at Arrandale. Would you like that?"

Fiona could scarcely contain her delight. But Ualan, the studious lad that he was, remained skeptical. "We're to go to Inverness," he pointed out.

"Aye, but we can change that. Would you rather go to a stranger? Or would you rather remain in the Highlands, with me?"

"I want to stay!" Fiona said.

Ualan eyed him skeptically. "Only three of us?"

"Only three of us," Rabbie confirmed. He'd made up his mind. No matter what else, these two children needed him as much as he needed them.

"But what of Barabel?" Fiona asked.

Rabbie smiled. "We'll visit often."

Fiona began to bounce on her toes. "I want to live with you. What is your name?"

"Rabbie, lass. Uncle Rabbie."

Ualan still hadn't said anything, and Rabbie looked at him, lifting his brow in a silent question.

"Only three of us?" Ualan asked again. "That's not a very big family."

"No. Sometimes, families are rather small. But maybe—maybe there will be four." He shrugged.

"Who?" Ualan persisted.

"*Och*, but you're a shrewd lad," Rabbie said, and told them about Bernadette and how he'd lost her family, too.

THE THREE OF them made the journey to Killeaven the next day. It was a bit of a slow go, as Rabbie could not ride with two children before him, and instead pulled them along in a cart behind his mount. Fiona chattered as they went along, her speech broken between Gaelic and English, the rush of words amazingly ceaseless.

Ualan remained silent. He'd been receptive to Rabbie's suggestion—perhaps because Rabbie had finally described it as an adventure for him—but he remained reticent. Ualan was eight years old now, with very few memories of his family. But perhaps far too many memories of being an orphan in an old woman's care. He did not come easily around to trusting adults, Rabbie noted.

When they reached Killeaven, Niall MacDonald walked out to greet them. "What's this, then?" he asked, grinning at the children. "Have you brought us guards?"

Rabbie smiled. "Is Miss Holly about?"

"I've no' seen her, no," Niall said. "Only the footman."

"Summon him, then."

The footman appeared at the door in an apron and was wiping his hands on the hem of it as he walked out of the house. His gaze slid to the children, then to Rabbie. "Good day, sir."

"Aye, good day. I'd like a word with Miss Holly, then, if you will summon her."

"Miss Holly is unwell," the man said, and dropped his apron, peering at Rabbie curiously.

"Summon her all the same," Rabbie said. "It's a matter of some importance, aye?"

"Very well," he said, and invited them to wait in the salon.

Inside, the children wandered around the room, taking in the furnishings. "Have I ever been here?" Fiona asked.

"No," Ualan said. He had stationed himself at the window. "You've naugh' been anywhere, Fiona."

"Is this where we shall live?" Fiona asked, and bounced onto a settee, testing it.

"No," Rabbie said. He could hear Bernadette now—she was coming down the stairs, her steps heavy. When she walked into the salon, Rabbie was taken aback—much of her hair had been pulled from the knot at her nape and her eyes were swollen. He panicked a wee bit—he didn't know if the children would go along with his plan with Bernadette looking such a fright. She was frightening *him*. "Miss Holly," he said.

"What is…what are you doing?" she asked, her voice dull.

"Allow me to introduce Miss Fiona and Mr. Ualan MacLeod."

"Pardon?" She turned her head to the children. Fiona had fled to Ualan's side and they were standing very close together at the window, gaping at her. Fiona shifted, trying to move behind her brother.

Bernadette lifted her hand and tried vainly to smooth her hair. "A pleasure to make your acquaintance," she said.

Neither of the children spoke.

She looked again at Rabbie. "I don't understand."

"Fiona and Ualan are the niece and nephew of Seona

MacBee. They alone survived…" He hesitated and glanced at the two of them. "Whatever might have happened, aye?"

Bernadette looked at them again. She managed a smile. The children didn't return that smile, but continued to stare at her curiously.

Now Bernadette put her back to them. "What is this about?" she whispered. "Why are they here?"

Rabbie spoke to the children in Gaelic, instructing them to remain at the window so that he might have a word with Miss Holly. Then he took Bernadette by the elbow and moved her as far from them as he could in the space of that room.

"I don't understand!" Bernadette said again. "What are you doing, Rabbie?"

"Helping you," he said. "You told me what happened to you, and then you banished me, aye? You didna want to hear my thoughts. You believed you knew what I'd think, you did."

"I beg your pardon?" she exclaimed, and glanced over her shoulder at the children, then moved closer to him. "What difference can your thoughts possibly make?" she said sharply. "I don't care what you think. I don't want to know what you think, because there is nothing that will change what has happened or what it means."

"That's where you're wrong, Bernadette. I *can* change it."

She snorted.

"I can change it," he said again. "I can love you—I *do* love you, with all my heart, aye? And I can keep you."

She shook her head, and Rabbie grasped her hand, pulling her closer. He leaned in and said, "If you canna bear me children, *leannan*, then I can bear them for you. I can give you happiness, and I will, gladly, I will. But you must believe it can be. You must believe there is another way."

She pulled her hand free and tried to move away, but he caught her by the waist.

"You're speaking nonsense," she whispered harshly. "You expect me to take in children I don't know?"

He had suspected she would react like this, and he was not going to debate it with her. He strode away from her, walked to where the children were standing and kneeled down. He took each of their hands in one of his and spoke softly in Gaelic to them. "Remember what I've told you. Do you remember how it makes you sad that you've no family?"

They both nodded.

"Miss Holly is sad, too. Don't fear her. It will be difficult at first, and she might seem frightening. But I know her—she is kind, and she'll be kind to you." The children glanced over his shoulder and stared at Bernadette. Neither of them seemed inclined to believe it.

"She looks wicked," Fiona whispered.

"She's unhappy," Rabbie said. "She needs a friend." He glanced at Ualan. "I need you both to befriend her."

"I don't like her," Fiona whispered.

"*Och*, lass, you don't know her. You didn't know me, either, and yet you gave me a chance. I think you can do the same for her." He looked at Ualan.

The lad shrugged.

Rabbie smiled. It was all he would get, and he tousled Ualan's hair. "Remember our plan. I'll come for
you tomorrow evening," he said in Gaelic, and kissed
both their cheeks, then stood. "You're Highlanders.
Be brave," he said, and with a wink, he walked away
from them.

Bernadette was hugging herself, watching him
warily. "What did you say? What is happening?"

"They are in need of a place to stay," he said.

It took Bernadette a moment to understand what he
was suggesting, and when she did, she panicked. "You
can't leave them here! We're leaving!"

"You donna leave for two days—"

"But you can't just *abandon* them," she said. "It's
madness! I'm English! Do they know that?"

"Aye, they know it," he said. "And they know to
judge each person on her own merits, aye? That courtesy was no' extended to their family, but they will
extend it to you. They know no' all *Sassenach* are the
diabhal. You'll show them that is true, just as you've
shown me. Help them, Bernadette."

Bernadette looked at the children. "No," she said,
her voice full of panic. But it was too late; Rabbie was
already at the door.

"Rabbie, no! *Wait!*" He could hear her running after
him, and she caught him on the drive, her hand on his
arm, and yanked him with surprising strength. "You
cannot leave those two children alone here!"

"They are no' alone, aye? They are with you."

"Charles won't—"

"I've sent our men to guard the house. I suspect

Charles can be persuaded to house two orphans in return." He shook Bernadette's grip from his sleeve and picked up the reins of his horse.

"Wait!" she cried again, and lunged for his arm, catching it. "I don't know what you mean to prove, but this isn't the way to do it. I can't keep those children. I don't know the first thing of it!"

"They are alone in the world with no one to care for them, like you, Bernadette. *I* am going to care for them. I will care for you, as well, if you'll allow it. Those two bairns donna fault you for anything that has happened in the past and neither do I. The only thing they want, the *only* thing, is to be loved. That's all I desire, as well. And I believe with all my heart that's what you want." He caught her chin in his hand and leaned closer. "I want to love you, Bernadette. I want to care for you. I want to keep you with me always. If you canna bear the burden of your past, I can. If you canna bear children, I can. You made me realize that I couldna neither live with sorrow nor cling to the past. Now it's time you learn the same." He kissed her lips tenderly, then let go of her and swung up on his horse.

"I'm to learn this because you've forced orphans on me?" she cried, sounding on the verge of hysteria.

"I'll be back on the morrow." He reined his horse around. "If those two can open their hearts to a *Sassenach* after what they've endured, then by God, you can open your heart to them. *And* to me. You've roughly a day to decide if you will take that chance and remain in Scotland, or if you will let your past define your future and return to the constant reminder of it in England."

He spurred his horse then and galloped away, leaving her standing there.

He wanted to believe that Fiona and Ualan would make her see the life they might have. With all his heart he wanted to believe it—but he didn't feel as confident as he thought he might. He supposed he thought she might have been more welcoming.

He hoped the bairns would not despise him after twenty-four hours with a grieving woman. He hoped Bernadette would wake up from her grief and recognize the promise in what he offered. Honestly, he didn't know if any of it would work. He didn't know if he was doing the right thing, or worse, if even he *could* do it. But he knew two things with all his heart: he loved Bernadette, and he did not want those children to be sent to a stranger in Inverness.

Rabbie rode away from Killeaven feeling a wee bit as if he'd put himself in a rowboat and pushed out to sea without an oar, without anything to guide him, and hoping for a favorable current.

CHAPTER TWENTY-FOUR

BERNADETTE WATCHED IN horror as Rabbie rode away—she was paralyzed with shock. What on earth would possess him, after all that had been said between them, to deposit two children at Killeaven and ride on? She was confused, she was angry and she very badly wanted something to kick.

She ran damp palms down the side of her gown and slowly turned around to face the house. Dear Jesus, what was she to do now? She started by taking several deep breaths to calm her galloping heart, then forced herself to return to the salon.

The boy and girl were standing in the very place Rabbie had left them. They eyed her as guardedly as she eyed them. Charles was there, too, and looked between her and the children and back again, utterly confused. "I can't say what this is about, Miss Holly, but I am certain you are aware you can't possibly return to England with two children in tow."

"No, of course not," she said. "They are... I understand they need a place to sleep for the night."

Charles sighed impatiently. "You're to be a nursemaid now? There is work yet to be done!"

"Yes, I know," she assured him. "But I'm feeling much better and I promise to help you—"

"Look here, Bernadette," he said, and stepped in front of her. "I don't care what you do. Just keep those two out of the way and out from underfoot. I've enough on my mind without worrying where they are or what they're into."

"I will," she said.

"And you might want to comb your hair," Charles added, and walked out of the room.

She glanced at the children. Their gazes were fixed on her. She tried to smile. "You mustn't pay him any mind. He's rather…" She tried to think of a word. "He's a bit occupied."

The little girl glanced uncertainly at her brother. What were their names, again? Fiona, yes, and…what was it? Ualan! Yes, that was it. How old were they? Bernadette guessed the girl to be around six, the boy a year or two older than that. She approached them nervously, still rubbing her palms on the sides of her gown, studying them. She hadn't even the faintest thought of what to do with them.

She reached them, and they watched her, but neither of them would speak. Bernadette sank down on her knees before them.

Fiona was quite comely, with strawberry-blond curls that framed her face and lovely blue eyes. Ualan's hair was more golden. He stood stiffly, but Bernadette could see the tremble in his hand. Was he afraid of her? Lord, she must look a fright, and she unthinkingly put her hand to her head again and felt her hair's unruliness. "Please forgive my appearance," she said.

"Aye, we know," Fiona said. "You're quite sad."

The girl's observation startled Bernadette. "Ah... yes," she agreed. "And I'm a bit surprised, as well. I wasn't expecting children."

The boy said nothing. He looked wise beyond his years, really.

"Are *you* surprised?" she asked them.

Fiona shook her head. Ualan didn't give her any indication of his feelings.

"Well, then." How did one speak to children? She hardly knew. "Are you hungry?" she asked.

The two children looked at each other. Fiona shook her head.

"Miss Holly?"

She glanced around. Charles had stuck his head into the room. "You must do something about the kitchen girl. She hasn't a care for the china nor the slightest idea how to pack it." He disappeared just as quickly as he'd appeared.

Bernadette was grateful for the task and rose to her feet. "Come," she said, and held out both hands to the children.

Fiona readily slipped her hand into Bernadette's without a moment's hesitation. Ualan kept his hands at his sides.

She led them to the kitchen, where Ina was sweeping up what looked like a broken teacup. "I did my best, I did," she said irritably to Bernadette. "He didna tell me how he wanted it done, did he?"

"Don't think of it," Bernadette said. "I'll do the packing." She would rather have something to occupy her hands than to stare at her two unexpected wards.

Ina put her hand on the small of her back. She seemed to notice the children then, and spoke to them in Gaelic.

Fiona responded.

Whatever she said caused Ina to smile, and she began a lively conversation with them. Fiona laughed and even Ualan had a small smile on his face. What in blazes had Ina said? What magic words had she uttered?

After several minutes of it, Ina said, "They're hungry, miss. Shall I prepare them a wee bite?"

Bernadette looked with surprise at the two of them. Why hadn't they admitted it to her? Did they think she might poison them? "Yes, please, if you'd be so kind."

So it was that Ina fed the children and laughed with them while Bernadette packed the china. She couldn't understand a word they said, but she listened to their young voices, the sound of their laughter, and her heart ached with longing. It was a cruel thing for Rabbie to have done. What did he think, that she would magically forget her misgivings and agree to this outrageous plan?

The very idea annoyed her, and she glanced irritably at Ina. "What else do they want? They don't seem to want to tell me."

Ina blinked. She looked at the children and asked them something. Both of them shook their heads.

"They donna want a thing, miss," Ina said. "They are quite happy to be here."

Bernadette snorted. "They may tell you that, but trust me, this is some grand jest."

"Oh, no, they mean it, they do," she said. "They were bound for Inverness and a stranger there. They are happy that a Mackenzie has taken them in."

"Inverness?" Bernadette repeated, and looked around.

"Aye, we were," Fiona said. "Because we havena any parents."

"That's no' *why*," Ualan said. "Because there are no more of our people in the Highlands."

Ina smiled sympathetically. "That happened to many of us, lad. That's why we all must keep together, aye?"

Fiona nodded enthusiastically. Ualan shrugged.

"What do you mean, a Mackenzie has taken them in?"

"They say they're to live with Mr. Mackenzie at Arrandale," Ina said.

"We'll visit Barabel, we will," Fiona added. "She taught me how to make a cake. Do you know how to make a cake?" she asked Ina.

"A wee one, I do," Ina said.

Bernadette turned around. She continued the packing, her hands moving by rote. Had Rabbie really taken them in? Did he truly intend to keep them, no matter what she said? Lord, had he gone and finally lost his fool mind? A man who was only days ago thinking of jumping off a cliff would now take children under his wing?

When she'd finished packing the china, and the children had eaten, she bade them to come with her so Ina might finish her chores.

"It's quite all right if they want to remain here, miss," Ina offered.

Bernadette was tempted. The children looked at her expectantly, and it occurred to her that perhaps she ought to inquire if Ina would like two orphans.

Charles ended all speculation, however, by striding into the kitchen. "The silver, Ina. You've forgotten it."

"Oh!" Ina said. She wiped her hands on a linen and hurried after Charles.

Bernadette looked at the children. "Well, then, that settles, it, doesn't it? You're tied to me," she said wearily. "Come along."

"Where shall we go now?" Fiona asked, hopping off a stool and sliding her hand into Bernadette's, uninvited.

"I haven't quite worked that out," Bernadette said, glancing behind her to see if Ualan followed.

She led them through the house in search of something to occupy her, or conversely, them, and found nothing. They ended up in her room.

"Sit there," she said, pointing to the bed. "I'll finish my packing."

"Are you leaving us, then?" Fiona asked as she bounced onto the bed.

"I'm leaving Scotland, darling." Bernadette opened her trunk and began to sort through her things.

"Uncle Rabbie said you might come to live with us at Arrandale," Fiona said. "We're all to live there. I've no' seen Arrandale, but Catriona said it is a house big enough for two children and some dogs."

"I'm terribly sorry, but Uncle Rabbie was mistaken," Bernadette said bitterly. How dare he give them that expectation? Couldn't he see how pointless this was? Couldn't he understand that one simply did not pick up two orphans and a lady's maid and form some sort of fictional family?

She realized that no one was speaking and glanced up. The children were staring at her. "What?"

"Do you have any children?" Fiona asked.

Bernadette's gut belly twisted a bit. "No."

"Why no', then?"

"She's no' married, Fiona," Ualan said darkly. "She has no family. She's alone, like us."

"Why will you no' come to live with us in Arrandale?" Fiona asked. "Uncle Rabbie said you might. Have you seen it?"

Bernadette dropped a pair of shoes and bent down to retrieve them. She'd seen Arrandale. She thought of being in Rabbie's bed. She thought of how she'd felt with him. Safe and adored and *wanted*. She swallowed hard. "Yes, I've seen it. It's quite nice."

"Then why will you no' come?" Fiona asked again.

"It's not as easy as that," Bernadette said, and picked up one shoe, but somehow managed to kick the other shoe under the bed skirt.

"Do you no' want a family, then?" Fiona asked curiously.

Bernadette felt light-headed. As if she was floating outside of herself. "It's rather difficult to explain grown-up things to a girl your age, Fiona. Is that what he told you?" she asked as she bent down on one knee to retrieve the shoe.

"He said we'd be a family, if you'd come."

"We're to be one all the same," Ualan said, correcting her. "But three is no' very many. Four is better."

Bernadette's eyes began to well again. She wanted a family. *She did.* But one could not simply summon a family out of thin air as he was trying to do. Life didn't work that way. "It's not possible for me," she said morosely.

"Why no'?" Fiona asked.

The girl was too inquisitive! "I told you, darling. For reasons that are too complicated for a girl to understand." She turned her head and smiled at Fiona, hoping that was the end of it.

It was not the end of it. The girl was determined. "Uncle Rabbie said we are to be a family because none of us have one. We donna have a family, do we, Ualan? They went away."

"Fiona! I've told you many times, they *died.* Even Uncle Rabbie said it. Will you no' listen?"

Bernadette paused and looked at the boy. She could see the anguish in his face. She could feel the anguish in her own chest. She knew the sort of agony he must live with every day and her heart went out to him. "My family, too," she said.

Ualan eyed her dubiously.

"Which is why I can't have a family now," she said morosely. "I lost mine." She rolled onto her knees to fetch the shoe that had been knocked under the bed's covers.

"But we're all to make a *new* one, because none of us has the old one any longer, aye?" Fiona said, as if Bernadette couldn't grasp the basic idea. She hopped off the bed and began to twirl. "I want a family as big as the Mackenzies. They have lots of children, aye? Lads and lassies."

"That's what children are," Ualan said, sighing. "Lads and lassies."

"Perhaps you donna care for lads and lassies," Fiona suggested. "Is *that* why you donna want a family?"

Bernadette felt herself flush. She put her hand down on the carpet. "I do," she said weakly. "I do like lads and lassies. I *do* want a family."

"Then you should have one," Fiona said with great authority.

Bernadette nodded. And then she put her other hand down. She was on all fours now.

"Are you ill, then? Mrs. Maloney was ill, too. She went to sleep and never woke."

That was precisely what Bernadette's life had felt like at times. As if she'd gone to sleep and never awakened from the nightmare.

"She died, too, Fiona," Ualan said. "That's what—she *died*."

"Will Uncle Rabbie die, too?" Fiona asked curiously.

"I donna know. Perhaps no' right away," Ualan said as he studied his hand.

To Bernadette's horror, a tear rolled off the tip of her nose. "I am so sorry," she choked out.

"It's all right," Fiona said.

"It's not," Bernadette said. "I am so sorry for Mrs. Maloney and for everyone who has ever gone to sleep and never awakened. And I'm so sorry for everyone who has ever gone to sleep and then awakened to something so awful they can't bear it."

Fiona stopped spinning. She and Ualan were staring at her, wide-eyed. Bernadette realized she was crying now, the pain burning in her head and heart. "I can't convey how very sorry I am for your loss, you lovely, lovely children. I'm sorry for Uncle Rabbie's loss, too, and mine. And I'm particularly sorry that I can't take back the things I've done or the consequences, and that I've ruined everything." She paused, gulping back a few sobs. She had lost so much following her heart's desire once and she understood that some of her tears now were the result of some deeply held terror that if she followed her heart's desire once more, she would lose again.

Fiona squatted down. "Donna be sad," she cooed, and patted Bernadette's head.

Bernadette rolled onto her bottom, her back against the bed. She tried to draw a long breath, but the breath caught in her throat and more tears fell.

"I'll help you no' be sad, aye?" Fiona offered. "I can sing and dance."

"Donna sing," Ualan said grumpily. "It hurts my ears when you do."

"I donna hurt your ears!" Fiona cried. "You're wretched, Ualan!"

"No one wants to hear you sing, Fiona!"

"No one wants to hear you *speak*!" she shouted, and shoved him. Ualan shoved her back. Fiona screamed at the top of her lungs.

"Stop!" Bernadette shouted, throwing up her hands. She pushed the two children apart before they fell into a brawl over her. And then she burst into tears again, overwhelmed by her desires, her hopes and the presence of two children she didn't know.

The children fell silent. Bernadette didn't know what she was doing, why she couldn't seem to stop, but she put her head down on her knees and wept.

Ualan kneeled down beside her. He very carefully put his hand on her hand. "Donna weep, madam," he said. "We'll be your friends."

Yes, that's what she needed. A friend. Bernadette lifted her head and studied his earnest little face. "Do you think you can?" she asked. "I've been quite a wreck since you've come."

Ualan frowned thoughtfully. "Aye, I *think* I can," he said gravely.

Bernadette couldn't help but smile. She wiped tears from her face. Fiona sat beside her, her legs straight in front of her, and leaned her head against Bernadette's shoulder. Bernadette slowly put her arm around Fiona. Ualan eased in beside her, too, and slipped his hand into Bernadette's.

She looked down at the two of them. Her heart was beginning to form out of its dust again. "You realize, do you not, that I'm English? And you're Scottish. Some people will not care for that."

"Uncle Rabbie says no' all English are bad men," Fiona said.

Bernadette smiled. "No, not all. What if you do not esteem me after a time? You might not care for me at all with a bit of time to know me."

"*I* esteem you," Fiona said. "You're bonny. But your eyes look verra strange."

"They do?"

"Aye, they look as if squads of bees have stung them," Ualan confirmed.

"Oh, that," Bernadette said, and put her arm around him, too. She noticed that he didn't resist, and in fact, settled in against her. "I've been weeping for quite a long while and my eyes have swollen."

"Why?" Ualan asked.

"Because I was alone and I didn't like it. Do you ever weep?"

"No," Ualan said. "Fiona does, quite a lot, she does."

Fiona agreed. "I'm sad, too, sometimes. I'm no' sad when Barabel allows me to help her make a cake. But sometimes, when Ualan says awful things, and I've no one to tell, I'm sad."

"I only say awful things when you say cake-headed things," Ualan pointed out, and Fiona didn't disagree.

"Do you know what I think would make me feel better? A walk."

"Aye, a walk!" Fiona said brightly, sitting up. "May we walk to the sea, then? Mrs. Maloney didna like to walk to the sea, she said it was too far and her legs pained her."

"Yes, the sea," Bernadette said, and as they stood

up, she pulled Charles's old boots from the trunk. She'd already packed them away.

They waited for her to put on her boots, then the three of them walked out of Killeaven, hand in hand, in search of Mr. MacDonald to walk along behind them. Perhaps the three of them were in search of more than that. Bernadette didn't want to think too carefully about it and risk losing the magic of that moment.

EVERYTHING WAS PACKED by noon the next day. Charles had gone with the first wagon of belongings to the cove to oversee the loading. Niall MacDonald and one of the men who had remained behind, but there had been no sign of the Buchanans since their first appearance. "Aye, the Buchanans are cowards, the lot of them," Mr. MacDonald had said the day before when he'd accompanied Bernadette and the children on their walk. "They'd no' come round with Mackenzies here."

She didn't know if that was true, but his confidence removed any worry from her head while she explored the path above the sea with two children. As the sun had shone down on them, and the children had collected rocks to show her, Bernadette began to wonder if perhaps Rabbie wasn't so mad after all.

Fiona and Ualan had spent the night in her bed, the three of them gathered together. "Like the dogs," Fiona had remarked.

Bernadette was to accompany Niall on the morrow with the last cart carrying the Kents' things. That afternoon, as Ualan and Fiona argued over something in the salon, Bernadette said goodbye to Ina and sent her on her way with the last of the pitiful wages Lord Kent had left for her.

"Will you come again?" Ina asked.

Bernadette smiled and shook her head. "Not here."

With Ina gone, there was nothing left to be done. Now that they were alone with Bernadette in the house, Ualan and Fiona chased each other on the terrace with sticks they pretended were swords.

Bernadette watched them idly. She was exhausted. She was emotionally and physically spent. But for the first time in several days she felt as if she could draw a clean breath. She felt as if her heart was actually beating, and not wrenching about in her chest.

The afternoon was growing late, and she walked out onto the drive to watch the sun begin its slide down behind the hills. She knew Rabbie would come, so it was no surprise to her when she heard a horse on the road approaching Killeaven.

She was standing just outside the entry, leaning against one of the columns, when he trotted onto the drive. He reined his horse to a halt, his gaze on her. He was assessing her, trying to determine her mood.

Bernadette gave him no indication. After he'd dropped two orphans here and ridden off, he didn't deserve to know her mood.

He came off his horse and walked forward. He looked grim, she thought, as if he expected the worst. He stopped a few feet from her and was at a loss for words as his gaze wandered over her. It seemed to require some effort on his part to finally ask, "How do you fare, Miss Holly?"

"Well enough," she said.

"And the children?"

"Oh, they are very well indeed. They are pretending at swordplay on the terrace."

He nodded. He put one hand on his hip.

Bernadette thought there had never been a more appealing man to walk these Highlands. She wanted to feel his arms around her. And she wanted to punch him in the mouth. "I take it you're still verra cross with me, aye?"

Bernadette said nothing.

"If it pleases you, my mother was appalled when I told her what I'd done," he said. "She thought it absurd and unkind to all parties involved."

"I agree with your mother."

His shoulders sagged almost imperceptibly. "Well, then… I'll collect them."

"Don't you mean to ask how we got on?"

One dark brow arched up, and he tilted his head to one side. "Dare I?"

"I think the three of us will agree that it was difficult. The children are loud, and they argue, and they require a lot of attention. I discovered I can be rather short when a child does not heed my advice."

He frowned darkly. "Aye, then, you've made your point, Bernadette," he said soberly. "I'll fetch them now."

"I'm not finished," she said, and pushed away from the column. "I also require a lot of attention. I hadn't realized just how much until…well, until I had it. I confess I fell very much apart, and I will confess that

I despised you terribly for doing such a wretched thing. But Fiona and Ualan were so kind to me, and they were attentive, and they promised if I made them beans for supper they would not complain, and then I realized, you are right, Rabbie. I've been living in my past as much as you have yours. But those two? They can't remember the past. They can only look to the future and what they see is bright and full of promise. From here on, I am determined to do the same."

His expression changed. He looked cautiously hopeful. "Speak plainly, then, *leannan*—what do you mean to say?"

"I mean to say, Rabbie Mackenzie, that I don't know if I can be any sort of proper mother to two orphans, if that's what you have offered. I don't know if I can be a proper wife to you…if that is what you have offered. But I am filled with hope and the desire to try—"

"Bernadette," he said, his voice full of relief. He strode forward and wrapped her in his arms, kissing her temple, her cheek. "*Diah*, how I longed to hear you say it. You have given life to my heart, *leannan*. I love you. I love you so."

"I love you, too, Rabbie," she said, smiling. "I didn't want to love you, God knows I wanted to despise you, and I was so angry with you for bringing Fiona and Ualan here as you did. But the moment I thought I would lose you, I was overcome with grief and sadness and… I don't want to lose you," she said, taking his face in her hands. "I don't want to look back anymore. I want to look forward, with you."

He groaned and kissed her neck.

"I want all that, but I have to know, Rabbie—have you really considered all that I've told you? Do you understand the sort of talk—"

"I donna care, Bernadette," he said, lifting his head. He dipped down to her eye level. "Do you hear me, then? Do you understand me? I *donna care*. I mean what I say—you have given me my life back, and for that, God as my witness, I will give you all that I have." He pulled her into his body, his arms around her, and he kissed her.

How had her fate brought her to the Highlands of Scotland? How had she discovered the happiness she was certain would elude her all the rest of her days? It was madness, it was magical, it was unbelievable, but Bernadette was a believer.

"Uncle Rabbie, *no*, donna do it!" Fiona cried from somewhere near by. "It's wretched!"

Rabbie and Bernadette broke the kiss and looked at Fiona. Bernadette laughed. Fiona ran forward, wrapping her arms around Rabbie and Bernadette's legs. Ualan didn't follow straightaway.

"*Och*, what do you stand there for, lad?" Rabbie said, and gestured for him to come.

Ualan smiled sheepishly and ran to join the hug.

EPILOGUE

IT IS AN early spring day, and they are gathered in the fields near Balhaire, Seona and her sister, her's sister's wee bairns, Seona's mother, too. Catriona has come down, as have Vivienne and Marcas and their brood. They have a basket of bread and fruit, and the dogs that have followed them lie about, panting, their snouts sniffing the air.

The wee baby, Seona's niece, is eight months old, and when Rabbie makes faces at her, she puts her fists to her knees and laughs. Her brother is almost two, and he walks about on chubby legs, bending over to pull wildflowers that he then drops on the heads of the dogs. None of the dogs pay him any heed.

Rabbie picks up his youngest nephew and holds him high overhead, telling him he's a bird, then jogs about with the lad overhead. Seona's nephew begs for a turn, and Rabbie lifts him up, kisses his cheek, then holds him high overhead. He laughs gleefully as Rabbie jogs around with him, flying like a bird.

When he puts the lad down, Seona says "You'll make a good father one day, Rabbie Mackenzie."

He hopes that is true. He falls to the ground beside

Seona. "One day," he says, and kisses her. "When I return from Norway, aye?" he asks, and smiles.

"You're a bold one," Seona says, and laughingly pushes him away. "I donna know what I'll think when you come back. Perhaps I'll have found another lad to amuse me."

He growls and kisses her again. "Promise me you'll be here when I return," he says, and takes her hand. "Donna agree to marry Gordon."

Seona laughs. "If I canna marry you, I'll marry no one, Rabbie."

It is the last day Rabbie will lay eyes on Seona MacBee.

RABBIE AND BERNADETTE married within a fortnight of that day. There wasn't a Mackenzie among them who thought they ought to wait, given all that had gone before. Lady Mackenzie was concerned that Bernadette's family was not present, but after a private meeting with Bernadette, she agreed to it. She understood better than anyone, Rabbie supposed, given her history with her late father. Bernadette would write to her sister, but she planned never to return to England.

The year that followed their wedding passed within a blink of an eye. It astounded Rabbie how, for two years prior, every day had passed with excruciating tedium. But now, it seemed that he was scarcely out of bed before the day had passed and it was time to retire again.

He was indescribably happy.

Today was Bernadette's birthday, and Rabbie had made her sit at the dining table at Arrandale with a scarf tied around her eyes. She put her hand out, searching the space around her, afraid that a child or something was lurking nearby to frighten her.

A dog startled her with a cold snout to her palm. They had three dogs now, all of them quite useless for anything other than lying in doorways and in everyone's path.

Bernadette scratched this dog behind the ears. "Woolly," she said, recognizing the dog. "You're not to be here."

"Donna look, *Mamma*!" Fiona cried. She was standing across the table from Bernadette. She'd begun to call Bernadette Mamma almost immediately. Ualan still called her by her given name, and Isobel, who had been no more than three years when she was found abandoned on the steps of the kirk at Balhaire, called her Mamma as well.

"I'm *not* looking," Bernadette said, and tipped her head back pretending to try and see.

Rabbie put his hands on his shoulders and leaned down. "Donna look, *leannan*, or I'll have your hide," he whispered.

"Will the torture never end? I can't wait another moment!"

"Shall I remove her blind?" Rabbie asked their brood.

"Yes!" they cried in unison.

He untied the blind and pulled the silk away from

Bernadette's face. She blinked, then looked down. There, on a silver platter, was the new pair of boots he'd had made for her. She gasped with delight, her face lighting with her smile. "They're my size!"

"Might I have the others back now?" Charles drawled.

Charles had remained on when he discovered Bernadette would not be making the voyage back to England. He'd come straightaway to Rabbie and asked if he might tend Arrandale. Bernadette had been surprised by it, but said she was happy to have her friend about.

They had no use for a butler at Arrandale, but Charles happily pretended to be one. Rabbie couldn't understand why an Englishman would be so eager to stay on in the Highlands. He was fairly certain there was something dire in England Charles hadn't wanted to face. He'd assumed a crime of some sort, and he would amuse Bernadette late at night, imagining all the crimes Charles might have committed in England.

And then, out of the blue, he announced that he intended to marry Ina. They were expecting a child. Apparently, Rabbie was not the only man brought back from the brink that long summer.

"You can have your boots, and I will even help you burn them," Bernadette said laughingly. She was delighted with her new boots and insisted on putting them on then and there and wearing them about the house for the rest of the day. Rabbie smiled every time he heard her clomping down one hall or the next.

That evening, when the children had gone to bed, he watched her brush her hair. It was his favorite time of day, watching her ready for bed. He could admire her at his leisure, could marvel that a woman as beautiful as she had married a Highlander like him.

She finished brushing her hair and climbed into bed beside him, and laid her head on his shoulder.

"Are you happy, then?" Rabbie asked.

"Quite," she said, sighing.

"You've no regrets?"

She smiled up at him in surprise. Every time he asked her, she gave him the same look of surprise. Rabbie couldn't help himself—he considered himself so very fortunate that he had to reassure himself from time to time that she'd not change her mind and would take this dream away. A year or so ago, he couldn't imagine that he'd ever know happiness again. That he'd ever have a wife he loved above all else. Not to mention children he loved. A year ago, he'd wanted death. Now he wanted life. A very long and happy one.

"Well?" he asked. "What say you?"

"I say I've never had the slightest regret," she said, and kissed his bare chest.

"Swear it?" he asked.

She crossed his heart with the tip of her finger. "Swear it."

He smiled. "I've one more gift," he said, and handed her an envelope that had arrived at Balhaire a few days ago.

Bernadette sat up on her knees to have a look at

the handwriting and gasped. "It's from Avaline!" She broke the seal and began to read.

It had been more than a year since she'd seen Avaline. They knew that Cailean and Daisy had taken Avaline and her mother to Chatwick Hall until some reconciliation with Lord Kent could be arranged. But then, quite unexpectedly, Lady Kent had died. Daisy had taken pity on the girl and had kept her under her wing, refusing to send her back to a man as odious as Baron Kent. And, for the record, Kent did not ask for his daughter to be returned to him.

There had been another development in the last year, too. Rabbie's father had been deviled by the idea that the Mackenzies' enemy, the Buchanans, would have a hand in the management of property so close to Balhaire. He'd come up with an idea. Rabbie's mother had implored her brother, Uncle Knox, a wealthy English lord, to negotiate a fair price for Killeaven. The plan was for Uncle Knox to hold it for Ellis until the young viscount reached his majority. Ellis had agreed to the deal at Cailean's request.

When they were able, the Mackenzie clan would buy the land and the estate from Ellis.

Rabbie watched as Bernadette eagerly read Avaline's letter, her eyes flying over the page. "Well, then?" he asked. "What does she say?"

"That she's in *love*," Bernadette said. "That her heart is singing with joy and something else that is quite illegible or covered by ink smudges, and that she hopes to be married very soon." She laughed with delight and looked up from the letter. "Do you believe it?"

"Aulay will be relieved to hear it." Rabbie chuckled.

"Aulay has given her no thought since he deposited her on the shores of England," Bernadette said with a laugh.

"Aye, and who is the lucky man?" Rabbie asked.

"She hasn't said," Bernadette reported, and read aloud some of the effusive praise of the gentleman. She turned the parchment over and gasped. She looked up at Rabbie with eyes as round as moons.

"What?" he asked, laughing.

"Ellis offered for her hand," she said. "And Avaline accepted!"

"Ellis!" Rabbie cried. "He's only seventeen!"

"Eighteen now. They are to be married at Christmas."

"Ellis," Rabbie repeated dubiously. "And *Avaline*?"

Bernadette burst into laughter. She tossed the parchment aside and crawled over her husband. He settled his hands on her hips, smiling up at her. "What are you doing, *leannan*?" he asked.

"I don't know! I'm delirious," she said, and kissed him.

His hands began to move on her, sliding over her hips, then up again, beneath her nightgown. "Delirious, are you?"

"With happiness," she said. "I still wonder if this is all true, Rabbie. I have yet to fully fathom that my heart's joy was revealed to me by a man standing on the edge of a cliff, preparing to jump." She laughed.

Rabbie smiled. That man had jumped a long time

ago. But he'd jumped instead into a marriage with this
woman and it was a far superior landing.

"Neither can I fathom it," he said. *"Tha gaol agam
art, mo graidh,"* he murmured.

"Oh, Rabbie. I love you, too," she said, and sank
into his arms.

* * * * *

*If you loved this novel, don't miss the other
wonderful titles in* THE HIGHLAND GROOMS
series:
WILD WICKED SCOT
SINFUL SCOTTISH LAIRD
Available now from HQN Books!

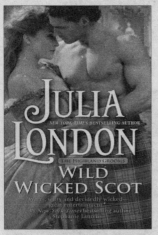

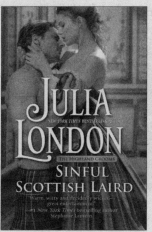

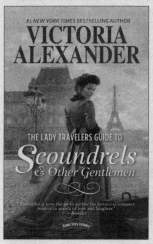

Get 2 Free Books,
Plus 2 Free Gifts—
just for trying the Reader Service!

HARLEQUIN

HISTORICAL

HH17